"IF A BOOK HAS JULIE GARWOOD'S NAME ON IT, IT'S GUARANTEED TO BE A METICULOUSLY WRITTEN ... AND THOROUGHLY ENGAGING STORY."
— *Sun Journal* (ME)

When Special Agent Grayson Kincaid first encounters Olivia MacKenzie, she makes quite an impression. The beautiful, tough young attorney has stumbled into the middle of an FBI sting operation and reduced it to chaos. Olivia has ticked off the wrong guy. He's FBI. But Olivia is even more intimidating. She's IRS.

Olivia is on the trail of an elaborate Ponzi scheme for her own very personal reasons, and her investigation has enraged some ruthless people and endangered her life. She's no stranger to tight situations, but she's smart enough to know when to call for help, especially if that help is tall, dark, and handsome.

Together, Grayson and Olivia make a great team to fight corruption, but they're also fighting an intense attraction—the one battle they're bound to lose.

"Kept me guessing until the very end."   —Fresh Fiction

"*Sweet Talk* took me by surprise ... hot romance ... danger, intrigue, and mystery."
—Guilty Pleasures Book Reviews

"Great storytelling! Very, very well-done, Ms. Garwood!"   —The Best Reviews

continued ...

MORE TITLES BY JULIE GARWOOD

JULIE GARWOOD

SWEET TALK

A SIGNET BOOK

SIGNET
Published by the Penguin Group
Penguin Group (USA) Inc., 375 Hudson Street,
New York, New York 10014, USA

USA | Canada | UK | Ireland | Australia | New Zealand | India | South Africa | China

Penguin Books Ltd., Registered Offices: 80 Strand, London WC2R 0RL, England
For more information about the Penguin Group visit penguin.com.

Published by Signet, an imprint of New American Library, a division of Penguin
Group (USA) Inc. Previously published in a Dutton edition.

First Signet Printing, June 2013

Ⓟ REGISTERED TRADEMARK — MARCA REGISTRADA

ISBN 978-0-451-41523-3

Printed in the United States of America
10 9 8 7 6 5 4 3 2 1

PUBLISHER'S NOTE
This is a work of fiction. Names, characters, places, and incidents either are the
product of the author's imagination or are used fictitiously, and any resemblance
to actual persons, living or dead, business establishments, events, or locales is
entirely coincidental.

The publisher does not have any control over and does not assume any
responsibility for author or third-party Web sites or their content.

To Aaron Michael Hass Garwood,
for your thoughtfulness, your generosity, and your love.
Welcome to the family.

PROLOGUE

The Pips were at it again. The four girls had vanished from the unit dragging thousands of dollars' worth of equipment with them and causing quite a commotion. The staff was frantic, desperate to find them before word of their disappearance leaked out. The only person not concerned was the man who held their futures in his hands. He insisted that the restless, mischievous adolescents had not escaped. They were pulling just another silly prank, no doubt orchestrated by Olivia MacKenzie, the ringleader. From the minute he'd looked into those gorgeous, sparkling blue eyes, he'd known she was going to be a troublemaker and a fighter.

He couldn't have been more pleased. Olivia gave the other Pips—Samantha Pearson, Jane Weston, and Collins Davenport—strength and a voice. Until she'd entered the program, the girls had been sullen, lethargic, and even borderline suicidal. And who could blame them? They spent most of their days in forced isolation, locked away from family and friends and the rest of the world. Members of the staff were constantly telling them how fortunate they were to have been chosen for the experimental program. Nurse Charlotte even insisted they were blessed.

The girls scoffed at the notion. All of them had a disease that, thus far, no drug had been able to conquer, and none of them felt the least bit fortunate to be human pincushions, subjected to a tremendous and sometimes unbearable amount of agony. The Pips were forbidden to call the wonder drug cocktail that was pumped into their veins poison, but that's what all of them believed it was. Excruciating pain followed each infusion, and by evening their bodies were covered with blisters from the tops of their heads to the bottoms of their feet. No, none of them felt blessed.

Though the youngest of the group, Olivia was the strongest and the toughest, and she had quickly stepped into the role of protector. Once she had gained her new friends' trust, she began to chip away at the boredom and, more important, the anger and the fear.

Pranks were Olivia's specialty. Within two weeks of her arrival, the nurses and the doctors grew hesitant to open their lockers for fear of what was going to jump out at them. Nurse Charlotte developed a twitch in her left eyelid after a rubber snake sprang at her, delighting the Pips to no end.

As the girls became more fearless, their repertoire of mischief grew. Each had a favorite trick.

Jane, the artistic one in the group, had a flare for design. She could sit for hours with a notepad and pencil drawing shapes, then connecting them into beautiful mosaics. She loved symmetry and color, so when the others suggested they TP the nurses' station, she objected. She thought that would be too crass. Instead, she decorated the space from ceiling to floor with streamers of every color of the rainbow.

Samantha, or Sam as she was called by her friends, was the adventurer. She was unafraid of risk, but she wasn't reckless. She went about each of the pranks methodically. Every situation was patiently examined and carefully planned to achieve the desired result. It took her a week to collect enough lime Jell-O to fill all the specimen cups. After warming them in the nurses' microwave for a few seconds, she slipped the little beakers of green liquid onto the lab cart and sent them downstairs for analysis. The girls laughed for days remembering the sight of the red-faced nurse on the phone apologizing and trying to explain the mishap to the lab tech.

Olivia had found it easy to bring Jane and Sam into the fun, but Collins had been more of a challenge. Because she was the most sensitive, it took her the longest to conquer her depression; but once she did, she was game for anything. Olivia designated her to be the decoy in their adventures. When the girls wanted to slip by the staff unnoticed, Olivia would send Collins to distract them. She was blessed with a sweet nature and a soft Southern accent that drew people to her, so when a teardrop or two would fall down her cheek, everyone would rush to console her. Once the tears began to flow, they'd huddle around her and give her their full and undivided attention. A couple of faint sobs, and she had them—especially the men—eating out of her hands. Little did her sympathetic audience know, the other three Pips were behind them, strategically placing furry fake spiders in unexpected spots.

In an attempt to keep the Pips calm and in their beds, their specialist, Dr. Andre Pardieu, gave each of them a deck of cards and took the time one afternoon to teach them how to play poker. They were quick learners. By the end of the month the Pips had taken him for more than three hundred dollars. They used the cash to buy pizzas and cake for Nurse Kathleen's birthday and a few other fun items to torment the staff.

After spending several weeks in the hospital, the Pips fell into a routine. Monday was poison cocktail day, and they were too sick to play any pranks. Tuesday, they were still too ill to do more than lift their heads off their pillows, but by nightfall the blisters would disappear, and they would begin to feel human again. They decided that Wednesday would be orange wig day; Thursday would always be freak-out-the-nurses day, and on Friday, as a compliment to their doctor—they all had a crush on him—they would speak his native tongue, French, which was a real trick considering the fact that only Olivia understood the language. Weekends were spent on target practice with their water guns, working jigsaw puzzles, and doing crosswords. Olivia's aunt Emma was what Dr. Pardieu called a coconspirator. She sent Olivia the water guns and wigs and other novelties. Whatever her niece requested, she got.

Dr. Pardieu also had a routine. Each morning when he walked into the unit, he greeted the girls the same way: *"Bonjour, mes petites pipsqueaks."*

And they responded, *"Bonjour, Docteur Pardieu."*

Olivia came up with a new idea one Thursday. After the doctor had made his rounds, she suggested a game of hide-and-seek to torment the nurses. She had broken into an empty storage closet the week before and discovered the rectangular room had enough space to fit all of them. It was at the end of the newly constructed south wing, which would be dedicated and opened for patients the next month.

The girls crept down the hall behind Olivia and slipped into the dark closet. They sat on the floor with their backs against the walls, two facing two, and stayed quiet while they strained to listen for every sound. The scent of disinfectant hung in the air around them. They could hear the supervisor calling their names as she clipped along the gray-and-white tile floor, her rubber-soled shoes squeaking with each step. When the sound faded, Olivia reached up and switched on the light.

All of them squinted against the sudden brightness.

"She's gone," Sam whispered, trying to stifle her laughter.

"Maybe we shouldn't stay here," Collins said. "We don't want her to keep looking for us."

"Are you kidding?" Olivia said. "Of course we want her to look for us. That's how we roll."

Jane was the most law-abiding of the four and whispered, "What if she calls the police? We could get into serious trouble." She was twisting the tube on her IV while she fretted.

Sam rolled her eyes. "She won't call the police," she said. "You worry too much."

"She could call our parents," Jane suggested then.

Olivia shrugged. "My mother has caller ID. As soon as she sees it's the hospital calling, she won't pick up. My disease is too stressful for her."

"You're joking, right?" Sam asked.

"No, I'm not. Mom has trouble coping."

"What does your father think?" Collins asked the question. "He's never come to visit you," she remarked, a tinge of sympathy in her voice as she reached over and patted Olivia's hand. The girls could always count on Collins for emotional support.

"None of her family has visited," Sam said.

"They're busy," Olivia answered with an indifferent shrug. "Mom flies back and forth between our homes in San Francisco and New York City. My parents have a strange marriage," she added, sounding very grown-up. "Mom adores him. She's . . . dramatic about it. I don't know how else to explain it. She doesn't have room for anything else in her life."

"Or *anyone* else," Collins said. Like daughters, she silently added.

"What about your father?" Sam asked again.

"Oh, he likes the adoration. At least he used to."

"No, I mean how does he cope with your illness? Is it too stressful for him, too?"

"Not really. He ignores it. Sometimes I think he pretends I'm at a sleepover. He used to call every week to see how I was doing. The last time I talked to him he asked me if I was having a nice time."

"Seriously?" Sam asked. She couldn't comprehend anyone being so oblivious. Her own family had taken her illness pretty hard, especially her four older brothers. Though they constantly reminded her that she was tough and could whip this thing, she knew on the inside they were worried.

"Seriously," Olivia insisted. "He loses track of time. At least that's what my sister, Natalie, tells me. She's always defending Mom and Dad. Nat would come see me if she could, but she's finishing college, and by the time she got off the plane here, she'd have to turn around and go back. She's ten years older than I am," she added.

"She hasn't called here in a while, has she?"

"She's very busy, too," Olivia responded.

"I talked to your sister once," Collins said. "You were getting X-rayed and couldn't come to the phone."

"Do you know this is the first time you've talked so openly about your family?" Jane remarked.

"Why is that?" Collins asked.

"Because it's embarrassing. I'm tired of making excuses for them," she blurted. "My family's dysfunctional. You're right, Sam. None of them has come to see me, and I don't think that's normal. Do you?"

All three girls shook their heads. "Exactly," Olivia said. "Aunt Emma is the only normal one. She doesn't like my father much, but I think it's because of the way my mother acts around him. Emma tries to hide how she feels when she talks to me, but I know. Once I heard her tell my mother she thought my father was shrewd with money but he was a nincompoop when it came to his family. She also said he was one of the most charismatic men she'd ever met."

"What does that mean?" Collins asked. "That he's smooth?"

"Polished, charming," Jane suggested. "Charismatic isn't a bad thing."

"My aunt made it sound bad. I wasn't supposed to be listening to the conversation, so I couldn't ask her what she meant."

"I don't know any charismatic men or women," Sam said. "At least, I don't think I do."

Olivia decided to change the subject. She wanted to talk about something else for a while. "If I get to grow up, I think I'd like to catch criminals. No matter how talented and clever they might be, eventually they all make mistakes," she said. "And they always get caught."

If-I-get-to-grow-up was a morbid game the girls played every now and then, though never in front of Dr. Pardieu, because they knew he would make them stop. Each time Olivia played, she changed what she wanted to become if she got to grow up. Last week she thought she wanted to become a chef. The week before that she was certain she wanted to become a physician just like Dr. Pardieu. The week before that she was determined to become a newscaster.

"You could become a detective or an FBI agent," Collins said enthusiastically. "It would be cool to carry a gun. Maybe I'll become an agent."

"You're a klutz, Collins," Jane said. "You'd shoot yourself. And besides, you'd probably cry every time you had to talk to a crime victim."

Her friend wasn't offended. "I probably would," she admitted.

"If I get to grow up, I'm going to become—" Sam began.

"A pilot," the other three Pips said in unison.

"Yes, a pilot," Sam agreed.

"Honestly, Sam, don't you ever think about any other careers?" Jane asked, clearly exasperated. "Why are you so stuck on being a pilot?"

"Let's see," Sam began. "My grandfather was a pilot; my father is a pilot; my four brothers are pilots . . ."

"And that means you have to be a pilot?" Collins asked.

"It's in my blood," she said with a shrug. "I have to fly."

No one argued with her. Then Jane said, "If we didn't have this horrible disease, we probably would never have met. Each one of us lives on a different side of the United States. Sam lives in Alaska; Olivia lives in California; Collins lives in Louisiana, and I live in upstate New York."

"I think fate would have pulled us together, no matter what," Sam said.

"It would have been nice if it hadn't been a terminal disease that brought us together," Olivia said.

Collins drew her knees to her chest. "My bum's getting cold."

"Mine, too," Olivia said.

The girls shifted to get closer to one another for warmth.

They didn't speak for a few minutes, and then Olivia broke the silence. "Aunt Emma thinks my father is going to leave my mother. She thinks that's the real reason he purchased the apartment in Manhattan." She had been worrying about the possibility that her parents would split up, and now that she'd told her friends about her family, she decided to tell them the rest. She felt closer to the Pips than anyone. Maybe it was because of what they were all going through together: shared laughter and shared pain.

"Divorce?" Collins asked in a bare whisper, as though the word would sting if she said it any louder.

Olivia nodded. "It will be a real nightmare if it happens."

"Why would your aunt give you such a worry?" Sam wanted to know. "You have enough to deal with. You don't need any more problems."

"Before I came here I made my aunt promise me she wouldn't keep anything from me, but I know she does sometimes. I want to know what's going on back home . . . the good and the bad."

"Divorce isn't such a big deal," Jane commented with a shrug. "You'll get through it."

"That's kind of callous," Sam told her.

"I'm being honest. My parents fought all the time. Everything got better once the divorce was final."

"What did they fight about?" Collins wanted to know.

"My big brother, Logan, mostly," she said. "Logan was getting into all sorts of trouble with drugs and alcohol. It's a miracle he graduated from high school. Mom protected him, made excuses for him. Dad cut him off, refused to give him any more money, but Mom would sneak some to him. Dad got sick of fighting all the time and left. That gave Logan the freedom to do what he wanted, and my mom would just give in. He even talked her into trying to up the value on my life insurance policy. Ghoulish, right?"

"Depends," Olivia said. "Who gets the money if you die?"

"Logan."

"Then, yes, it's ghoulish."

"The insurance company wouldn't do it. I'm a bad risk," Jane said.

"You should stay alive just to spite your brother," Sam said.

"I plan to," she replied, smiling. "So, you see, Olivia, my family is as wacked as yours."

"I don't think so," Olivia argued. "I could tell you stories that would turn your hair gray."

"We don't have any hair, remember? The wonder drugs made it all fall out," Sam said.

"We were already bald from the chemo when we got here," Collins reminded them. She gently brushed her fingertips across her bare forehead as though sweeping a stray lock into place. Exaggerating the lilt of her Southern accent, she said, "So you're going to have to take my word when I tell you I had the most fabulous blond hair."

"You, Olivia, and Sam could all be movie stars," Jane said.

"So could you," Olivia countered.

"I'm so thin and pale. I have these dark circles under my eyes and—"

Olivia wouldn't let her continue. "The medicine has just been rougher on you than on the rest of us. When it's over, you'll see your beautiful self again."

Jane wasn't convinced. "But Collins has blond hair and blue eyes—"

"Fabulous blond hair," Collins interrupted, smiling.

Jane rolled her eyes, then continued on. "Olivia, your eyes are such an intense, brilliant color of blue, so I'm guessing your hair is blond, too."

"Nope," she said. "Dark auburn," she corrected. "You've got pretty hazel eyes. I'll bet your hair is light brown, Jane."

"You're right."

"Sam, you're the easy one," Collins said. "Your eyes are green, so I think you're a natural redhead."

"I used to have dark brown hair, almost black," she said.

"When this is over . . . if we make it . . ." Jane began.

"We'll make it." Olivia's voice was emphatic.

"I'm not ready to die yet," Sam said.

"Neither am I," Collins whispered. "I have too much living to do, and I haven't even gotten started."

"But will you three still be my best friends?" Tears sprang into Jane's sunken eyes. There was no question that she was the most frail member of the group. Her pale skin looked almost translucent. Her voice was weak as she added, "No matter where we end up, no matter what we're doing . . . okay?"

"Absolutely," the others responded.

They made fists and gently tapped one another's knuckles to seal the promise.

"Friends forever," Sam whispered.

Olivia nodded. "Till death do us part."

ONE

Twelve years later

Olivia MacKenzie was certain she would have been offered the job if she hadn't punched the boss during the interview. But knocking the man senseless turned out to be a real deal breaker.

The CEO of one of the largest investment firms in the country, Eric Jorguson, was now being questioned by an FBI agent. He wasn't cooperating. The agent had taken Jorguson to the opposite side of the terrace and was trying to get him to calm down and answer his questions. Jorguson was busy screaming at Olivia, threatening to have her killed and also to sue her because she'd broken his jaw. She hadn't done any such thing, of course. The man was exaggerating. She'd smashed his nose in, not his jaw. A waiter wearing the name tag TERRY pinned to his black vest stood next to her trying to soothe what he referred to as her extreme case of nerves. She wanted to punch him, too.

"You're in shock," he told her. "That's why you look so calm. The guy tears your dress and gropes you, and it's only natural for you to go into shock. Don't you think? That's why you're not crying and carrying on."

Olivia looked at him. "I'm fine, really." Now *please* leave me alone, she silently added.

"Hey, look," Terry said. "They're arresting Jorguson's bodyguard. What's the guy doing with a bodyguard, I wonder." A few seconds later he answered his own question. "He must need one. Especially if he attacks other women the way he attacked you. You think you'd like to go out with me sometime?"

She smiled to ease the rejection. "I don't think so."

"You're still in shock, aren't you?"

Olivia was angry, not hysterical. She stood by the table with her arms folded across her waist as she patiently waited for the FBI agent to get to her. She had been told it wouldn't take long.

Terry tried twice more to engage her in conversation. She was polite but firm each time he attempted to get personal.

She watched the agents while she tried to figure out how she had gotten into this bizarre situation. Job hunting wasn't supposed to be dangerous. She had already interviewed with three other Fortune 500 companies without incident. Before she had gone to those interviews, however, she had done quite a bit of research. She didn't have that luxury with Jorguson Investments. Because the position had just become available, she'd had less than a day to study the company's prospectus. She should have looked more closely before she agreed to the preliminary interview. Should have, could have, she lamented.

She hated job hunting and all the inane interviews, especially since she really liked her current job and the people she worked with. But there was talk of cutbacks. Serious talk, and according to some of the other employees, Olivia didn't have seniority. She would be one of the first laid off. It was important to her that she stay in her current job until she accomplished what she had set out to do, but it didn't look like that was going to happen.

The only constant in Olivia's life right now was the mortgage. It had to be paid, no matter what, which was why she had to have job options.

She had gone to the office an hour earlier than usual this morning, finished two case files by noon, and headed over to Seraphina, a lovely restaurant with a stunning view. The five-star restaurant overlooked a manicured terrace, with tables strategically placed under a canopy of tree branches. Beyond was the river. Lunch was going to be a treat. She'd never dined at Seraphina because of the expense, but she'd heard that the food was wonderful. Grossly overpriced, but wonderful. No peanut butter and jelly sandwich today.

The hostess showed her to a table on the south side of the terrace. It was such a beautiful day with just a slight nip in the air, perfect for lunch outside.

The preliminary interview with Xavier Cannon, the company's lead attorney, had gone well, she thought, but he hadn't answered some of her more pressing questions and had suggested instead that she ask Jorguson. Cannon also mentioned that, if Jorguson liked her, he would offer her the job during lunch.

Jorguson was waiting for her. She spotted him across the busy terrace. He held an open folder in his hand and was reading a paper inside it. As she drew closer she could see that it was her résumé.

For about twenty seconds she thought he was quite a charmer and a rather distinguished-looking man. He was tall and thin and had a bright, white smile.

He stood and shook her hand. "Bring the lady a drink," he snapped impatiently to a passing waiter.

"Iced tea, please," she said.

The waiter had already moved her chair for her, and she sat before Jorguson could come around the table to assist her.

Jorguson's cell phone rang, and without offering an apology or an excuse for the interruption, he turned his back to her and answered. His voice was low and angry. Whoever he was talking to was getting a dressing-down. His vocabulary was crude.

So much for charming, she thought. She tried to focus on her surroundings while she waited. The linen table-cloth draped all the way to the ground, and in the center of the round table was a crystal bowl of fresh-cut flowers in every color. She looked around her and smiled. It was a really pretty day.

Jorguson finished his call. He slipped the phone into his suit jacket and gave her his full attention, but the way he was staring at her quickly made her uncomfortable. She was about to ask him if something was wrong when he said, "You're stunning. Absolutely stunning."

"Excuse me?"

"You're very beautiful," he said then. "Xavier mentioned how pretty you were, but I still didn't expect . . . That is to say, I wasn't prepared . . ."

Olivia was horrified by his close scrutiny. His leering inspection made her skin crawl. Jorguson wasn't just unprofessional; he was also creepy. She opened her linen napkin and placed it in her lap. She tried to turn his attention so he would stop gawking at her.

Typically she would have waited for him to lead the questioning, but the awkward silence and his inappropriate behavior compelled her to speak first.

"This morning I had a few minutes, and I pulled up your prospectus. Your company is quite impressive," she said. "But there was a note that last year you were investigated by the FBI—"

He rudely cut her off with a wave of his hand. "Yes, but of course nothing came of it. It was simple harassment." He continued. "They didn't like some of my clients and wanted to make trouble, which was ridiculous. I should have sued, but I didn't have the time."

Sue the FBI? Was he serious or just trying to impress her with his power. His arrogance was overwhelming.

"You're a brand-new attorney, aren't you?" he asked.

"Yes, that's correct."

"Only two people ranked higher than you on the bar. I cannot tell you how remarkable that is. Still, you don't have much experience with contracts."

"No, I don't," she agreed. "How did you find out about my scores? That's confidential—"

He waved his hand in the air again, dismissing her question. The gesture irritated her. She admitted then that pretty much everything about the man irritated her.

"There were quite a few others who applied for the position, and most of them have more experience than you, but when I discovered you were Robert MacKenzie's daughter, I moved you to the top of the list."

"You know my father?" She couldn't hide her surprise.

"Everyone who's anyone knows who your father is," he replied. "I know people who have invested in your father's Trinity Fund and have made a handsome profit. Very impressive," he stated with a nod. "I'm considering adding the fund to my own portfolio. No one plays the market like your father does. He seems to have a knack for choosing the right investments. If you're half as clever as he is, you'll go far, young lady."

Olivia wasn't given time to respond. He'd already moved on. "You'll be wonderful working with our clients. With that smile of yours, you could get them to sign anything. Oh yes, they'll be as dazzled by you as I am," he gushed. "And I have several powerful clients. Xavier will guide you. Now, then, what questions do you have for me? I have a potential client meeting me here at one, so this will have to be a quick lunch."

"Did the SEC investigate when—"

He interrupted. "No, the SEC will never investigate me," he boasted. "I'm protected there."

"You're protected? How?"

"I have a friend, and he has assured me . . ."

Her eyes widened. "You have a friend at the Securities and Exchange Commission?"

Color crept up his neck. His eyes darted to the left, then to the right. Was he checking to make sure no one was listening to the conversation?

He leaned in to the table and lowered his voice. "I don't have any worries there. As I just said, I won't be investigated, and since you're going to be working closely with me, I don't want you to be concerned."

Working closely with him? That thought made her cringe.

"About this friend . . ." she began.

"No more questions about the SEC," he snapped. He wasn't looking into her eyes now. He was staring at her chest. The longer he stared, the more indignant she became. She considered snapping her fingers several times in front of his eyes to get his attention but, wanting to remain composed and professional, decided to ask a question about the investments he'd made.

Jorguson was slick; she'd give him that much. He danced around each question but never really gave her any satisfactory answers.

The topic eventually returned to the SEC. "Who is your contact?" she asked, wondering if he would tell her. He was so smug and arrogant, she thought there was a good chance he might. She also wanted him to assure her that everything he did was legal, and she thought it was odd that he hadn't offered any such affirmation.

"Why do you want to know? That's confidential information."

He was staring at her chest again. She folded her napkin, smiled at Terry the waiter when he placed her iced tea in front of her, and handed him her menu.

"I won't be staying for lunch."

The waiter hesitated, then took her menu, glanced at Jorguson, and walked away.

Olivia was disheartened. The salary at Jorguson Investments was good, really good, but it had taken less than five minutes to know she couldn't work for this man.

What a waste of time, she thought. And money. She could have worn one of her old suits, but she'd wanted to stand out, so she bought a new dress. It was expensive, too. She loved the fit and the color, a deep emerald-green silk. It had a high V-neck, so there was no need to wear a necklace. Diamond stud earrings, which were so tiny you could barely see the sparkle, and a watch were her only jewelry. She wore her hair down around her shoulders and had taken the time to use a curling iron.

Olivia looked at Jorguson. The degenerate was still staring at her chest. And for this she had curled her hair?

"This isn't going to work," she said.

She tried to stand. Jorguson suddenly bolted upright, grabbed the top of her dress, and ripped it apart. The silk material tore, exposing her collarbone and part of her black bra.

Appalled, she slapped Jorguson's hands away. "What do you think—"

"Are you wearing a wire? You are, aren't you? That's why you asked me who my contact was. That investigation stalled, sweetheart. It's not going anywhere. The

FBI's been after me for two years now, and they've got nothing. I know for a fact they're following me. They won't ever get anything on me. They like to go after successful entrepreneurs. I'm an honest businessman," he shouted into her chest. "Now where's the damn wire? I know it's in there somewhere."

Olivia was so shocked by his behavior, she bounced between disbelief and outrage. She shoved his hands away, pulled her top together, and said, "If you try to touch me again, you'll regret it."

He tried again, and she retaliated. She heard a crunching sound when she punched him and felt a good deal of satisfaction. It was short-lived. A giant of a man with a thick neck and bald head appeared out of nowhere. He was wearing a tailored black suit, but he looked like a thug. He was at the other end of the terrace and heading toward her. As Jorguson was screaming and holding his nose with one hand, he was waving to the big man and pointing at Olivia with the other.

"Martin, see what she did to me?" he howled. "Get her, get her."

Get her? Was he twelve? Olivia could feel her face turning red. She kept her attention centered on the bodyguard as she jumped to her feet. His suit jacket opened, and she saw a gun. He hadn't reached for it, though, and was glancing around to see how many people were watching.

She was in trouble, all right. She thought about taking off one of her stiletto heels and using that as a weapon, but she decided she could do more damage with it on. She spied Terry watching from the doorway with a cell phone to his ear. She hoped he was calling the police.

"Do you have a permit to carry that gun?" she demanded of the bodyguard, trying to make her voice sound as mean as possible. Now, why, in God's name, had she asked that? What did she care if he had a permit or not? She was slowly slipping her hand inside her purse to get to her pepper spray. She couldn't find it and realized then that, when she'd changed purses, she'd left the spray at home on her bedside table. A lot of good it would do her there.

The thug named Martin, zigzagging around the tables, was getting closer. The man was built like a sumo wrestler. Olivia figured she was on her own. The other diners were already beginning to scatter. She stepped back from the table, dropped her purse into the chair, and waited for the man to reach her. If he touched her, she'd kick him where it mattered most, and if he blocked her, she'd go for his knee or his midsection.

Jorguson, holding his bloody nose, was backing away but still pointing at her and shouting. "How dare you touch me. You're going to be sorry. I know people who will hurt you. You don't hit me and get away with it. Don't you know who I am and what I can do? One phone call is all it will take," he screamed. "You're a dead woman, Olivia MacKenzie. Do you hear me? A dead woman."

Of course she'd heard him. She thought everyone within a ten-block area had heard him. She refused to give him any satisfaction by reacting, though, and that was probably why he was becoming more outrageous with his threats.

Her attention remained centered on the bodyguard. She thought he would do his best to intimidate her in front of his employer, maybe even try to get her to apologize to Jorguson—hell would freeze before she'd do that—but he surely wouldn't touch her. Not in front of all these people.

Or maybe he wouldn't care who was watching. Jorguson had shouted his intent to have her killed. Would this bodyguard try to top that crazy threat?

There was a wall of windows in the restaurant facing the river, and diners were crammed together, their faces plastered to the glass. Some had their cell phones glued to their ears; others were using the cell phone cameras to record the incident . . . for YouTube, no doubt. Certainly, most of them had witnessed Jorguson ripping her dress and then screaming after she'd punched him. The man had howled like an outraged hyena. Surely they'd heard his ridiculous threats, too.

The bodyguard took Jorguson's orders to "get her" to heart. He lunged. He grabbed her upper arm and twisted as he jerked her toward him. Pain shot up into her neck and down to her fingers. His grip was strong enough to break her bones.

He glanced over his shoulder at the crowd before turning back to her. "You're coming with me," he ordered.

A woman rushed out of the restaurant shouting, "You leave her alone." At the same time, two men in business suits ran past the woman to help Olivia.

"Let go of me," she demanded as she slammed the heel of her shoe into the top of his foot.

He grunted and let go. Olivia got in a solid kick, and he doubled over. But not for long. He quickly recovered and, roaring several grossly unflattering names at her, straightened and reached for his gun. His face was now bloodred.

Good Lord, was he going to shoot her? The look in his eyes suggested that he might. Apparently, Martin had forgotten his audience, or he no longer cared he was being watched. His impulse control had vanished. He had the most hateful look on his face as he pulled the gun from the waistband of his pants. The two businessmen coming to her aid stopped when they spotted the weapon.

"I said you're coming with me," he snarled as he lunged.

"No, I'm not." She threw a twelve-dollar glass of iced tea at him. He ducked.

"Bitch." He spit the word and tried to grab her again.

"I'm not going anywhere with you. Now get away from me."

The gun seemed to be growing in his hand. She backed away from him, and that infuriated him even more. He came at her once more, and before she could protect herself, he backhanded her. He struck the side of her face, his knuckles clipping her jaw. It was a hard hit and hurt like hell. The blow threw her backward, but even as she was falling, she didn't take her eyes off the gun.

She landed on her backside, winced from the impact on her tailbone, and quickly staggered to her feet.

She understood what the expression "seeing stars" meant. Dazed, she tried to back away.

The thug raised his gun again, and suddenly he was gone. Olivia saw a blur fly past her, tackling the bodyguard to the ground. The gun went one way, and the thug went the other, landing hard. Within seconds her rescuer had the man facedown on the grass and was putting handcuffs on him while reading him his rights. When he was finished, he motioned to another man wearing a badge and gun who was rushing across the terrace.

With one of his knees pressed against the bodyguard's spine, the rescuer turned toward her. She suddenly felt lightheaded. She could have sworn she saw an ethereal glow radiating all around him and the sound of a singing choir echoing overhead. She closed her eyes and shook her head. The blow to her jaw must be making her hallucinate. When she opened her eyes again, the vision and the choir were gone, but the man was still there, looking up at her with beautiful hazel eyes.

"Who are you?" he asked as he hauled the bodyguard to his feet.

"Olivia MacKenzie," she answered. She sounded bewildered, but she couldn't help that. The last few minutes had been hair-raising, and she was having trouble forming a clear thought.

"Who are *you*?" she asked.

"Agent Grayson Kincaid. FBI. Are you all right?"

"I've been better."

"Maybe you should sit down."

The bodyguard finally found his voice. "I was protecting my boss."

"With a Glock?" Kincaid asked. "And against an unarmed woman?"

"She kicked me."

A hint of a smile turned his expression. "Yeah, I saw."

"I'm bringing charges."

"You attacked her," Kincaid snapped. "If I were you, I'd be real quiet right now."

The bodyguard ignored the suggestion. "Mr. Jorguson has known for a long time that the FBI has been tailing him and listening in on his private conversations. What you're doing is illegal, but you people don't play by the rules, do you?"

"Stop talking," Kincaid said.

Another agent grabbed hold of the bodyguard's arm and led him away. He didn't go peacefully. He was shouting for a lawyer.

"Hey, Ronan," Kincaid shouted.

The agent dragging the bodyguard away turned back. "Yeah?"

"Did you see it?"

Ronan smiled. "Oh yeah, I saw it all. After I put this clown in the back of the car, I'll go get Jorguson."

Olivia glanced around the terrace. In all the commotion she hadn't seen him slip away.

Kincaid nodded, then turned back to her.

"The gun is under the table," she offered.

"I'll get it," Kincaid said.

He walked over to her, and she flinched when he reached out to touch her. Frowning, he said, "I'm not going to hurt you. I just want to see how bad it is."

"It's fine," she insisted. "I'm fine."

He ignored her protest. He gently pushed her hair away from the side of her face. "Your cheek's okay, but he really clipped your jaw. It's already starting to swell. You need to put ice on it. Maybe I should take you to the emergency room, have a physician look at your arm, too. I saw the way he twisted it."

"I'll be all right. I'll ice it," she promised when he looked like he wanted to argue.

He took a step back and said, "I'm sorry I couldn't get to him faster."

"You got here before he shot me. He really was going to shoot me, wasn't he?" She was still astounded by the possibility and getting madder by the second.

"He might have tried," he agreed.

She frowned. "You're awfully nonchalant about it."

"I would have taken him down before he shot you."

Her cell phone rang. She checked the number, then sent the call to voice mail. Out of the corner of her eye, she saw a man rounding the corner of the building and glaring at her. He stormed toward her, just as Kincaid bent to retrieve the bodyguard's gun.

"What the hell's the matter with you?" the man shouted.

Since he was wearing a gun and badge, she knew he was also FBI. "Excuse me?"

"You ruined a perfectly good sting. Were you wearing a wire? Did you get anything we could use? No, I didn't think so. You weren't supposed to be here until one. We weren't ready."

The agent screaming at her was an older man, late fifties, she guessed. His face was bright red, and his anger could light fires.

He moved closer until he was all but touching her, but she refused to be intimidated. "Stop yelling at me."

"She's not with the FBI," Kincaid said.

"How . . ." The confused agent took a step back. He looked at Olivia, then at Kincaid.

"I'd know if she was. Your undercover woman hasn't shown up yet."

"Two months' planning," the agent muttered. He pointed at Olivia. "Are you wearing a wire? Jorguson seems to think you are. Are you with a newspaper or—"

"Poole, leave her the hell alone," Kincaid said.

Poole was staring at her chest. Uh-oh. Olivia knew where this was going.

"If you think you're going to look for a wire, be advised. I'll punch you, too," she warned.

Distraught to have his investigation fall apart, Agent Poole stepped closer and said, "Listen, you. Don't threaten me. I could make your life a nightmare." He put his hand in front of her face and unfolded three fingers as he said, "I'm F . . . B . . . I."

She smiled. It wasn't the reaction he expected. "You want to talk nightmares?" she said. She put her hand up to his face and unfolded her three fingers. "I'm I . . . R . . . S."

TWO

Olivia was still waiting with Terry the waiter by her side. He tried several more pickup lines, and when none of them worked, he finally shrugged and went back into the restaurant.

Agent Kincaid had told Olivia to stay put until he and the other agents dealt with Jorguson and his bodyguard. He hoped by the time they returned to her Agent Poole would have calmed down. Unfortunately, that didn't happen. Poole's expression bordered on homicidal. His eyes bulged, his jaw dropped, and his face contorted in a scowl. Had Kincaid not been so angry with him for deliberately ignoring orders, he might have laughed.

It was apparent that Poole still didn't want to believe that Olivia was just an innocent bystander. He planted his hands on the table and leaned forward. "Someone tipped you off that we were running this operation, right? You're with a newspaper or one of those trashy television shows, aren't you? Are you doing an exposé on Jorguson or something? If you are, I'll shut you down," he threatened.

"IRS," she quietly repeated.

"I want proof."

She reached into her purse and pulled out an oblong laminated card. "Here you go."

Kincaid thought she sounded almost cheerful, which didn't make any sense considering what she had just been through. She should have been on her last nerve, but Olivia MacKenzie's calm demeanor was impressive ... not to mention her stunning beauty. Her eyes were a clear violet blue. Her complexion was flawless, and her lips were lush and full. From what he could see, her body was just about perfect, too. Full breasts, narrow waist, and long, shapely legs. It was one hell of a challenge not to stare at her. He hadn't experienced a reaction like this since he was a teenager.

"Okay, then," Olivia said. She snatched her ID from Agent Poole and slipped it into her purse. Then she tried to leave. "Good luck with Jorguson and Martin." She turned toward the parking lot, but Kincaid stopped her by grabbing hold of her hand. "Not yet."

"Not yet?" she repeated, looking up at him. "I really should return to work, and I'm going to have to go home and change clothes first."

Ignoring her protest, Kincaid gave Poole his full attention. "Shut this down and go back to the office," he said, his voice decisive and abrupt. "You and I need to have a word as soon as I'm finished here."

"How long will that take?" Poole demanded.

"As long as it takes."

"Yes, sir." Poole gave Olivia one last glare and took off.

"He looks like I just ruined his life," Olivia remarked.

"Isn't that what you do at the IRS?"

She could hear a smile in his voice. "Pretty much," she agreed. She tugged her hand away from his and asked, "Where exactly are we going?"

"Inside."

She stopped. "Oh, I don't think ..."

He took her hand again and pulled her along toward

the restaurant doors. She gave up on protesting. She could have argued, but she didn't think anything she said would matter. Agent Kincaid looked like the kind of man who was used to getting his way. The air of authority about him was a bit daunting, and she had the feeling he wasn't going to let her go anywhere until he was finished with her.

He was being awfully familiar with her, holding her hand. Was he making sure she wouldn't bolt? The on-lookers who were beginning to return to their tables parted to let them pass.

Five minutes later she was sitting alone at a table in a private dining room, waiting for Agent Kincaid to come back. A waiter had brought her a glass of ice water. She reached into her purse and retrieved her inhaler. All the commotion on the terrace had made her a little short-winded. She had been treated with some powerful drugs when she was a child, and one of the side effects was a touch of asthma. She never went anywhere without her inhaler.

She decided to call her boss, Royal Thurman, to let him know she was going to be late. He wouldn't really care, she knew, but it was the courteous thing to do. His phone went to voice mail, and she had just finished leaving a message when another call came in. She didn't recognize the number, but as soon as she heard the loathsome voice, she thought she knew who it was. Carl Simmons, her father's attorney, was on the line threatening her again.

"You were told to stop interfering," he said in a muffled whisper. "This is your last warning."

"Who is this?" she demanded, knowing full well Carl wouldn't tell her. Still, there was always the hope his temper would get the better of him, and he'd let it slip.

"You're forcing us to silence you. Do you want to get hurt?"

"You can threaten me all you want. I'm not going to stop."

Olivia didn't wait for a response. She ended the call and placed her phone on the table just as Agent Kincaid walked into the room. He had a small plastic bag with him.

Her hands were shaking. The phone call had gotten to her, but she didn't want the agent to notice, so she put her hands in her lap. He pulled out a chair, sat down facing her, and handed her the bag of ice. Then he asked her to tell him what led up to Jorguson's attack.

She held the bag against the left side of her jaw while she talked. Twice during her explanation she put the bag down, and each time, he picked it up and put it back in her hand.

"Did you happen to hear any of Jorguson's threats, Agent Kincaid?" she asked.

"Call me Grayson," he said. "And, no, I didn't hear the threats. Tell me."

She repeated what Jorguson had shouted and added, "He was furious and out of control. 'One phone call and you're a dead woman.' He actually shouted that. He didn't seem to care who was listening. You and the other agents were planning to catch him today, weren't you? I'm guessing I was in the wrong place at the wrong time, and somehow that really botched up your plan."

"It wasn't the right plan to begin with," Grayson admitted.

She could hear the irritation in his voice and surmised that the fault for the fiasco lay at the feet of Agent Poole, though Grayson wasn't going to say it.

"What happens to Jorguson now?" she asked.

"We're taking him in. We're not through talking to him."

"I'm sure his lawyers are already on their way."

"It doesn't matter how many lawyers he has circling him. Jorguson isn't going anywhere until I'm finished with him. Can you recall what he said to you?"

She repeated everything she remembered of the conversation and added, "You might want to ask him who his friend at the SEC is. I doubt he'll tell you, but it's worth a shot. I'm not even sure he was telling the truth. He's a braggart and very full of himself."

"Jorguson knew you worked for the IRS?"

"Yes. Maybe he thought I was out to get him."

"Are you?"

"No."

"Would you tell me if you were?"

She didn't answer the question, but said, "Do you think I would have interviewed for a position in his company if I were investigating him?"

He laughed. "Good point."

"Any other questions, Grayson?"

"No, I think that's it," he said. "I have your phone number. If I think of anything else, I'll call you." He handed her his card and added, "And if you remember anything pertinent, you call me."

"Yes, I will," she agreed. She laid the bag of ice on the table and stood to leave. With a sigh she said, "Too bad Jorguson couldn't have waited until after lunch to attack me."

"That is a shame," he said with a smile. He handed the ice back to her. "Let's eat."

She laughed. "I was just kidding. I should go. I've got so much to—"

"Aren't you hungry? I'm sure you must be, and I am, so let's eat. You took a hit for the FBI. The least we can do is offer you lunch. If you like seafood, the chowder's great."

"Do you eat here often?"

"Every once in a while."

Olivia was torn. She loved seafood chowder. Really loved it. If the iced tea was twelve dollars a glass, she could only imagine what the chowder cost. She would insist on paying for her own meal, so the question was, did she want to spend a small fortune on lunch? No, she should go home, change her clothes, and eat a peanut butter sandwich. It would be dry because she was out of strawberry jam. Come to think of it, she was out of bread, too. And she really wanted chowder, now that Grayson had mentioned it.

Nope, she was going to be practical. Money didn't grow on trees, according to her mother, even though as a child, Olivia never once thought that it did.

It didn't take much coaxing to get her to stay, especially after Grayson argued that it would be a professional courtesy.

Grayson removed his suit jacket, and she couldn't help but notice how broad his shoulders were and how muscular he was. He was certainly in shape, and she wondered how often he worked out to stay so fit. Dark brown hair and deeply tanned skin, he looked as though he'd just stepped out of an ad in a sports magazine. She also noticed how impeccably dressed he was. His suit was definitely designer label. The cut and fit were perfect. Probably Armani or Prada, she guessed. His shirt was crisp, and his tie had a subdued design in a dark hue. For such a big man, he certainly wore his clothes well.

By comparison she was a mess. After she gave the waiter her order, she went to the ladies' room to freshen up and got a good look at herself in the mirror. She had grass in her hair and a gaping tear in the top of her dress. If that weren't enough, the left side of her jaw was already turning purple. She looked as though she'd been in a barroom brawl.

There wasn't much she could do to improve her appearance. She brushed her hair, put on some lip gloss, and tried to stop feeling embarrassed. Why did she care what Grayson thought about her appearance? After today, she probably would never see him again. She already knew he was out of her league. She had very little experience with men, but she had a feeling that Agent Grayson Kincaid was the James Bond of the FBI: a gorgeous man who loved women. Olivia knew she had no business judging him without knowing anything about him. She'd bet a month's salary she was right, though.

She returned to the table, and while they waited for their orders, they talked about living in D.C., and he asked her several questions about her work. He seemed genuinely interested. By the end of lunch she was over her bout of nerves and was glad she had stayed. Once she tasted the chowder, she stopped obsessing about the cost. It was worth the price. She sat back, crossed one leg over the other, and asked, "Did you grow up around here?" She was curious to know if he would share any personal information.

"No, the family lived in Boston until I was in my teens. Then, because of my father's business, we moved to Washington, D.C."

"You travel a lot, don't you?"

"I used to, before I joined the FBI."

"Ever been to Europe?"

He smiled. "Yes. What about you? Have you traveled much?"

She shook her head. "I've lived in San Francisco and D.C. Except for a few business trips, that's it. No, wait," she added. "I went to Colorado."

"To ski?"

"No. One of my best friends went through the Air

Force Academy. I attended her graduation. Samantha's a pilot. She flies those sleek little jets now."

A waiter cleared the table while another placed fresh glasses of iced tea and dessert menus in front of them. His eyes were on Olivia, and he nearly knocked her glass over. She grabbed it before it spilled.

Grayson understood. It was difficult not to stare at her. He waited until they were alone again and then asked, "What about you? Where did you grow up?"

"San Francisco until I was eleven. Then I moved to D.C. I've been here ever since."

When he frowned, she realized the little slip she'd made. She hadn't included her family when she told him she'd moved. Maybe he hadn't noticed and was frowning about something altogether different. She hoped so. She didn't want to talk about those first years in D.C. It was too personal and too painful to relive, and she certainly didn't want to talk about her odd family.

Grayson's phone beeped, indicating he had a message. Olivia smiled. The distraction was just what she needed. "Why don't you check it? I don't mind."

He shook his head. "It can wait. You said you moved to D.C. Just you?"

She pretended not to understand. "D.C.'s my home now. The crime's a problem and you have to be so careful, but I love the energy. Don't you?"

"You didn't mention family. You moved alone?"

So much for distracting him. Grayson was an FBI agent, she reminded herself. Guess he was trained not to be distracted.

"Yes, I moved here without family."

"And you were just eleven years old."

"Yes."

She suddenly felt as though she was being interrogated, and she didn't like it one bit.

"Boarding school?" he asked.

Sure. Why not? "Something like that."

Grayson knew he was making her uncomfortable, but he couldn't figure out why. What was she hiding? Olivia checked the time and reached for her purse. He didn't want her to leave just yet. He took a drink and casually asked, "Married?"

The question surprised her. "No. You?"

"No. Ever gotten close?"

She smiled and relaxed. "No. You?"

"No."

She laughed. "You're FBI. You could find out anything you wanted to know about me."

"Yes. It wouldn't be as much fun, though."

Grayson had a beautiful smile. She thought he might be flirting with her now, but she couldn't be sure. She wasn't good at this. It was peculiar. Less than two minutes ago she couldn't wait to get out of here, and now she wanted to stay.

"You're with the IRS," he said. "You could find out all about *me*."

"You know I can't do that. I can only work on the cases I'm assigned," she said, and before he could pose another question, she asked, "How did you end up in the FBI?"

"I finished law school and didn't know what I wanted to do. None of the offers appealed to me. My cousin, Sam Kincaid, worked for the FBI. His specialty is languages," he added. "He's also an attorney, and he thought I'd be a good fit. Turns out he was right."

"A law degree would certainly give you a leg up in the FBI."

"Yes," he agreed. "Okay, now it's my turn. How did a nice girl like you end up working for the IRS?"

"During my third year of law school, I worked as a

law clerk for Judge Bowen because I wanted to get as much experience as I could in family law. After I passed the bar, my goals changed, and I decided to learn about investigative work and tax law. I'm now an attorney with the IRS."

"An attorney, huh?" He didn't know why he was surprised, but he was. He had pictured her sitting in a cubicle somewhere checking tax returns.

"Isn't everyone in Washington an attorney? I think it's a prerequisite to living here."

He laughed. "That's about right."

The waiter presented the check inside a black leather folder. When she argued that she should pay the bill, Grayson slipped his American Express card inside.

"Next time you're attacked during an interview, you can pay for lunch."

The likelihood of such a thing happening was ridiculous, but she decided to be gracious and thanked him.

"Why were you interviewing with Jorguson's company?" he asked.

"Cutbacks, and since I'm one of the newer employees, I have to assume I'll be one of the first to go. I was exploring other options," she explained. "I hope I can stay with the IRS a little longer, though. I have a goal to accomplish there. I'm learning so much about how to investigate financial crimes. I hound the investigators with all my questions. They've been very patient with me."

"Would you stay with the IRS permanently if you could?"

"Yes, I would. When I first started, I wanted to learn and then move on. My primary interest is children's advocacy, but I now know I can't do that full-time because I'd burn out too quickly. Working for the IRS is a nice balance. I had assumed the work would be boring, but as it turns out, it isn't."

"So what's your goal at the IRS?"

"It's not important," she dismissed with a shrug.

Grayson tilted his head and studied her, wondering what he was missing. Olivia was being evasive, and he felt that she was leaving out an important detail. She reminded him of his nephew, Henry. Talking to the eight-year-old took endurance, and getting the full story was nearly impossible.

He leaned forward. Olivia instinctively folded her hands in her lap and waited. She hoped he hadn't noticed how tense she was. She knew he wasn't through questioning her, and she also knew she was confusing him. Too late, she realized she shouldn't have mentioned anything personal, especially her goal.

"Let me recap," he began, sounding very much like a professor now.

"You want to recap?"

He ignored the laughter in her voice. "Yes, I do. You said you enjoy working at the IRS. Is that correct?"

She slowly nodded. "Yes."

"Assuming the cutbacks don't come, you'd stay with the IRS."

"That's right."

"Even after you accomplish your goal?"

"Yes."

"What about children's advocacy?"

"I'm doing some work on weekends and evenings when necessary for Judge Bowen and Judge Thorpe. It can get intense."

"Is this goal of yours legal?"

She laughed. "Yes."

Grayson suddenly realized how much he was enjoying this bizarre conversation. He liked being with her. When she smiled, a dimple appeared in her right cheek, and her eyes fairly sparkled. Damn, she was pretty. Everything about her appealed to him. Whatever perfume she was wearing was a real turn-on. It was so feminine and sexy. So were her legs.

"Aren't you going to tell me what your goal is?" he asked.

She gave him the sweetest smile she could muster. "No, not really."

THREE

To his credit, Grayson didn't pressure her to explain. She wondered how he would have reacted if she'd oh-so-casually said, "My goal? I want to put my father in prison . . . or die trying."

Okay, maybe the "or die trying" was a little over the top, but she was more certain than ever that she had to do something to stop him.

Everyone has a breaking point, and Olivia would never forget the night several months ago when she'd reached hers. She had just passed the bar and wanted to celebrate with her aunt Emma. The day hadn't started out great. In fact, it was hellish. It was a Saturday, she remembered, and there were a hundred things she'd wanted to get done before nightfall. Unfortunately the best-laid plans . . .

She had overslept a full hour because she forgot to set the alarm on her iPhone; her right front tire had blown out while she was driving sixty miles per hour on the highway; she had tripped over a small pothole she hadn't noticed when she was crossing the street, skinning both knees; and the strap on her favorite purse had snapped. The most upsetting offense of all: the leather on her brand-new shoes got scuffed. Needless to say, by five o'clock she wasn't in the best of moods.

Emma would fix that. Just being around her aunt made everything better. Olivia changed her clothes and headed over to Emma's gorgeous colonial house to have dinner with her. Her aunt was such a sweet, loving woman; she had a knack for making everyone she was with feel good. Olivia would leave her frustrations and worries at the door, and she knew that by the time she sat down to a delicious dinner prepared by Emma's longtime cook, Mary, she'd be laughing and having a fine time, listening as Emma regaled her with the most wonderful stories about her travels around the world. Whenever she spoke of her late husband, Daniel, her voice would soften and sometimes her eyes would get misty with her memories. After all these years, Emma's love hadn't waned, and some of the stories she told were so romantic.

Olivia missed her uncle very much. He had been a kind and generous man, and though he was an extremely successful businessman with tremendous demands on his time, he never left any doubt that Emma came first. It was obvious to everyone who knew them that they were crazy about each other. While Olivia knew better than to wish for marriage and happily ever after, she loved listening to her aunt talk about him and their life together.

Olivia arrived at Emma's house at dusk. She drove through the gates and up the long driveway that circled in front of the three-story Georgian mansion. A dark sedan sat parked near the steps that led to the main door. Olivia didn't recognize the car, and as she got closer she could see the figure of a man sitting in the driver's seat. She had to pass the car to reach her usual parking space behind the house, and when she was a few yards away, she recognized the man. He was Carl Simmons, her father's attorney. He was looking down at his phone and didn't turn his head or look in her direction. Olivia felt a knot forming in her stomach. If Carl Simmons was here, that meant her father was inside with Emma. She hadn't counted on running into her father tonight, and she didn't look forward to the encounter. She pulled around the house and parked outside the garage as was her habit when she had lived with Emma. She entered through the back door, and as soon as she walked into the kitchen, she could hear raised voices. The housekeeper, a robust woman named Harriet, looked relieved to see her.

"What's going on?" Olivia asked.

Harriet put her finger over her lips in an unspoken command to keep silent, then motioned for Olivia to follow her into the laundry room. She pulled the door shut behind her and whispered, "I'm so thankful you're here. Mary certainly got hold of you quickly, didn't she? She only just went upstairs to get her phone so she could text you."

As if on cue, Olivia's phone beeped, indicating she had just received a text.

"No, I stopped by to have dinner with all of you. I heard shouting when I came into the kitchen."

"It's a fight," Harriet said, nodding for emphasis. "A big one. Your father and your aunt are having it out. Something terrible happened and Emma is enraged. Mary and I have never seen her like this. And your father is getting meaner and meaner. He threatened her, Olivia, and he's saying such terrible things about your mother."

"The fight's about my mother?" she asked, trying to understand.

Harriet shook her head. "I don't think so, but your father dragged your mother into it. From what I overheard, it's about some charity that lost money."

The poor housekeeper was beside herself with worry.

She kept folding and refolding a dish towel. "Emma never raises her voice," she whispered. "So you can see how serious this situation is."

"Yes," Olivia agreed. "Harriet, you said my father threatened Emma?"

"He did. Something to do with your mother. Whatever it was upset Emma."

Olivia opened the door. "All right. I'll go in now and see what I can do."

"May I offer a suggestion?"

"Yes, of course."

"If I were you, I'd listen at the door to find out what's going on. Once Emma sees you, she'll stop the argument, and you'll never know what it was about."

Harriet was right. Since Olivia was a little girl, Emma had tried to shield her from any unpleasant family conflicts. Even though Olivia was an adult now, Emma continued to protect her.

Olivia didn't like the idea of eavesdropping on a private conversation, but she thought she just might linger at the door for a few minutes to get the gist of the argument. That wouldn't be considered eavesdropping, would it? Of course it would, she admitted. But right or wrong, she was still going to do it.

As it turned out, she couldn't lean against the door because Mary had gotten there first. That didn't matter, though. Olivia could hear every word from down the hallway.

Her father's voice was furious. "If you try to make trouble, I'll leave Deborah, and you know what that will do to her. She says she can't live without me. Shall we find out?"

"Do it," Emma challenged. "Leave my sister. You've made the threat to divorce her how many times now? I'm not giving you any more money to stay with her. I made that mistake years ago, and I won't make it again. My sister may be a fool but she deserves better, and if she can't see it, then she'll have to wallow in self-pity when you leave."

"If Deborah does anything crazy, it will be on your hands."

"Are you suggesting she might harm herself? What do you suppose that will do to your reputation, Robert? Investors want stable managers, and they don't like scandal. Tell me," she continued, "did you ever love Deborah?"

Olivia stopped a few feet from the door. Mary, Emma's cook for the past twelve years, a sturdy German woman who always wore her silver-gray hair pulled back in a tidy bun, stood in front of her, unaware that she'd approached. Looking embarrassed to be listening in on a conversation that had become so personal, Mary turned to leave and saw Olivia standing behind her. After giving her a sympathetic smile and a pat on the arm, Mary went down the hall toward the kitchen. Olivia stepped up to the door. It was open a crack and the voices were loud and clear. She waited for her father's answer to Emma's question, but she didn't hear one.

Then Emma asked, "Are you capable of loving anyone but yourself?"

"The question's ridiculous. You still haven't told me what you plan to do—"

"About Jeff Wilcox?" Emma asked. "That depends on you. Are you going to stand by and do nothing while Jeff goes to prison because of your lies?"

Olivia leaned forward and peeked in to her aunt's study through the tiny opening in the doorway. She saw her father pick up a magazine from the desk and flip through it nonchalantly as he responded. "Yes, that's exactly what I'm going to do. Stand by and do nothing. I didn't put a gun to his head and force him to give me the money and make the investments for his charity."

"Believe me, if I had known that he was going to do that, I would have put a stop to it immediately. If Daniel were alive, he would never have let Jeff get involved with you."

Olivia recognized the name. Jeff Wilcox had been her uncle Daniel's protégé. He was the son of close personal friends of her aunt and uncle, and when he had graduated from college, he had gone to work for Daniel. Olivia was away at school at that time, but she remembered seeing Jeff at a couple of gatherings. She'd heard her aunt and uncle speak of him many times. From what they said, he was a courteous and easygoing young man who often expressed his gratitude for the opportunity her uncle had given him and the kindnesses shown to him by her aunt. Shortly after her uncle died, she'd heard that Jeff had taken a position with a charitable organization.

"He knew there were risks," she heard her father say.

"You set him up," Emma cried. Olivia had never heard her aunt so upset. "You lied to him. He would never have invested the charity's funds if he had any inkling that they weren't safe. I know Jeff. He's honest and decent. He has a wife and a new baby now. He wouldn't risk that. Have you no conscience?"

"I only did what he asked," her father answered. "It's not my fault if his board of directors thought he misappropriated the funds. I offered him several investment strategies, and he made the final decision."

"Decisions based on the lies you told him," Emma countered.

"Wilcox isn't such an upstanding citizen," he snapped. "Greed was his downfall. He demanded a fee from me for investing the charity's funds, and I've got the signed papers to prove it."

"Lies, all lies," she cried out. "Jeff would never—"

"It's his word against mine," her father snapped. "And when the authorities investigate, they'll see that the evidence is on my side. The documents clearly show that there were risks with the investments and no guarantees. Documents that he signed, I might add."

Olivia had heard enough. She took a deep breath, opened the door, and walked inside. Neither Emma nor her father noticed her. They stood with their backs to the door. The window was on her father's right and she could see his reflection. His eyes were cold and his jaw was clinched.

"How much did Jeff Wilcox give you?" Olivia asked.

Robert MacKenzie turned to her, the contemptuous scowl gone, replaced by a dazzling smile. She'd been told that women adored him and that, if he hadn't decided to go into the Wall Street world, he could have made millions as a movie star. Tall and fit, with thick silver-tipped hair and eyes as blue as hers, he was considered devastatingly handsome, but it was his charm that captured his clients. Men believed they were in his inner circle, and women thought he wanted them in his bed. He had never cheated on his wife, though, for to do so would diminish his carefully constructed persona. He had learned to use all of his attributes to captivate and to hypnotize. Besides, money was far more important and arousing than sex. Very few people knew the real Robert MacKenzie, the devil hiding beneath the angel's wings.

"Hello, darling. How long have you been standing there?" he asked.

"Not long," she lied. "I just heard you talking about Jeff Wilcox. What have you done to him?"

"Nothing. Your aunt was misinformed," he said, shaking his head and never letting the smile fade. "As usual," he added. He walked over to her, put his hands on her shoulders, and leaned down to kiss her on her cheek. "How are you feeling? Are you taking your medicine every day?"

It always came back to her health. She believed it was her father's way of reminding her that she was flawed in his eyes. He knew how to manipulate her and make her feel inferior. When she was younger, it had worked, but no longer.

Olivia looked at Emma to gauge her reaction. Her aunt's gaze was locked on Robert, and her face was flushed with anger.

Olivia stepped back, then walked over to stand next to her aunt in a show of loyalty. "Father, I haven't had to take medicine for years. You know that." Turning to Emma, she said, "Tell me about Jeff Wilcox."

"Don't answer that," Robert ordered. "Olivia doesn't need to concern herself with business matters, especially in her weakened condition."

"Will you stop—" Olivia began to protest.

Her father cut her off when he said to Emma, "My daughter is so starved for affection, she'll believe anything you say, Emma, and she'll try to help because you've shown her that you care. If you get her involved in this, the stress could prove to be too much for her."

"For God's sake, Robert, your daughter has grown up and is quite healthy. Stop trying to make her an invalid."

"Tell me about Jeff," Olivia repeated. She folded her arms and leaned back against the desk, leaving no doubt that she wasn't going to budge until she got an explanation.

Her father refused to respond. Emma didn't have any such qualms. "Jeff became the manager of the Walden Foundation. They help the indigent and the homeless by providing housing and job programs. They've had a tremendously successful track record. The man who started the charity had, himself, been homeless and had been helped by a kind stranger. When Walden's luck turned, he vowed he would help others, and he started the charitable foundation. He died several years ago, but he left thirty-two million dollars for his charity to continue, and Jeff was brought in as its director. The position was perfect for Jeff. He always wanted to do work that would make a real difference in the world. And he was doing a great job, I understand . . . until he met your father."

"Jeff gave him the money to invest," Olivia said.

"That's right."

"And now it's gone," she concluded.

"Yes," her aunt said. "All of it squandered in risky investments."

"The risks were clearly explained," her father argued.

Emma ignored his protest and continued. "The board of directors had allowed Jeff autonomy to make these investments because he had given them assurances that everything was in secure funds. Of course, when the investments went under, they called for an investigation. Your father had guaranteed that all of the investments were protected and had the highest ratings possible, and Jeff, being the trusting and decent man that he is, believed him." She shot Robert a look of contempt.

Olivia's father shook his head and smiled condescendingly at her. "He was lying, Emma. The papers he signed clearly show he was made aware of the risks."

Emma turned back to Olivia. "The prosecutors are involved now. They're claiming that Jeff not only mishandled the money but also that he did it knowingly and with the intent of lining his own pockets. If there's a trial and he's convicted, he could go to prison and be taken away from his wife and his baby—all for something I know he didn't do."

Olivia turned to her father. "How much did you make on these investments?"

Her father gave a slight shrug and answered, "It's not my responsibility to keep people from making stupid decisions. If Wilcox had chosen to invest in my Trinity Fund, he wouldn't be in this mess, but he insisted on another route."

"How much?" Olivia insisted.

"My five percent commission for the transactions was a low fee, considering the circumstances."

"So you walked away with over a million and a half, and Jeff Wilcox faces prison—not to mention the charity that is destroyed."

"I've wasted enough time talking about this," her father said as he began making his way to the door. "I have to be back in New York for an event tonight."

Olivia could barely control her anger. Her chest was tight, and she desperately needed to use her inhaler, but she didn't dare in front of him. It would be one more thing to mock, and it would prove to him that she was, indeed, inferior.

She had known that her father's business activities were suspect in the past, but it was as though she was seeing him without a filter for the first time. Even his attire seemed disingenuous, with his hand-tailored suit and his handsome cashmere scarf draped around his neck. Olivia watched him slip on a black wool coat that was impeccably cut and a perfect fit.

"Father?"

"Yes?" he said as he put on one leather glove and reached for the doorknob.

"This has to stop. You can't continue to hurt people this way."

Her father turned back to her with a compassionate smile. "Get some rest, Olivia. You look pale. That terrible disease you have . . . it's lurking under your skin . . . waiting. You never know when it could come back." He left without saying good-bye.

Monday morning, Olivia applied for a job with the IRS.

FOUR

"I don't know what I was thinking," Olivia told Jane. "Agent Kincaid asked me how I ended up working for the IRS, and once I started explaining . . . it got away from me."

"Did you tell him you're investigating your father?"

"No," she replied. "But I went on and on about reaching my goal, and he naturally wanted to know what the goal was. I wouldn't tell him, of course. I barely know the man. He has to think I'm crazy."

The two women were sitting side by side in beige leather recliners in what they called the Dracula room of St. Paul's Hospital. Olivia was giving blood her friend would receive the following afternoon.

Dressed in black silk pajamas and a hot-pink robe, birthday gifts from Sam and Collins, Jane had come down from her hospital room to keep Olivia company. Jane's long honey-brown hair was up in a ponytail and she looked pale, terribly pale. Dr. Pardieu had ordered the blood transfusion and had told Jane that it would help immensely. It had in the past, he reminded her, and there was no reason to think it wouldn't help now.

"You shouldn't care what other people think."

"I know," Olivia agreed. "But Grayson's . . . different. I do care what he thinks about me, and honest to Pete, I don't have the faintest idea why." She sounded bewildered.

"Grayson?"

"Agent Grayson Kincaid. He told me to call him Grayson."

"Do you think you'll ever see him again?"

"Probably not," she said and was surprised by the stab of disappointment she felt. "Let's talk about something else. Did I mention that Jorguson told me he admires my father and that he knows people who have done quite well investing in his fund?"

"He must not have heard that you're trying to stop him."

"How could he have heard? Every time I make an inquiry or lodge a complaint, it's squelched. No one's calling me back, the SEC . . ." She took a breath. "It's frustrating, but I'll keep trying."

"Tell me everything that happened at the interview," Jane said. "Start at the beginning."

Since Jane was looking so sickly, Olivia decided to accommodate her, and by the time she was finished, Jane had a stitch in her side from laughing so hard.

"Let me get this straight. You asked Jorguson's bodyguard if he had a permit to carry a gun? The man's pointing a . . . What did you call it?"

"A Glock. Agent Kincaid called it a Glock."

"Okay, then, he's pointing a fancy Glock at you, and you want to know if he has a permit?" Jane thought, given the circumstances, the question was hilarious, and she couldn't stop laughing.

Olivia handed her a tissue to wipe the tears from her cheeks. "I watch way too much television, don't I? On all those police shows the detectives ask the criminals if they have permits. I was trying to think of something to say to get him to stop coming toward me. It's illegal for him to even carry the gun. I don't know why I didn't point that out."

"Weren't you scared?"

If an outsider had asked her that question, she probably would have pretended that it was no big deal, that she hadn't been scared at all. She wanted people to think she was a tough, no-nonsense kind of woman. Only Jane and the other Pips knew the real Olivia. They understood her vulnerability because they were just like her.

"Oh yes, I was scared," she said. "But I was also so astonished by his behavior I could barely think what to do, and I was angry, really angry. People shouldn't bring guns to five-star restaurants."

"Is that a rule?"

Olivia laughed. "It sounded like one, didn't it? I guess I just didn't want to die in such a lame way."

"Getting shot during an interview *is* a lame way to die."

She shrugged. "I can think of better ways. Don't laugh at me. I'm giving you my blood, which happens to have antibodies you need, so be nice to me."

A nurse came into the room to check Olivia's IV. After saying hello, Jane switched to French as she continued the conversation. Because of their crush on Dr. Pardieu, all the Pips eventually had become fluent in his language. It was their way of saying thank you to him for saving them.

"I'm always nice to you," Jane said. Then, in the blink of an eye, she became melancholy. "What if the transfusion doesn't work this time? What if I don't feel better and I have to start chemo again?"

"The transfusion will work," Olivia assured her.

"You're a real contradiction—you know that?" Jane said. "You're such an optimist with everyone, but when it comes to yourself, you only see the negative."

Dismissing her criticism, Olivia responded, "The transfusion helped in the past, and there's no reason to think it won't help now. You're just a little anemic, that's all. Don't stop trusting Dr. Pardieu. He's taken good care of all of us."

Jane was in the mood to feel sorry for herself. "But you and Collins and Sam have all been cured. I'm the only one struggling after all this time. I don't understand it. I was feeling great until a few weeks ago."

"We're in remission," she corrected. "Not cured."

"Dr. Pardieu said you're safe now," she said. "And none of you have had any symptoms for years. I'm the difficult one." Jane knew she sounded pitiful, but she didn't care. She usually tried to be the positive, upbeat one, but she knew she didn't have to put up any shields with Olivia or the other Pips. She could cry like a three-year-old if she wanted to and not worry that any of them would think less of her.

"You've always been difficult," Olivia said, smiling. "Sam says you can be a real pain in the . . ."

Jane burst into laughter. "I guess I'm not going to get any 'there, there, you poor thing' from you."

"When did you ever get any of that from me?" She shifted position in the recliner and winced when the needle moved ever so slightly.

"Never."

"If Dr. Pardieu isn't worried . . ."

"He says he isn't."

"Has he ever lied to any of us?"

"No. In fact, he's been brutally honest."

"So, if he isn't worried . . ."

Jane smiled because she realized she was actually feeling much better. A little whining wasn't such a bad thing after all. "If I don't have to do another round of chemo, I'm going to participate in the art show at the

Scripts Gallery. The artists have to be there," she explained. "I'll have four paintings on display. Maybe I'll get lucky and sell one or two."

"Are you low on funds? I could give you—"

"I've got more money than I know what to do with from my mom's life insurance. I'm just saying, getting paid for my work is validation. I want you to come to the gallery, okay?"

"Let me know when and where, and I'll be there."

"Logan's going to try to come to the show, too."

"Your brother's out of rehab?" Olivia's surprise was evident in her voice.

"Yes," she replied. "And he's doing really well this time. He seems serious about his sobriety. He's going to meetings every single day, and he's trying to make amends."

"Like?"

"He comes to see me every evening on his way home from work."

"Logan has a job?"

"He's working as a mechanic at Roger's Rent-A-Car company. He helps out at the counter, too. Logan says the owner is giving him more responsibility, and he doesn't want to let him down. He worries about me. He never used to."

"He was too drunk and too stoned to worry about anyone." She saw Jane's expression and hurriedly said, "I'm sorry. I shouldn't have said that."

"No, it was true, but not any longer. He brings me carryout and told me that when I get home, he'll come over and cook for me."

"Maybe rehab worked this time," Olivia said, though she didn't hold out much hope. Jane was an eternal optimist. Olivia wasn't. Logan hadn't gone willingly; rehab had been court mandated. Jane's older brother had been a mess for as long as Olivia had known Jane. He drank alcohol like water, and his drug of choice was cocaine.

She hoped for Jane's sake that Logan had decided to change his life. She was about to ask another question about Logan when he walked into the room. He was tall, gaunt, and painfully thin, but there was a light in his eyes Olivia hadn't seen before. He put his finger to his lips to let Olivia know he didn't want her to say anything, then quietly snuck up behind Jane. He leaned down and whispered, "Boo."

Jane jumped. "Logan, will you stop doing that," she demanded. "Why you think it's funny to scare people is beyond me."

He laughed. "Hi, Olivia. How are you doing?"

"I'm fine," she answered.

He turned to Jane then. "I've been all over this hospital looking for you. What are you doing here?"

"Olivia's giving me her blood," Jane said. "She's keeping me alive with her antibodies." She realized she shouldn't have joked when she saw Logan's expression. He looked stricken. "I'm going to be fine."

"Don't try to protect me," he said. "I know you're sick. Always tell me the truth, okay? I can handle it."

"Jane's anemic, that's all," Olivia said, trying to help Jane downplay her illness.

"And your blood will make her better?"

"Yes, that's right," Jane said and then hastened to change the subject. "What about the art show? Did you get permission?" Turning to Olivia, she explained, "Logan has a nine o'clock curfew at the halfway house."

Logan grinned. "Yes, I got permission. I can stay out until ten thirty." He leaned down and kissed Jane on the cheek. "I've got to go. I've got a meeting in thirty minutes."

Jane waited until Logan had left the room and then said, "What do you think?"

Olivia smiled. "I think he's on the right track."

"I do, too. He's different now, in a good way. He's been clean and sober over a hundred and twenty days. That's the longest he's ever gone," she added. "And he isn't hanging out with all those losers anymore. I wish Mom were alive to see his recovery."

Jane took a breath. "Okay, we're through talking about my brother. I've got really funny news to tell you. You'll never guess what Collins did. I'm not supposed to tell you because she wants to, but you need to be warned so you won't laugh the way I did. She was furious with me. I couldn't help it," she added. "I swear you'll never, ever guess."

"Is she in trouble?"

"No."

"Just tell me."

"She took the exam and she passed. Aced the interviews, too. In fact, they actually recruited her."

"They?"

"FBI," Jane said. "Collins has decided to become an FBI agent. It's kind of ironic, don't you think? This news coming on the same day you have a run-in with the FBI?"

"It wasn't a run-in. It was a mistake," Olivia argued. "Collins in the FBI—that's a good one." She laughed. Miss Sensitivity an agent? Not possible."

"I'm not joking. Can you picture it? Collins carrying a gun?"

"Dibs on telling Sam."

"I already tried," Jane said. "I got voice mail. She'll get back to me when she can."

Olivia's cell phone rang, interrupting their conversation. Before she looked at the iPhone screen, she checked her watch.

"Talk about a pain in the backside," Olivia said. "Natalie's right on time."

"Your sister's on time? On time for what?"

"She's been calling every night for the past five nights at exactly seven o'clock."

"You better answer it. You may explain after you talk to her . . . if you want to explain . . . unless it's private . . ."

Exasperated, Olivia said, "You know I tell you everything."

Jane nodded. "I know. I was being sensitive. It's a new thing I'm trying. Now answer your damned phone. I want to hear what's going on."

Olivia didn't want to talk to her sister, but she knew that, if she didn't answer the call now, Natalie would continue to phone her every fifteen minutes until she got hold of her. Her sister was as tenacious as a junkyard dog, and in some instances just as mean.

"Hello, Natalie. What's new?"

Her sister wasn't in the mood to be chatty. "Did you talk to Aunt Emma yet?"

Olivia counted to five before she answered the question, hoping to get rid of some of her anger before she spoke. It didn't help. "No, I did not." Her voice was emphatic.

"She's home from London."

"Yes, I know."

She could hear Natalie's long, drawn-out sigh over the phone. "Don't you care about our mother?"

Here comes the drama, Olivia thought. She really wasn't in the mood to put up with Natalie's antics tonight. She'd had enough drama today.

"Is Mother there with you?" she asked.

"Yes."

"May I speak with her?"

"She's on the other line talking to our father . . . you know, Robert MacKenzie, the man you've been ignoring."

Olivia couldn't resist a bit of sarcasm. "I thought I was ignoring our mother."

"Don't be rude," Natalie snapped.

Olivia vowed she wouldn't let her sister goad her into an argument, no matter how abrasive she became, and so she remained silent.

Another sigh, then Natalie said, "All I'm asking is that you talk to Aunt Emma and convince her to come to our father's birthday party."

"His birthday isn't for several months," Olivia stated.

"These big celebrations take time. It's going to be an amazing event," she said, enthusiasm lacing her words. "One of Dad's assistants booked the grand ballroom at the Morgan Hotel over a year ago, and we're expecting as many as three hundred guests."

"Three hundred for a birthday party?"

"It's amazing, isn't it?"

Amazing was obviously Natalie's word of the day. "Yes," she said. "Amazing. But here's my question. Dad lives in Manhattan. Why is he having a birthday party in Washington, D.C.?"

"Oh, there's going to be another party in New York."

"Two birthday parties?" she asked and began to laugh. "Isn't that a little narcissistic?"

"Dad didn't want to exclude anyone, and all those men and women who invested in the MacKenzie Trinity Fund want to celebrate with him. He's made them all rich."

"I'm betting they were already rich."

"Yes, but Dad's a financial genius, and he has more than doubled their investments. So many of his investors live in D.C., and that's why he decided to throw a party there, too. There's going to be at least three senators and twice that many congressmen attending the party and a couple of ambassadors, too." Natalie sounded starstruck.

"Was every investor invited?"

"No. That would have made the number of guests well over a thousand. Just the high-income investors were invited. I'm telling you, it's going to be amazing."

"It sounds like it will be," she said to placate her sister.

"So you understand."

"Understand what?"

"Aunt Emma has to be there," she cried out. "For God's sake, pay attention. You know how important Emma is. And powerful. How many boards do you think she's on? And she's a huge patron of the arts."

"She's on three boards."

"She's an influential member of society," Natalie said. She sounded calmer now, more in control. "If she doesn't attend the birthday party, it will be noticed. People will talk, and Mother will be embarrassed."

"I don't think Aunt Emma cares what people say."

"But Mother does," she snapped. "This is tearing her apart. She can't stand the rift. It's terrible that Emma won't talk to her."

"I believe it was our mother who started the silent treatment when Emma told her she'd changed her trust. Our mother and father aren't getting any of her money."

"Mother doesn't care about that," Natalie insisted. "She's just happy that you and I are still beneficiaries. We'll both get large sums when Emma's gone, and I will gladly hand it over to our father to invest. Unlike you, I'm loyal."

Her sister's callous and mercenary attitude was making Olivia sick. "Wasn't the money you got from Uncle Daniel's trust enough, Natalie? Now you can't wait to get your hands on more?"

Olivia heard Natalie's husband, George, in the background telling her to hand him her phone. Then he was on the line.

"Olivia, George Anderson here."

"For God's sake, George. She knows your last name," Natalie said.

"We understand your aunt Emma joins you for dinner every Sunday."

"When she's in town," Olivia said.

"Yes, and you cook for her."

"I don't cook, George. We go out." She knew she was irritating him with her interruptions, and she couldn't help smiling.

"At one of the dinners, perhaps you could mention your father's birthday party and request that she attend. Is that so difficult?"

"Apparently it is," Olivia said.

"Don't be sarcastic," he chided. He turned away from the phone. "There's no reasoning with her, Natalie."

Her sister came back on the line. "Who cares who started the silent treatment. Emma needs to do the right thing and call Mother," she said in a near shout. "And by the way," she continued on a rant now, "shame on you, Olivia. Do you realize how cruel you're being to the family? If you don't show up for the party either, how would it look? It wouldn't just be hurtful—it would be disloyal."

Olivia muted the phone. "Natalie wants to know if I realize how hurtful I'm being to the family."

Jane put her hand out, palm up, and wiggled her fingers. "Let me talk to her. Come on, give me the phone." Jane's face wasn't pale now. In the space of a few seconds, her complexion had turned bright pink. "I'll set the record straight."

Olivia smiled. Jane had always been her champion.

She hit the MUTE button again and said to Natalie, "Aunt Emma has a mind of her own. You know that."

"But she'll do anything for you because she feels . . ."

Natalie had suddenly stopped. Olivia's determination not to get pulled into an argument flew out the window. "She feels what?" she demanded angrily. "Go ahead, say it."

"Okay, I will," she said defiantly. "She feels sorry for you. She always has, ever since you got sick. Why do you think she moved to D.C.?"

"Oh, I don't know. Maybe because she loved me and knew the rest of you had pretty much written me off."

"We did no such thing."

"Emma wanted me to have a home to go to when I was released from the hospital. And she wanted me to have at least one visitor when I got out of isolation."

"You do like to dredge up the past, don't you?"

Olivia closed her eyes. She couldn't do this anymore.

"Natalie, do me a favor."

"What?"

"Stop calling me."

She didn't give her sister time to argue. She disconnected the call, dropped her phone into her purse, and turned to Jane to tell her what Natalie wanted.

"Why is she so hell-bent on getting your aunt Emma to attend the party?"

"According to Natalie, everyone who matters in D.C. society knows who Emma is, and if she isn't at the party, it will be noticed, and that will embarrass my mother."

"Is Natalie working for your father now?"

"No," she answered. "She's just helping out with the birthday parties. She and her husband, George, still run that Internet company. From what I understand, it's doing quite well. They sell everything from shoes to kitchen sinks. They have so many people working for them, they can afford to take time off."

"Is George a believer, too?" she asked.

Olivia laughed. "A believer? Do you mean under my father's charismatic spell?"

"Yes, that's what I mean."

"Yes, he is. According to Natalie, our father has doubled their money. She boasts that they could retire now if they wanted."

The nurse walked into the room carrying a glass of orange juice. She handed the drink to Olivia and unhooked the IV.

"You know the drill," she said. "Drink all the orange juice, sit back, and relax. If you feel dizzy, push the CALL button."

Olivia's cell phone rang. Certain it was Natalie calling again with a renewed attack, she didn't bother to look at the screen.

Her greeting wasn't very polite. "You're driving me crazy. You know that? Absolutely crazy."

A deep male voice responded. "Yeah? Good to know."

Agent Grayson Kincaid was on the line.

FIVE

Grayson had spent the rest of his afternoon putting out fires caused by the Jorguson debacle, but as busy as he was, he couldn't get Olivia MacKenzie out of his head, and that irritated the hell out of him. His response to her didn't make any sense. After all, he'd been with the woman for only an hour. It was purely a physical reaction, he reasoned. She had a beautiful face, an amazing smile, an incredible body. He would have to be a eunuch not to notice or react.

He sat at his desk reading through a file and cross-checking it with the data on his computer screen, but every now and then she'd pop into his thoughts. Disgusted with his lack of focus, he shook his head in an attempt to clear it and started over again on page one.

Agent Ronan Conrad knocked on his door, opened it, and leaned in. "Have you got a minute?"

"Sure. Come in."

The office was claustrophobic. Ronan had to shut the door in order to pull out the one chair so that he could sit. In the process he banged his knee on the metal desk.

It was a cold, uninviting space. The gray walls were bare, and there weren't any personal items, like family photos or mementos, on the desk. The only window was the size of a postage stamp.

"I like what you've done with the place," Ronan said, grinning.

The two men were good friends. They had gone through training together and had been assigned to the same team now for four years. Their work ethic and dedication were very similar, though their backgrounds couldn't have been more different. Ronan grew up in a large working-class family in the inner city. He attended a state university on an athletic scholarship and upon graduation entered the Marines. After serving several years on a special ops team, he returned home to attend graduate school and was recruited by the FBI.

Grayson, on the other hand, had been dealt a different hand. He was born into a family of wealth and prestige, and in the D.C. area was considered a blue blood. He entered the academy after earning his law degree at Princeton. His inheritance from a trust fund handed down by his grandfather was substantial, but Grayson had made several wise investments and had turned a large fortune into an even larger fortune. If the truth be known, he didn't need to work for a living.

Coming from two such dissimilar circumstances, one would assume that the two men would be worlds apart, but the opposite was true. They had bonded after the first couple of weeks of training. Ronan initially had his doubts when he'd learned of Grayson's privileged background, but his opinion quickly changed. There wasn't anyone in their class who trained harder or studied longer. Grayson excelled at every test the academy threw at him, and soon a friendly rivalry developed between the two friends, each one pushing the other to a higher level. By the time they graduated from the academy, both men had won the admiration and respect of the instructors and all the other trainees.

"How do you like filling in for Pensky?" Ronan asked, crossing his arms and leaning his chair back on two legs.

"She's back Monday, thank God. I hate being cooped up in this office. I feel like I'm in a tomb."

Ronan looked around the room. "I think the utility closet is bigger," he remarked. "Maybe you'll get to use it."

"Why would I want to do that?" Grayson asked. He rolled his shoulders to work out the stiffness. He'd been leaning over the file folders for hours now.

"Word is, the job is yours if you want it. Pensky's going to retire next year. Maybe sooner."

Grayson shook his head. "I don't want it."

"If you end up getting custody of your nephew, you probably won't want to be running all over the country. Pensky's job would be perfect for you."

"I'm hoping my brother will step up and start acting like a father."

"Come on, Grayson. You know that's not gonna happen. At least not anytime soon."

Ronan had known Grayson's brother, Devin, almost as long as he'd known Grayson. He'd met him shortly after graduating from the academy. Devin had the same upbringing as Grayson, but the two brothers were polar opposites. Grayson had a strong work ethic and a fierce sense of duty and loyalty to family, but Devin was irresponsible and self-centered. Since his wife's death several years ago, he had become quite the jet-setter. He liked the action in Monte Carlo and Dubai, and he loved women. He was the ultimate playboy and, sadly, often forgot he had a son.

Ronan knew it was difficult for his friend to talk about his family, and he doubted anyone else in the office knew about the situation.

"You're lucky your brother isn't dragging Henry all over Europe."

"I wouldn't let that happen."

"Is Henry still living with your father?"

"Yes," he answered and then abruptly changed the subject. "What's happening with the Harrison investigation?"

"That's what I wanted to report. Those brothers are crazy, plain crazy. I enjoyed arresting them, and I have to admit I wish they had resisted. I would have loved to punch all three of them."

"Are they in lockup?"

Ronan nodded. "And they're not going anywhere. They were denied bail."

"No bail? That's good."

"After you dropped the case in my lap—why are you smiling?"

"Because that's exactly what I did. It's called payback."

Ronan looked surprised, then conceded. "Yeah, okay. I guess I deserved it after the Brody case."

"You guess? Do you know how many interviews I had to do with those freaky cult members?"

"I heard it was hilarious," Ronan said.

"I still don't know how you did it. One day you're running the investigation, and the next it's on my desk."

"It took finesse," Ronan boasted. "Someday I'll teach you a few of my tricks." Turning serious, he asked, "What about Poole? Have you talked to him yet?"

"Yes, and he agreed to a transfer."

"He agreed?"

"Yeah, well, I didn't really give him a choice."

"And in return?"

"I won't detail his latest screwup in his personnel file. Of course, his superior will, but I won't. I won't add fuel to the fire."

"You're too soft, Grayson," Ronan said with feigned disgust. "I almost got that out with a straight face. You're a hard-ass, just like me."

"Maybe," he allowed. "What's going on with Jorguson? Have you heard anything?"

"No, not yet. The only reason we got dragged into the middle of the investigation was because of that hothead Poole," he remarked.

Grayson disagreed. "We weren't dragged into the investigation. We were doing a favor for Agent Huntsman."

"Poole was told to shut down the operation, and he completely ignored the order. That's about the third or fourth time he's disregarded Huntsman's instructions, right?"

"Right," Grayson said.

"He should be fired or forced to retire."

"That's Huntsman's call, not ours, but I agree with you. Poole needs to get out."

"It's a good thing we made it to the restaurant when we did," Ronan said. "I don't think Poole would have gotten to the bodyguard before he hurt Olivia MacKenzie."

"You remembered her name."

Ronan nodded. "I remember everything about her," he admitted. "And I didn't even speak to her. You interviewed her. What's she like?"

"Smart," he said.

"And?"

"And what?"

"And drop-dead gorgeous."

Grayson smiled. "That, too."

"So you did notice."

"Of course I noticed," he said. "I'm not blind."

"Huntsman doesn't have the evidence to prove Jorguson is laundering money for some of his clients, so he's decided to do some pushing. I helped him get statements from six strong witnesses who saw Jorguson attack MacKenzie at the restaurant, and we have the cell phone video. Huntsman hasn't contacted her yet to find out if she'll testify. He's charging him with battery. It's not much but—"

Grayson interrupted. "If that's the only charge, Huntsman has to know it will never get to court. Jorguson's attorneys will either get it thrown out or plea it down."

"Of course they will," he agreed. "But Huntsman is going to keep them busy, flood them with paper. I honestly don't know what he hopes to accomplish," he said.

"He's frustrated."

"Yes, he is," Ronan agreed.

"I just finished my report and sent it over to him, and when he reads it, he'll realize there's a better way to go after Jorguson."

"What better way?" Ronan wanted to know.

"Apparently Poole didn't mention Olivia's occupation to Huntsman. He was probably embarrassed because he couldn't intimidate her." Thinking about it made him smile.

"What am I missing?" Ronan asked.

"Olivia MacKenzie works for the IRS. Therefore, Jorguson attacked . . ."

"An IRS agent." He laughed. "Oh, that's sweet. Huntsman's going to love it. Did Jorguson know? Of course he did. He was interviewing her, right?"

"Right."

"I'll contact MacKenzie—"

"No, I'll do it." Grayson heard how eager he sounded and quickly added, "I want to get out of this office. I can't breathe in here."

He thought he'd been smooth, but Ronan wasn't fooled. "So you are, in fact, interested in her?"

"I'm interested in helping Huntsman nail Jorguson. I already interviewed Olivia, and I think I should finish it up."

"A phone call would probably—"

"No, I should do it in person."

Ronan stood. "Okay, I'll get her phone number for you, and you can set up a time to meet."

Without thinking, Grayson said, "I've already got it programmed in my phone."

"But you're not interested," Ronan said as he strolled out of the office.

Grayson could hear his laughter through the door.

SIX

Grayson wanted to meet with Olivia to discuss the Jorguson investigation, at her convenience, he insisted, as long as it was Saturday at five o'clock. It was the only time he had available, he explained, and he wanted to get this all tied up before Monday.

"There are some discrepancies I'd like to go over as soon as possible regarding the incident with Jorguson."

"Discrepancies? How could there be any discrepancies? There were at least twenty people watching," she said. "Some of those people were recording with their phones. And just for the record, Agent Kincaid, it wasn't an incident. It was an attack."

"I know," he said, placating her. "Jorguson's attorneys are calling it the alleged incident, and Jorguson's version of what happened is quite different from yours."

"You're joking."

"Sorry, no." He heard her sigh. "Olivia?" he said after a long minute of silence.

"I'm thinking, Grayson."

He liked the way she said his name. She dragged it out so he'd hear her frustration. He smiled in reaction. "Five o'clock. I can either come to you, or we could meet somewhere."

"You want to meet Saturday night?" she questioned. Didn't the agent have a life outside of the office?

"Early Saturday night," he corrected.

Ah, so he did have plans, probably a late date, she speculated as she took another sip of the orange juice the nurse had given her.

Jane was checking messages on her phone and wasn't paying any attention to the conversation.

"Three o'clock works better for me," she told him.

"No, that won't work for me. I'm tied up until four thirty."

"Then it will have to wait until Monday."

"No."

"No? Can't you be a little flexible? I have plans, and I can't change them."

"What plans?"

He sounded suspicious. Was he simply curious, or didn't he believe her? Olivia pictured Grayson tackling that horrible bodyguard, saving her from certain harm, and she decided the least she could do in return was cooperate.

"I'm going to a formal affair," she said. "I have to get ready and be at the Hamilton Hotel by seven thirty. If clearing up discrepancies will only take ten or fifteen minutes, then fine, we'll meet at five."

"It could take longer than that. What's the formal affair?"

"The Capitol League Benefit."

"That's Saturday night? I thought it was next weekend." Grayson had received an invitation and had respectfully declined, but he had also made a substantial donation to the charity because he believed it was a good cause.

"Then you're planning to attend?"

He thought about it for a second or two, then said, "Yes."

She felt a little burst of pleasure that took her by surprise.

"Then perhaps we could meet at the hotel. It shouldn't take all that long to discuss Jorguson's blatant lies, should it? Unless you have plans . . . or if you have a date and it would be rude to leave her while you discussed . . ."

"Jorguson's lies?"

She could hear the amusement in his voice. "Yes. Do you have a date?"

"No."

"Really?"

He laughed. "Really. I'm working, remember? The Jorguson investigation."

"That's right."

"What about you? Do you have a date?"

"No," she said. "I sound boring, don't I?"

"Olivia, there isn't anything boring about you," he said, and before she could respond to the compliment, he asked, "Were you planning to go alone?"

"Yes. My aunt is being honored at the event, and I promised her I'd attend. I was planning to meet her there. Unlike us, she has a date."

"Who is your aunt?"

"Emma Monroe."

"Why don't I drive you to the hotel? We can talk on the way there."

"Yes, all right."

"Listen . . . I might as well . . ."

"Yes?" she asked when he hesitated.

"I might as well take you home after . . ."

"That would be lovely."

"What time?"

"Seven."

"I'll see you then."

He ended the call, turned back to his desk, and noticed Ronan standing in the doorway. He didn't ask him if he had listened to the awkward conversation. The look on his face told Grayson he had.

"Man, that was painful," Ronan said. "What happened to you?"

Grayson shrugged. "Damned if I know."

Olivia told Jane about her conversation with Grayson while she wheeled her friend back up to her hospital room.

Always the artist, Jane asked, "Give me a visual. What does he look like?"

"He's tall, well over six feet, and he has dark hair, a really great mouth, and a firm jaw. Good bone structure . . . you know, patrician," she explained. "His eyes are intriguing. Now that I think about it, he's very sexy and quite handsome."

"You sound surprised. Didn't you think he was handsome when you met him?"

The elevator doors opened, and she backed the wheelchair in, then waited for Jane to push the eighth-floor button. "Yes, I did think he was nice-looking, but . . . you know . . . he's FBI . . ."

"Would I want to paint him?"

"Oh yes, you would. He wouldn't let you, though. From the little I know about him, I think he'd be mortified if you even suggested it. He's an agent, very strait-laced and professional. So, of course, a relationship is out of the question. He's interesting, though. Very sophisticated. No rough edges. Aunt Emma would like him."

"And you're going out with him tomorrow night."

"No, I'm going to the Capitol League Benefit. He's going to drive me there and drive me back home."

"Will he go inside with you?"

Olivia laughed. "Of course he will."

"Then you've got yourself a date."

"It isn't a date," she argued. "It's work related. We'll be discussing the Jorguson investigation."

"How romantic."

Olivia pushed the wheelchair into Jane's room and parked it in the corner while Jane got back into bed. There were two thick books on her bedside table, a biography and a book about addiction recovery. On top of the volumes was an AA pamphlet. Jane was obviously taking her brother's new sobriety seriously, and Olivia knew that her friend would do anything she could to help Logan stay on the right path.

Olivia didn't want her to be disappointed again. She decided not to mention the reading material or bring up the fact that Logan's addiction wasn't just alcohol but also cocaine. Maybe AA would work for that recovery, too. For Jane's sake, she hoped it would.

Olivia stood at the foot of the bed and waited for Jane to get settled. Her arms folded across her chest, she was frowning at her friend as her thoughts went back to their conversation about Grayson Kincaid.

"What?" Jane asked when she noticed how serious Olivia looked.

"I don't want tomorrow night to be romantic. How crazy would it be for me to get involved with him? Even assuming he would be interested . . ."

"Of course he would be interested. How could he not? You're fairly intelligent, somewhat sweet when you aren't being bitchy, and beautiful."

"Bitchy? Fairly intelligent?"

Jane laughed. "Only *you* would focus on the nega-
tives. I did say beautiful."

She shrugged. "It doesn't matter, because as soon as
my father is arrested . . . if I ever find the evidence to get
him arrested . . . I'll become a leper. No one in this city
will want to be seen with a MacKenzie. My family will
call me a traitor, and, in fact, that's what I am. They can't
be surprised by what's coming, though. I've pleaded with
Natalie and her mule-headed husband, George, and my
mother—who, by the way, is a completely lost cause—to
get their money out of my father's investment firm, but
no one will listen to me. I don't want to hurt them, but I
don't know what else to do. If he continues, he'll not only
ruin them—he'll destroy the lives of hundreds of other
innocent people."

"Do you have any solid evidence yet?" Jane asked.

"No," Olivia admitted. "But I know I'm right. My entire life I've seen how my father operates. He's very
charming. He has a way of getting people to believe he's
the most sincere and candid person they've ever met,
and he looks very successful, so when he presents an investment opportunity, they trust him. Sometimes I think
he actually believes what he tells them. It's almost like a
compulsion and he can't help himself."

Olivia wished she could look away and let things play
out, but she couldn't. She knew what was coming and she
couldn't just stand by as more and more people got
sucked in. She'd seen it happen before. When she was
young, she knew her father was different from other
dads, but it wasn't until she was older that she realized
what he was and finally could see what he'd been doing.

One of his first ventures was in oil. He had convinced
hundreds of people that geologists had discovered incredibly rich oil deposits off the coast of Texas. All he

needed was enough money to invest in the drilling equipment to extract it. People gave him millions because he assured them that they were taking a small risk. He made them believe they were going to make a hundred times what they'd put in. People were greedy. No one knew how much drilling actually went on, but within a year he announced that the wells had come up dry; the geologists were mistaken. The investors walked away with a loss, but somehow Olivia's father moved on to bigger and better.

He formed another company a couple of years later. This time he invested in technology. He managed to find enough people to believe that he had collected a group of engineers who were on the verge of developing a revolutionary battery, one that would solve all the country's energy problems. That turned out to be a flop, too, but while the investors lost every dime and the company went under, her father's lifestyle became more lavish.

Those were just a couple of his so-called business ventures. Now he'd gotten even bigger. With his new firm, he'd collected massive amounts of capital from investors, big and small, with promises of phenomenal returns. Somehow he'd convinced them that their money was safe, but there was no way he could maintain the big profits he'd been claiming.

"Is there any way he could be legitimate this time?" Jane wondered.

Olivia thought about Jeff Wilcox facing prison because of her father's lies. How many more were there? She shook her head. "No, it just doesn't make any sense. I try to warn people, but until I find proof, no one will pay any attention to me." She took a breath. "Actually, that's not quite true. My father's law firm, Simmons, Simmons and Falcon—or as I like to call them, Slimeball, Slimeball and Slimeball—did get wind of what I'm trying to do, and they're trying to stop me. They sent a nasty threatening letter. If I don't desist with what they called my insane and inflammatory accusations, they'll have me arrested."

"On what charges?"

"They don't have any. It's all bogus. I haven't done anything illegal. They're just trying to scare me. If they were to try to sue me, they'd have to let me see my father's financials, and trust me, Jane, they'd kill me before they'd let that happen."

"Good God, Olivia. Don't talk like that."

"They should all be in prison."

"Then go after them. Just don't . . ."

"Don't what?"

"Don't get killed."

Olivia laughed. "That's the plan."

SEVEN

Olivia was ready by six thirty Saturday night and spent the next half hour catching up on e-mails. She wore a black floor-length gown. The silk hugged the curves of her body, but it wasn't obscene, by any means. The scooped neck showed a little cleavage, nothing that would have men ogling, she thought. Her neck was bare, and her only jewelry was a pair of teardrop diamond earrings that her aunt Emma had given her for her birthday. Her hair was swept up in a cluster of curls. A few tendrils escaped at the base of her neck.

Grayson was five minutes early. She opened the door and stood there staring up at him, speechless. The man was even more sexy in a tux. James Bond, all right, she thought. No, she corrected. Better.

Neither of them moved for a few seconds, and then Grayson said, "You look nice." He sounded hoarse.

"Thank you. So do you," she said as she stepped back. "Please, come inside. I'll just get my purse and wrap."

He stepped into a small foyer and followed her into the living room. Olivia lived in an upscale neighborhood on the edge of Georgetown. The building was old; the third-floor apartment was spacious and comfortable. Tall arched windows and worn hardwood floors were the backdrop for her overstuffed sofa and two matching chairs. The walls had been painted a pale blue, the windows were trimmed in white, and the furniture was a soft yellow color. A black square coffee table sat in front of the sofa with a stack of books on one side and a white vase filled with fresh daisies in the center. Colorful rugs brightened the area.

He noticed a pair of worn tennis shoes under the coffee table and a pair of flats in the doorway of a small room off the living area that Olivia obviously used as an office. Her laptop sat on an old, dark cherrywood desk that had been beautifully restored. Bookcases flanked the desk, the shelves bowed from the heavy books.

Grayson was an armchair architect at heart and appreciated the unique features of these older buildings. He would have loved to see the rest of the apartment.

Olivia came back into the living room and noticed Grayson staring at her ceilings. He caught her watching and said, "I like the moldings."

"I do, too. That's one of the reasons I bought the apartment."

"Ten-foot-high ceilings? That's rare."

"Yes."

"Bet it gets cold in here in the winter, doesn't it?" he asked when he noticed the old-fashioned radiators.

She pointed to the afghan draped over a chair. "I wrap up in that."

He nodded. "How many bedrooms?"

"Two."

"One large, one small?"

"No, both are quite spacious."

"Has the kitchen been remodeled?"

Puzzled by his interest, she answered. "Yes, the whole building was remodeled a few years ago."

"How long have you lived here?"

"A little over two years. Are you interested in the neighborhood? Thinking about moving?"

Grayson didn't explain that he bought buildings, renovated them, and either sold them or rented them out. It was an expensive, yet profitable, hobby.

"Just curious. Are you ready?"

He took the key from her and locked the dead bolt on their way out. Neither said another word until they were in his car and on their way.

"Tell me what Jorguson is saying happened," she began.

He glanced at her. "You attacked him."

She was properly outraged. "That is absolutely not true."

"Special Agent Huntsman has been after Jorguson for some time. He wants to know if you'll testify should he take him to court."

"Yes," she said without hesitation. "But do you really think it will get that far?"

He grinned. "Those were the exact words my partner, Agent Conrad, said. Jorguson knew you worked for the IRS, so, in fact, he attacked a representative of the IRS, didn't he? It's my understanding the Internal Revenue Service doesn't like it when one of their own is assaulted."

She laughed. "No, they don't."

"Huntsman wants to push this."

"I'll help in any way that I can," she promised.

"How much research did you do before your interview with Jorguson?"

"Very little," she admitted. "I didn't have the time. A big mistake on my part. I never should have gone to the interview."

"Jorguson's client list is filled with real bad . . ." He started to say "asses" but substituted "people" instead.

She laughed. "Bad people? You sound like one of my kids."

"One of your kids?"

"The kids I represent. When we had lunch, I thought I mentioned I do some work on the side for Judge Bowen and Judge Thorpe."

"Yes, you did mention it. It just jarred me to hear you call them your kids."

"When they're in trouble, they are my kids. In most cases, I'm all they have." Her voice had turned serious, passionate.

"I've got a feeling it's enough."

"Tell me more about these bad people."

"Jorguson Investments is legit as far as Huntsman can tell; however, some of his clients have brought in copious amounts of cash. One in particular, Gretta Keene, was very active. Her base was in Belgium but she operated in the United States for several years. The federal government took action a few months ago to have her deported. She disappeared before that happened."

"Where's all the money coming from? Drugs?"

"Among other endeavors, we suspect."

"So let me go out on a limb here. If and when I talk to Agent Huntsman, he's going to tell me Jorguson is money laundering for either the mob or perhaps one of the drug cartels."

He smiled. "Maybe."

She switched gears. "Did you talk to Jorguson about his threat to have me killed? 'One phone call and you're a dead woman.' I believe those were his very words."

"He denied threatening you. When I mentioned the number of people who heard him, he said they were all mistaken. While he was spewing his ridiculous lies, his two attorneys' heads were nodding up and down like they were bobbing for apples. We happened to have a video from one of the waiters' cell phones and played it for him." He grinned as he added, "His expression was priceless."

"Bet he changed his story then."

Grayson nodded. "As a matter of fact, he did. The alleged incident was all a big misunderstanding, and he was bluffing when he pretended to threaten you."

"He actually said he pretended to threaten me?"

"I can't make this stuff up," he said, laughing.

"What else did he say?"

"He'd love it if you would come work for him."

"The thought of seeing that pervert every single day sends shivers down my spine."

"Then that's a 'no'?"

They'd stopped at a red light, and Grayson glanced over at her with a warm smile. Olivia was suddenly tongue-tied, and her heart skipped a beat. She didn't know what to make of her physical reaction to him. She was usually so professional and composed, and this was a business evening, wasn't it?

"You're blushing," Grayson said. "How come?"

She didn't answer his question.

The light turned green, but Grayson didn't notice. When Olivia had turned in her seat to face him, the slit in her gown exposed part of her thigh. Her skin was golden, and he wondered if the rest of her was as flawless. The driver behind them honked, and Grayson's gaze was pulled back to his driving.

"Have you ever been to the Hamilton?" he asked.

"No, I haven't. It only just opened a couple of months ago. I've stayed at the one in Boston. It's beautiful and quite elegant. Have you been to this one?"

"Yes, I have. Aiden Hamilton threw a party a couple of weeks before the grand opening. I've known Aiden and his family for some time now. My cousin, Sam, helped on a case for Aiden's brother-in-law, Alec, and he introduced us. Sam and Alec are both FBI."

"How was the party?"

"Good," he said. "I ran into a lot of old friends I hadn't seen in a while. I was ready to take my date home when Alec suggested we play a little poker. I got home at six the next morning."

"And your date?"

"I took her home and came back for the game. She wasn't happy about that."

"Did you win any money?"

"Aiden decided to join us, so, no. When he plays, he wins. I lost the girlfriend and a lot of money. Had fun, though."

"You don't sound too broken up about the girlfriend."

"The relationship wasn't going anywhere," he said. "And, hey, it was poker."

"And she didn't understand. I do," she said. "I love poker."

He raised an eyebrow. "Yeah? You really like to play?"

"I do."

"Any good?"

"I think I am."

He grinned. "We'll have to see about that."

They pulled into the circle drive in front of the hotel, ending the conversation. Two attendants rushed forward to open their doors. Grayson's BMW was whisked away by the valet, and he took hold of Olivia's arm and walked by her side up the wide steps to the entrance.

The Hamilton Hotel faced Pennsylvania, a busy and noisy street, but as soon as they walked through the doors, Olivia felt as though she'd entered another world. There was a perfect blend of old-world charm and sleek contemporary touches. Massive columns stretched to the ceiling of a soaring lobby, and grand curved staircases on either side led to a wide mezzanine overlooking the main reception area. The polished brass balusters on the steps were topped with a carved railing of rich mahogany. Every table and chest was adorned with fresh flowers. Beautiful marble floors were covered in rich Oriental rugs, and the luxuriously upholstered furniture was overstuffed, inviting guests to linger and relax in this elegant and quiet setting, forgetting the turmoil and demands of the outside world.

All seven Hamilton Hotels were known for unparalleled luxury, absolute discretion, and impeccable service. The hotels catered to discriminating clientele and were dedicated to protecting privacy. Because of the chain's reputation for pampering guests and taking care of their every whim, dignitaries, politicians, lobbyists, and celebrities had already booked the four ballrooms in this hotel well into the future.

The Capitol League gala was being held in the largest ballroom, which was located on the first floor at the end of a long, wide corridor. Outside the large double doors leading into the ballroom was an open area with a magnificent fountain. Directly beyond were tall windows overlooking the serenity gardens.

Two Capitol League attendants stood side by side at the doors. Olivia pulled her invitation from her beaded clutch and handed it to one of them. Grayson noticed the man was so preoccupied staring at her, he barely glanced at the card.

There was already a crowd gathered inside, but the flow was good, and it was surprisingly easy to get from one side of the ballroom to the other.

Olivia hadn't attended many of these events. When she could afford it, she donated to causes that were close to her heart, most having to do with children in need, yet she rarely went to the parties, and for that reason she knew very few people attending the celebration.

Grayson, on the other hand, was the man of the hour. He seemed to know everyone, or rather, most of the guests seemed to know him. He was immediately surrounded by friends and donors. A senator on the finance committee stopped to talk about his reelection campaign and to ask what Grayson thought about a certain stock. Olivia wasn't sure what to do. This wasn't exactly a date, so she didn't think she should stay and listen to his conversations with friends. Or should she? Feeling a bit awkward, she decided to find her aunt Emma, but when she tried to step away, Grayson took hold of her hand and pulled her in to his side. He wasn't at all subtle. She gave him a disapproving frown. He responded by winking at her.

Olivia decided to be accommodating and humor him, and as it turned out, she was very happy she did. She soon lost count of the number of powerful men and women he introduced her to. She patiently stayed beside him for a good twenty minutes, smiling until her face felt frozen, and chatting amicably with the CEO of a cereal conglomerate, a Nobel Prize winner for physics, a real estate tycoon, an Internet software whiz, two art gallery owners, a couple of ambassadors, and a congresswoman. She even had a brief, though surreal, conversation with a senior adviser to the president of the United States. The topic was yoga, of all things.

The second there was a lull, Grayson suggested they go find her aunt. Then James Crowell stopped Grayson to say hello. Olivia recognized him from the cover of *Time*.

Crowell was Person of the Year and she believed it was a well-deserved honor. He was a genius and a self-made billionaire and, like Bill Gates and Warren Buffett, had donated most of his fortune to charity. Olivia was starstruck. Crowell was one of her heroes because of all of his humanitarian efforts. How did Grayson know him? It was obvious that Crowell liked Grayson, and from their conversation and their ease with each other, she concluded they had been friends for some time.

Just who was Agent Grayson Kincaid? The real Bruce Wayne?

Grayson watched Olivia as Crowell shook her hand and walked away.

"Your face is flushed," he remarked.

"I admire Mr. Crowell. He's done a lot for the poor in this country." She turned to Grayson and said, "May I ask you a question?"

"If it will get you to quit frowning, sure."

"I'm not frowning. This is my puzzled expression."

"Yeah? Good to know. What's the question?"

"You are with the FBI, aren't you? It isn't just a hobby, is it?"

He laughed. "Yes, I'm with the FBI, and, no, it isn't a hobby."

"So if I were to look in your garage, I wouldn't find a Batmobile?"

He looked at her as though he thought she was crazy. Shaking his head and looking very serious, he said, "Of course not."

She felt foolish for making the comparison and for asking such a silly question.

Grayson put his arm around her waist and pulled her close so that an elderly couple could get past. Then he leaned down and whispered into her ear.

"I keep it in my cave."

EIGHT

Was there anyone Grayson didn't know?

"It's so good to see you again, Grayson," Aunt Emma said when they found her.

He took her hand and bent down so that she could kiss his cheek. "It's always good to see you, Emma."

"How is your father?"

"Doing well, thank you. He's sorry he couldn't be here tonight to celebrate with you, but he had another engagement he couldn't cancel. He sends you his best wishes."

Emma turned to Olivia. "I had no idea you knew Grayson," she said to her niece, who was standing there with her mouth open in astonishment. Olivia gave Grayson a scolding glare for not telling her he was acquainted with her aunt, but before she could say anything, Emma continued. "You look lovely, dear." She kissed her on both cheeks. "I'm so pleased you're here."

Olivia thought her aunt looked radiant. She was a petite woman, just five feet three inches, and Olivia, at five feet six inches and in stilettos, towered over her. Emma had never had any face work done, but with her genes and her bone structure had aged beautifully. She had silver hair, cut short with just a hint of curl. She wore a silver floor-length gown, the cut simple and elegant. Her crystal clear eyes never missed anything, and her smile could melt the coldest of hearts.

Another acquaintance asked for a minute with Grayson, and while he was turned away, Olivia whispered to her aunt, "Are any of the others coming tonight?"

"The family? No," Emma answered. "They're all in New York."

"Have you spoken to my mother yet?"

"No, dear, I haven't. Now go and find your seats. The ceremony is about to start. I've been told that there won't be any long-winded speeches tonight, thank heavens. Three of us are receiving the Brinkley Humanitarian Award, and none of us feels we deserve it. It's . . . humbling," she admitted. "I tried to talk my way out of this, but the committee said this event could raise a lot of money, so here I am." She stepped closer and whispered, "Tomorrow I expect to hear all about how you met Grayson Kincaid. I always thought you and he would make a good match, but you're so stubborn about letting anyone interfere—"

She abruptly stopped when Grayson joined them. A few minutes later the ceremony began.

Olivia was so proud of her aunt. She was being honored for her contributions to the community, specifically for creating a medical scholarship for cancer research and for funding a new pediatric oncology ward at the children's hospital. Olivia knew how pleased Emma's late husband would be. When he died, Uncle Daniel left her with a large fortune, and she had put it to good use. From the response the audience gave after her considerable accomplishments were listed, it was apparent that Emma was well loved and appreciated by everyone.

As soon as the music started and couples headed to the dance floor, Olivia asked Grayson if he was ready to leave. He draped her wrap around her shoulders and followed her out of the ballroom.

Aiden Hamilton intercepted them just as they were crossing the lobby. He reminded Olivia of a model in *GQ*. Was everyone in Grayson's life perfection? Impeccably dressed, Aiden looked as though the tuxedo had been invented with him in mind. He was tall and terribly fit, and he approached them with a wide smile. The greeting between the two men was a bit humorous. Grayson slapped Aiden on his shoulder, and Aiden retaliated in kind. Then they shook hands like gentlemen.

Grayson introduced Olivia to his friend, and after pleasantries were exchanged, Grayson asked him, "How long are you in town?"

"Just overnight," he answered. "I leave for Sydney first thing in the morning."

"Are you building another hotel?"

Aiden nodded. "Hopefully," he said. "We built one in Melbourne and didn't run into any problems, but we're having trouble with permits in Sydney. It will work out," he added. "What about you, Grayson? Still working twenty-four/seven?"

He shrugged. "Pretty much."

"I wish we had time for a poker game," Aiden said. "I'm sure you still have a few dollars left for me to win."

"Your luck is bound to run out someday, Hamilton," Grayson countered. "I'll get my revenge."

Aiden turned to Olivia. "Sorry to bore you with this chatter," he apologized. "I'm sure you don't want to hear about our poker games."

"Actually, Olivia is quite a poker player, too," Grayson said.

Aiden looked at her admiringly. "Is that so?"

"I learned when I was a little girl," she explained. "My friends and I loved to play. We haven't had much opportunity lately."

"Then perhaps the next time I'm in town, you can join

us," Aiden offered. He smiled warmly and took her hand. "It was a pleasure meeting you."

Grayson pulled her hand away. "We were just leaving," he said abruptly. He put his arm around Olivia's shoulder and turned her toward the door. She nearly tripped, trying to keep up with him.

Olivia thought that Aiden Hamilton was one of the most attractive men she'd ever met. He was a real charmer who, no doubt, could have any woman he wanted, whenever he wanted, but she didn't see a reason for Grayson to be jealous. In her mind, he was much sexier.

Once they were in the car and on their way, she asked, "Tonight . . . how did you know all those people?"

"I run into them now and then at different events, and I don't know all of them, just some."

But you do run in their circle, she thought. He was so at ease with the movers and shakers in D.C., and she realized, there wasn't any question; she was completely out of his league.

"Thank you for introducing me to James Crowell. It was the highlight of the night for me."

Grayson thought about all the people he had introduced her to, including several A-list celebrities, and yet she was most impressed by a short, skinny, balding man who, without seeking publicity or fanfare, had made a real difference in the world. The fact that she recognized what Crowell had done made Grayson like her all the more.

"The men and women who met you tonight, including James Crowell, won't forget you because, frankly, you're pretty unforgettable, Olivia, and if there are cutbacks and you have to leave your current job, you have a connection with all of them."

"You were networking," she said.

He shook his head. "No, *you* were networking. You just didn't realize it."

She didn't know how to react. She wasn't used to people doing nice things for her, at least not lately. "Then tonight was about helping me."

He nodded. "And clearing up a few details about your interview with Jorguson."

"Right, Jorguson. Our discussion could have been done over the phone, couldn't it?"

"Yes," he admitted. "But this was more fun."

She agreed. "Then thank you. I did have fun tonight. Meeting James Crowell was a dream come true."

He laughed. "Yeah?"

Grayson loosened his tie as he steered the car into traffic. He didn't say anything for several minutes and seemed perfectly relaxed. He was a real enigma, a man who was just as comfortable tackling thugs as he was socializing with the rich and powerful.

Olivia wasn't good at small talk, and the silence was making her feel uneasy. She took a breath and blurted, "You make me nervous, but you know that, don't you?"

"Uh-huh."

She expected him to ask her why he made her nervous and wondered what she would tell him, but he didn't ask. Maybe he knew why and could explain it to her. She really had enjoyed herself tonight. It had been a long time since she had gotten all dressed up and gone out with such a handsome man. A long, long time.

She should get into the game, she thought. Then she remembered her father and what was coming, and she pushed the notion of getting involved with any man aside.

Her cell phone rang. She didn't recognize the number. "This is Olivia MacKenzie."

One of her clients was on the line. "Olivia, it's Tyler." The voice was hushed and brimming with fear. He had said her name once, and so she put up one finger. "Everything's fine, Olivia." Two fingers up. "I just wanted you to know that I'm back home with my uncle and aunt, Olivia, and everything is okay."

She heard someone speaking in the background, and then Tyler said, "They don't want you to worry and have to look for me. You won't, will you?"

"Now that I know you're okay, Tyler," she said, deliberately saying his name so he would know she understood the threat, "I won't worry."

"I've got to hang up now." His voice dropped to a whisper. "He just went into the kitchen. There are two other men here, and they're really mad. They say my uncle wants too much money. They have guns, Olivia. I'm so scared . . . Should I hide? I'm going to hide."

"I'm on my way."

The line went dead. Olivia quickly found the address recorded in her phone and rattled it off to Grayson. "A little boy is in danger," she said and then repeated what Tyler had told her. "I'm sorry. There isn't time for you to take me home so I can get my car. Besides, I'm going to need your help. We have to get there quickly."

"Call nine-one-one and request a squad car to meet us."

Grayson had pulled onto the ramp and was now blazing down the expressway. He also called for backup and was patched through to his partner, Agent Ronan Conrad.

"Ronan, where are you?"

"On my way home. What do you need?"

Grayson told him where he was headed and filled him in on the situation. "I'm on my way," Ronan answered.

"We'll be there in five minutes," Grayson said.

"Make it faster," Olivia urged, her voice strained. "Five minutes might be too long."

He pushed the accelerator. "Tell me about Tyler."

"He's ten years old and was removed from his uncle's house and put in a safe house. The Purdys—the uncle and the aunt—are drug dealers, and they were using Tyler to deliver the product."

"Which is?"

"Cocaine and meth. Mostly meth these days," she added. "The aunt and uncle are twisted. The aunt has this thing about blood and family. Inside that sick mind of hers she believes she owns Tyler now that his parents are in prison."

"It doesn't sound like the kid ever had a chance," he remarked.

"Judge Bowen was his savior. He put Tyler with a good family and severed all parental rights. The aunt and uncle were never given custody, and there's a restraining order, but that means nothing to them."

"Why did you hold up three fingers?"

"That's the number of times he said my name. It's a code the kids and I have. If he says my name once, I know he's in trouble. The more times he says it, the more dangerous the situation. I never know who might be there with him listening or coaxing him when he's talking to me."

"Have you ever been called when it wasn't an emergency?"

"No, never," she said emphatically. "These kids understand real danger, and they wouldn't exaggerate. There's too much at stake to cry wolf."

The neighborhood they drove into was in the heart of gang territory. A few of the owners of the cookie-cutter houses had at one time tried to keep up maintenance, but the vast majority had let their homes go to seed. Half of them had already been abandoned and condemned. Grayson drove past a house that was falling apart. One side of the porch had collapsed, and the front lawn had been turned into a junkyard. There was a rusted-out washing machine and a stripped-down motorcycle blocking the broken sidewalk. It was impossible to tell if there was any grass because every inch of the yard was layered with trash. The air smelled of mildew, rotting garbage, and despair.

Three blocks west was the Purdy house. Grayson slammed on the brakes, threw the car in PARK, and said, "Stay in the car, Olivia." His voice was calm, almost soothing.

He pulled his tie off and tossed it on the seat as he got out of the car. His jacket followed. Opening the trunk, he reached for his bulletproof vest and slipped it on. He was adjusting the Velcro straps when Ronan arrived. He took the corner on two wheels and came to a hard stop inches from Grayson's car. Grabbing his vest, he walked over to Grayson, saw Olivia, and nodded to her.

"How many inside?"

"Four adults, but there could be more."

They could hear sirens wailing in the distance. "Are we waiting for additional backup?"

"No, there's a boy inside. We can't wait."

Grayson bent down to look at Olivia and once again ordered her to stay inside the car.

"Be careful," she said. "I've been to court with these people. They're . . . sadistic."

His nod indicated he'd heard her. He pulled his gun free, and with Ronan at his side headed to the house.

The streetlights were dim, but Olivia could see that the Purdy house should have been condemned years ago. At least half of the shingles were missing from the sagging roof, and the aluminum siding had been torn off both sides. The wood on the front porch looked as though it had been torched, and there were holes in the porch floor. In the shadows, she could just make out Grayson kicking in the front door.

Olivia didn't realize she was holding her breath until her chest started to hurt. Two shots were fired in rapid succession, then another and another. A man came running around the side of the house. He had a gun in his hand and was glancing over his shoulder. He appeared to be young, in his late teens. Dressed in a filthy tank top and jeans, he had a crazed look in his eyes.

He headed to the street but didn't make it. Ronan came at him from one direction, and Grayson from the other. The man fired wild, and a second later they had him facedown in the dirt.

Two squad cars arrived. The policemen ran to Grayson, and after he filled them in, they rushed into the house.

Where was Tyler? Was he safe? He knew to hide, but would he come out for the FBI or the police?

Olivia glanced in the rearview mirror and saw three men she was pretty sure were gang members. They were half a block away and were walking toward her. One of them picked up a board from the gutter, but an older man in the middle of the three shook his head, and the board was immediately tossed back into the street. Were the three simply curious to know what was going on, or were they wanting a fight?

The police brought out two of the most frightening-looking men Olivia had ever seen. They were handcuffed and shouting for lawyers. Odd how even the most drugged degenerates with burned-out brains still understood the law and knew how to manipulate it. Odd and disgusting.

Grayson and Ronan were both talking to a police-man, but she noticed their gazes were locked on the group that had stopped in the street a couple of houses away. Their number had increased from three to six. A child, no older than six or seven, ran down the street to join them.

Olivia watched as the leader of the group grabbed the little boy by the arm and pivoted him in the opposite direction, yelling, "Marcus, I told you to stay inside. Now, go home."

The boy started to protest, but when the older man gave him a hard shove, he reluctantly walked away with slouched shoulders, dragging his feet.

Olivia turned back to the house and saw something moving on the roof. Oh God, it was Tyler. In the moon-light she could see him creeping along the ridge.

She flew out of the car and called to Grayson. "Tyler's on the roof."

Grayson rushed back inside, and a minute later he was reaching for Tyler from the second-story window. The boy wouldn't budge, but when Grayson pointed to Olivia, he began to inch his way down the slope.

While she waited for them, yet another squad car arrived. When one of the policemen asked how many bodies were inside, Ronan answered, "Two in the kitchen, one male, one female."

The front door opened, and Tyler flew across the porch and down the stairs. He ran to Olivia and nearly knocked her off her feet when he threw himself into her arms.

She hugged him tight. "Are you all right? They didn't hurt you, did they?"

His head was tucked under her chin, his voice muffled when he answered. She could feel him trembling, and he was crying softly.

"I did it the right way, didn't I?" he asked. "I said

your name when I called you on the phone, just like you told me to if I was in trouble."

"Yes, you did it just the way we practiced. You're very brave, Tyler."

"I knew you'd come for me."

"Of course. Are you ready to let go of me yet?"

He stepped back. "You smell good. How come you're all dressed up?"

As she walked to Grayson's car and opened the back door for him, she explained that her aunt had received a special award.

One of the gang members who had been watching shouted to Tyler. "Is she going to put you in juvie?"

Another yelled, "What'd you do, kid?"

Tyler turned to the group. "I'm not going to juvie, and I didn't do anything wrong." He pointed to Olivia and said, "She's my lawyer. I called her, and she came right away. She's taking me back to my new home." His voice was filled with pride.

The leader of the group, a hard-looking man who was probably still in his twenties but looked fifty, motioned to his friends to stay where they were as he walked over to Olivia. Grayson was suddenly standing in front of her.

The man stepped to the side so that he could see Olivia and asked, "Are you really his lawyer?"

"Yes," she answered. "I'm Tyler's attorney."

The man glanced warily at Grayson, then said, "Uh . . . do you have any cards on you with your phone number in case one of us needs a lawyer? I didn't like my last one. He didn't do anything to help me."

She didn't know how to answer him. The thought of representing a gang member made her shudder.

Although he didn't realize it, Tyler came to her rescue. "You have to go through court to get her," he said, sounding very grown-up. "The judge gave her to me."

The explanation seemed plausible to the man. He nodded and headed back to his friends. He suddenly stopped, then turned to Grayson. "You got the kid out just in time. Another couple of hours would have been too late. Those fools decided they would make their own meth. Cut out the middleman," he added. "They were going to start cooking tonight. They would have blown themselves up and taken the kid with them."

Grayson wanted to get the boy away before the bodies were carried out. He and Ronan had surprised the aunt and the uncle when they burst into the house. Startled, the woman had thrown a meat cleaver at them and then she and the uncle reached for their guns and began shooting. Grayson heard Ronan mutter, "Son of a bitch," a scant second before he shot her.

Olivia waited while Grayson and Ronan wrapped up things with the police. She had put Tyler in the backseat. After he'd snapped on the seat belt, she'd covered him with Grayson's jacket. Clearly exhausted, the child was sound asleep minutes later.

She called the foster mother and filled her in on what had happened, assured her that Tyler was all right, and estimated that she'd have him back home within an hour.

When they were finally on their way, Grayson said, "One of the policemen told me they'd been to the aunt and uncle's house this evening looking for Tyler. They searched the house but couldn't find him. The foster mother reported him missing when he didn't come home in the carpool from soccer practice."

"The aunt was probably waiting to grab him," she said. She looked back at Tyler to make sure he was sleeping and then asked in a whisper, "Are they both dead?"

"Yes."

She was pleased he didn't embellish. "I shouldn't feel

relieved, should I? It's just that they were such vicious people, and they wouldn't have left Tyler alone. The drugs made them evil."

He shook his head. "No, they were already evil. Drugs made them bolder. Does Tyler like where he's living now?"

"Oh yes, very much," she said. "The foster mother is a loving woman. He's very comfortable there."

"Would he tell you if he weren't?"

"We've got a secret code for that, too."

As they drove toward Tyler's new home, Olivia was thinking how fortunate it was that Grayson had been with her tonight.

"I'm glad you were with me. It made it so much easier. Thank you."

He pulled onto the expressway and cut over to the middle lane. "You're welcome. Tell me, what would you have done if you'd been home when Tyler called? You told me there wasn't time for me to take you home to get your car. Would you have driven into that neighborhood alone?"

She knew he wouldn't like the answer. "I always call for backup," she said. "And usually the squad car beats me to the address."

"But not always?"

"No, not always."

His frown was fierce. "What about tonight? What would you have done?"

"Tyler was on the roof. I would have signaled to him not to move because the roof wasn't stable. Then I would have figured out a way to get him down."

"What if he was inside the house, and you heard him screaming?" he asked. "Then what?"

She didn't hesitate to answer. "I would have gone in after him."

Even though Grayson knew that's what she was going to say, it still infuriated him.

"No training, no weapon ... What would you have done? Shout at them?"

"If I heard Tyler scream, I would have gone in," she insisted. "And so would you."

Only after she made that statement did she realize how foolish it was.

"Of course I would have," he snapped. "I've been trained for situations like this, and I carry a weapon."

"This conversation is ridiculous. Tyler's safe, and that's all that counts. It all worked out."

He wasn't ready to let it go. "It's amazing you're still alive."

He had no idea how truthful that remark was. "Yes, it is," she agreed.

"You've never been close to death, and maybe that's why you're such an optimist."

Never been near death? Try two years' worth, she thought. And optimistic? Her friends were constantly telling her she was too negative. What would Grayson think if he knew this about her?

The discussion finally ended when they reached the foster home. Grayson carried Tyler inside and put him in his bed. The child never opened his eyes.

It was three in the morning by the time they reached Olivia's apartment. Unaccustomed to such late hours, Olivia was exhausted. Grayson, on the other hand, looked as though he'd just started the evening.

He parked in front of her building. The doorman rushed outside to tell him he had to move his car, but then he saw the weapon at his side and stepped back.

"It's all right, John. He's with the FBI," Olivia said.

"Is everything okay, Miss MacKenzie?"

"Yes. Everything's fine," she said. She stopped at the

elevator and turned to Grayson. "You don't have to come up with me."

"Sure I do."

He pinned her to the wall when he reached around her to push the button.

"You're still nervous with me, aren't you?"

She looked up into his eyes. She was barely inches away from him. All she had to do was tilt her head ever so slightly and lean in, and she'd be kissing him. She didn't give in to the urge.

"No. I'm no longer nervous with you." It was a blatant lie, but she thought she'd told it well.

He wasn't buying it. He flashed that adorable smile again. He could get anything he wanted with that smile, she thought. And probably did. That reminder helped. She knew women threw themselves at him, but she wouldn't be one of them. He wasn't her type.

She laughed. Talk about a whopper of a lie. That was the big daddy of them all.

The elevator doors opened on three. He stepped back to let her out first, then followed.

"What's so funny?"

"I was just thinking you're not my type, and that was funny to me because . . ."

"Yes?"

"Because you are."

He frowned. "Your type?"

You're every woman's type, she thought. She didn't tell him that, thank God. Instead, she said, "I'm tired. I'm not making much sense."

Her apartment was at the end of the hall. She got her keys out of her purse and unlocked the door. Grayson pushed it open and backed her inside. His eyes never left hers as he put his arms around her.

"I had a lovely time tonight," she said, remembering

the awards gala. "It was really nice . . ." She realized what she was saying. "Except for the two people you had to shoot and except for . . . Oh God, Grayson, just kiss me. I won't stop talking until you do."

He pulled her closer, and his lips brushed over hers. It was a quick middle-school kind of kiss, a prelude, she quickly realized, to driving her out of her mind. As soon as she put her arms around his neck, he stopped teasing her. His mouth opened and his tongue delved inside to rub against hers. She tightened her hold. His mouth was doing magical things to her, and every nerve in her body reacted. It was the most erotic kiss she'd ever experienced, and she never wanted it to end. He made love to her with his tongue, and when he lifted his head he could have taken anything he wanted.

She sagged against him. Taking a deep breath, she let go of him and stepped back so he could leave, even though she wanted him to kiss her again. She wanted . . . him.

"Be sure to lock the door," he said in parting. His voice was a rough whisper.

And he was gone. Her hand shook as she flipped the dead bolt. She kicked her shoes off, walked into the bedroom, and dropped down on the bed.

She knew she was going to be thinking about that kiss for a long time, and she wondered . . . had it meant anything to him?

NINE

Olivia was having a lazy Sunday afternoon. She read *The Washington Post* and *The New York Times,* did two crossword puzzles, played three games of Words with Friends on her iPhone, and was now talking to Samantha and Collins on a conference call to give them an update on Jane. It had been two months since her last transfusion, and she was back in the hospital again.

Although she didn't mention Grayson Kincaid to them, Olivia couldn't stop thinking about him. She wasn't sure why she didn't tell them about him. Maybe it was because she didn't want to make a big deal of their relationship. Besides, there really wasn't anything to tell, was there? In the two months since the awards gala, he hadn't called her. Of course, he never said he would. In fact, his last words to her were a reminder to lock her door. How romantic was that?

At the very least, he owed her an update on Jorguson. She hadn't heard a word about the investigation.

For the first full week after their alleged date, she was certain he'd get in touch with her. The second week she convinced herself that he was too busy to call but that he would eventually get around to it. After three full weeks had passed and not a word, she decided hell would freeze over before she went out with him. She had wasted enough time thinking about him and vowed she wouldn't spend one more second remembering that amazing kiss. Yeah, right. That was pretty much still all she could think about.

Would he have kissed her if she hadn't asked him to? Now that was the million-dollar question.

Olivia realized she was daydreaming again while she was still on the conference call. Sam and Collins were discussing Jane's medical issues, and she forced herself to pay attention.

"Why didn't the last transfusion help?" Collins asked.

"How do you know it didn't?" Olivia said.

"Because she's back in the hospital," Sam pointed out.

"Dr. Pardieu told Jane he wanted to run a couple of tests, that's all. He insists he's not worried, and we trust him, don't we?"

"Of course we do," Sam said. "We wouldn't be here if it weren't for him. I'm sorry I can't give her blood."

"We all have the same blood type," Collins reminded. "That's why we were put in the experimental program. I don't understand why Dr. Pardieu won't take some of ours, Sam."

"Mine just happens to work better for her," Olivia answered. "You know, if you're so worried, you could talk to Jane about this."

"Isn't it too soon for you to give blood again?" Sam asked.

"No," Olivia assured. "It's been almost eight weeks. If she needs it again, there wouldn't be a problem."

"I wish I were there. I can tell how Jane's feeling just by looking at her."

"She's going to be fine," Collins insisted. "But you know the last thing she needs now is stress. Olivia, Sam told me that creepy brother of hers is hanging around again."

"Actually, Logan is really trying this time. I think he might make it. He lives in a halfway house, and he's working. Jane says he hasn't missed a single day."

"That's different," Collins admitted.

"He cares about Jane, and he's trying to make up for all the pain he's caused."

"That will take a lifetime," Sam said.

"If Jane can forgive him, we can, too," Olivia said. "She went back into the hospital last week, and Logan has been there every day. He comes to see her on his lunch hour and after work. When she's home, he brings her dinner. He's trying, Sam."

"Okay, I'll give him another chance," Sam said. "Listen, I've got to go. Quickly, Olivia, tell me how your search is going."

"I can't get access to my father's records, so I've run into another dead end," she answered. "I have been able to get copies of some of the statements for his fund, though, and reading them is like gazing at the stars and trying to identify each one. There are lists of thousands of investments. Some of them I recognize as legitimate but the rest are really obscure. It appears that there are a great many in foreign countries. It also appears that the portfolio changes constantly. I swear he's Houdini. He might be committing the perfect crime because I can't find the fraud."

"You can't find it *yet*," Collins said. "There's no such thing as a perfect crime. At least that's what they tell me."

"Are you still determined to become an FBI agent?" Olivia asked.

"Yes," she answered emphatically. "And I think I'll be a good one."

"When do you begin your training?" Sam asked.

"I'm still waiting to hear. I know the academy will be a challenge, so I've decided to get a head start. I've been going to a firing range to get some practice."

"Have you shot anyone yet?" Sam asked with feigned alarm.

"Of course not," Collins answered indignantly, "but there have been a couple of close calls."

She shared a few stories about her first experiences with a firearm. By the time the friends ended their conversation, she had them laughing uproariously.

Olivia had just disconnected the call when another came in. Her boss, Royal Thurman, was on the line. He had never called her at home before, and an alarm was sounding inside her head. Something bad was coming, she thought.

"There's a problem I need to discuss with you," he began in his deep baritone voice. "Do you have any time this afternoon? My wife and daughters are shopping at Tysons Corner, but they're going to meet me for dinner at Neeson's Café at six. My girls love their macaroni and cheese. The restaurant is quite close to you, isn't it?"

"Yes, sir, it is."

"Could you stop by the café at five? It's important, Olivia, or I wouldn't bother you at home."

She didn't ask him to explain what the problem was or even to give her a hint. She was supposed to have dinner with her aunt, but Emma had decided to go to Palm Springs early for a seminar to get away from the cold.

"I'll be there," she told him.

Don't borrow trouble, she warned herself. The nurses used to say that to her when she was worried about the results of one of her tests. And for a long while, the results had been bad. It didn't seem to matter if she borrowed trouble or not. She took a deep breath. This wasn't the chemo isolation unit, and she was now an adult. If Thurman was going to fire her or let her go because of cutbacks, so be it. She'd find another job. But wouldn't he do it during office hours?

Olivia had told her boss about her horrid interview with Jorguson. He hadn't laughed, but she could tell he wanted to. He'd assured her that, when the cutbacks came, he would do everything he could to protect her.

Maybe that had changed.

Fortunately, she didn't have long to stew about all the possibilities for the meeting. It was already three thirty. She jumped into the shower, washed and dried her hair, and pulled it back in a ponytail. She dressed in a heavy, dark green sweater, skinny jeans, and knee-high boots. She even took time to put on some makeup and dab perfume on her wrists.

She pulled on her heavy sheepskin coat, a bright red wool scarf, a knit cap, and gloves. The inside of her coat had a large pocket, so she put a credit card in it, added her driver's license, three twenty-dollar bills, her cell phone, and her keys. She zipped the pocket closed and headed to the elevator.

John was on duty in the lobby. "It's awful cold out there," he warned.

"I'm going to Neeson's to meet my boss," she said. "It's close."

"I love Neeson's. They've got the best mac and cheese in the city. My stomach's grumbling just thinking about it."

"Would you like me to bring you some?"

"Oh no, no. I wasn't hinting." He opened the door for her.

"I'll get you some," she promised as she walked past.

The blast of frigid air entering her lungs as she stepped outside reminded her that she'd left her inhaler in her apartment. She turned to run back up to get it but changed her mind. Neeson's Café was six short blocks away from her building, and if she took her time, she'd be fine. She didn't want to keep Mr. Thurman waiting.

By the time she was halfway to the restaurant, she was frozen solid. It was bitterly cold, and there was a wet, blustery wind. The lighted display on the bank across the street said it was eighteen degrees. She increased her pace the last two blocks. When she walked into the tiny vestibule, the warm air stung her cheeks, and her lungs felt like they were burning.

Although she was ten minutes early, Mr. Thurman was already there in a large booth in the back of the nearly empty restaurant. He looked relieved to see her. It was bad, all right. She reminded herself not to borrow trouble and almost laughed at the notion.

Mr. Thurman, the ultimate gentleman, helped her with her coat and hung it up for her, then waited until she was seated before he slid into the booth across from her. He pushed his empty coffee cup to the side and stacked his big hands on the table. When a waitress came over with a coffeepot and refilled his cup, Olivia requested hot tea and an order of mac and cheese to go.

"I'll get right to it," Thurman said. "I was about to sit down for Sunday breakfast when I received a call from Carl Simmons of Simmons, Simmons and Falcon. You're familiar with the law firm?"

"Oh yes."

"I wasn't," he said. "I mean to say, I'd heard of the firm, but I'd never had a conversation with any of them until today. You can guess what the topic was."

She smiled. "Me."

"Exactly so," he said. "You must also know that the firm represents your father."

"Yes, I know. But why would he call you?"

"Carl . . ." He paused to smile and said, "He insisted I call him by his first name because he's certain we will become good friends who—according to him—will help each other. I could almost hear him winking over the phone," he added. "I didn't care for the man one little bit."

"What did he want?"

"He felt it was his duty to warn me about you. He believes you may be abusing your position as counsel for the IRS. I asked him what proof he had, knowing full well there wasn't any, and he hemmed and hawed. Then he got to his obvious agenda. He specifically mentioned your father. Simmons believes you're trying to manufacture evidence to discredit him. If that happens, his investors will lose faith in him, and before you know it, they'll remove their money, and his fund will go belly up."

"And it will be all my fault."

"Exactly so."

"I'm not manufacturing evidence, sir."

"I know that, Olivia," he said, his voice kind and sympathetic. "I'm merely repeating what he said to me."

"I've worked on cases I've been assigned and only those cases," she assured him. "I certainly haven't looked at my father's file. That would be illegal, and besides, what would be the point? It's all a fairy tale. I came to the IRS to learn."

"You told me about your father before I hired you, remember? You do exceptional work. Researching your father's dealings outside of your job hasn't interfered with that."

"But?"

"But I want you to be ready for what's coming. Simmons hinted . . . strongly hinted," he stressed, "that you were mentally unstable and needed help. He also suggested that your family is determined to see that you get it. He kept saying 'in my opinion' and seemed to think slandering you is perfectly okay if he's only giving his opinion."

"That's a new tactic."

"He didn't come right out and say that you're unfit, but I'll tell you, Olivia, he's going to try to get you fired. He'll go over my head, but I don't think he'll be successful. If what you say is true about your father's investment fund, I'm guessing that Simmons is raking in profits right along with him. He isn't going to let you ruin it for him. He's shrewd, all right. He'll get out right before the bubble bursts. I've seen it before, and it saddens me to say I know I'll see it again. Greed has a way of overtaking morals."

The hot tea was placed in front of her along with a carryout bag. She thanked the waitress and handed her a twenty-dollar bill.

She stared out the window and wasn't surprised to see snow falling. "I can't find anything," she whispered.

"Could your judgment be impaired because of past experiences with your father? Could you be wrong about him now? What if he's innocent? Have you considered that he might have learned some valuable lessons over the years and has made up his mind to be honest in his dealings? Your father is thought by many to have a special knack when it comes to picking stocks. His portfolio performance is quite impressive."

She wondered if he realized how naive he sounded. "No, I don't believe he's learned any lessons. I think he's just gotten better at hiding his crimes."

"From what I've heard, his fund has gone through the roof," he pointed out. "His clients have made enormous profits."

"Oh, sir, you aren't one of his clients, are you?"

He laughed. "And suffer your wrath? No, of course

not. I just want you to consider the possibility that your father might be a changed man."

Mr. Thurman wasn't familiar with the details of her father's history. He, therefore, wasn't convinced that her father was doing anything wrong, and she didn't have any evidence to prove that he was. Still, her boss was loyal to her. After pointing out the possibility that she could be mistaken, he let it go.

His family arrived promptly at six. They asked her to have dinner with them, but she declined, explaining she had made plans to see her friend who was in the hospital.

"We're supposed to get snow tonight," Mr. Thurman said. "If you have to drive, be careful."

Olivia counted herself lucky to have such a great boss. He genuinely cared about her. She knew he was trying to protect her from being laid off, and now he was trying to help her with the Carl Simmons situation.

She had just left the restaurant when her cell phone rang. She stepped back inside the warm entry to answer.

Judge Bowen was on the line. "Olivia, I just received a call from an attorney named Carl Simmons . . ."

"Oh no. What did he say?" she asked. "No, let me guess. In his opinion, I'm unstable and making things up."

The judge chuckled. "Yes, he did say something like that, though he did coat it with his concern for you and the well-being of any children who may be in your charge. He was playing me, Olivia, and you know how much I hate that. He didn't come right out and say it, but he implied that you were unfit, and he felt it was his duty to caution me. He said the occasional case I give you involves vulnerable children, and I should be aware that, because of your fragile state of mind, if anything were to happen to one of the children, I could be held responsible. Did you know you're about to have a nervous breakdown?"

"No, I didn't," she replied.

"Of course, Simmons insisted that he was telling me this in the strictest of confidence," he said with obvious disgust. "He added that your father is being urged to have you committed for a seventy-two-hour evaluation."

Olivia was shaking with anger. "I'm so sorry you were dragged into this."

"I know what this is all about. Simmons's firm represents your father . . ."

"That's right."

"And you're probing."

"Yes, I am."

"I warned Simmons you could sue him for slander, and he assured me that it would never happen. He said he was only trying to protect the innocent, and that he had proof of your irrational acts. He brought up a couple of names. Just a second . . . I wrote them down." He paused and she heard papers rustling. "Here they are: a Frank Greeley and a Kimberly Mills . . ."

She had to think for a second. "Yes," she said. "They were involved in two different cases I handled for Judge Thorpe. Greeley was a real hothead. He claimed that I had manufactured lies that he was an abusive father. 'Crazed with power,' I believe were his words. Of course, the bruises and welts on his four-year-old little girl didn't give him much credibility. Mills also called me crazy. She had been called to the office for a meeting about an abuse charge. I happened to walk in just as she'd grabbed her little boy and was about to backhand him. I knocked her down, and she began screaming that I was a lunatic. In both instances, the parents filed a complaint, but nothing came of them. It would take some fancy footwork for Simmons to create a case."

"There's more, Olivia."

She rubbed her temple and took a deep breath to calm down. "Yes?"

"He also alluded to drugs you had taken in the past that may have had a lasting effect on your mental state and impaired your judgment."

She was speechless.

"Olivia?"

"Yes?"

"I know you're a private person, and I hate asking, but was there ever a time . . ."

"The drugs?"

"Yes."

"When I was a child, I went through chemotherapy."

The judge was outraged on her behalf. "If you can find grounds to sue him, I'll testify," he said. "I'd love to see you tie up all his firm's assets and paralyze them."

"I don't know if that will happen, but thank you for your support," she responded.

"I think I'll give Judge Thorpe a call and give him a heads-up. He'll probably get a real kick out of the drug accusation."

Once she got past her anger, Olivia realized she shouldn't have been surprised that Carl Simmons had contacted Mr. Thurman and Judge Bowen. The slimeball had been calling her on a regular basis and threatening her. The scare tactics weren't working, though, and that must have been exceedingly frustrating for Carl. It was a natural progression to go to her employers. Poke the bear, he's bound to attack. And she'd certainly been poking and prodding. Of course they would retaliate.

It was a pity he hadn't come right out and slandered her. According to Judge Bowen, Simmons came close a couple of times, but the creep knew what he was doing. Olivia understood his plan. He would try to discredit her, destroy her reputation, and attack her character. She also knew that the next attack would be even more despicable but within the law.

Slimeball was smart, but she was smarter, she told herself. Eventually she would nail him for his part in ripping off innocent people, stealing their life savings, while he was living the high life. His day in court was coming.

She pulled her coat collar up around her neck, adjusted the scarf, and started walking home. The snow was coming down in sheets, and there was already more than an inch on the sidewalk. Had the temperature dropped? She couldn't make out the numbers on the bank, but she thought it felt colder because her face was stinging, and her lungs struggled to take in the frozen air. She tugged on her scarf and pulled it up over her mouth and nose. Why hadn't she gone back for her inhaler? She would love to sprint home, but she couldn't. Her chest was already tight, and she was wheezing. She had to slow the pace.

There wasn't any traffic, and she was the only person on the street. The snow was swirling down all around her, and the only sound was the gushing wind. The streetlights looked like they were covered in gauze. As bitterly cold as it was, she thought it was beautiful. Her street looked like a holiday greeting card. Everything was so clean and white, and all the little lights in the windows of the apartments were glowing. It was almost magical.

Being the pessimist that she was, she reminded herself that tomorrow it would all be a mess. Slush from cars would splatter against the windows, and the snow would turn brown and gray from being trod upon. But tonight it was pretty.

No way she was going to drive to the hospital, though. She had already slipped twice crossing streets, and people—including her—were crazy when they drove in snow. Olivia decided she'd make herself a cup of hot tea and call Jane to check on her. She didn't feel guilty. She was going to see her friend tomorrow after work when she donated more blood for her. They'd have a nice chat then.

There was an SUV illegally parked at the end of the block. Though she couldn't see him, she knew the driver was inside because the motor was running and the windshield wipers were moving. Must be waiting for someone, she thought as she crossed the street and hurried on. She switched the carryout bag from one arm to the other and tried to take a deep breath. She could really use her inhaler now. The green awning over the entrance of her building was weighed down by the snow. She could tell the walkway had been shoveled, but it was quickly filling up with fresh flakes.

She was almost home when she heard an odd popping sound. She pictured a giant champagne bottle being uncorked. Out of the corner of her eye, she saw the SUV coming toward her. Then she saw John through the window of her apartment building. He was standing behind his desk. He smiled when he spotted her and hurried to unlock the door.

All of a sudden there was rapid gunfire, bullets whizzing all around her. She understood what was happening and knew she needed to get to safety, but her legs wouldn't cooperate. She felt an excruciating jolt of pain in her thigh, then another jolt near her shoulder that was so forceful it knocked her back. The third jolt sent her spinning into the wall. Her head slammed against the brick, and her body crumpled to the ground. The world began to reel in a chaotic blur, with images of snow and lights and brown bags flying through the air. She tried to get up, but a dizzying fog rolled over her, and everything went black.

TEN

She made the ten o'clock news.

Grayson had the television on and was half listening to the end of a *Dateline* interview with a congressional lobbyist while he finished his third report on his laptop. He hit the SEND button and closed the lid. It was Sunday evening, and he was only now finishing work.

He put the laptop back in his briefcase on the table next to his nephew's school backpack. In the two months since Henry had come to live with him, Grayson's apartment had lost all semblance of order. The backpack was lying open; papers were sticking out every which way, and the report on volcanoes that was due tomorrow wasn't there. Grayson searched the living room, then went back into the den. He tripped over some LEGOs and a remote-control robot Henry was building, and found the report on the sofa, half hidden under Henry's tennis shoes.

Grayson made sure the entire report was there, then put it back in the yellow folder and added it to the papers he'd already straightened inside the backpack. The child would probably still lose at least one assignment before he got to class if history was any indication, but he was getting better at organization. He no longer left his backpack in the car.

Grayson went into his bedroom and was about to change out of his jeans and sweater when he heard the newscaster say that a young woman had been gunned down in front of her apartment building. A conversation about the city came back to Grayson. Washington, D.C., could be a dangerous place to live, and one had to be careful, but the energy here made the city irresistible. Hadn't Olivia said that? He smiled, remembering.

A day didn't go by that he didn't think about her, and if his life hadn't gotten so damned complicated, he thought he'd most likely be with her right now.

He picked up the remote to turn up the volume. The lead into the news was over and a commercial was playing. He stood in front of the flat screen and waited. He assumed the shooting had something to do with the gang war going on, and he was curious to know where it had happened.

Then Ted on Channel 12 announced that he was reporting live from Georgetown. Grayson stopped breathing. "Ah, hell," he whispered. "Don't let it be Olivia." The sick feeling in his gut contradicted the hope. He told himself he was overreacting. It had been two months since Jorguson had threatened her, but he had calmed down since then.

The newscaster said the name of the street; then the camera switched to the chaotic scene in front of an apartment building. Her apartment building. Grayson recognized the doorman. What was his name? John, he remembered. The man's face was gray. Grayson could see his hands shaking as he clutched something that looked like a paper bag against his chest. He was standing in the background talking to a couple of detectives. Grayson didn't recognize either one of them.

It was Olivia. Had to be. Even though he had spent only one evening with her, she had made a lasting impression. She was a beautiful, smart, and caring woman, and the way she handled that terrified little boy was something to see. The world needed Olivia MacKenzie.

His cell phone rang. Ronan's greeting was brisk. "Are you watching the news? Olivia MacKenzie was shot multiple times, and she—"

"Is she alive?"

"Yes," he answered, reacting to the fury in Grayson's voice.

"Where is she?"

"They took her to St. Paul's. It's the closest trauma center," he explained. "I talked to Detective Cusack, and he told me Olivia's in surgery now."

"How bad is it?"

"She got hit three times."

"I'm going over to the hospital."

"I'll meet you there."

Grayson had just put his gun in his safe. He got it out and shoved it back in its holster, then picked up his badge. His hands shook. That surprised him, and he realized he needed to get his anger under control.

He went down the hall and quietly opened the door to one of his spare rooms to check on Henry. His nephew was sleeping soundly. He pulled the door closed and went into the kitchen. The housekeeper, Patrick, was sitting at the table making a grocery list. Grayson told him where he was going and headed out.

The snow was still coming down hard, and the roads were like an ice rink. There were car accidents everywhere. Grayson drove his SUV and took as many side streets as he could to avoid getting slammed by other drivers. He parked the car in the doctors' lot close to the hospital door. The security guard didn't give him any argument once he showed him his badge.

He got directions to the surgical floor, and in a hurry,

he took the stairs. The floor was nearly deserted. A scrub nurse was rushing by. He stopped her and asked where Olivia MacKenzie was.

"She's still in the OR," she said. "Are you family?"

"FBI," he answered. "Where are the guards?" he asked then.

"I'm sorry? There aren't any guards on this floor."

He didn't show any reaction to that news but asked, "Could you find out her condition and how much longer she'll be in there?"

"Yes, of course. The surgical waiting room is right down that hallway," she said, motioning to her left.

"Which OR is Olivia in?"

She pointed to the doors at the end of the hallway on the right.

"I'll wait here." No one could get past him as long as he blocked access to the OR.

The nurse promised to be right back. She rushed down the corridor, then picked up a wall phone directly outside the OR doors.

He pulled out his cell phone and started making calls. Within minutes he'd arranged twenty-four-hour protection for Olivia.

He refused to even consider the possibility that she might not make it. The idea was simply untenable. It was bizarre, this connection he felt, but he didn't try to reason through it.

Ronan arrived a few minutes later. His dark hair was covered with snow. He brushed it off as he walked down the hallway.

"How is she?" he asked.

"Still in surgery. A nurse is checking on her condition."

Ronan looked around. "There's no one here. No police, no hospital guards . . . What the hell?"

"I've got agents on the way."

"This is our case then?"

"Oh hell yes."

"Good," Ronan said, nodding. "Do you think Jorguson's responsible? He did boast that he was going to have her killed."

"That was two months ago. He's threatened a couple of other attorneys since then. He's a hothead, and I know he's got some badasses for clients, but I still don't think this was his work."

"I'm not marking him off."

"I'm not either," Grayson agreed. "I'm just saying I don't think it's him."

"Who besides Jorguson would want her out of the way?"

"She works for the IRS. That could open up all sorts of possibilities. Who knows what some disgruntled taxpayer might do."

"I don't believe they've released her name yet, which means they haven't notified the family. Probably still trying to locate them." Ronan walked down to the surgical waiting room to see if anyone was there. He returned a minute later. "It's empty."

"After I get an update, I'll call Olivia's aunt."

The nurse he'd asked to check on Olivia interrupted. She was smiling. "The patient is on her way to recovery. She's going to be all right. The surgeon said he would be out in a few minutes to talk to you. He also said she's a very lucky young lady."

Grayson felt as though he could take a deep breath again, so great was his relief. Ronan noticed. He waited until the nurse had left, then asked, "You only had one date with Olivia, right?"

"Right."

"Did you . . ."

Grayson knew what he was asking. "What the hell, Ronan."

"So that's a no, you didn't."

They both heard the bell indicating the elevator doors were about to open. Each put his hand on the grip of his weapon and waited. Two detectives stepped out. The younger one was the spitting image of the actor Tom Cruise, down to the thick brown hair and square jaw.

"Doesn't that guy look like . . ." Ronan whispered.

"Yeah, he does," Grayson agreed.

Both detectives were eating sandwiches and chatting. They stopped when they saw Grayson and Ronan. The older one, wearing part of his sandwich on his mustache, called out, "Who are you?"

"FBI," Ronan answered.

"You don't need to be here. We've got this."

"No, you don't." Grayson didn't raise his voice, but the look in his eyes showed he was in charge.

"This is our case," the Tom Cruise look-alike snapped. He had a definite swagger as he walked toward Grayson.

Grayson wasn't impressed with his rooster tactics. Neither was Ronan, who said, "No, this isn't your case. It's ours."

"We were assigned this at the scene," Mustache told them. "Didn't see either of you there."

"So you knew this woman was gunned down, that it was a hit, right?" Grayson asked.

"Yeah, of course," Mustache replied.

"But you didn't think to post guards?"

The two detectives glanced at each other. Then Mustache said, "She's in surgery. We were going to wait and see if she made it . . ."

Grayson spotted the surgeon at the end of the hall. He was talking to the nurse.

"You deal with them," he told Ronan as he walked toward the OR doors.

He heard Cruise say, "I'm gonna make some calls."

Ronan responded, "You do that."

After Grayson talked to the surgeon, he made the dreaded call to Emma Monroe, Olivia's aunt. It hadn't taken him long to get her cell phone number and to find out she was in Palm Springs for a seminar.

Emma knew something was wrong as soon as she answered the phone and heard Grayson's voice.

"Olivia's going to be fine," he began.

"What happened?" she demanded before he could continue. "Was there an accident?"

"No, there wasn't an accident," he said, and then explained what had happened to her. He also told Emma what the surgeon had said and ended by repeating once again that Olivia was going to be fine.

Emma was beside herself. "Three gunshots? Someone shot her three times? Who would do such a thing to a lovely, kind . . . She's been through so much . . . She's had so much pain and now this. You find out who did this, Grayson." She went from shock to fury.

"I will," he promised.

"Where was she shot?"

"Right hip, left shoulder, and left side," he said. He'd already given her that information, but he knew she was having trouble taking it all in.

"Someone needs to contact Dr. Pardieu. I hope the surgeon has already called him," she said.

"Dr. Pardieu?"

"Andre Pardieu. He's her physician. Grayson, I'm going to get on the first flight I can find . . . No, I'll charter a jet," she decided. "I should be there—"

Grayson interrupted. "The city's snowed in, Emma. No flights in or out."

"She shouldn't be alone. She needs someone to watch out for her."

"There will be someone with her at all times," he promised. "No one's going to get to her."

"Has anyone called her parents and her sister?"

"I'll check," he said.

"I'll call them. They're all in Miami, celebrating with some new investors. Olivia's father purchased a mansion overlooking the ocean."

Grayson could hear the disapproval in her voice, which told him there were family issues. He didn't care about that. His total focus was on finding out who wanted Olivia MacKenzie dead.

Little did he know just how high that number would be.

ELEVEN

Olivia could have sworn Tom Cruise stopped by to say hello. Then Grayson appeared and shooed him away.

She floated in and out of consciousness. Everything was a blur, and visions swirled around in her head: snow and paper bags flying through the air and John's face at the window and a thin crimson line streaming across the white earth. Then, out of the fog, Grayson's face appeared. Why was he there? Did he want to kiss her again? She couldn't focus enough to find out, and she drifted away once more.

The next time she came to, she felt something cold on her head. She forced her eyes open and saw Grayson leaning over her. She closed them again. She was hallucinating. Focus, she told herself. She knew she was dreaming and needed to make herself wake up. Yet, when she looked again, he was there. He was no illusion.

When he moved the cold pack on her head, she felt the throbbing pain. She opened her mouth to complain but nothing came out. Her throat was so sore.

Finally in a raspy voice she managed to whisper, "What is it with you and ice?"

"What is it with you getting hit in the head?" He

smiled as he added, "The nurse wants you to keep this on your bump."

"Bump?"

"I think you slammed your head into the brick wall outside your building."

"Why would I want to do that?"

He didn't have a ready answer to her question. She struggled to sit up and felt pain all the way down to her toes.

"Be useful. Help me sit up."

"You are sitting up."

She closed her eyes. "Go away." She wanted to stay awake, but the fog was descending again and she couldn't fight it.

The next time she woke up, she was lucid and feeling half human. She looked around. She was in a room filled with vases of flowers, and Dr. Andre Pardieu was standing at the foot of the bed, reading her chart.

"Bonjour, Docteur."

"Ah, you're back with us," he said.

"I have to give Jane some blood."

"No, not now. You need to rebuild your strength. Then you can help her."

Their conversation continued in rapid French. Grayson stood in the doorway listening. It was apparent the physician had great affection for Olivia. Grayson could have sworn he heard him call her Pipsqueak.

At the end of their talk, Dr. Pardieu switched back to English. "Now that I see you're all right, I'll keep my plans to go to France. I'll be in Paris for a conference, and then I'll be going on a holiday with my family. If you need me, you know how to get hold of me." He kissed her on the forehead before he left the room.

Olivia was looking out the window when Grayson walked in, and she hadn't noticed him watching her. He wondered how anyone could look that good after being shot three times. Her face was pale, but she was still beautiful. Her dark auburn hair spilled out on the pillow behind her.

She caught him staring at her. Those clear blue eyes locked on his. Then he walked over to the window ledge and leaned against it. He folded his arms across his chest and said, "How are you feeling?"

"All things considered, pretty good," she replied.

What was he doing here? she wanted to ask. How did he get involved in this? One silly kiss, then two months without a word. Message received, she thought. He obviously hadn't wanted to have anything to do with her and had moved on. Damn it, so had she.

"Are you ready to answer some questions?" he asked.

"Yes."

"Do you remember what happened?"

"I do remember," she said, surprised that she did. "But it won't help much. There was a black SUV parked at the end of the block. The motor was running, and I remember thinking that he was waiting for someone. Guess he was waiting for me, wasn't he?"

"Apparently so."

The topic of the conversation was horrific, she thought, yet they were both acting and sounding so casual about it. Olivia knew Grayson must be used to dealing with attempted murders and all sorts of other awful happenings. He was a pro at this sort of thing. Nothing much seemed to faze him. She, on the other hand, was a novice.

"Could you see anyone in the SUV?"

"No, the windows were tinted, and it was snowing. Visibility wasn't good. The driver was on my side of the street. And that's it, Grayson. That's all I know." She smiled and waited for his next question.

"That's it, huh?" he said.

"I should call my aunt. I don't want her to worry."

"I talked to her."

"You did? You didn't upset her, did you?"

"No, of course not. Hearing that you'd been shot three times didn't upset her at all."

She ignored his sarcasm. "She's in Palm Springs."

"No, she's on her way here."

Olivia asked him about her boss and her friend Jane, but she didn't mention her parents or her sister.

"Just a couple of questions, and I'll let you rest while I go talk to Judge Bowen and Judge Thorpe," he said.

"They're here?"

He nodded. "So is your boss, Thurman. They're in the waiting room discussing their contempt for an attorney named Simmons."

"I'd like to see them."

"There are about twenty other people waiting to say hello and make sure you're all right."

"I'll talk to Judge Bowen, and—"

"After I talk to them," he said. "But before I go ... do you have any idea who might have done this?"

"Don't you mean, who wants me dead?"

"Yes."

She started wiggling fingers on her right hand, then her left, as she counted. Then her right hand again.

"At least fifteen people would like to get rid of me," she said.

"Did you include Jorguson?" he asked.

"No," she answered. "Should I? That makes it sixteen people who would like me to disappear. I'm sure there are more. I'll be happy to write their names down for you."

He thought she was joking. He walked over to the side of her bed, towering over her. "This is a serious matter, Olivia," he said.

"I am being serious, Grayson."

"Your aunt told me she couldn't imagine anyone would want to harm you. She said you're sweet and kind-hearted."

"I'm not." She sounded disgruntled.

He wasn't going to argue with her. He turned to leave and stopped, remembering the other question he wanted to ask. "When we were having lunch, you told me you had a goal you wanted to accomplish."

"Yes." She'd hoped he'd forgotten the conversation.

"Does your goal have anything to do with the number of people who would like to get rid of you?"

"Yes."

He waited for her to explain, but she remained stubbornly silent. "We aren't playing twenty questions," he snapped. "What's your goal, Olivia?"

She knew he would eventually find out what she was trying to do. What did she care if he thought she was a vindictive, traitorous daughter? Doing the right thing was more important than the guilt she felt.

"I'm going to put my father in prison."

After talking to Judge Bowen, Judge Thorpe, and Royal Thurman, Grayson understood their contempt for the attorney Carl Simmons. Suggesting that Olivia was a drug addict at a very young age when, in fact, she had gone through chemotherapy was despicable, and Grayson personally wanted to throw the bastard into a wall.

He spent the next several hours finding out all he could about Olivia that wasn't on her résumé. Her aunt Emma was a great help. Despite the weather, she had managed to get back to D.C., and they sat together in the nearly deserted hospital cafeteria discussing Olivia's past and her contentious relationship with her immediate family. Emma began by telling him about the experimental program Olivia and three other young girls were part of and a little of what they had endured.

"Olivia wouldn't be happy I'm telling you about this," Emma said. "She's a very private person. Her relationship with her parents was strained even back then. I didn't realize for a long time that none of them—her father, her mother, nor her sister—ever came to see Olivia when she was allowed visitors at the hospital. Olivia was all alone."

Grayson didn't show any reaction to what she was telling him, but he now understood why Olivia helped kids who didn't have anyone to watch out for them. She knew what it was like.

"Tell me about her father."

"Robert MacKenzie is one of the most charismatic men you'll ever meet. He could sell you a beach house in the Arctic. He walks into a room, and he owns it. Do you know what I mean?"

"Yes," he replied.

"In the past Robert has run several companies. Each one ended up going under, yet Robert did quite well. He got his salary and bonus when he resigned. He's always lived extravagantly. When he bought a home in New York, I thought he would divorce my sister, but that didn't happen. She's still with him."

"He was CEO of these companies?"

"Yes. It was all legal," she said.

"Now he runs his own investment firm?"

"That's right, the Trinity Fund, and it's quite successful. On paper anyway. Olivia knows several people who have given her father their retirement funds to invest. They all get quarterly statements showing how well their investments are doing. She's seen how her father works, and she's convinced this is just another one of his scams."

"She thinks he's running a Ponzi scheme?"

"If he is, she hasn't been able to prove it. Shall we head back upstairs? I'd like to say good-bye to Olivia and find out if she needs me to bring her anything."

Grayson walked by Emma's side to the elevator. He was lost in thought. "What do *you* think of Robert MacKenzie?"

"I agree with Olivia. He should be in prison."

The number of people on Olivia's enemy list made sense now. She'd been asking questions and probing, bringing attention to her father's firm. She probably had already gone to the SEC, and the men raking in the money wouldn't like that one little bit.

A woman in a wheelchair was coming out of Olivia's room when they arrived. A slender young man was pushing the chair. Emma introduced Olivia's friend Jane and her brother, Logan, to Grayson.

Logan extended his hand and said, "You're gonna catch this guy, right?"

"Yes," Grayson assured him.

"When are you going home, Jane?" Emma asked.

"Tomorrow," she said. "I'll come back in a month or so when Olivia's strength is back."

"Olivia is giving Jane some of her blood," Logan explained. "It's got antibodies she needs. Right, Jane?"

"Yes," she said. "Olivia's worn-out, so I wouldn't stay long. Now, if you'll excuse us, Logan has a meeting to attend."

"And you need rest," he told Jane.

Emma and Grayson watched until they turned the corner. Then Emma said, "Jane doesn't look at all well, does she? She's so pale."

Grayson thought Jane's brother looked just as sickly. When Emma went on into Olivia's room, he stopped to go over the schedule with the agent on duty tonight. After that, he called Ronan to talk about Robert MacKenzie's investment firm and found out that Ronan had already dug into Olivia's family and had come up with all sorts of possibilities for those relatives who might want Olivia out of the way. He wondered if Olivia knew that her brother-in-law, George, had a gambling problem and had recently taken out another mortgage on his home to pay some of his debts.

By the time Grayson ended his conversation with Ronan, Emma had left and Olivia was alone. He checked his watch as he entered her room. He needed to head home soon. Now that his nephew was living with him, he tried to eat dinner with him as often as possible to give him some kind of stable home life.

Olivia was fighting sleep. The television was on, and she was trying to watch the news. Her eyelids kept closing on her. She saw Grayson and asked, "Why are you here? I didn't think I'd ever see you again. Were you assigned to this investigation?"

"No," he answered. "I asked for it."

The pain medication was kicking in, and she was feeling a bit loopy. "Because of Jorguson."

"No, because of you."

She frowned. "Let's get something straight."

"All right," he agreed. "What?"

She looked at him. "What?"

"You wanted to get something straight."

She remembered. "You better understand, Grayson. I'm never going to ask you to kiss me again."

He smiled. "You won't need to."

His cell phone rang, interrupting the moment, which was a good thing, he thought, because he was seriously thinking about kissing her. He knew that he wouldn't give in to the urge, but he didn't like the fact that he wanted her.

His nephew was calling to remind him that he had to build a solar system and that Grayson had promised to help.

"What solar system?"

"*The* solar system," Henry stressed.

"This is the first I'm hearing about this, Henry."

"I was sure I told you, and I thought you said you would help me."

"When is it due?" he asked, thinking that he would make time this weekend to help him.

"Tomorrow."

Ah, come on. "Tomorrow?"

"Yes, and we need stuff."

"What stuff?" Grayson wondered.

"Stuff to make it. Like Styrofoam and string maybe."

Grayson noticed that Olivia's head was back on her pillow and her eyelids were at half-mast, but she was smiling. She obviously thought the conversation was amusing. He didn't. This parent "stuff" was a bitch.

"Okay. I'm on my way home." He ended the call and said, "I guess you got all that."

"How old is he?"

"He turned nine two weeks ago."

"And you need to build a solar system?"

"Apparently so. I'll be driving all over town looking for supplies. I better get going."

"Good luck," she whispered and fell sound asleep.

TWELVE

The night before Olivia was released from the hospital, her aunt Emma came to visit and insisted that Olivia move into her home to recuperate. Olivia refused. She told her aunt she wanted to sleep in her own bed and not be fussed over. In truth, she didn't want to put Emma in any danger, and as long as the shooter was still out there, everyone around Olivia was at risk.

As Emma was leaving, Grayson and Ronan walked in. Emma smiled at the agents and said, "Grayson, in all this confusion I forgot to ask about your father. How is he doing?"

"Better," he answered but didn't expound.

Olivia was curious to know what had happened to his father but thought it would be intrusive to ask. She'd have to wait until she and Emma were alone to find out the details. Not that it was any of her business, she reminded herself. She had made up her mind to maintain a professional relationship with Grayson and not to ask any personal questions.

"Please give him my best," Emma said. She turned to Olivia. "I'll be here early tomorrow to drive you home."

Grayson stepped forward. "I . . . We feel it would be best if I took Olivia home . . . for security reasons," he said.

"All right," Emma responded. She gave Olivia a kiss on the forehead and left.

Grayson had a list of questions he wanted to ask Olivia, particularly about her brother-in-law and the debt he had incurred. Did she know about it? Did her sister? From what he had discovered thus far, Olivia's relationship with her family was strained at best. In the days she had been in the hospital, he hadn't seen any member of Olivia's immediate family come to visit.

Unfortunately, he didn't get the chance to ask any of his questions. A constant stream of visitors, several phone calls, and her exhaustion overrode his agenda. He decided to wait until tomorrow to talk about her family.

The following morning, he drove her home from the hospital but didn't bring up the obviously uncomfortable subject of her relatives. When Grayson announced that an off-duty policeman would be arriving soon to keep watch outside her door, she protested. As long as she stayed inside her apartment, she insisted, she was safe. Grayson listened to her argument and ignored it, stating emphatically that the guard was not negotiable.

They had just reached her apartment and Olivia was fishing through her purse for her key when a door at the end of the hall opened and an elderly woman wearing a pink chenille bathrobe stepped out. Her thin white hair was held away from her bony face by two bobby pins, and her lips were pursed to give a breathy whistle. When Olivia looked in her direction, the woman crooked her finger and motioned for her to come closer.

"Hello, Mrs. Delaney," Olivia said as she approached the woman.

"Olivia, dear, I need milk." As she spoke, Mrs. Delaney was peering around Olivia and looking suspiciously at Grayson.

"I'm sorry," Olivia said. "I'm afraid I won't be going to

the store for a few days, but I'll be happy to get you some milk when I shop again."

Mrs. Delaney looked perturbed. "All right," she said. "I'll call down to John and have him bring me some when he comes to work tomorrow, but he always buys the wrong kind. I specifically ask for two percent, and he inevitably brings me whole milk. That's just too rich for me. My nervous stomach won't tolerate it."

"I understand," Olivia answered patiently. "I'll be sure to let you know when I'm going to the supermarket, and you can give me a list."

"Good," Mrs. Delaney said and turned to go back into her apartment. "Get me some of those lemon cookies, the ones with the icing on top, not the plain ones like you got me last time." Grayson and Olivia could hear her adding to her list even as she was closing the door.

"She doesn't like to go out in the cold," Olivia explained.

"Sounds like she's rather particular."

"A little," Olivia laughed. "She's all alone, and I don't mind helping out when I can."

Grayson took the key from Olivia's hand and inserted it into the lock. "You may act tough, but you have a soft heart, Olivia MacKenzie." He pushed the door open and stepped back so she could go inside.

Olivia was happy to be home. Her aunt had sent her staff over to clean the apartment, restock the refrigerator and pantry, and do Olivia's laundry. There were fresh apples and oranges in a wooden bowl on the kitchen island, chicken noodle soup ready to be warmed up, and fresh baked bread.

"If you aren't too tired, I'd like to talk to you about your family," Grayson said.

"Okay, but I don't know what I can tell you that would help." She was emptying her purse looking for her cell phone. She finally found it and went into her office to plug it into her charger.

When she returned, Grayson had removed his suit jacket and was tugging at his tie. She noticed what he was doing but didn't comment. If he wanted to get comfortable, that was fine with her. She would still be able to maintain her distance. He wasn't a friend; he was her protector.

That reminder should have helped keep it all in perspective, but he looked great in a suit, and with the jacket off, he looked even better. She had forgotten what a muscular frame he had. Her side was throbbing, her shoulder stung, and her hip felt as though there was still a bullet inside the bone. She was a wreck, and yet she could still lust after him. She could have blamed her thoughts about ripping his clothes off on her pain medication, but she hadn't taken any today.

"I'd like to discuss your brother-in-law," he continued.

"George? There's not much to say about him. I haven't been with him all that much. I've usually just talked to him on the phone, and it's always been superficial. You know, 'How are you?' ... 'Fine' ... 'How are you?' Then he'd hand the phone to my sister. George isn't much of a talker. He's a bit ... stiff," she said. "He makes Natalie happy, though."

"How long have you known him?"

"Almost ten years. I met him several months after they were married."

"You didn't go to their wedding?"

"No, it was in San Francisco, and I was here in D.C. It wasn't possible for me to leave."

Olivia never talked about her illness, and he wondered if she knew that he had found out all about her time in the experimental program. According to her aunt, Olivia only discussed those years with her other family, the three girls who went through the program with her. He also knew that her surrogate father was Dr. Andre Pardieu.

He forced himself to finish his questions so she could rest. "Do you know anything about their financial situation?"

Olivia sat on the easy chair and put her head back on the cushions. "He and Natalie started an Internet company several years ago, and they're doing very well. Natalie invested most of their profits with our father, God help her. I tried to talk to her, make her understand what a scam it all was, but she's sipped the Kool-Aid and is a believer. Like my mother," she added. "She likes to paint a picture of the perfect family. She thinks Natalie is the perfect daughter; George is the perfect son-in-law . . ."

"And you?"

She closed her eyes and smiled. "Imperfect," she said very matter-of-factly. "So she usually doesn't include me when she talks about her family. Natalie has become an only child. These days my mother considers me a traitor."

"A traitor to the family?"

"Yes," she answered. "And I guess I am. I have to stop him. He can't go on ruining lives and destroying families. I used to think he couldn't help himself, that it was all just a game to him, but now I know better. Money is everything to him. He's obsessive about bringing in more and more. He lures his rich friends to give him their savings and their trusts to invest, and he also targets large pensions and charities.

"The more difficult the potential client, the more my father thrives. My aunt Emma won't let him near her money, and it's making him frantic. He hates losing, and he's determined to find a way to force her to give him everything she has. It won't happen, but he'll go to prison still trying."

Olivia struggled to get up. Surprised by how much that action drained her, she headed to her bedroom. "I'm going to change clothes," she said. "Help yourself to something to eat and drink."

"Want me to warm up some soup for you?"

"That would be nice."

She walked down the hall but stopped at her bedroom door and looked back at him. "My mother idolizes my father, and she only has room in her heart for him. She can't help the way she is. It's like he has this mind control over her."

"Does she know what he's doing? Is she part of it?"

"No." She was emphatic. "And if you showed her absolute proof, she wouldn't believe it or see it. Honest to God, I think she'd throw anyone under the bus to protect him."

"Including you?"

She didn't answer. "I think, once my father is behind bars, my mother might open her eyes. Then again, she might not. She might want to crawl in the cell with him."

"Olivia?" he called when she walked into her bedroom.

She stepped back into the hallway. "Yes?"

"Why would your mother think you're imperfect?"

She sighed. "I got sick, Grayson. That made me imperfect."

She really hoped he was through asking questions about her family tonight. He was dredging up all sorts of emotions she didn't want to feel. She shut her bedroom door and changed into a pair of blue-and-white flannel pajama bottoms and a blue T-shirt. That little bit of effort exhausted her, and she sat down on the side of the bed. She fell back, rolled to her side, and closed her eyes. She would just rest for a few minutes and then have some soup, she told herself. After that, she'd send Grayson home and get a little work done on her computer.

Fifteen minutes passed and Olivia hadn't come back to the living room. Grayson opened the bedroom door a crack and looked in. Her hair covered the side of her face, and her arms were crossed over her chest. Grayson pulled the covers back on the king-size bed, then lifted Olivia into his arms. He held her close against his chest for a minute, liking the feel of her warm body against his. He gently placed her between the sheets and covered her. He brushed her hair back and stroked her cheek. Her skin was so soft, so smooth.

"There's nothing imperfect about you, Olivia."

THIRTEEN

Ronan thought Olivia's brother-in-law, George Anderson, looked good for the shooting and wanted to put him at the top of the list.

Grayson wasn't convinced.

Ronan opened his desk drawer, pulled out a Nerf football, and tossed it across the office to Grayson. Throwing the football while they brainstormed had become a ritual, providing the cavernous office was empty.

"I'll put Anderson in the top five," Grayson said. "But there are others who look better, like Carl Simmons and his crew, and unfortunately, Olivia's own father. Any one of them could have hired men to silence her. Did you know she was calling the SEC?"

Ronan smiled. "Good for her."

Grayson tossed the football back to Ronan. "Olivia's been asking a lot of questions about the Trinity Fund. There could be someone connected with the SEC who doesn't want an investigation."

Ronan nodded agreement. "Let's talk about Anderson."

"Yeah, okay. He owes three hundred thousand to a bookie named Subway, and every week the interest escalates."

"Every week?"

"Every week," Grayson repeated. "If Anderson continues to let the loan ride, in six months he could owe as much as, what . . . six hundred thousand?"

Ronan tossed the football as he answered, "Right. So I'm gonna go out on a limb here and suggest that Subway isn't a bookie. He's a loan shark."

Grayson nodded. Then Ronan asked, "Does Olivia know about her brother-in-law's gambling problem?"

"I doubt it. I'm going over there in a little while to talk to her about him. She mentioned that George is in town and wants to stop by tonight."

"And what did you say?"

They were throwing the football faster and faster until it was rocketing across the office.

"I said he's not getting in unless I'm there. The guard knows," he added.

"What about Anderson's wife, Natalie? Do you think she's aware of her husband's gambling problem?"

"I don't think so," he said. "He could get some money out of the Trinity Fund to pay off the loan—they have close to four million in an account with her father—but he hasn't taken any."

"Because she'd find out."

"That's what I'm thinking. She's put a great deal of her own money in the account. Her uncle, the late Daniel Monroe, was very wealthy. He set up trust funds for his two nieces so that they'd each get a large sum. The minute Natalie got her money, she turned it over to her father to invest."

"What about Olivia's fund?"

"She gets hers next year."

He then told Ronan what he'd discovered about Simmons, Simmons and Falcon. He'd looked into their banking practices and their accounts and had uncovered that Carl Simmons was a silent partner to Robert MacKenzie.

"Carl Simmons is slandering her, spreading lies about

her to get her to stop asking questions. How much do you want to bet her father knows what he's doing?"

Grayson nodded. "If things work out, I'll get to see him in action in a few weeks at the Morgan Hotel."

"The big birthday party?"

Grayson nodded. "I haven't crashed a party in a while. It should be interesting." He tossed the football back to Ronan and stood. "I'm leaving."

"You're going over to Olivia's now?"

"Yeah. Henry's sleeping over at a friend's tonight."

"Not that I'm keeping tabs," Ronan said, "but it appears you've been spending an awful lot of time at Miss MacKenzie's apartment."

"What can I say?" Grayson answered with a grin. "I take my investigations seriously, and I'm very thorough."

"Uh-huh," Ronan drawled with a good deal of skepticism.

The fact of the matter was, Grayson had looked for excuses to see Olivia. Even when a question could be answered with a simple phone call, he'd insist that it needed to be done in person. He couldn't resist being with her. What he was feeling was so new to him, he couldn't explain it. The only thing he knew for certain was that Olivia MacKenzie was different from any other woman he had ever met, and the more time he spent with her, the more he wanted.

He was walking toward the stairs when Ronan asked, "Are you still being a gentleman?"

"With Olivia?" he said, pretending not to understand.

"No, with her dog."

He laughed. "She doesn't have a dog, and, yes, I'm still being a gentleman."

And it was killing him.

*   *   *

It had been three weeks since Olivia had been shot, and the only time she had left her apartment was to go to the doctor to have her stitches removed. She was beginning to feel like a caged animal. Her routine was so boring. She got up early every morning, dressed, then went into her office and logged on to her computer with her password. Since there weren't any distractions, she got caught up with her cases fairly quickly.

The only exercise equipment she owned was a treadmill, and since she couldn't go to the gym and use the elliptical trainer like she used to, she got on her treadmill twice a day to break up the boredom. Some days, when her asthma wasn't bad, she would run; other days she walked so slowly she felt as though she was crawling.

Collins came over two Sundays in a row and stayed for a couple of hours each time. Then she'd go back to the firing range to work on accuracy. Olivia still trembled thinking about Collins carrying a gun.

Jane stayed at home because of the weather. Washington was having an unusual winter. It was bitterly cold, and snow kept blasting the city. She lived in a town house near Dupont Circle and was busy renovating it to be a studio for her painting. Olivia had missed her art show, but Jane told her all about it. She'd sold three paintings and felt validated and invigorated.

Sam called only a few times, but then she was in Iceland, so she kept in touch by e-mail. She wrote long, rambling letters about the jets she was flying and didn't complain at all about where she was stationed.

All three of Olivia's friends dated, but none of them had ever been in a serious relationship. Though they were healthy today, they lived with the fear that their luck would change. And how could they put a man they loved through that kind of worry? They had decided to be practical. Happily ever after wasn't in the cards for them.

*   *   *

Olivia had just finished answering a couple of e-mails. She closed her laptop and checked her watch. Remembering that Grayson was coming over, she went to her bedroom to change clothes. She stayed casual in a pair of fitted jeans and a white blouse she didn't bother to tuck in. She brushed her hair and dabbed on a little perfume and lipstick.

George would also be arriving soon. He'd said he wanted to have a serious talk with her. Olivia wondered if Natalie would be with him. She was positive she knew what George wanted to talk about: getting Aunt Emma to invest in Trinity Fund to show her loyalty and support to the family. Olivia's response wasn't going to change, no matter what George said. Invest in Trinity? Absolutely not.

How could Natalie and George be so blind?

Grayson arrived just after she straightened up her living room. She'd gathered up all her newspapers and magazines, put them in a recycle bag, and was folding her afghan when she heard the doorbell. She tossed the afghan on the back of the sofa.

She always felt a little catch in her throat whenever she saw him. Tonight was no different. He wasn't wearing a suit. He was as casually dressed as she was, in jeans and a camel-colored sweater. His gun was at his side. That hadn't changed.

He looked wonderful, she thought, but then he always did. She stepped back and waited while he hung up his coat in her hall closet.

"You're early," she said. "George won't be here until eight."

"I wanted to talk to you before he got here."

He went to the sofa and sat down. She followed. "Talk about George?"

"Did you know he had a gambling problem?"

Her expression confirmed she hadn't known. She looked shocked, then shook her head. "He doesn't seem the type. He's so . . . stuffy."

She sat down next to him and listened in growing astonishment as he described the hole George had dug himself into.

"He owes that much?"

Grayson repeated the amount. He thought her reaction to the news was comical. Her cheeks turned pink, and she was sputtering. "How could anyone . . . He borrowed from . . . How stupid is he?"

"Are you asking me?"

"A loan shark? He really went to a loan shark?"

"Yeah, he did," he said, smiling. "And, yeah, it was stupid. People do stupid things all the time. It's why I have a job. You work for the IRS . . . Don't you deal with stupid all the time?"

She laughed. "Yes, I guess I do." She thought about George for a second. "Natalie's going to kill him."

"You don't think she knows?"

"George is still breathing, so, no, I don't think she has any idea."

Olivia hadn't meant to sit so close to him. She didn't want to move, though. She loved the way his eyes crinkled at the edges when he smiled. She stared into those eyes and said, "May I ask you a question?"

"Sure. What do you want to know?"

"It's not about the investigation," she said.

"Okay. Shoot," he told her.

"Do you ever think about kissing me?"

He smiled at her again, and she felt as though she was melting. "Yeah, I do. All the time," he said as his hand moved to the back of her neck.

"All the time, Grayson?" she asked, her tone teasing.

He pulled her toward him, and his lips covered hers in a kiss that was outrageously carnal. His mouth was hot, and his tongue stroked hers until she was desperate for more. She could have stopped him, but that was the last thing on her mind.

For Grayson, the kiss was consuming and extremely arousing. When he came to his senses and realized what was happening, he took her by the shoulders and gently pushed her away. "We can't do this now." His voice was harsh.

Olivia was feeling dazed. One kiss and she was shaking. What would happen if he made love to her? She'd probably disintegrate. She threaded her fingers through her hair and took a breath. Grayson had disappeared into her kitchen. She needed to apologize. She knew she was putting him in an awkward position. He was an agent investigating a crime, and she was the victim. Getting personally involved was not a good idea. Their relationship should stay professional . . . shouldn't it? Her head was telling her yes, but her heart was screaming no.

When she entered the kitchen, Grayson was standing at her refrigerator. He had the door open and seemed to be looking for something in particular.

"What would you like?" she asked.

That was a leading question. "I don't know. Something to drink."

She pushed the door closed. "There are all sorts of drinks in the beverage drawer. It's behind you."

It looked like a regular drawer to him; the exterior was the same dark cherrywood as the cabinets. He opened it, pulled out a bottle of water, then closed it.

"Nice," he said, making a mental note for his next remodel. "I like it. I should put one of these in my kitchen. My nephew is always in the refrigerator."

"Henry?" she asked.

"Yes," he answered.

"He's living with you?"

"Yes, ever since my father's heart attack."

"I'm sorry. Is your father going to be okay?"

"Yes," he replied and said nothing more.

That was it? Just yes? No explanation at all. Okay, she got the message. His personal life was off-limits. She felt like a fool now because she had all but begged him to kiss her. Again.

Olivia leaned against the sink and folded her arms across her waist. She was irritated with herself. She had broken her vow not to ask personal questions, to let him volunteer whatever he wanted to tell her.

"Do you mind if I look at your cabinets?" he asked.

Since he already had opened the door above the sink and was looking at the wood, she didn't bother to answer.

"I rehab houses," he explained. "This wood is nice. I like the grain. Did you choose it?"

"Yes."

"I also like the granite."

He suddenly moved and pinned her against the sink. Then he leaned down and kissed her. It was quick and very nice.

"What was that for?" she asked, bewildered.

"To get you to quit frowning."

He brushed his mouth over hers again. "Know what else I like?"

"No, what?" she whispered.

He stepped back. "Your sink."

She walked past him. "You're such a flatterer."

He followed. "Hey, I really do like your sink."

She rolled her eyes. "You want to kiss me; you don't want to kiss me. You kiss. Then you don't kiss. Make up your mind, for Pete's sake."

He laughed. There was a knock on the door, and his mood changed in a heartbeat. "Go sit down. George is here."

"He's early," she said. "Guess he didn't have any trouble finding the place."

"He's never been here before?"

"No."

He waited until she was seated, then unlocked the door and opened it. George was a big man, almost as tall as Grayson. He needed to lose some weight, at least sixty pounds. He carried most of the extra pounds in his chest and stomach. Heart attack waiting to happen, Grayson thought.

George introduced himself to Grayson but couldn't look him in the eye.

"Are you staying or leaving?" he asked.

"Staying," Grayson said firmly.

"Why? There's a guard right outside the door. She doesn't need one inside, too. He patted me down, which I found a bit insulting."

"Come sit down, George," Olivia called. She wanted to get up and properly greet him at the door, but Grayson had insisted she sit.

"I see no reason why he—"

"I'm staying," Grayson repeated.

"Grayson's with the FBI," Olivia explained. "They're investigating the shooting."

Olivia's brother-in-law stopped arguing. He took his coat off and started to hand it to Grayson. He quickly changed his mind and draped it over a table. It immediately fell to the floor, and George didn't bother to pick it up.

He was used to others taking care of his needs, Grayson thought.

George looked around the living room before taking

a seat in one of the chairs facing the sofa. Olivia didn't care if he liked her home or not. After Grayson and she were finished talking to him, he wouldn't be coming back.

"How are you feeling?" he asked Olivia.

"I'm fine," she answered.

He turned to Grayson. "Have you got any leads on who shot Olivia? I'm sure it's one of the people she's going after for not paying their taxes. A lot of people hate her . . . I mean . . . hate the IRS."

Grayson didn't say a word. He simply stared at George until he flinched and looked away.

"Where's Natalie?" Olivia asked.

"In Miami with your parents."

"Does she know you're here?"

"Of course. In fact, she suggested I come talk to you."

Here we go. "Talk to me about what?" she asked innocently.

"You simply have to talk to Emma and convince her to put her money in Trinity," he blurted.

"No. Was there anything else you wanted to talk about?"

"Don't dismiss me," he snapped. "This is important. People . . . influential people . . . know she hasn't invested. When she does, they'll follow suit."

"No."

"This is killing your mother and your sister."

"What's killing them?" she asked. She tried to sound worried but couldn't pull it off.

"This hold you have on Emma. She'll do whatever you tell her to do."

"She will not. She's an intelligent, strong, independent woman." And you're a moron, she silently added.

"But you've got this special hold on her, ever since you gained her sympathy when you were sick."

"I gained her sympathy? Are you kidding me?"

"I'm simply stating what I know to be true."

"You know, George, until today I thought you had at least half a brain. I don't think that any longer. You're as blind as Mother and Natalie when it comes to Father's scam."

George huffed and started to get up. He glanced at Grayson, and quickly sat down again. "You're the one who's blind. Do you realize how much money Natalie and I have made?"

Grayson took over. "Why don't you use some of it to pay off your loan?"

Feigning ignorance, he said, "What loan?"

"The loan from your bookie. Subway calls himself a bookie, right?"

"Listen here," he shouted. "That's private . . ."

"Natalie doesn't know about the loan, does she?" Olivia asked.

He seemed to deflate in front of her. His shoulders slumped as he hunched over, and his head dropped.

"No." He sounded as though he wanted to cry. "She'll divorce me if she finds out."

"You're going to have to take that risk. You can't ignore a loan shark—"

"He's a bookie," he snapped. He buried his face in his hands. "I've been such a fool. I started out placing a couple of bets on some college basketball games, and before I knew it, I was in over my head."

"How does getting Emma to invest in Trinity help you?" Olivia asked.

"It doesn't," he answered. "I'm just trying to help your parents and Natalie. It's very important to them that the firm continues to grow, and Emma is so influential. If her friends knew she'd put her faith in the fund, they'd follow suit."

"And you could take some of your money out for your debts?"

"No, I can't do that . . . not without Natalie finding out about the gambling."

She was getting sick to her stomach. "Tell Natalie, and for God's sake, get your money out of that fund before it's too late."

"You're not going to be reasonable, are you?" He paused for a moment, and Olivia could almost see his mind racing. "Now that you know about my debts . . . what about you?"

"What about me?"

"You could borrow against your trust. Don't you get it in two months?"

"No, a year and two months," she corrected.

"What happens to the trust if Olivia dies before she gets it?" Grayson asked.

Without hesitating, George said, "It all goes to Natalie."

"And you."

"Well, yes, we're married—" He stopped abruptly. "Wait . . . You don't think I would ever harm Olivia."

Grayson didn't answer. He didn't think George had the nerve to shoot anyone. He could see him hiring people, though.

"And once she has the money, if anything were to happen to her, it would go to whomever she's named in her will," Grayson said.

George pretended he didn't know anything about a will.

Grayson continued. "And I'll bet you know how much is in Olivia's trust, down to the last dollar."

"Olivia was given more than Natalie because of her illness. At least, that's what Natalie and I believe."

"George, it's time for you to leave," Olivia said.

He didn't protest. Once he had his coat on, he said, "You won't talk to Emma?"

How many times did she have to say it? "No."

She didn't walk him to the door. Grayson did. After he locked it, he said, "What does your sister see in him?"

"You haven't met my sister yet, have you? When you do, you'll understand."

"Understand what?"

"He's perfect for her."

"I see."

She touched his arm. "I don't think George would have harmed me, but I'm glad you were here."

"Me too," he said. He took her hand. "You know, if you need anything . . . that is, if you get scared or want to talk, you can call me."

"I know," she answered with a warm smile. "Thank you, Grayson. I don't know that I could have handled all this without you."

He looked away from her and didn't say anything. He seemed preoccupied. "I should get going," he said finally.

She watched him turn off the kitchen light and walk to the closet to get his coat . . . only, he didn't get it. He pulled it off the hanger, then hung it back up. He stood there deep in thought for a few seconds; then he circled the living room and turned off all but one lamp. The room was cast in shadows. He stopped at the fireplace, picked up the remote from the mantel, and pushed the ON button. Fire licked the logs, the gas feeding it until the flames were high.

The living room was warm and cozy now.

He silently watched the fire for a couple of minutes with his hands in his pockets, and then he began to walk back and forth, staring at the floor as though he were looking for answers to some unsettling question.

Olivia observed his peculiar behavior. She was getting

a crick in her neck as he paced in front of her. She thought he might be trying to work something out about the investigation, or he was thinking about her lovely relatives perhaps, maybe even thanking God they weren't in his family. He'd met only George. She wondered how he was going to react when he met the others. She should probably take his gun away before she introduced them.

"Grayson? What are you doing?" she asked, breaking the silence. She'd been sitting too long. She stood and stretched her arms over her head to get the stiffness out of her shoulders and immediately regretted the action. "Ouch," she whispered, grimacing. Her shoulder and side were healing nicely, but stretching wasn't such a good idea yet.

Grayson had stopped pacing. She looked up at him, and the intensity in his eyes made her breathless. She went to him. Stopping just a foot away, she faced him. "What's going on?" she asked softly. "Tell me what you're thinking about. Maybe I can help you."

He almost laughed. "Yeah, okay. I'm thinking I'm not gonna be able to keep my hands off you much longer. Wanna help me with that?"

FOURTEEN

He'd rendered her speechless. Fortunately, the condition didn't last long.

"I thought you were thinking about George."

"Why would I be thinking about him?" he asked, clearly exasperated.

"Because he was just here," she reminded. "And you're angry."

"I'm not angry." His jaw was clenched, and he was frowning at her.

"Yes, you are ... and so I assumed you were thinking about my brother-in-law. But you weren't."

"No."

His eyes looked deeply into hers, and she suddenly realized what was going on inside him.

"You want me," she said. It was a statement, not a question.

Her surprise irritated him. "Hell yes, I want you. And guess what, sweetheart. You want me, too."

Her hands went to her hips. "You can't know that."

"Sure I can. Are you going to be honest with me and admit it?"

He took a step toward her. He was definitely trying to intimidate her, she thought, and she was having none of it. She stood her ground.

"That isn't the question here."

"Yes, it is."

"There's no need to raise your voice, Grayson."

"You're yelling, Olivia."

She was having trouble catching her breath. She guessed grabbing her inhaler wouldn't be very romantic, but then he was glaring at her now, and how romantic was that?

"Yes, I want you," she admitted. "Does my honesty please you?" She wagged her finger at him. "It doesn't matter, so tuck your ego away. I will not distract you, and having sex with you . . . Stop smiling. Having sex . . ."

"Will distract me?"

"Exactly so."

Grayson wanted to take her into his arms and kiss every inch of her. God, she was beautiful and so damned passionate.

"You will get fired," she said.

He had to force himself to pay attention. "I what?"

"Get fired."

He shook his head. "No."

"This isn't funny, Grayson. You'll get into trouble."

He shook his head again. "I mean . . . if they found out . . . Oh, for the love of God, stop looking like you want to laugh. I'm thinking about you."

"I'm thinking about you, too."

He went back to the hearth, picked up the remote, and turned the gas off. The fire flickered and sputtered, then went out.

Olivia felt a stab of disappointment the second he turned away from her. Yet she was determined to help him make the right decision, no matter how it affected her.

"You have to think about this, base your decision on logic, not lust."

Grayson turned around, and his eyes never left hers as he walked toward her. He stopped just inches away, and though he wanted to take her into his arms, he forced himself to wait. He needed to hear her say the words first.

"Do you want me to touch you, Olivia?"

His voice was gritty with emotion, and she could see the passion in his eyes. She knew she could end this now. She could lie and he would leave ... except, she didn't want him to leave, no matter how complicated it became. And so she simply gave him the truth. No coyness, no lies, no games. "Yes," she whispered. "I do want you to touch me."

"Now?"

She sighed. "Oh yes. Now."

He reached for her, pulling her into his embrace. She wrapped her arms around his neck and began to place soft kisses along his jaw and the side of his neck. She teased his earlobe with her tongue and knew he liked what she was doing because he tightened his hold and pulled her against him.

He growled low in his throat as he roughly twisted her hair into his fist and jerked her head back. His open mouth came down on hers and his tongue sank inside to mate with hers. The scorching kiss went on and on until she was shaking with desire and could barely stand up. Her fingers slid into his hair, and she clung to him.

Panting, she stepped back. "Grayson." His name was said with a groan.

He swept her up into his arms and carried her to her bedroom. She put her head on his shoulder and closed her eyes. Her heart was racing; she couldn't catch her breath, but all she could think about was touching him. She loved his scent, so earthy and clean and male. It made her want to get even closer to him.

Grayson lifted her chin so she'd look at him. "Are you sure? Your wounds—"

She silenced him by putting her finger on his lips. "I'm okay," she said.

He slowly put her down, and she stepped back, her gaze locked on his as she began to unbutton her blouse. She was trembling so, she could barely get her fingers to work. He was quicker. In seconds he pulled off his sweater, then his T-shirt, and was bare-chested.

Her heart beat faster and faster. The dark hair sprinkling his bronzed skin tapered to a V at his waist. His upper arms and chest were all muscle. Grayson was one fit man. One perfect man.

She was suddenly feeling self-conscious.

"Let me," Grayson said. He gently pushed her hands away and finished unbuttoning her blouse. Then he slid it down her arms.

Her bra was lacy and sexy as hell, her breasts full. Grayson reached for the clasp and removed the garment. It dropped to the floor. He was desperate to touch her. He slowly glided his fingers down to the small of her back. "You're so soft everywhere, so beautiful."

Olivia's breasts rubbed against his chest, and an electric sensation coursed through her body. His skin was warm, his muscles hard beneath. She could feel his strength and power under her fingertips, and his dark curly chest hair tickled her breasts when she moved. The erotic feeling intensified when she put her arms around his neck and her breasts rubbed against him again.

Resting the side of her face against his chest, she could hear his pounding heart and knew he was as excited as she was. It had happened so quickly. She wanted to kiss him, to touch him everywhere.

He unbuttoned her jeans and pushed them to the floor so she could step out of them. When he slipped her panties down, she felt a tingle that started at her toes and shot up through her body. Olivia watched as he slipped out of his own clothes. He was so magnificent, so perfectly sculpted, like one of Michelangelo's statues.

She pulled the covers back, and Grayson followed her down onto the sheets. He covered her with his body. Bracing his weight with his arms, he lifted up and stared into her eyes.

"You feel so good," he told her.

He clasped the sides of her face and finally kissed her. He wasn't gentle. His mouth took possession of hers, his tongue forcing her to respond. He couldn't get enough of her.

The kiss went on and on until Olivia was burning in every cell of her body. Her fingers glided over his hot skin, caressing his shoulders and his back while her hips moved erotically against his hard arousal.

Grayson ended the kiss and looked at her. He could see the passion and knew she wanted him as much as he wanted her. He kissed her again, then moved slowly down her body. His lips gently nibbled on her neck and the valley between her breasts.

His thumbs brushed across her nipples, once, then again. Her body responded by arching against him, and she moaned softly, telling him without words how much she liked his touch. He began to caress her breasts, then leaned down and took one nipple into his mouth, sucking hard. She cried out and moved restlessly against him. She couldn't keep still. Her hands stroked his shoulders, and she shifted under him until she was cuddling his arousal and forcefully moving against him. Her toes rubbed against his legs. His skin was hot, and she could feel his strength, but it didn't overwhelm her, for he was being so incredibly gentle, so loving.

His hands were everywhere, stroking, teasing. He was

gentle and rough, and he was driving her wild. She wanted to make him as crazed as she was. Her hands slid down between their bodies, and she caressed his arousal. She knew he liked that because he groaned and tightened all around her. He couldn't take the torment long. His mouth claimed hers again in a hot, wet kiss that ignited the fire inside her.

She arched up against him. "Now, Grayson," she demanded. She was close to screaming if he didn't end the teasing and come to her.

He moved between her thighs and looked deeply into her eyes. When he thrust inside, he was immediately surrounded by liquid heat. She was so tight, so perfect for him. She drew her legs up to take more of him, and he groaned again. He began to move, slowly at first, and then with growing need. Losing all control, his mind was consumed with finding release for both of them. It was a blissful, pulsating torture as he reached higher and higher peaks of ecstasy. She dug her nails into his shoulders and arched up against him each time he withdrew, quickening the pace. Suddenly, she tightened and squeezed him, crying out his name with her climax. He couldn't stop his own release. He held her in his arms while he lost himself in her.

Her orgasm overwhelmed her, consumed her. The world seemed to splinter into a million brilliant stars, and she felt as though she had skyrocketed to the heavens and was slowly floating back to Earth. She was stunned by the intensity. She had never lost control like this, and it was terrifying. Yet Grayson had held her, whispered to her, telling her she could let go, she could trust him. And, oh God, how she did.

"Wow."

One word, that was all, but it was enough to tell her how pleased and satisfied he was. She recovered before he did. His breathing was still harsh, and she could feel his heart racing. Then she realized she was having just as much trouble. She was still tingling everywhere and continuing to stroke his back and his shoulders.

Grayson lifted his head and smiled at her. She looked properly ravaged, and that gave him an arrogant satisfaction. Her lips were red, and he could see the passion still there in her beautiful eyes.

"I love your mouth," he whispered before he kissed her again.

Realizing he was probably crushing her, he gathered enough strength to roll away from her. He lay on his back and took a deep breath. He was amazed it was taking him so long to clear his mind. Making love to Olivia was like nothing he'd ever experienced before. It was different. *She* was different.

"You said, 'Wow.'"

He could hear the laughter in her comment. He rolled to his side, propped his head with his arm and said, "No, I didn't."

Her eyes were closed, but she was smiling. "Oh, but you did, Agent Kincaid. You said, 'Wow.' Is that your sweet talk?"

"Did you want sweet talk?"

"No. 'Wow' pretty much said it all."

He trailed his fingers from her neck to her stomach. "You screamed my name."

"I didn't scream."

"Oh, but you did, Miss MacKenzie."

His mood darkened in the space of a heartbeat. He stared at the scar from the bullet wound on her shoulder and was suddenly enraged. He wanted to kill the man who had hurt her and hoped he got the chance. She was lucky, the surgeon had told him. Both the injury to her shoulder and her side were considered minor. The bullets had gone straight through and hadn't hit anything vital. The hip was more serious because the bullet had lodged in bone.

"Does this still hurt?" he asked as he gently traced a circle around her shoulder.

"No."

"What about this?" He circled the small, raw wound on the side of her waist.

Olivia shivered. He was giving her goose bumps. "No."

He touched her hip. "And this?"

"Better," she admitted.

"What about your throat?"

She frowned. "What about it?"

"Does it hurt from screaming?"

She smiled. "I did not scream."

"Only one way to prove it," he told her.

Suspicious, she asked, "How?"

He pulled her into his arms. "I gotta make you scream again."

Olivia was curled up against his side, sound asleep. Grayson wasn't going to spend the night, but he was too comfortable and content to move. He decided he would call Ronan tomorrow and remove himself from the case. He'd still follow what was being done, might even make a couple of suggestions here and there, but that was all. He couldn't sleep with Olivia again and run the investigation at the same time. Actually, he supposed he could; he just wasn't going to.

Maybe he'd stay with Olivia until early morning after all. He'd get up at five and leave. Yeah, that's what he would do. He pulled the covers up and yawned loudly. Olivia scooted closer and put her head on his shoulder.

He had made her scream twice, and he was damned proud of that accomplishment. He was thinking about how aggressive she had become after her second orgasm. She'd pushed him onto his back and proceeded to drive him crazy with her hands and her mouth and her tongue. Her enthusiasm staggered him. He realized he was getting hard again, and was seriously thinking about waking her up, when his cell phone rang. He gently lifted her off him, grabbed his phone from the bedside table where he'd put his gun and holster, and answered.

Henry was calling. "Uncle Grayson. I think I'm sick. Can you come get me?"

Grayson sat up. He heard the worry in Henry's voice but didn't ask for an explanation because he knew what was wrong. Henry was homesick. As much as the boy wanted to sleep over with friends, he couldn't seem to get through an entire night. Grayson had thought about Henry around ten o'clock, and when he didn't call, he had thought Henry had finally gotten over his problem.

He was getting better, though. He'd made it until eleven thirty this time.

"It's okay. I'll come get you."

After he'd dressed, he kissed Olivia on the forehead and nudged her.

"I've got to go. You're okay?"

"I'm fine," she told him. "Good night."

She disappeared under the covers. He stood there for a minute and then began to laugh. Had he been wanting some praise or a testimonial about their time together, he would have been disappointed. Apparently she wasn't much for sweet talk either.

FIFTEEN

Grayson asked Ronan to take over the MacKenzie investigation and to assign another agent to assist. Ronan refused.

The football was flying across the office as the two men argued. It was late, after nine in the evening, and both Ronan and Grayson were sitting at their desks catching up on paperwork. They had already discussed pending investigations, none of which was pressing, and then they began to talk about the progress on Olivia's case. That was when the argument started.

"I'm serious," Grayson insisted. "I'm going to remove myself from the investigation. I'll talk to Pensky tomorrow."

Ronan hurled the football to Grayson. "No, don't talk to her. I'll take the lead, but you're staying on. You can assist. Or . . ."

"Or what?"

"Distance yourself from Olivia until we get the shooter."

That was easier said than done. Grayson couldn't get her out of his mind. All he wanted to think about was taking her to bed again. "I don't know if I can distance myself."

"Jeez, Kincaid. What happened to your discipline?"

Ronan feigned disgust, which made Grayson laugh. "I don't know what the hell happened to it."

"It's different with her?" Ronan asked, serious now.

"Yes."

"Okay, so you care about her."

"Of course I care." He was getting irritated. He put a spin on the football and sent it spiraling back to Ronan.

"Tell me how you can walk away."

"I'm not walking away—"

Ronan interrupted. "Do you think someone else— besides me, of course—could do a better job protecting her and finding the shooter? You'd put her safety in someone else's hands?"

"I trust you to do the job," he snapped, "but no one else."

Ronan was hitting a nerve. Grayson didn't want to leave the case, but he didn't know how he was going to keep his objectivity.

"I'm not working this without you," Ronan said. "Don't talk to Pensky. All right?"

Grayson snatched the football from the air and held on to it as he thought about his options. Finally, he gave in. "Yeah, okay, for now anyway. I'll find a way to keep my distance."

"Good." Ronan swiveled in his chair and picked up a notepad from his desk. "I've got another name to put on the list of suspects."

"Yeah? Who?"

"Jorguson's bodyguard. Remember him?"

"The tank? That's what I felt like I was hitting when I tackled him. His name is Ray Martin."

"Jorguson fired him, blamed the whole incident on him."

Grayson laughed. "I thought he blamed Olivia. Didn't he say it was all her fault?"

"For a little while he did. Then it became a misunderstanding. Jorguson just found out Olivia's going to testify against him, and now there's a court date set."

"His attorneys will delay, probably keep it out of court for at least a year, maybe two."

Ronan didn't disagree. "Jorguson pointed the finger at Martin. He said after he was fired, Martin ranted to some people that it was all Olivia's fault, actually said he was going to get even with her."

"Who did he say that to?"

"According to Jorguson, Martin made the threat in front of him and his assistant, Xavier Cannon. He claims he said it to a couple of clients. We've checked them out, and these clients have less-than-stellar reputations themselves."

"They're setting up Martin so the heat's off Jorguson."

"Could be," Ronan agreed. "Guess what Martin drives?"

"Tell me." He spun the football with one hand, then sent it in a high arc across the room.

"Brand-new black SUV. Ford Explorer, to be exact." Ronan caught the ball and lobbed it back. "There's more," he told him. "I sent two agents over to his place. Martin lives a couple of blocks from that drug house we broke into to get the kid for Olivia."

"Gangland."

"Yes," he said. "The agents showed up to bring him in for questioning, and right there in plain sight on the table was a whole display of weapons. Gave the agents cause to search the rest of the house. They found an arsenal. Turns out Martin has a thriving business on the side selling guns to the neighbors. He said he just wanted to help them protect their homes."

"Now see, that makes him a nice guy."

"That's what I was thinking."

"What about George Anderson?" Grayson asked.

"I did what you suggested and had one of our agents in Las Vegas check out the loan shark, figuring he's like all the others—you know, a real businessman who breaks legs and arms to get his clients to pay up but doesn't see the feasibility in killing them because then he'd never get paid. Anderson's loan shark, Subway, is different. Every now and then one of his clients turns up dead. Looks like he's sending a message to other slackers. Word is, he gave Anderson a deadline. He's got three months to pay it all back."

"Do you think Anderson would know how to find a shooter?"

"No, but I think Subway would have names, and if Anderson mentioned how much money his wife would get if Olivia were dead, then, yeah, I think he'd help him find a driver and a shooter. He might have hired them for Anderson."

"Anderson's a weasel . . ."

"Is he capable of hiring a hit?"

Grayson didn't have to think about it. "To save himself, yes. But then, so is Martin."

"Then there's also the possibility it was random. It could be a gang initiation. She was about the only person out during that freakish snowstorm. A blizzard that early in the season is unusual, and weathermen had only predicted flurries, so how does a kid anxious to get in a gang pass the test when there's no one around to kill? Maybe Olivia was just a handy target."

Grayson realized he was holding the football and tossed it back to Ronan. "She's made a lot of people who haven't paid their taxes very angry."

Ronan offered yet another option. "What about the kids she's helped? One of their relatives or guardians could be out for vengeance."

"I've talked to Judge Thorpe and Judge Bowen, and they gave me the names of the boys and girls she's been assigned. I tell you, Ronan, some of the places she's gone into, some of the god-awful situations those kids were in . . . I would have unloaded my gun on all of them once I got the kids out."

"No, you wouldn't have. You would have wanted to, but you would have taken them in."

"I swear I don't know how she does it," Grayson said. "She admitted she likes working for the IRS, partly because it's more mundane and balances out the horrors she sees in the other job."

"Were there any suspects? Relatives of these kids who want her dead?"

Grayson caught the ball, tucked it under his arm, and shuffled through a stack of papers on his desk until he found the one he wanted. He skimmed over it and said, "Two cousins of one little boy. Guess she really nailed them in court. They each got twenty years."

"So we've got motive . . ."

"Neither one of them have the connections outside of prison or the funds to hire a hit. I've got a few others I'm still checking out, but nothing looks promising."

"I want it to be Carl Simmons, her dad's attorney. After I interviewed that son of a bitch, I really wanted it to be him. Listening to all the trash he was talking about Olivia, trying to get her fired, calling her crazy . . ."

"She's been getting threatening phone calls," Grayson said. "She thinks it's Simmons. He disguises his voice, but she's pretty sure it's him. He only calls her cell phone number . . ."

"Were you able to trace the number back?"

"Every call came from a different public phone."

"Every call?"

"Olivia told me there have been four in all."

"Is she scared?"

"No, she's angry."

Ronan nodded. "You know who Simmons reminds me of? A game show host. He's got this phony yellowish-brown tan and these capped teeth that are a little too big for his mouth, and the color is beyond white. Creepy smile, too. He's tall and skinny, and when he opens his mouth, it's freaky."

"A real lady-killer, huh?"

Ronan laughed. "Funny thing is, he could be. I'd like it if he was the shooter," he repeated. "I'd like it a lot. Put his tanned ass in prison."

Grayson tossed the football into an open file drawer and turned his computer off. "Olivia's due to go back to work," he said. "How much longer will there be a protection detail?"

"I'm getting pushed now to end it," Ronan said. "Another week, maybe, but the budget . . ."

"I understand," Grayson said. "I'll take over and pay for it. I don't want her to know that, though. I'll hire some off-duty policemen I know and trust." As he grabbed his coat and put it on, he added, "I'll help out, too."

Ronan was searching for one of his gloves. He knelt on one knee and located it under the desk across from him where he'd tossed his coat. "For how long?" he asked.

"Until we make an arrest."

Ronan followed Grayson outside. "That could take a while. I look at the list and I ask myself, who doesn't want to kill her?"

It had been two weeks since Olivia had seen Grayson. The last time they were together, they had spent several

passionate hours making love. Then nothing . . . not even
a phone call to say, "Hello, how are you doing?"

She knew she probably should have been furious with
him, but she wasn't. After the first time he'd kissed her,
she hadn't seen him or heard from him for two long
months. It took a shooting to get him to remember her.
Maybe this was going to be a long hiatus as well. Grayson was a busy man, she reminded herself, with a nine-
year-old he was now raising—though she didn't know if
that was a temporary or a permanent situation—and his
father, Edward Kincaid, was recovering from a massive
heart attack.

Emma had given her the details about his father's
condition. She said that the cardiac surgeon had called
the heart attack the widow-maker, and if Grayson's father hadn't gone to the emergency room when he'd first
experienced symptoms, and if the cardiac surgeon hadn't
been right there to take over, Edward Kincaid wouldn't
have made it.

Olivia understood why Grayson couldn't take time
for her. No, she wasn't angry with him, but she was
damned irritated. How long would a phone call take? Or
even an e-mail or a text? No time at all. Exactly.

It was Friday afternoon, and she was about to do a
favor for a coworker so that he and his family could
leave early to catch a flight to Miami for a long weekend.
She had volunteered to drop off some papers, and she
was looking forward to her errand. The company she was
going to visit unannounced was called Nutrawonder
Works, a vitamin distribution company. It was owned
and operated by William Hood, who, according to the
notes she'd been given, had raised suspicion that he'd
been ripping off the government for several years. The
IRS wanted to go through his records to prove it and
also to find evidence that he had been ripping off his

employees as well by falsely reporting contributions to their pension fund. The word *bully* was underlined in red on the report.

Olivia didn't plan to walk into Nutrawonder alone. She was going to take an armed IRS agent with her, but as it turned out, that wasn't necessary. Just as she picked up the phone, Grayson walked in.

She put the phone down and watched him walk toward her. Don't stare, she told herself, yet she continued to do just that. Her mind scrambled for ways to get over her nervousness, and the advice she'd once been given before ascending a podium to speak in front of a crowd popped into her head: Think of him naked. She tried that trick, but a picture of his magnificent body appeared and had her suddenly feeling breathless and hot. Okay, that was a bad plan. Don't think of him naked, she told herself.

She could feel her cheeks getting warmer. She opened her desk drawer, took out her inhaler, and used it. God, how telling was that?

Grayson stopped in front of her desk. "Are you ready to leave?" he asked casually. "I'll drive you home."

She was still too rattled to come up with a witty and stinging reply. She nodded, then shook her head. "The policeman drove me here."

"I've sent him home. Another guard will be at your front door at ten tonight. Until then, you've got me."

No apology, no excuses, and not a hint of embarrassment or guilt. All right. If that was the way he wanted to play it, she'd go along. She could be just as aloof.

"I have to make a stop before I go home. I need to drop off some papers."

"That's fine."

"It's not going to be a pleasant meeting. You might need your weapon."

"Yeah, okay."

He was Mr. Cool, leaning against the desk looking relaxed and . . . mellow. Yes, that was the word to describe him: mellow. Her nerves were raw. She had worried and wondered about him for the last two weeks, but here he stood, calm and collected. Obviously, he hadn't been thinking about her. She wanted to kick him and kiss him at the same time.

She put the papers she was going to take to Nutrawonder in a legal envelope and sealed it. Then she got her purse out of the bottom drawer and started throwing personal items inside. Her cell phone went in first, then her indulgences: M&M's, a protein bar she'd been carrying around for a couple of months but refused to eat because the last one tasted like sawdust, and a cold bottled water she'd just gotten out of the refrigerator.

"You forgot your inhaler," he said. "It's in your middle drawer."

"No, I have one in my purse. I always keep an extra one here."

"You might want to check. I saw two in your drawer when you opened it."

He didn't miss anything, did he? She might have two in her desk, but she always carried one with her . . . except today. She ended up emptying everything in her purse onto her desk and realized then that she had put the one she always carried with her in the drawer.

"Oh . . . I didn't realize . . . I don't do that. Thanks for noticing."

What else had he noticed? How nervous she was? That was a given, she decided. She put the inhaler where it belonged and was ready to leave. Even while she was telling herself she didn't care, she was wishing she'd taken the time this morning to put on something a little fancier. Her pale pink silk blouse, black pencil skirt, and black flats were so ordinary. She could at least have worn high heels or boots. What had she been thinking? That it was freezing outside, that's what. Wearing high heels in this snow was asking for a broken ankle. And when she wore boots, her feet always got hot while she worked at her desk. Still, she should have put a little effort into her appearance. She hadn't even bothered to put her hair up or curl it. The thick mass was down around her shoulders. She nervously pushed a strand away from her face as she walked toward him.

He lifted her coat from the rack and held it out for her. "What happens when you forget it?"

"My inhaler?"

She put her coat on and turned toward him. Grayson took her scarf and wrapped it around her neck, gently lifting her hair out of the way. They stood inches apart.

"Yes, your inhaler," he said. "What happens when you forget it?"

She stared into his eyes. "I get into trouble."

"Olivia?"

She jumped. One of Mr. Thurman's assistants, a sweet, older woman named Violet, stood in the hallway. "Mr. Thurman wanted me to tell you that the team is on their way to Nutrawonder and will wait in their cars until you give them the word."

"Thank you, Violet."

The assistant took a step closer to Olivia. She glanced at Grayson, smiled, and then said, "I hear Billy Hood is a nasty piece of goods, if you know what I mean. Would you like to borrow my pepper spray?"

She smiled. "No, thanks. I've got something better." She tilted her head toward Grayson as she walked past Violet. "I've got him."

SIXTEEN

Billy Hood was indeed a nasty piece of goods, though, after meeting him, Grayson had a few more succinct words to describe the bastard.

Nutrawonder's offices were located outside the city and just a mile off the interstate in a run-down industrial area. The building was old and in need of paint. The linoleum floors were cracked and split, and the desks of the employees were crammed together. It was around sixty degrees inside, and Grayson noticed that some of the men and women were wearing their coats as they worked at their computers.

Hood's office was upstairs. Unlike the sterile first floor, the second floor had been remodeled. There was a garish neon-blue carpet, new furniture, and dark paneled wood in the reception area. The temperature was much more pleasant.

The woman sitting behind the desk was wearing enough makeup to spackle an entire wall. She had a fashion magazine open in front of her and was casually turning the pages with unnaturally long, curved, polished nails, completely ignoring Olivia and Grayson.

"We close in five minutes," she said, without looking up. "Besides, Mr. Hood isn't available. He's on the phone in his office, but he isn't available to anyone. You'll have to make an appointment. Mr. Hood doesn't see anyone without an appointment." She finally raised her head. "Do you want to leave your name or your card . . . or something?" she asked. She was staring at Grayson while she twirled a strand of hair in her fingers. "Or your phone number?"

Olivia rolled her eyes. She glanced at Grayson to see how he was reacting to Miss Spackle. He didn't seem affected. He was probably used to getting hit on, she supposed, and for some reason that irked her. She walked past the receptionist, opened the door to Hood's office, and went in. The receptionist didn't notice until Grayson followed Olivia.

"Hey, Billy isn't available," she called out. "I mean, Mr. Hood isn't available."

Grayson stopped in the doorway. "You can go home now," he told her as he was pulling the door closed.

Hood was talking on his cell phone. Grayson spotted a suitcase behind the door.

"Just make sure you bring your passport, Lorraine. I'll meet you at the airport." He looked up from his conversation and saw Olivia and Grayson standing there. "Hold on a second." He pointed to the door. "I'm talking on the phone," he snapped. "Get out of my office." He looked at Olivia, lingering on her legs, and said, "I guess you could stay, darling."

Olivia shook her head. "I'm not your darling. Now get off the phone."

Hood was an unpleasant-looking man. There were deep wrinkles in his forehead and above his cheekbones. Olivia attributed them to scowling most of his life. His beady eyes were a little too close together and his jowls hung low like a bulldog's. She knew he was married, and she wondered if his children looked like him—God forbid—or like their mother. She pushed the silly thoughts aside and focused on the task at hand.

Hood ended the call and slipped the cell phone into his pocket.

"Who are you?" he demanded.

Olivia gave him a friendly smile. "Where are you going, Mr. Hood, if you don't mind my curiosity? I noticed the suitcase, and I did happen to overhear you telling Lorraine not to forget her passport."

"California," he answered. "Napa."

"Lorraine doesn't have a driver's license to show at the airport?" she asked in her most pleasant, noncombative voice.

"Of course, she has a driver's license."

She tilted her head and looked puzzled. "You are aware that California is still part of the United States."

"Maybe I don't want to tell you where I'm going. Did you ever think of that? For all I know you could be . . ."

"What?" Grayson asked.

Olivia stood on one side of the desk, and Grayson was on the other, looming over him. Hood swiveled his neck and blurted, "Spies."

Olivia looked at Grayson with mock surprise. "Mr. Hood appears to be a little paranoid. Perhaps it's because Lorraine isn't his wife."

"Ah."

"My personal life is none of your business."

She nodded. "You're right—" she said as she pulled the legal papers out of her envelope.

She was about to tell him that his finances were definitely her business when he interrupted. "You're working for my wife, aren't you? You're spying for her. How dare she not trust me." He pointed to the door again, and just as Olivia was about to explain who she was and why she was there, he started cursing her. "Get out of my office, you bloodsucking bitch." He added several more gross names before he took a breath.

Olivia pretended to be both shocked and thrilled. Her hand flew to her throat, and she gasped. She sounded excited when she said, "I didn't know we got to use dirty words, Mr. Hood. Let me have a turn." She dropped the papers on his desk in front of him, placed her card with the bold IRS letters visible, leaned in, and said, "Prison."

Grayson listened to the conversation with great amusement. Olivia's handling of Hood was truly impressive. He had seen many sides of her since they'd met. He knew she was loving and gentle. He had seen that side when they'd rescued Tyler from the drug dealers. He had witnessed her steely determination when she stood up to George. He definitely had seen her passionate side with her uninhibited lovemaking. And today, he was getting a glimpse at her wicked sense of humor, a side he thoroughly appreciated.

Hood, on the other hand, wasn't amused. "Go ahead. Do another audit. You won't find anything. I'm still leaving on vacation. I'm going to—"

"California?" she asked, helping him remember the lie he'd just told.

"Yes, bitch, California."

"I'm afraid you're going to have to put that trip off for a while."

He tried to grab her arm. Grayson put a death grip on his shoulder. "Don't touch her unless you want to get hurt. You don't want to get hurt, do you, Billy?"

Hood glared at Grayson before turning to Olivia again. "Lorraine's going to be pissed," he muttered. "How long do I have to postpone my trip?"

"Ten to twenty with good behavior would be my guess."

Olivia texted the leader of the audit team, but there wasn't any need. They were already in the building.

Since Grayson was watching Olivia, Hood made the mistake of assuming that he wasn't paying any attention to him. He slowly reached into his desk drawer.

Grayson slammed the drawer shut, and Hood howled in pain. His fingers were trapped, and Grayson wasn't letting him pull them out.

"Now, see, Billy," Grayson said, his tone mild. "That has to hurt."

"You broke my fingers," he screamed. "You broke my fingers."

Olivia was surprised by Grayson's actions but didn't comment. A moment later she understood the reason behind the brute force.

"Let's see what you keep in your drawer," Grayson said.

"That's private property. You have no right . . ." He stopped protesting when Grayson produced a handgun. "I have no idea how that got there."

"Yeah, right."

"It's not loaded."

"Oh?" Grayson pointed the barrel at Hood. "Then if I pull the trigger . . ."

"Don't!" he shouted. "Okay, okay, it's loaded. It's for protection in case someone tries to rob me. I wasn't going to shoot anyone. I'm telling you I didn't even remember the gun was in my drawer."

Olivia and Grayson were through talking to him, but it took another twenty minutes before they were able to leave Nutrawonder. After refusing to cooperate, Hood was led out in handcuffs, shouting that he'd been set up and a lawyer would prove his innocence.

Once Grayson and Olivia were back in the car, he asked, "Did you know the gun was there?"

"I had a suspicion."

"Then you noticed him reaching for the drawer."

"No, I noticed you noticing him reaching for the drawer."

Olivia saw the muscle in his cheek flex as he clenched his jaw.

"I wouldn't have gone into the office alone," she said. "There would have been at least one armed agent with me. When I'm alone, I'm more observant, and, yes, I know I should always be observant, so stop the scowl."

"You're right. You should always be more observant. You take risks, Olivia. Dangerous risks."

"I beg to differ. I don't normally go into situations like the one today. I was doing a favor for a colleague."

"Did he warn you about Hood?"

"Yes."

"Damn it, Olivia, you need to be more careful."

"I was being careful."

"Yeah, right."

"Don't take that tone with me."

"What tone?"

"You're snapping at me."

She looked disgruntled. For some reason her expression eased some of his anger away.

"I care about you," he said quietly.

She didn't acknowledge his statement for a long while, and Grayson didn't pressure her. He had just parked the car when she whispered, "I care about you, too. If I didn't care, I never would have . . ."

"Let me touch you?"

"I was going to say I never would have touched you."

She rushed to move the subject away from sex because, from the moment she'd seen him, she'd wanted to rip off his clothes and have wild, arrestable sex.

"Your job is more dangerous than mine," she said. "I don't have a bulletproof vest in the trunk of my car, and I don't carry a gun."

"Do you worry about me?"

She didn't answer because they had just arrived at her apartment building. Grayson followed her upstairs. When he got a whiff of her perfume, he instantly reacted. Her scent had the power to drive him crazy. It was so damned sexy.

He hung up her coat and then his. His suit jacket followed. Olivia went into the kitchen and opened the refrigerator to search for something she could munch on. She wasn't really hungry yet; she was feeling the tension of having Grayson in her apartment again. She decided on a Jell-O cup. It had zero calories, and it would keep her hands and her mouth busy. She pulled out a spoon and turned around to finally answer him. She knew he wasn't going to let it go.

He stood in the doorway, waiting. She pointed the spoon at him and said, "Yes, I worry about you, but I don't want to. Besides, what's the point? Worrying is wasted energy. What will happen will happen no matter if I worry or not, and when it does, it's usually bad."

"Interesting," he said. "All this time I thought you were an optimist."

"I don't live in the clouds."

He crossed the kitchen and backed her into the corner. "Here now, gone tomorrow. Is that your attitude?"

She waved the spoon in front of his face and tried to push him away. "Something like that," she said defiantly.

"You're always optimistic with kids, aren't you?"

"Of course."

"What about your friends, Jane and Samantha and Collins? Are they as pessimistic as you are about their futures?"

She was taken aback. "I know you've met Jane, but how do you know about Samantha and Collins?"

"Emma told me about them." He took the Jell-O and

spoon from her and put them on the counter. Then he put her hands around his neck.

"She shouldn't have . . . What are you doing?"

"Kissing you," he answered. He tugged on her earlobe with his teeth and knew she liked that. He felt her tremble.

"Stop it." She tried to sound irritated instead of breathless.

"You like it."

Since she'd tilted her head to the side to give him better access to her neck, she couldn't tell him he was wrong. "Yes," she whispered.

"I'm keeping my distance." His fingers slid through her silky hair, and he gently turned her to look up at him. His mouth came down on top of hers. She never wanted the wet and hot sensation to end. As he made love to her with his tongue, she clung to him, and when he tried to end the kiss, she pulled him back to kiss her again.

He was shaking with desire when he finally backed away. "Olivia, it happens so fast with you," he whispered. "All I have to do is get near you, and I want it all. I thought it was your perfume that was such a turn-on, but it isn't. It's you."

She understood. When she got close to him, all she could think about was making love to him. She tucked her head under his chin so she wouldn't be distracted and asked, "What did you mean about keeping your distance?"

His chin dropped down and he rubbed it lightly across the top of her head. "I'm keeping my distance from you until we make an arrest."

"This is your idea of keeping your distance?"

He hugged her. "Apparently so."

He let go of her and walked out of the kitchen. She followed. "Where are you going?"

"To bed."

She opened her mouth to protest, then closed it. Grayson took her hand and started toward the bedroom.

"We have to have sex," he said very matter-of-factly.

"Why?"

"You know why. You're here now, but you could be gone tomorrow. We need to take advantage of the time we have."

"That's not funny," she snapped, pulling on his hand.

"Yeah, it kinda is."

She was furious with him. "I could die tomorrow," she argued.

"Yes, you could." He'd removed his tie and was now working on his shirt. His smile was tender. "But you're here now."

"You're being cruel, Grayson."

"No, I'm not. Take your clothes off, sweetheart."

She couldn't believe his gall. Did he think that all he had to do was snap his fingers and she'd strip for him? she wondered, even as she removed her blouse and reached for the zipper on her skirt.

"This is just lust." She made the statement as her skirt dropped to the floor. She pulled the silky camisole over her head and tossed it behind her. Her bra and panties followed. "Sex is a way to release pent-up tension . . . you know, anxiety. But it's primarily lust. That's all it is."

Saying it out loud didn't make it true. Olivia was already emotionally invested. She wanted Grayson to touch her, yes, but there was another reason besides the physical. Her feelings for him were growing.

Grayson was watching her expressions. In the past minute she'd looked happy, then angry, and now . . . disgruntled. He was pretty sure he knew what was going on in that stubborn mind of hers. He was pushing her and she was pushing back.

He had already undressed. He dropped down on the

bed, and before she realized what he was going to do, he'd pulled her down until she was straddling him.

"No, it isn't just lust. It's much more."

She acted as though she hadn't heard what he'd said and tried to kiss him. He wouldn't let her. "Admit it."

"No."

If this was a game of who was more stubborn, she would win hands-down. She brushed her lips over his and whispered, "No," once again.

His mouth covered hers, and he kissed her hard, thoroughly. He fell back on the bed, forcing her to stretch out on top of him, then rolled over until he'd pinned her beneath him.

Her fingers spread upward through his hair as she kissed his chin, then lower, until her lips were pressed against the pulse at the base of his throat. She could feel his heartbeat under her lips. She rubbed her pelvis against his in an attempt to drive him out of his mind. She wanted him to beg her to stop the erotic torment and come to him. Oh yes, she would make him beg.

The plan backfired. Five minutes later she was begging him. When it came to sex, how could she have thought she was superior to him? My God, he was a master. He knew what she liked, where to touch and stroke and how to make her respond. He made her burn with passion. She was writhing in his arms as she pleaded with him to come to her.

Grayson was determined to make her admit the truth to him before he let her climax. The effort nearly killed him. He used his last shred of discipline as his hands and his mouth moved over her sweet body. His forehead was beaded with perspiration, and he was aching with his need, yet he continued to hold back.

"It's a hell of a lot more than lust between us, isn't it?" he demanded.

His hand slid between her thighs. She relented. "Yes," she cried out. "Happy now?"

"Damn right," he whispered gruffly. He lifted up and looked at her. Her eyes were misty, and it was his undoing.

"Grayson," she groaned. "Gloat later."

He moved between her thighs and thrust inside her. She arched up against him, taking him deeper. He wanted to make it last, this glorious rapture, but he couldn't control his body any longer. Or his desire. Olivia was as wild to find fulfillment as he was, and both climaxed together.

Long minutes passed while they tried to regain their senses. Olivia couldn't understand how something that was so wonderful could keep getting better.

"Are you okay?" he asked as he tried to find the energy to roll away from her.

She nodded against his shoulder. He moved onto his back and pulled her with him. She felt like a rag doll, a very content rag doll. She probably looked like one, too, with her hair hanging over her face.

"Did you enjoy hearing me plead?"

He smiled. "Yeah, I did."

She rolled on top of him, stacked her hands on his chest, and stared at him. He looked arrogantly pleased with himself. And why wouldn't he? She'd caved and given him a little hint of the truth. She hadn't told him she loved him, but she'd come close.

"I'll get even with you," she whispered. "I'll make you beg."

He laughed. "I look forward to it."

He caressed her back, his touch gentle now, sending shivers down her arms and legs. "I love your scent."

"I thought you loved my mouth."

"That too."

She tried to roll off him, but he wouldn't let her, so she laid her head on his chest and rested her hands on his arms. His biceps were firm and taut, and she marveled at him. He was so powerful, so protective. She had never been this uninhibited with anyone. Yet, when she was with him, all she wanted to do was melt into him and let his courage and strength enfold her. He made her feel safe.

With a contentment she'd never experienced before, she lay quietly, feeling his rhythmic breathing against her cheek.

After a few minutes passed, she said, "Why does Henry live with you?"

The unexpected question jarred him. "His mother died several years ago, and Henry moved in with his grandfather. Then, when he became ill, Henry came to live with me."

"What happened to Henry's father?"

"His father is my brother, Devin. After his wife died, he went a little crazy. She . . . stabilized him, helped him focus. Now he travels a great deal. I guess you could say he's become somewhat of a jet-setter these days."

"Does he love Henry?"

"Yes, he does. He just doesn't like being a father. Since he's out of the country so often, I've gained full custody."

She rolled to her side and her fingertips moved over his skin in featherlight strokes. She circled his navel and moved lower.

"Henry has to come first," she said.

"I know," he said. He grabbed her hand to stop her from tormenting him, then pulled her into his arms. "I'm hungry," he told her.

"Me too," she whispered. "What would you like?"

He tilted her face up toward him, kissed her brow, then her cheek. "You," he answered.

"Me?"

"Yeah. I want you."

No other words were necessary.

SEVENTEEN

What started out to be a lovely, thoroughly satisfying evening ended up in a fight.

They reluctantly left her bed, and because Grayson didn't want the intimacy to end, he followed her into the shower. Olivia was shocked by how quickly she could want him again, and though she was a little clumsy and in jeopardy of drowning, she did get him to beg her to come to him. By the time he gave in, she could barely stand. Grayson lifted her up, wrapped her legs around him, and made love to her again.

The man had far more stamina than she did. He had already dressed and was in the kitchen looking for something to eat before she had dried her hair. She put on jeans and one of her favorite T-shirts. It was old, a little frayed around the bottom, and a little too tight across her breasts, but she loved the feel of the soft fabric against her skin. Besides, after what she'd done in bed and on her knees in the shower, being self-conscious about a tight T-shirt was ridiculous.

Grayson was guzzling a bottle of water, leaning against the kitchen island when she joined him. His gaze was locked on her as he slowly put the bottle down.

"You're beautiful. You know that?"

She shook her head. "Not a lick of makeup on and I'm beautiful. You've overdosed on sex."

He laughed. "That's not possible. I can never get enough of you."

The way he was looking at her, the intensity in his expression as he watched her, indicated he meant what he said. He looked as though he was thinking about dragging her back to bed. She was suddenly embarrassed and didn't have any idea why.

He noticed she was blushing and thought that was hilarious.

"Sweetheart, considering what you just did with that sweet mouth of yours—"

She interrupted. "I'd rather not discuss what we did."

She nudged him out of her way so she could open the refrigerator. "Would you like chicken Parmesan with pasta?"

"Sure," he said.

She handed him the casserole dish. He lifted the lid and said, "Did you make this?"

"Oh God, no. My aunt's cook, Mary, brings meals over. She thinks I'm wasting away."

"You've got a great body," he remarked, and before she could react to the compliment, he asked, "What can I do to help? I'm starving."

She put him to work making a salad. It didn't take any time at all to warm the chicken and pasta. She sliced hot French bread, and dinner was ready. They sat at the small table in the alcove overlooking the street. Grayson turned the plantation shutters so no one could look in.

He ate like a starving linebacker. "Does your aunt's cook . . ."

"Mary," she supplied.

"Does Mary bring food every day?"

"Sometimes, or she'll bring a week's worth of dinners.

She puts all of them in the freezer with instructions on each, and all I have to do is slip one into the oven or the microwave, and dinner's ready. I keep telling her she doesn't need to continue cooking for me, but she's like my aunt Emma. Neither one of them will listen."

"When did she start cooking for you?"

Olivia stared at her plate while she thought about it, twisting the pasta around and around her fork, barely aware of what she was doing.

"When I was finally released from the unit . . . the hospital unit," she explained. "I moved in with Aunt Emma and Uncle Daniel. They'd purchased a house in D.C. about eight months before."

"Why didn't you go back home to San Francisco?"

"I had to continue to see Dr. Pardieu, and I would never leave Jane and Collins and Sam. They were still undergoing treatment."

He nodded to let her know he understood. "You're very loyal."

"They're my sisters." Her voice was emphatic. "We protected one another."

"From what? The outside world?"

She shrugged. "Something like that. Mary had just started working for Emma. At the time I was released, I was weak and thin, and from Mary's horrified expression, I assumed I looked bad. I was suddenly encased in a bear hug, and Mary told me she was going to fatten me up. I remember thinking of the story *Hansel and Gretel*."

"The witch was going to fatten them up before she cooked them."

She nodded. "Mary wasn't a witch, though. She was and is an angel. Unfortunately, I'm still not fattened up enough to suit her."

"Emma moved here for you, didn't she?"

"Yes." She put her fork down and pushed her plate

aside. "I thought when I went off to university and later when Uncle Daniel died, she would move back to San Francisco, but she loves it here, and she doesn't want to move."

"Mary has a key to your apartment?"

"Yes, of course."

"Who else has a key?"

"Jane and Collins. Neither one of them has ever used her key, though."

"What about Samantha?"

"Jane and Collins live here, and in an emergency they know they can come stay with me. That's why they have keys. Emma's house is always open to all of us, too," she added. "But Sam's in Iceland or somewhere thereabout. She doesn't need a key."

Olivia carried her dishes to the sink. Grayson followed and nudged her out of his way. "I've got this."

She was happy to let him clean up. She sat on a stool at the island, watching him. His back was to her so she could stare at him. He could easily overwhelm her, she thought. Can't let that happen. But he was so . . . bigger than life. So wonderful and sweet and sexy and . . . She suddenly wanted to wrap her arms around him and hold tight.

Snap out of it, she told herself.

He turned and saw her watching him. "Is something wrong?" he asked. "You're frowning."

Fortunately, her cell phone rang, and she didn't have to come up with a suitable answer. She wasn't going to tell him the truth, that he scared the hell out of her, making her want things she could never have.

She didn't recognize the phone number, but as soon as she heard the voice, she knew exactly who was calling.

"Olivia, this is Eric Jorguson. Now, don't hang up on me, please. Hear me out."

"What do you want?" she asked quietly. She tapped Grayson on his shoulder, and when he turned to her, she whispered Jorguson's name.

Jorguson continued. "I want to apologize for my behavior at the restaurant."

"That happened some time ago."

"And you're wondering why I'm apologizing now? Is that it? I know it's long overdue. I jumped to the wrong conclusion. I should have reasoned it through. You're Robert MacKenzie's daughter, and if I can trust him with my money, I can certainly trust that you wouldn't be part of anything so underhanded as wearing a wire. I completely overreacted." He paused and then said, "The other reason I'm calling is to offer you a position."

She nearly dropped the phone. "You want me to come work for you?" She shivered with repulsion over the possibility. At least she didn't gag.

"Yes, I most certainly do. Once I understood you weren't working for the FBI, I realized what a catch you would be. I really want you to consider working for me."

He then explained in great detail what the position would be, and when he casually mentioned the starting salary, she nearly dropped the phone again.

Grayson was leaning against the sink, a dish towel in hand, watching her intently. He looked like he was about to grab the phone and throw it against the wall.

"I hope you don't mind, Olivia," Jorguson went on, "but I did have a look at your financials."

"My financials?" she repeated, dumbfounded by his temerity.

He either didn't hear how strained her voice was, or he didn't care. "And I noticed you have never accepted any money from your relatives. You're making your own way on your own terms, and I admire that. Yes, I do," he insisted. "I also found out what your annual salary is, working for the IRS. In one year with me, Olivia, you'll make more than five times that amount.

"Besides salary," he continued, "there are other benefits, and you'll only work with three of my top clients."

He listed their names, and Olivia thought they sounded familiar. Probably from the FBI's Most Wanted List, she surmised. Hmmm. The possibilities were growing. She might be able to help Agent Huntsman nail him. Wouldn't that be lovely?

"I'll have to think about it," she said.

"Yes, think about it. Take all the time you need. Now, one last thing . . ."

"Yes?"

"I want to tell you how sorry I am that Ray Martin, my personal assistant, went after you the way he did."

"Do you mean when he attacked me and hit me?" And you were yelling, "Get her, get her"? she thought but didn't add.

"No, I mean when he drove by your apartment building and shot you. I want you to know he was no longer working for me. I had already fired him after the incident at the restaurant, and I believe he blamed you and wanted revenge."

"You're certain it was him?"

"Oh yes. You won't have to worry about thugs like Martin bothering you when you work for me. You'll be protected."

And on he continued, raving about his luxurious offices and how very lucky she was to be one of his chosen.

As soon as the call ended, she looked over at Grayson and said, "I don't know if I want to laugh or throw up. Get this. Jorguson said he's invested in my father's fund." She laughed. "He's going to lose every penny."

"Huntsman will want to know about this. I'll tell him. What else did Jorguson say?"

Grayson followed her into the living room, and she plopped down on the sofa. He stood on the other side of the coffee table and asked her to repeat the entire conversation.

Olivia was still flabbergasted when she finished. "How can he do that? Call me as though there weren't still charges pending for the attack?"

"He wouldn't call unless he was convinced his attorneys were making it all go away. They've evidently managed to shift all the blame onto Martin." He thought for a second and said, "He didn't give you any concrete reasons why he thinks Martin is the shooter?"

"Not really," she said. "Other than saying Martin wanted revenge because Jorguson fired him. That's more of a guess on Jorguson's part, isn't it? Could Ray Martin be the shooter?"

"He doesn't have an alibi, said he was home watching *Sixty Minutes*."

"Really?" She didn't know why she thought that was funny, but she did.

"Really," he insisted. "Couldn't remember what was on, though. We don't have proof yet that he was involved with your shooting, but we can prove he's been selling guns to his neighbors, and we found his stash."

"He's got a bad temper," she added. "I've seen it."

"Yes, he does," he agreed. "He tried to throw a chair at an agent during questioning. He's got a short fuse, and he could kill someone. One of the guns we found, an old .45, was used in a shooting last year. Only prints on it were his. Martin's going away for a long time."

"What if he has something to offer in return for a lighter sentence? Maybe he could give you Jorguson and some of his clients."

"He'd have to give up Gretta Keene along with Jorguson to get any consideration, and that's not going to happen."

"I thought you told me Keene vanished right before she was deported."

"We don't think she ever left the country. She's still running her operation here, and we believe Jorguson is still laundering her blood money."

He sat down next to her and called Ronan. He was waiting for him to pick up when Olivia said, "You know, I could take a leave from the IRS and maybe use some of my vacation . . ."

Ronan answered. "Hold on," Grayson said. Turning to Olivia he asked, "For what purpose?"

"Do you realize the data I'd have access to if I were to work for Jorguson? You told me Agent Huntsman has been after him for some time now. I'd like to help. This would be an opportunity . . . Stop looking at me like you think I'm crazy."

"Do you actually believe he'd let you near anything illegal?"

"I could snoop around, find out how he communicates with Keene and how he—"

"There's no way in hell you're going to work for that bastard."

"I really think I'm the one who should make that decision."

Thus began what Olivia would later refer to as the blowout. Grayson had a dark side, and she didn't like it one little bit. He thought he could intimidate her and almost did, but she gave as good as she was getting. At least, she thought she did. But in the end, the FBI trumped her.

"Are you really that stubborn?" she demanded.

"Apparently I am," he countered.

In the heat of the moment, Grayson had forgotten Ronan was on the line. His friend was on his way to pick up a date. He tried a couple of times to get Grayson to talk to him, then gave up and listened.

Grayson argued, "You can't be that naive, Olivia. The only reason Jorguson wants you working for him is to keep an eye on you, and to keep you from testifying against him. That's also the reason he would pay you an obscene salary."

"I realize—" Olivia began, and that was as far as she got. She didn't get in another word for several minutes while Grayson lectured over the foolishness of her suggestion.

The sharp whistle from the phone reminded him that Ronan was still waiting.

"Jorguson called Olivia," Grayson explained to him.

"I gathered as much," Ronan said. "I could hear you shouting at her. Olivia's just trying to be helpful," he said in her defense. "It's a stupid idea, going to work for that creep . . ."

"Damn right it is."

"*But*," he said, all but shouting the word, "don't tell her that. She means well."

While Grayson talked to his partner, Olivia went into the kitchen to get a bottle of water. When she returned, she paused to glare at him just for the sheer pleasure of it, then took a drink and sat down next to him.

Grayson finished his call, put his arm around her, and said, "I didn't mean to shout at you."

She rolled her eyes heavenward. "Yes, you did."

"Yeah, you're right. I did."

She made the mistake of looking up at him. He kissed her then, distracting her. He took the bottle out of her hand and gulped down a long swallow before handing it back.

With a calmer voice now, Olivia said, "I was only offering to help."

"I understand," he answered, "but these are dangerous people who have done terrible things. If you knew
more about them, you'd see."

Olivia decided to let Grayson win this battle. So much
for her superspy ambitions. She realized she couldn't in-
filtrate Jorguson's operation or help Agent Huntsman.

Letting the subject of Jorguson drop, she said, "I hope
Ray Martin is the man who tried to kill me. He's your
main suspect, isn't he?"

"No."

"No? Why not?"

"It doesn't feel right."

"What does that mean?"

He shrugged, which, in her opinion, wasn't much of an
answer.

"He had motive," she said. "I got him fired."

"If everyone who got fired—"

"Revenge is a powerful motive."

"There are other powerful motives and other people
who stand to gain much more than satisfaction or revenge if you're out of the way. Why do you want it to be
Martin?"

"It would make it easy."

"That isn't a reason."

He was gently stroking her arm. She put her head
down on his shoulder. "I don't want it to be a relative."
The fact that she considered it possible that her father or
mother or her sister or brother-in-law could go to such
lengths made her sick. "You haven't met my father yet,
have you?"

"No, I haven't."

"Why?"

"I wanted to find out all I could about him before I

met him. I've talked to a lot of people who know him and have worked with him and for him."

"I'll bet every one of them sang his praises, even the ones who lost money."

"Pretty much," he agreed. "Ronan has taken the lead on the investigation. He's met him. He flew to New York and questioned him."

"But you're trying not to form an opinion until you meet him?"

"No, that's not possible. I know what he's done to you, sweetheart. I've got a real strong opinion."

There was anger in his voice. Grayson had become her champion, and she was a little overwhelmed. A long, quiet minute passed before she spoke again.

"When will you meet him?" she asked.

"At his birthday party here in D.C. next weekend."

She bolted upright. "You can't go to his party."

"Of course I can," he said. "Want to come with me?"

"Absolutely not. You're not going either," she insisted. "And quit shoving my head down on your shoulder. I mean it."

"Do you know you're even more beautiful when you're mad?" he said.

She wasn't having it. "Saying I'm beautiful isn't going to sway me, Grayson, so you can stop the phony flattery."

"It's not flattery, Olivia. You are beautiful."

She shook her head.

"What do you see when you look in the mirror?" he asked.

The question surprised her. "It depends."

"On what?"

"If I'm all dressed up and everything works, I feel pretty."

"What do you mean, if everything works?"

Before she could stop him, he lifted her up onto his lap and put her arms around his neck.

"I'm not a puppet, Grayson. You can't just put me where you want me."

He ignored her criticism. "What do you mean, if everything works?"

"You men . . ."

"Yes?"

"You have it so easy. Put on a suit and walk out the door. It's far more complicated for a woman. I'll give you an example. If I were to wear my all-time favorite white, wickedly sexy dress—which I happen to love with all my heart, as shallow as that sounds—and if my hair is just right, and my complexion is clear, and the makeup works, then I'd feel and see a pretty woman when I look in the mirror."

"It's kind of complicated, isn't it?" he remarked, trying not to laugh. "What happens when you're not dressed up?"

She didn't tell him the truth, that some days she felt like that ugly twelve-year-old in the hospital, fighting blisters and welts. "I look and feel drab sometimes. Yes, drab," she repeated, jabbing him in his chest. "Don't you dare laugh at me. I'm not so different from other women. We all have insecurities about our appearance."

He laughed anyway. She was primed for a fight. Apparently, he wasn't. She leaned in and kissed him, teasing him with her tongue. She knew he liked that because he tightened his hold around her.

"I'm not above having sex to get what I want," she purred.

He laughed again. "Glad to hear it."

EIGHTEEN

Olivia was going stir crazy. Work kept her busy during the days, but nights were difficult. She became quite the little housekeeper. She organized her kitchen cabinets, painted the guest bathroom a pale pink, decided she didn't like the color, and then painted it a dark blue. That didn't work either, so with her bodyguard at her side, she went back to the paint store a third time and purchased a can of taupe paint. Only after it was on the walls did she realize she'd painted it the original color.

It seemed to her that she was constantly tripping over the bodyguards following her around. She was allowed to go to work or stay home. There were no other options as far as Grayson was concerned. Even Aunt Emma's house was considered out-of-bounds.

An off-duty policeman drove her to work, then returned at five or six, depending on her schedule, to drive her home.

Another guard sat outside her office.

Olivia put her foot down about the twenty-four-hour protection, insisting that it was ridiculous to have a guard standing outside her apartment door. Once she was inside her home and had locked the dead bolt, she was perfectly safe. Besides, there was a doorman on duty twenty-four hours a day in the lobby. She gave Grayson the same argument about work. There was absolutely no reason for a bodyguard to sit outside her office.

Grayson relented as long as she promised not to go anywhere alone. He gave her five different cell phone numbers to call for the bodyguards. One of them would always be available to accompany her.

She breathed a sigh of relief when she got the news that Ray Martin was behind bars. He had been denied bail—the prosecutor convinced the judge that Martin was a flight risk—and Olivia didn't think it was coincidence that there hadn't been another attempt on her life since he was locked up. She pointed out the obvious fact to Grayson, but every time she brought it up, Grayson asked the same question: What did Martin have to gain by killing her? Revenge apparently wasn't enough of a motive to suit him.

Monday evening she video-chatted with Samantha, who couldn't stop raving about her jet.

"I wish you could go up with me," Sam said. "You'd love it."

Olivia thought she might like it, too. "As long as you're the pilot, I don't think I'd worry."

"Tell me about Jane. How is she doing?"

"Have you talked to her?"

"She was throwing up when I called and couldn't come to the phone. Logan answered. He told me he's really worried about her. He said she's losing weight, and he can't understand why the doctor can't fix her."

"Fix her?"

"Yes, that's what he said. Olivia, has it come back?" she asked, fear radiating in her voice.

"Dr. Pardieu says no, there aren't any signs that our disease has come back, but her cell count is down, and her symptoms aren't consistent. He's still in France. I'll be happy when he gets back and can take over again."

"When are you giving her blood?"

"Soon," she answered. "The hospital will let me know."

"Collins is there. She can give her blood, too."

"Yes," she agreed. "Maybe Jane's just got a bad case of the flu. Some viruses stay in your system a long time, don't they?"

"I think you're reaching," Sam said. "I feel so helpless. So does Logan," she added.

"Jane's brother has only just reconnected with her, and it's heartbreaking for him to see her so ill. He was never around when she was in the unit with us."

They continued to talk for another ten minutes. Sam told her there were several good-looking men around her, but she wasn't interested in any of them. "I'm so much younger than most of them," she said.

Olivia told her about Grayson and how she had gotten so involved with him.

"His nine-year-old nephew lives with him."

"How come?" Sam asked.

"The child's mother died, and the father is absent."

"That's too bad," she said. "I know what you're thinking. You're just like me. We're fatalists."

"Yes."

"We can't plan futures. Happy endings don't exist for any of us."

"Maybe we shouldn't live our lives . . . waiting. You know?"

Sam agreed. "I'm going to cram all I can into the time I have."

By the time they said their good-byes, Olivia was feeling an overwhelming sadness, but she didn't allow herself to wallow in self-pity long. Since she was stuck at home, she decided to catch up on her reading. She had two unread novels and at least twenty-five journals stacked on her desk.

When she couldn't read another article without falling asleep, she went shoe shopping on the Internet. After that, she decided to do a little investigative browsing. She remembered Grayson mentioning a couple of Jorguson clients. One name in particular, Gretta Keene, came to mind first, so she decided to focus on her. She typed her name into the search engine and was surprised by the number of articles she found. As it turned out, the woman had quite a résumé. According to the reports, she was a Belgian emigrant who had become a major player in the American drug scene. After a long investigation by the government, she was finally charged with drug trafficking, but the case never got to court because of a technicality. Shortly after her release, the Belgian government instigated their own attempts to have her extradited. They were anxious to get her back so they could prosecute her for murder. Unfortunately, before any formal action could be taken, Keene disappeared, and she hadn't been heard from since.

In her research, Olivia saw Jorguson's name mentioned several times as a business associate, but he wasn't linked to any criminal activity. If the FBI was so convinced that Jorguson was laundering money for Keene, Olivia surmised they had some pretty good evidence, just not enough to convict him. She now understood their determination to connect the dots and to prove that Keene and Jorguson were working together.

Olivia was really getting into her research and thinking it was kind of fun—that is, until she happened upon photos of a crime scene, bloody bodies amid bags that were to be filled with drugs. The article printed with the pictures stated that Keene was believed to be connected to the killings, but that hadn't been proven either. Olivia found several more references to the same incident, and those led to other articles. After an hour, Olivia couldn't look at another crime scene or read about another bloodbath between rival drug cartels. These people were monsters. If Jorguson was aiding them in any way, Olivia prayed the FBI would catch him soon.

She turned off her computer and looked at the clock. The evening was still young, so she decided to try to make dinner. She chose a recipe from her one and only, new, never-before-opened cookbook and went to work. The result was a disaster. Emma's cook, Mary, saved her from starvation. Olivia pulled one of Mary's chicken-and-noodle casseroles from the freezer and popped it in the microwave. As she sat at her kitchen island eating out of the casserole dish, her thoughts went to Grayson.

She thought about him all the time. Whenever she had a spare minute, there he was. As far as her relation-ship with him went, she was certain that, when the threat was over and he was convinced that the proper arrests had been made, she wouldn't see him again. And that was for the best, she believed; yet, whenever she thought about never seeing him again, she'd feel an ache deep within her chest.

Was this just a fling? Maybe . . . except, she didn't do flings. She knew exactly what had happened and finally found enough gumption to admit it. She'd fallen in love with Grayson. What she didn't understand was how she had allowed herself to be vulnerable. This was all her fault. She couldn't blame Grayson for any of it. He'd never done anything to lead her on or make her think he had these feelings for her. She had likened him to James Bond when she'd first met him, and she'd seen all the movies. In every one of them Bond made love to the woman and moved on. And so would Grayson. Wasn't that for the best?

Olivia decided not to think about the future.

*   *   *

On Friday she left work early—Fridays were always slow for some reason. She arrived home, changed into jeans and a periwinkle-blue sweater, and went to the kitchen to see what she could microwave.

Grayson changed the plan when he showed up at her door and told her he was taking her out.

He looked wonderful. His face was ruddy from the bitter cold outside. His coat collar was up, and his hair was damp from the falling snow.

Olivia hadn't seen him since last Sunday when he'd dropped by unexpectedly. He had been able to stay for only a few minutes then, but he'd called her every day, sometimes twice, to check on her. Now, with him standing in front of her, she wanted to throw herself into his arms. Resisting the nearly overwhelming urge, she forced herself to step back so he could come inside, and still not trusting herself, she put her hands behind her back.

"Come on. I'm taking you to dinner," he repeated.

"You don't tell me we're going out to dinner. You ask me. That's how it's done. And then I decide if I want to go or not."

His hand moved to the back of her neck, and he jerked her toward him. His open mouth came down on hers, his tongue penetrating, tasting, teasing, tempting. When he lifted his head, she sagged against him.

She came to her senses and moved away from him. "We can't go out to dinner," she said as she walked into the kitchen. "It wouldn't be safe. Those were your words, Grayson." She opened the refrigerator, then closed it. "You told me I couldn't go to a restaurant or a shopping center or—"

"I remember what I told you. Office and home. I don't recall adding paint store to the list."

The bodyguard had told on her. She said, "We went in at closing and were the only customers."

Grayson noticed the open cookbook on the island. "Did you already make dinner?"

Her chin came up. "Risotto."

He looked around. "Where is it?"

"In the sink . . . soaking."

When he saw the wooden spoon sticking straight up out of the gluelike substance, he began to laugh. He took the spoon handle and attempted to move the congealed goo in the pan, but it wouldn't budge. "When did you make this?"

"Last night," she answered. "Grayson, it's not that funny."

"Yeah, it is."

She opened the refrigerator again. "Thank goodness for Mary."

"You don't want to go out?"

"You were serious? Of course I want to go out. I'm going crazy staying in all the time. I'm getting a vitamin D deficiency, for Pete's sake. I need sun and fresh air. I'm even trying to learn how to cook, and if that doesn't tell you how far gone I am, I don't know what will."

"A vitamin D deficiency?"

She folded her arms. "It's real."

"Where we're going you'll be safe."

Suspicious, she asked, "Where? Your office? No, I've got it. Vending machines at the police station."

"My place."

She shook her head. "I can't be around Henry. It wouldn't be safe for him."

"He isn't home tonight. He went to a movie with his grandfather and then is spending the night. It's the only other place he'll sleep."

Curious to see what his home was like and desperate

to get out of her apartment, she agreed. "Okay, but no funny stuff."

He grinned. "Funny stuff?"

Ignoring him, she rushed into her bedroom to get her shoes.

Grayson was holding her coat when she returned. She slipped it on, grabbed her purse and cell phone, and unlocked the dead bolt. Grayson saw her inhaler on the table and picked it up.

"What are we having for dinner? Are we doing carryout?"

"I'm cooking for you."

"You cook?" She sounded shocked.

It was a short ride to Grayson's building, a grand five-story structure at the intersection of two quiet streets in a very exclusive neighborhood.

"I'm guessing you're a minimalist," she remarked.

Grayson used an app on his iPhone to open the iron gates that led to a parking garage below the building.

"How do you figure that?" he asked.

"Your home," she explained. "I'm guessing it's sleek, modern. Everything has a function. Am I right?"

The garage was empty. He pulled into a parking slot next to the elevator. "Have you forgotten I have a nine-year-old living with me?"

"Okay, cluttered minimalist."

"Until Henry moved in, the only furniture I had was my bed and a chest of drawers. The living room was empty. Once I'd finished remodeling, I planned to put it on the market. Everything changed, of course. I ordered furniture, and the last of it just arrived."

"Are you still thinking you'll sell?"

He shook his head. "Henry needs stability, so no more moving."

"Are you the only tenant living in the building?"

"Yes. I bought the building, remodeled the top floor, and the architect I hired is working on plans for the others."

"You should have become an architect."

"No, it's just a hobby."

The elevator doors opened to his foyer, gleaming marble floors and a wide-open space. The living room was straight ahead. Facing them was a wall of windows, and the view was spectacular. Area rugs in muted tones adorned dark hardwood floors. The furniture was sparse and did have the sleek lines she'd imagined. Two mahogany leather club chairs sat adjacent to a taupe overstuffed sofa. The contemporary fireplace was encased in black granite that went all the way to the ceiling. There were lots of neutrals, and on the wall next to the fireplace was an abstract painting she thought might be a Richter original. Beautiful splashes of color and thick drapes gave the room dimension and texture.

The dining room was surrounded by windows as well. On the round, dark cherry table, she noticed a pad, no doubt to protect it from the LEGO kit strewn about.

There was evidence of a nine-year-old everywhere. A handheld video game was on the arm of a chair; a pair of gym socks were under the dining room table, and there were three other LEGO kits half completed behind the sofa.

To the left of the foyer was a long hallway. From what she could see, there were at least three bedrooms. To the right was another hallway that led to the kitchen and the pantry beyond. Grayson took her coat and hung it in the hall closet. She followed him, but stopped at the entrance to a gourmet chef's dream come true.

"This kitchen is practically the size of my entire apartment," she said.

Stainless steel, granite, and sleek lacquered cabinets

everywhere she looked. All of the appliances appeared to be brand-new: two double-size ovens, a microwave, an espresso machine, a coffeemaker that had so many buttons it looked like it could run NORAD, a huge stove with eight gas burners, and a few other electrical gadgets she had never seen before.

The granite island was twice the size of hers. She pulled out one of the four barstools and sat.

"Do you know how to work all of these appliances?"

"Sure I do." He was at the sink across from her washing his hands. "But Patrick, our housekeeper, runs the kitchen," he explained.

"Housekeeper?" she asked.

"That's what Patrick calls himself, but he's more like a manager. He runs the house and he also helps with the renovation projects I take on. He needed a place to live at the same time Henry was moving in with me, so it's worked out for everyone. He keeps Henry and me on schedule and somewhat organized. Would you like something to drink? A glass of wine or . . ."

"Just water for now."

He got her a bottle, opened it, and handed it to her. "I'll get dinner started and then go change out of this suit."

"May I help?"

"No, you relax. I've got this."

"So what's your plan?"

He moved to the other side of the island to face her. Then he looked at his watch. "It's six thirty-five. I'll change my clothes and fix dinner. By eight twenty we should be finished. That's when I'll hit on you."

"Oh?"

"Yes. Then, at eight forty, I'll hit on you again. My plan is to wear you down," he added.

She nodded and very seriously said, "I see."

"At eight fifty-five you'll give in just to get me to stop nagging you. Besides . . ."

"Besides what?"

"Let's face it, sweetheart. I'm good. You've told me so."

"When did I . . ."

"Every time I touch you and you moan and beg me to—"

She put her hand over his mouth. She could feel her cheeks warming, knew she was blushing. "I can't argue with the truth." She took a calming breath. "And then?" she asked, trying to maintain a somber expression.

"At approximately one in the morning, we'll get dressed, and I'll take you home." He smiled as he added, "And that's my plan."

She leaned forward. "That's all well and good, but I was asking you what your plan was for dinner."

He laughed as he came around the island and leaned down to kiss her. "You taste good," he whispered.

"Grayson, you know we can't . . . not here . . ."

He rubbed his lips over hers. "Yeah, I know. Want to hear my secondary plan?"

"You like messing with me, don't you?"

"I kinda do. I like the way you blush."

She nudged him. "Go change your clothes."

"Come with me."

She pushed him again. "Oh no. I'll wait here."

As soon as he left the kitchen, she went to the window to look out. She could see over the rooftops for blocks. Down below, traffic was moving slowly, and there were no pedestrians on the sidewalks. Snow flurries were expected, and the temperature had plummeted.

She turned and surveyed the apartment. There was a rectangular table with four chairs near the window. Henry's backpack was in the center of the table with two action figures. A deck of cards was stacked next to a notepad and pen. On the chair was an iPad.

Grayson returned wearing a pair of jeans and a light-blue cotton shirt, open at the neck with sleeves rolled up. Olivia insisted on helping prepare dinner. He grilled salmon he'd been marinating, made a spicy lemon-pepper sauce, and added steamed vegetables and brown rice. He let Olivia do the microwaving of the vegetable steam bag, but after seeing the result of her attempt to cook risotto, he wouldn't let her near the fish.

She didn't think he'd noticed during dinner, but when they were rinsing the dishes and putting them in the dishwasher later, he said, "You should have told me."

"Told you what?" she asked, handing him a glass to rinse.

"That you don't like salmon."

"It looked delicious."

"You didn't taste it."

"Okay, I don't like salmon. I'm sorry."

"I would have fixed you something else."

"You went to so much trouble, I didn't want to be impolite," she explained. "Does Henry like your cooking?"

"My nephew has a very limited palate. Chicken fingers and mac and cheese are his favorites. Patrick can get him to eat vegetables, but I can't."

Grayson's cell phone beeped with a text. He read the message and sighed. "Henry's coming home from the movie. He was supposed to spend the night with his grandfather, but ..."

"He'd rather sleep here?"

"No, his grandfather ... my dad ... has a friend coming over to spend some time with him. She just called him to let him know she's back in town."

"Do you have time to take me home?"

He shook his head. "They're on their way now, but as soon as Patrick gets back, we can leave. It shouldn't take too long."

"I don't mind waiting, and I'd like to meet Henry."

He took a plate from her hand and said, "I'll finish here. You look tired. Why don't you relax, and I'll brew a cup of coffee?"

"If you don't mind, I'd prefer tea if you have it," she said.

"Tea coming up," he said.

Olivia sat in one of the club chairs and picked up a comic book from a stack on the side table. As she thumbed through the pages, reading about a superhero in a slick purple suit who could teleport himself anywhere in the world, she began to feel a tightness in her chest. She recognized the signs of her asthma immediately and walked to the hall closet to get her purse. She pulled her cell phone out, then her lipstick, comb, billfold, tissues . . . no inhaler.

Grayson saw what she was doing. "Your inhaler is in my coat pocket."

Startled, she asked, "How did it get in your coat?"

"You left it on the table, so I grabbed it."

It was such a thoughtful thing to do. "Thank you."

She was thinking how terribly sweet he was until he started lecturing her.

"You need to pay attention and make certain you've always got an inhaler with you, Olivia. I've done some reading on asthma, and an attack can get out of hand. I don't understand how you can be so cavalier about it."

She used her inhaler and put it in her purse. Then she walked into the living room. She stopped in front of the windows.

"This view is spectacular."

He stood behind her and put his arms around her. "Don't want to talk about inhalers?"

"Not really," she said. "I'll admit I've become a little too careless about my asthma. I'll try to do better."

He turned her around, tilted her face up with his hand under her chin and kissed her. He meant only to give her a quick kiss, but in no time at all it got out of hand, and before he realized what he was doing, he'd lifted her up, her pelvis pressed against his, his mouth ravishing hers.

She didn't hear the bell on the elevator. Grayson did and reluctantly let go of her.

The doors hadn't completely opened when Henry bounded out, shouting, "Uncle Grayson!"

"I'm right here, Henry. You don't need to shout."

Henry remembered the intercom and pressed it. "I'm home, Grandfather." Turning back to Grayson, he said, "He let me ride up by myself. Who's she?"

"A friend," he answered. "Put your coat away and take your shoes into your bedroom." Henry had already kicked them off. "Then come meet her."

He was back in two seconds, which told Grayson he'd opened his bedroom door and tossed his coat and shoes in. He slid across the marble and walked over to Olivia. Grayson made the introductions.

Olivia thought Henry was a charmer. There were a few similarities to Grayson in bone structure, high cheekbones and square jaw, and he definitely had the same smile. Henry was tall for his age and lanky. He stared up at her with big brown eyes for a good twenty seconds without saying a word. She stared back.

Grayson watched the two with amusement.

Henry broke the staring contest. "Do you work in the FBI?"

"No."

"Why not?"

"I don't want to."

"She's an attorney, Henry," Grayson explained.

"You are, too."

"Yes."

He looked at Olivia again. "Do you go into the court to help good people or bad people?"

"She has two jobs," Grayson said. "She works on taxes for the IRS," he said, trying to simplify it for him.

"I don't know taxes."

"She's also a children's attorney."

Henry was fascinated by the idea. "Kids can have their own lawyers? You could work for me."

"Yes, I guess I could," she said. She walked over to the sofa and sat. He followed and sat beside her.

"How was the movie?" she asked.

"Grandfather didn't buy the premise. That's what he said."

Grayson sat in an easy chair facing them. "Did he explain what 'premise' meant?"

Henry nodded. "He did, and he said he didn't believe a car could turn into a robot."

Transforming one item into another was the topic of conversation for the next ten minutes, and then the three of them moved to the dining room table. While Grayson caught up on his e-mails on his laptop, she and Henry worked on constructing a filling station with LEGOs.

She heard, "You're doing it wrong," at least ten times, and she noticed that every time Henry said it, Grayson flashed a smile. Henry thoroughly enjoyed that she was so inept.

"Grandfather says I need a woman," Henry casually remarked.

That statement got Grayson's full attention. Olivia didn't seem fazed. "For what purpose?"

"To boss me probably. Olivia, when we're finished, do you want to see my room?"

She was trying to cram a tiny cube into the base of the attached car wash. She couldn't resist teasing him.

"I already saw your room. It's very nice. I liked your bed. I rolled around in it and tested the pillow. Nice and firm."

Henry was giggling. "No, you didn't."

"Oh yes," she countered. "Then I went through all your stuff, played some video games, and when I was finished, I went into your closet and tried on some of your clothes."

He had a good laugh. Then he told her she was connecting the LEGOs all wrong again. She handed him the tiny piece and said, "You fix it. I'll watch."

"Olivia, will you write down your phone number in case I need my own lawyer?"

"Henry, she doesn't—" Grayson began.

She interrupted. "I don't need to write my number. I'll give you one of my cards."

He followed her to the entry where she'd left her purse and patiently waited while she searched for the case with her cards. She found it and gave him one.

"Are you worried about something?" she asked.

"No, but I'm going to try out for soccer."

She wanted to ask him to explain why he thought he'd need an attorney for soccer and would have if the elevator bell hadn't sounded. A few seconds later Patrick arrived.

She had expected a much older man, but Patrick was in his early forties. He was very tall, at least six feet five, and with his lean frame, he had the physical attributes of an NBA player. He shook her hand and shot Grayson a sly look of approval before heading to his room to change.

"Patrick plays basketball most Friday nights," Henry told her.

He then asked her to play a card game with him. Since Henry was having such a good time with Olivia—he was clearly winning—Grayson waited until his nephew had gone to bed to take her home.

Olivia was quiet in the car, her mind jumping from one thought to another.

"Do you worry that Henry's father will come home and take him?"

"No."

"Why not?"

He smiled. "Because my brother knows what's best for Henry, and right now he needs stability."

"But what if . . ."

"Olivia?"

"Yes?"

"Do you like to worry?"

She started to say no, of course not, then decided to think about it. "I guess I'm used to worrying."

"So, you do admit you're a pessimist."

"I'm a realist."

Grayson didn't argue. "Henry likes you."

"That's because I have the sense of humor of a nine-year-old. He gets me."

"What about me? Do you think I get you?"

She turned toward him. "Probably not."

He didn't look at her as he said, "Oh, I know exactly what's going on inside that illogical mind of yours."

She took immediate umbrage. "Excuse me? Illogical?"

"About some things, yes, you're definitely illogical," he said. She opened her mouth to disagree, but he changed the subject. "Ronan told me you're reading up on a couple of Jorguson's old clients."

"I was thinking I might—"

He cut her off. "You aren't still considering going to work for that prick, are you? Because if you are, you should know I'm not gonna let that happen. If you think I'll stand by and watch you put yourself in danger, you're out of your ever-loving mind."

Olivia was surprised by his reaction. In the space of a few seconds, he had worked himself into a lather. "You care that I—"

"Damn right, I care."

She put a hand up. "Don't yell at me."

"I'm telling you, Olivia, I won't let you—"

"I'm not going to work for Jorguson. And don't you dare say, 'Damn right, you're not,'" she rushed to add when he looked as though he was about to say just that. "I made the decision, not you."

"If you want to think—"

"Grayson, I'm not going to argue with you."

He took a breath. "Yeah, okay. Tell me why you were looking at Jorguson's connections."

"I've been stuck at home every night, and I haven't been able to find anything on my father, so out of sheer boredom, a little curiosity, and . . ."

"And what?"

"My ego," she said. "I guess I thought I might find something that would help the FBI's investigation."

"Did you find anything?" he asked.

"I discovered a great deal about Gretta Keene and some of the horrific crimes she might have committed. If Jorguson is involved with any of them, I hope you can find the proof you need to bring him down."

"We will," he assured her.

Grayson noticed a car parked in a no-parking zone just around the corner from Olivia's apartment and called it in. The plates were registered to a woman who lived one block over. He parked in front of Olivia's building, and she waited until he came around to get her. He was being a gentleman, but he was also protecting her. She noticed he always made himself the target whenever they walked anywhere. It was all part of his job, he'd told her. She'd argued she wasn't the president, and he shouldn't have to take a bullet for her, but he'd simply ignored her.

They entered her apartment building, and when the elevator doors opened on her floor, he walked out first. He took her key from her, unlocked her door, and followed her inside. After he'd checked every conceivable place for someone to hide, he came back into the living room. Just as he was taking off his coat, Ronan called.

"Where are you?" he asked.

"Olivia's."

"Ah."

"Ah? What the hell do you mean by 'ah'?" he asked, inwardly cringing over how defensive he'd sounded. He went into Olivia's study and shut the door so that he would have some privacy and said, "Look, Ronan, I know I said I was going to distance myself from this investigation . . ."

"Yeah, you did say that."

"And you've gotta be thinking it's Friday night. What am I doing in her apartment, right?"

"Actually—"

Grayson didn't let him get any further. "I know I shouldn't have gotten involved with Olivia, but I swear from tonight on I'll distance myself. So stop bringing it up."

"Grayson, what the hell's wrong with you?"

He had the answer, but he didn't say it out loud. Guilt. He knew what he should be doing and what he shouldn't. Yeah, it was plain old guilt.

"Are we done?"

"Depends," Ronan said. "If you've finished ranting, I'll tell you why I called."

Grayson leaned against the desk and closed his eyes. He had been ranting.

"Ray Martin wants a deal."

"That son of a bitch bodyguard punches Olivia and pulls a gun on her, and he wants to deal. The hell with that."

"You're not being reasonable."

Grayson knew he was right. "What does he want to deal with? What's he got to offer?"

"He'll give us the name of the weapons supplier and will testify against him."

"Come on. You can't trust—"

"He says he has proof."

"Like what? A receipt?"

Ronan laughed. "Something like that. What do you think? If it's legit, would you press to make a deal?"

"I can't be objective," he admitted, and as soon as the words were out of his mouth, he was appalled. He really couldn't be objective, and how in God's name had he allowed that to happen? Hell. "If Martin's the bastard who tried to kill Olivia, there isn't going to be any deal made."

"You weren't convinced he was the shooter," Ronan reminded him. "Have you changed your mind?"

"No, I'm still not convinced, but as long as he remains a suspect . . ."

"Okay. I won't argue." He sounded resigned.

"Ronan, he punched her and pulled a gun on her. He ought to get a firing squad for that."

"Are we still doing firing squads?"

Grayson ended the call a minute later and went into the living room. Olivia had kicked off her shoes and was sitting on the sofa with her feet up on the ottoman, her iPad in her lap. She looked up when Grayson entered the room, saw his dark expression, and asked, "What's wrong?"

He threaded his fingers through his hair and continued to frown at her. "Listen . . ."

"Yes?"

"I just told Ronan I couldn't be objective, and that's just not acceptable. This can't go on. I need to be able to concentrate on the investigation, but you're messing with my mind, Olivia. I can't allow that to continue."

She put the iPad on the coffee table and sat up. "I'm what?"

"You heard me. You're messing with my mind. I've got to get my focus back, stay away from you while I work. I feel like I'm missing something, some detail that might make a difference, but every time I'm with you I get sidetracked. It's not your fault. You're a very seductive woman."

He thought he was giving her a compliment, but she wasn't pleased. "I distract you."

"Yes. Not on purpose, but, yes, you do," he said firmly.

"What did you mean when you said you feel like you could be missing something?"

"I'm not paying attention, damn it. My focus is all screwed up. I don't know how else to explain it. This is totally not like me. I've got to get back on track."

"Okay, I'll help."

He almost laughed. "You'll what?"

"I'll help you focus. Why is that funny?"

"Olivia, you're the problem."

She took exception. "And you're not? How about I won't touch you and you won't touch me? I have as much self-control as you do, probably more."

He laughed. That reaction didn't sit well.

"You think you're stronger willed than I am? Really?"

"Of course," he responded, as if there was no doubt.

"I'm not going to argue with you. You believe one thing; I believe another. I'm hungry for something sweet. Would you like something?"

"No," he replied. "Tell me what you found out about Gretta Keene. Anything that might be helpful?"

Olivia got up, tossed her hair over her shoulder in what Grayson thought was a deliberately provocative gesture, and went into the kitchen. She came back a minute later with a cherry Popsicle and a plate. "Are you sure you don't want anything?"

"No," he said curtly. "Now talk to me about Keene and then I'm out of here."

She put the plate on the table, tore the paper off the Popsicle, and said, "I just love these."

"Gretta Keene," he reminded her.

He watched her use the tip of her tongue to lick the side of the Popsicle.

"I'm sure Agent Huntsman knows all there is to know about Gretta, but I did discover she's quite a micromanager. She has to oversee every detail, no matter how small."

Her tongue slowly slid up one side and down the other. Grayson couldn't take his gaze off her mouth. He knew what she was doing, and he was amused. Still, he couldn't look away.

"Gretta has trust issues." She put the tip of the Popsicle in her mouth, her full, luscious lips closing around it. Then she took a bite and chewed. She was savoring the icy cold feeling against her tongue. "She won't move away from the money or underlings."

"She what?" He was having a hell of a time concentrating. She was driving him crazy, and she knew it. How could eating a Popsicle be so sensual, so erotic, and such a turn-on?

She repeated what she'd just said and then took another bite. When a drop of the red juice began to slide downward, she slowly drew her tongue across her lower lip to catch it.

"Gretta wants to keep the men who work for her under her thumb at all times so none of them will branch out on their own and become competitors. There was one employee who went against her orders, and she made an example of him. He was tortured before he was killed. I think she's here because she has to watch Jorguson, especially if a lot of her money is going through his firm."

Olivia sucked the last bit of the Popsicle into her mouth and put the stick on the plate.

Grayson watched her carry her plate back into the kitchen. He loved the way her hips moved when she walked. Reluctantly, he reached for his coat and pulled it on.

"I'll check in every now and then," he said, his voice gruff. "But you don't go anywhere alone. Got that? You call one of the numbers and get one of your guards to go with you."

She walked him to the door. "For how long do I have to—"

"For as long as is necessary," he said. "And by the way, your little seduction didn't work."

His restraint was rapidly shredding, and it was taking all of his concentration to keep from grabbing her.

She didn't act innocent or protest that she didn't know what he was talking about. She stepped out of his way so he could leave, waited until he was closing the door, and then whispered, "Oh, I think it did."

NINETEEN

A week had gone by without a word from Grayson. Olivia kept telling herself she was happy and relieved that he'd stayed away. She was feeling guilty for the seduction game she played with the Popsicle. It wasn't really fair. He was just trying to do his job, and their relationship was getting in the way. They had been acting like horny teenagers who couldn't keep their hands off each other, and it had to stop. It wasn't right for either of them. Grayson had his job to think about, and she had her heart to think about. She was getting too emotionally involved, and since the relationship couldn't go anywhere, separating herself was the only decent thing to do.

She wondered if he would ever get married and decided that, yes, of course he would. He'd probably have children, too. He should, anyway, because he would be such a great father. He was so loving and patient with Henry.

Every time she thought about her bleak future, she'd get depressed, and yet she couldn't seem to stop thinking about it. Others might try to convince her that she could have a normal, happy life with a marriage and a family, but she knew better. She had seen the anxiety and suffering that illness could cause, and just the mere possibility that it could rear its ugly head again, as she feared it had done with Jane, made her determined never to let anyone she cared about go through that heartache and sacrifice.

On Friday evening Emma called and insisted that Olivia have dinner with her. Olivia was delighted to have the chance to get out of her apartment for an evening, but that meant she had to call one of her guards to drive her. She had promised. All five guards were nice, polite gentlemen who took their job seriously, but she was getting sick and tired of having to rely on them. She longed to be able to get in her car and go wherever she wanted whenever she wanted. Boring but necessary chores, like grocery shopping or picking up her dry cleaning, now appealed to her. Even though she hated shopping for clothes, she needed a new pair of running shoes, but a trip to the mall was out of the question because there was always the worry of bullets flying all over the food court while the man who wanted her dead tried a second time to kill her.

Her patience was running out, yet every time she was close to throwing up her hands and yelling, "Enough already," she'd get a look at herself in the mirror and see the raw bullet scars. She'd then decide she needed to be patient a little longer. Besides, the FBI wouldn't be paying for protection unless they felt there was a real threat. Right?

Ronan accidentally let the cat out of the bag. He called with a question about Simmons, Simmons and Falcon. He wanted to know how long the firm had been working with Olivia's father. She didn't have the answer but said she'd try to find out for him.

"While I have you on the phone, I'd like to ask you something," she said.

"Okay." Ronan was sure she was going to ask about Grayson.

"The FBI wouldn't be paying for these bodyguards if—"

Before thinking, he said, "They aren't paying. They stopped. . . . I mean to say . . ."

Olivia sat up straight, bristling at what he was trying not to tell her. "Who's paying the bodyguards?" There was no immediate reply, so she asked, "It's either Grayson or Emma, isn't it? Tell me."

Ronan sighed. "Grayson's paying." He rushed to add, "He wants to keep you safe, Olivia."

"Yes, I know. Did you have any other questions?"

Ronan heard the stiffness in her voice. "It doesn't matter who's paying. If you go anywhere, you call for a bodyguard first. Understand?" he said sternly.

"Good night."

"Olivia . . ." he began, but it was too late. She was gone.

She found her car keys, locked the door after her, and took the elevator down to the garage. What an idiot she was, not to have figured it out sooner. If she truly needed a bodyguard, the FBI would have continued to provide the protection. How dared Grayson do this behind her back! She could take care of herself.

By the time she reached her car, she began to calm down. Maybe she was being too hard on Grayson. After all, he'd obviously acted out of concern. He felt there was still a threat out there, and he wanted to protect her. True, his intentions were good, but he should have been honest with her, shouldn't he? She made up her mind to pay him every dollar he'd spent on the bodyguards. Only then would her pride be salvaged.

She would prove that she could be cautious and self-sufficient. She wouldn't allow herself to be blindsided again.

She took caution to a whole new level. She carried her pepper spray in one hand and held her key fob in the other, one finger hovering over the panic button. She even checked to see if there were any red lights blinking under the car or in the backseat. Killing someone with a bomb wasn't all that unusual. She wasn't being paranoid; she was being smart. She even made certain she wasn't being followed and took several side streets to get to her aunt's house. She arrived alive and well.

Mary had set the table in the dining room. She and Harriet stayed in the kitchen, no doubt to eavesdrop because they knew the topic was going to be Olivia's father.

Emma greeted her with a kiss on each cheek. Her aunt always looked so put together. Olivia had never seen her in what she called casual clothes, and the thought of Emma putting on a pair of jeans made her smile. It was such an outlandish picture. Tonight Emma wore a fitted charcoal-gray wool dress with a high round neck. The skirt was straight and ended just below the knees. Her midheel shoes matched the dress exactly. They were a beautiful suede. Her only jewelry was her wedding ring—she'd never taken it off after Daniel died—and a jeweled broach in the shape of a hummingbird. Standing next to her, Olivia felt like a hobo.

She straightened her sweater and said, "I should have taken the time to put on a dress, but I had only just changed out of my clothes from work when you called." She realized she was making excuses and paused. "I should have changed out of these jeans at least."

"You're fine, dear. You worry too much, but then you always have been a worrier. Come sit and we'll have dinner."

Olivia didn't have much of an appetite. Two fudge bars and a grape Popsicle had dampened it. Olivia loved junk food, mostly freezing-cold junk food. It was a dark secret only her friends knew about. The cold had soothed the sores in her mouth after the chemotherapy, and ever since, she craved the icy sweet comfort. Half of her freezer was stuffed with Dove bars, Fudgsicles, Popsicles, and various flavors of ice cream. The other half was reserved for Mary's healthy casserole dishes.

Tonight, Mary had prepared a roast turkey with root vegetables for dinner. She entered the dining room with a large platter and held it for Olivia to serve herself. Olivia didn't want to hear Mary tell her she was too thin and needed to put some meat on her bones, as she had often done in the past, so she took a portion of everything and said, "This smells wonderful."

After Mary returned to the kitchen, Emma said, "Catch me up. What have you been doing?"

Having sex with Grayson, thinking about having sex with Grayson, and having more sex with Grayson. Emma would be horrified if Olivia blurted out those thoughts.

"I've been doing some research on a few of the names connected to Eric Jorguson." She then explained who and why, and when she was finished, Emma asked several questions.

"It was a wasted effort," Olivia told her. "Aside from the fact that I made myself sick reading all the awful things these monsters have done, I couldn't find anything that might help Agent Huntsman."

"What else have you been up to?"

"Trying to figure out who shot me. And work has been busy." She put her fork down and talked a bit about her job.

Emma asked, "What about your father? What have you done about him?"

"I've sort of put him on the back burner . . . It's so frustrating," she admitted. "Word has gotten out that I'm trying to stop him and . . ." She didn't finish her sentence. Time for some honesty, she decided. "I've been seeing Grayson," she began.

Emma didn't seem surprised. She smiled.

"You knew?" Olivia asked.

"Yes, dear. You were explaining why you've put your larcenous father on the back burner," she reminded.

Olivia felt cowardly because she didn't want to admit to her aunt that she feared the repercussions of the truth, that when it all came out and her father was arrested and charged, life would change dramatically. There was going to be such anger, such hate, and it would all be directed at her family. Her father would be safe behind bars and probably become a celebrity with the other prisoners because of his oh-so-clever scams, but the rest of them would be fair game for the press and for all those people who had lost their life savings. Even though Olivia knew it had to be done, she dreaded what was coming.

"There's a young man sitting in a jail cell waiting to go to trial for a crime your father committed," Emma said.

Olivia was surprised. "Jeff Wilcox? Why is he in jail?"

"He was arrested. The prosecutors feel they have enough to convict him."

"Didn't the court set bail?"

"Yes, but they've revoked it. I asked Mitchell to check into it, and he says they're trying to force Jeff into making a deal, but he's refused, and so they've come up with some excuse to keep him in jail until his court date."

"Who is Mitchell?"

"Mitchell Kaplan is one of my attorneys. He's also a financial adviser and a dear friend. I believe you've met him."

If she did, she didn't remember. "Is he representing Jeff?"

"No. Jeff's attorney is Howard Asher. Mitchell said he's a deal maker. That's all Asher does, make deals, and ninety-nine percent of them are bad deals. He'll do anything to stay out of court. Mitchell told me that Asher doesn't know what he's doing. A public defender would have been a better choice. Jeff doesn't have the resources to fight this. He doesn't have any income, and his poor wife is at home trying to hold on until this is all sorted out." She stared at Olivia a long minute and then said, "And you, young lady, are just the one to sort this all out, aren't you?"

"Yes, ma'am, I am."

"No more back burner . . ."

"No."

Emma nodded. "I feel responsible for what's happened to Jeff. Your father used Jeff's friendship with me to get close to him. Did you know, if it does go to trial, your father is going to testify against Jeff?"

Olivia was beginning to feel the familiar tightness in the pit of her stomach again. "No, I didn't know."

"Your father won't want it to go to trial. It would bring too much attention to him, and heaven forbid, his attorneys might not be able to keep his records hidden."

"I promise you, my focus is back where it should be."

Focus. That was the word of the week. Grayson had told her he needed focus. She did, too. He'd also told her he felt as though he could be missing something because he hadn't been giving the investigation his full attention. She'd distracted him. Now she felt the same way. She had allowed Grayson to distract her from her investigation into her father's dealings.

"I'm going to help," Emma continued. "Mitchell Kaplan is one of the best attorneys in the country, and investment fraud is a specialty. He's agreed to take this case on, but you have to hire him. Mitchell made me promise that I would step back from this. He believes if my financial assets are in any way connected to this, your father will try to attach them."

Olivia agreed. "He's been trying to get your money into his Trinity Fund for a long time now."

"I would say there's a love/hate relationship between us, but the fact is, there has never been any love." Emma pushed her plate aside and, sitting back in her chair, folded her hands on the table. With a steady voice of authority she said, "I have an unwritten agreement with Mitchell, but you need to give him a small retainer. After this is all over, I'll transfer money into your account to pay his full fee. I can't do that now, though, because—"

"It could come back to you."

"It probably will anyway, dear, but it's best not to have a paper trail leading to my door. I also want you to give Jeff's wife a check, enough to make ends meet. Do you have enough to do that?"

Olivia nodded. "Yes," she said. And if she ran out of money before this was sorted out, she would take out another mortgage on her apartment. Whatever it took, she would make things right.

"You need to go see Jeff as soon as possible, before any deals are made."

"I'll go tomorrow."

"Take a check over to Mitchell on your way. I'll give you his card."

"Tomorrow's Saturday," she reminded. "Will he be in his office?"

"Yes, he will, and he's expecting you at ten o'clock. You could messenger the check over, but I'd like you to meet him, and he certainly wants to meet you."

She didn't ask why. "What about Jeff? Does he know what you're doing?"

"What *you're* doing," she corrected. "And the answer is no. You're going to have to explain it all to him."

"I'm a MacKenzie. How am I going to get him to trust me?"

Emma smiled. "You'll find a way."

TWENTY

For Olivia, Saturday started at four thirty in the morning with a call from a police station across town.

The officer on duty apologized for the early hour. "Judge Bowen told me to call you. We have a little girl here who needs protection . . . your kind of protection. The judge doesn't want her in the system. It has something to do with a trial that's coming up," he told her. "He said you'd help the child disappear for a while."

"I'll be right there."

Thank goodness for GPS, or she never would have found the police station. The paperwork didn't take as long as usual because the judge had already signed the order. By eight o'clock she had nine-year-old Lily Jackson settled in her new, though temporary, home.

When she got in her car and checked her phone, there was a message from Mitchell Kaplan moving their meeting to eleven. Olivia was thankful for the extra time. She drove back to her apartment, showered, and changed into a dark blue dress. She left her hair down but used a barrette to keep it out of her face, then put on her earrings and watch. Since there was still a little time to spare, she went through her briefcase again to make absolutely certain she had all the necessary papers for Jeff.

She'd already written her check to Mitchell Kaplan and tucked it in her purse, along with another one for Jeff Wilcox's wife.

Coat and scarf on, she headed out. The elevator doors opened, and there stood Grayson. She was so surprised to see him, she froze, but only for a second or two. She stepped into the elevator and pressed the button to the garage.

"Hi." Not very original, but it was the best she could do.

Grayson didn't look happy to see her. "What are you doing?"

When she didn't immediately answer, he pushed the button to stop the elevator. "I said, what are you doing?"

"Errands."

"No."

"No?" She didn't shout the word, but she wanted to. Instead, she pushed his hand away from the buttons. "Ronan told me you've been paying for my bodyguards, and I want you to know I'm going to reimburse you for every dollar you spent, but, Grayson, you really should have told me what you were doing."

"I'm going to keep you safe, no matter how much you fight me," he countered. He nudged her chin up so she would look him in the eye and said, "Damn it, Olivia. I don't want anything to happen to you."

She thought he was going to kiss her, but he suddenly stepped back.

"I am safe," she insisted. "And, of course, I'm being cautious."

"Were you cautious when the elevator doors opened?"

"I usually have my pepper spray at the ready," she countered.

"Usually?"

His voice was deceptively soft, a bad sign she recognized from past experience. Grayson was about to lecture the hell out of her.

"Push the button to the garage. I have an appointment I can't miss."

He started to argue, then changed his mind and pushed the button to the lobby.

"I'll take you."

"I'm perfectly capable—"

"I'll take you. Where are you going?"

"First to an attorney's office, then to jail."

Mitchell Kaplan was going to be a godsend for Jeff Wilcox. Olivia had taken time the night before to look up some of his cases and was impressed. Kaplan's adversaries called him a barracuda, and that was exactly what Jeff needed.

His nickname certainly didn't fit his appearance. Kaplan reminded her of a teddy bear. He was short, a bit round in the middle, and wore thick wire-rimmed glasses. He was also soft-spoken and reserved. Although Olivia and Grayson spent only a short time with the attorney, they both liked him.

"Where are they holding Wilcox?" Grayson asked.

"Mr. Wilcox has been held close to his home in Fairhaven. It's a decent facility, but I had my assistant check this morning before I sent you there to talk to him, and I learned that last night he was moved to Beaumont."

"That's ninety miles from here. Wilcox won't last long there."

Kaplan nodded.

"Why did they move him?" Olivia asked, and then

before Grayson or Kaplan could explain, she asked, "Why won't he last long?"

"Fairhaven is to a country club what Beaumont is to Attica," Grayson explained.

"My assistant was told he was moved because of over-crowding. It's a game they're playing, trying to force Mr. Wilcox to take the deal he's been offered. There are serious charges, and I'm sure the federal prosecutor would like to save the taxpayer the expense of a trial."

Kaplan went over the documents he was sending with Olivia and then said, "Please tell Mr. Wilcox I'll get the ball rolling right away to get him released, but I can't do anything until he signs the paper retaining my services. I'll plan on being at the jail to see him later today. By now I imagine Mr. Wilcox is feeling beat down."

"Then you'll be able to get him out of there today?" she asked.

Kaplan nodded. "He'll be under house arrest, but he'll be home."

Olivia handed him an envelope containing the retainer check and pulled the other envelope from her purse. "Would you see that he gets this, as well?" she asked. When Kaplan gave her a questioning look, she continued. "It will help his family get through the next couple of months," she explained.

Smiling, Kaplan took the envelope. "Of course."

Olivia thanked him and was walking out the door with Grayson at her side when Kaplan said, "Mr. Wilcox's useless attorney is meeting with him late this afternoon. I'd try to get there before he does."

Once they were out in the hallway, Olivia whispered to Grayson, "This is going to sound really paranoid. The deal that's being pushed on Wilcox—I've got a feeling my father has something to do with it."

He nodded. "It does sound paranoid, but I'm not dismissing the possibility."

"What if Wilcox's inept attorney has made a deal of his own to pressure Wilcox to cooperate?"

"Who would make the deal? Your father?"

"Simmons," she suggested. "He's one of my father's attorneys. I wouldn't put anything past him, and he and my father would have good reasons not to want this to go to trial. Kaplan would bring them into it, and there goes my father's low profile."

As soon as she clipped her seat belt in place, she said, "I'm nervous about meeting him."

"Wilcox?"

"Yes, Wilcox," she said. "I don't know if he'll remember me, but as soon as he hears my last name, he'll probably spit in my face."

"I won't let that happen. Start with 'I'm going to get you out of here,' and I guarantee he'll listen."

"You can't stop him from—"

"If he does anything to you, I'll coldcock him."

As much as she hated to admit it to herself, she was glad he was so protective. "Can you take the time to go with me?"

"You're not going without me."

"What about Henry?"

"Basketball camp all day with Patrick. As long as I'm back by eight tonight, I'm good."

"Why eight?"

"I've got a date."

Her reaction was instantaneous. She felt as though he'd just coldcocked her and immediately recognized that she was being illogical. She wanted him to move on, so shouldn't she be happy that he had a date?

"That's nice." She tried to sound pleased, but her

voice betrayed her, coming out raspy, as though she'd just gargled vinegar.

Grayson pulled onto the highway. "Traffic isn't bad. It shouldn't take us all that long to get there."

"Did you just meet this woman, or is she someone you've known for a while?" she asked. "I'm just curious," she rushed on. "Making conversation."

"What woman?"

"You said you had a date tonight."

"Yes, I do."

"I see."

"Aren't you going to say 'That's nice' again?"

"I was just . . ."

He glanced at her. "Making conversation."

"Exactly. Where are you going?" She hurriedly added, "You don't have to tell me, unless you want to tell me."

"A birthday party."

"A birthday . . ." The light dawned. "Oh no, you aren't."

He started to laugh. "Yes, I am."

"Grayson, we talked about this. You're going to my father's birthday party? Is that what you're saying?"

"That's what I'm saying."

"I don't want you to go." She knew she sounded like a petulant child.

"Really? Why didn't you say something sooner?"

"I did say . . ." She realized he was teasing her. "I mean it."

"What are you so worried about?"

She looked out the side window while she tried to put into words what she was feeling. "I'm related to him."

"Olivia, we all have at least one family member we'd rather not be related to," he said. His brother immediately came to mind.

"Just one? I've got a plethora."

Had she not sounded sincere, he would have laughed again. "I want to see him at work."

At work? She thought about it for a minute and understood. "Yes, he will be working, dazzling people. He'll make sure everyone loves him."

"But I won't."

"I know." *Because of what your father did to you.* She remembered Grayson saying those very words to her. He knew what Robert MacKenzie was all about. He couldn't be swayed.

"Who's going with you?"

"No one," he said. "I'll be working. Did it bother you when I said I had a date?"

"Of course not." It was an outrageous lie, and she was pretty sure he knew it.

"When we go out on a real date—and we will be going out on a real date—"

"I don't think we should—"

He cut her off. "Once I'm convinced we have the right man behind bars and it's safe out there for you, we should celebrate."

She started to object but changed her mind. What could one date hurt? A celebration date, nothing more. "Yes, okay. One date."

"I'd like you to wear the white dress you've told me about. You've made me very curious to see it."

"Oh, I don't know about that. My coveted, one-of-a-kind white dress? If I were to wear the dress, there would be rules you'd have to follow."

"Rules? Like what?"

"Like no red wine. And you couldn't eat any pasta with red sauce. Now that I think about it, I should probably give you a list of what you could and couldn't eat. Maybe it would be better if you didn't eat at all."

"I don't usually fling my food around when I eat."

"One tiny little splat, and the dress is ruined," she warned. "It's vintage, 1960. It can't be replaced."

"I'm not taking you out to dinner and not eat."

"I guess I could wear a raincoat."

He whistled and shook his head. "That dress must be something else."

The banter was fun, and Olivia was beginning to relax, but her lighthearted mood changed with a phone call. Her sister wanted to harass her one last time to make Emma attend the birthday party. Natalie had blocked her phone number on the display so that Olivia would answer the call.

Olivia denied Natalie's request yet again, but her sister was not ready to end the conversation.

"I wanted you to know that all of us have suites at the Morgan Hotel. Mom and Dad are in the presidential suite, and George and I are in a smaller suite on the same floor. The top floor, of course," Natalie bragged.

"What's happened to you?" Olivia asked. "You and George made a lot of money with your Internet company, honest money," she qualified, "and you never acted like this."

"Like what?"

Like a greedy fool, she silently answered, but since she didn't want a fight, she didn't say it aloud. "Is there something else you want, Natalie?"

"Mother would like you to stop by before the party."

"So she can drag me along? No, thank you."

Natalie exploded. "Aren't you ashamed of yourself? You should be," she shouted. "You're so damned selfish."

And on she went. Olivia held the phone away from her ear and waited for the rant to end. She knew Grayson could hear every word. The people in the Ford Explorer in the next lane could probably hear.

Turning to him, Olivia quietly said, "I just realized I haven't had anything to eat since last night. I had to get up at four thirty, and by the time I got back to the apartment, I was in too much of a hurry. Think we could stop for a bagel or something?"

Natalie had gone into warp speed, screeching. The more she ranted, the louder she got.

"You left your apartment at four thirty? What the hell for?" Grayson asked.

Great. Now she was going to have shouting in both ears. "It was closer to four forty-five."

"That makes a big difference. Where did you go?"

Olivia started to answer, but Natalie's voice had just gone up another decibel. She was demanding to know if Olivia knew she was such a bitch.

"Hold on," she told Grayson before putting her phone back to her ear. "Yes, Natalie. I do know I'm a bitch."

Warp-speed screaming again.

"I'm waiting for an explanation," Grayson reminded, ignoring her sweet smile.

"I drove across town to a police station to pick up a nine-year-old little girl. She's a new client," she explained.

He nodded. "Which police station?"

"Oh, you wouldn't know it."

"I know all of them. Which one was it?" he repeated.

She didn't want to tell him because the station was located in such a bad area, and she knew he wouldn't take the news well. He coaxed it out of her, though. Thankfully, Grayson was neither a screamer nor a screecher. She couldn't imagine him ever behaving like her sister. Grayson's voice was soft but firm. Sometimes he could be downright scary, but he was never scary with her. Angry, yes—scary, no. He always got his point across, and when he was displeased with her, she knew it.

He didn't ask her if she knew she was crazy — that was a Natalie move — but his look suggested he thought she might be.

Olivia put her phone to her ear again and, interrupting her sister's tirade, said, "Good-bye, Natalie." She took great delight in ending the call.

"In the middle of the night . . . What would you have done if your car had broken down?" he asked her.

"I'd stay in the car, keep the doors locked, and call you."

"You'd call me?"

That took a little wind out of his anger. "I'd also call for a tow. Now, can we please stop and get something to eat? We should probably find a drive-through. I want to get there before Wilcox's attorney."

At her insistence, they stopped at a McDonald's. She ate a chicken wrap and drank a Diet Coke and told Grayson it was delicious.

"It doesn't take much to make you happy," he remarked.

She smiled as she sipped the last of her Coke. "I'm a simple girl at heart," she said. Carefully folding the wrapper and napkin so that no crumbs would fall, she placed them in the paper bag.

"Have you figured out what you're going to say to Wilcox?" he asked.

She had given some thought to the conversation, but she couldn't know how Wilcox would react to seeing her. Would he remember her? Would he freak out when he heard her name? She practiced a couple of approaches on Grayson and was feeling pretty good about her plan . . . until she walked into the jail. She was immediately sorry she'd eaten anything because her stomach started doing flips. The rancid smell of what she suspected to be rotting mice in the walls was overwhelming, and everything looked old and decayed. The few pieces of furniture were broken-down and ready for the dump. Grayson told her the jail was going to be closed just as soon as a new facility was finished, but with budget cuts, no one knew exactly when that would be.

The air in the cell block was heavy with sweat. The cells were so crowded, there was barely room to walk around. A jailer with dark circles under his eyes and a weariness to his gait led Jeff Wilcox into a small interrogation room. Wilcox sat on one side of a small wobbly table. He looked scared and overwhelmed.

He saw Grayson's FBI badge and said, "Am I being charged with mail fraud, too?" His voice was flat, with little emotion.

"No," Grayson answered.

"Shouldn't my attorney be here for this interrogation?"

"It's not an interrogation. We're having a conversation," Grayson said.

Wilcox was focused on Grayson and was obviously afraid of him or possibly what he thought he was going to hear from the FBI agent. Olivia had time to study the man. The longer she watched him, the angrier she became on his behalf. She was seeing one of her father's victims up close and personal.

"You're going to fire your attorney," Grayson said very matter-of-factly. He stood next to Olivia with his arms folded across his chest, his stance relaxed.

"Why?"

Grayson looked at Olivia. "Do you want to start explaining?"

Jeff Wilcox turned to face her then, and his eyes widened.

"Hi, Jeff," she began. "I don't know if you remember me. I'm Olivia—"

He almost came out of his chair. "MacKenzie," he finished. "I remember you." His demeanor changed immediately to anger. "You're that bastard's—"

She cut him off. "Listen carefully. Yes, I'm that bastard's daughter, and I know what he is. I'm here to help you." She rushed to continue before he could turn away from her. "You have a new attorney. His name is Mitchell Kaplan. Have you heard of him?"

"Of course, I have. He's famous. I can't afford . . ."

"I'm paying for his services," Olivia said.

"Did he agree to take my case? Does he know what I've been charged with?"

Before Olivia could answer, he listed them. "Investment fraud, securities fraud, investment adviser fraud, and my attorney says, if I take the deal, they won't add mail fraud."

"What is the deal?" Grayson asked.

"Twenty-five years. Solid twenty-five years." He put his head in his hands. "I swear to God I didn't do anything wrong. I swear it, but my attorney said that, given the atmosphere, the prosecutor could add another twenty and get it."

She thought he might start crying. Who could blame him? She put her briefcase on the chair across from him, pulled out a manila folder, and placed it in front of him.

"I know you're innocent, and I know what you're up against. Mr. Kaplan has written you a letter. Please read it, and then if you agree, sign the attached paper authorizing him to take over your defense. You can either choose to let Kaplan prove your innocence or . . . not. It's up to you."

She could see the confusion in his eyes. He wanted to believe but was afraid.

"Why do you want to help me?"

Tears came into her eyes. "I told you why," she said, her voice shaking. "I know what he is, and he has to be stopped. I would like your help to do that, but even if you can't, or won't, I'll still keep trying until I succeed."

"Read the letter," Grayson suggested.

"How do I know this is real?" He looked at Olivia and said, "Your father showed me investment statements on official letterheads, and it was all a fake."

"Read the letter, Wilcox," Grayson repeated more firmly. "You've got nothing to lose and everything to gain."

His hands shook as he opened the envelope. Olivia's hands were shaking, too. She hadn't realized how anxious she'd been about this meeting. She felt as though she'd just put herself through a wringer. Her nerves were stretched tight, and she could only imagine how Jeff was feeling.

Jeff looked up from the page he was reading. "Mr. Kaplan says he'll have me out of here by tonight. Can he do that?"

"If he says he can, then he can," Olivia replied. "You'll be under house arrest, but you'll be home with your wife and your baby."

Jeff was starting to believe. She could see it in his eyes. She watched him go through the rest of the folder, scouring every page.

"There are copies of all these papers for you to keep."

"Does either of you have a pen?"

Jeff signed two papers, one firing his current attorney, Howard Asher, and another retaining Mitchell Kaplan.

He'd just handed the papers back to Olivia when Asher walked in.

"What's going on here?" he bellowed.

Asher wasn't what she'd expected. Because Olivia had heard how inept the man was, she had made the assumption that he was young and inexperienced and perhaps had only just passed the bar. Asher was in his late thirties or early forties. He was dressed in a business suit and tie, but there was still something disheveled about him. She noticed the expensive Rolex watch he was wearing when he reached out to shake Jeff's hand.

She decided he was also sleazy when he wouldn't stop giving her the once-over. Her chest and legs seemed to captivate him.

"This is for you," Jeff said, reaching out with the signed document in his hand.

Asher was still staring at Olivia when he asked, "What is it?"

"A paper I signed, firing you," Jeff answered.

That got his attention. He whirled around and snatched the paper. "What's this about? You need an attorney, Jeff."

"Mitchell Kaplan will be handling my defense."

Asher's mouth dropped open. "Kaplan? You can't afford Mitchell Kaplan. You've got to be kidding."

"Mr. Kaplan has agreed to represent me."

Asher shook his head. "Prove it."

"I don't have to prove it. You're fired. That's all you need to know."

"It's too late," Asher stammered. "We've made a deal."

Jeff looked to Olivia for help.

"Then you're in trouble, Mr. Asher," she said, "because Jeff hasn't agreed to any deals."

"Exactly who did you make this deal with?" Grayson wanted to know.

Asher looked as though he needed to sit. His face was gray. "This can't be happening. How did you ever get Kaplan interested . . ."

"I think we're done here," Olivia said.

"Wait . . . Now, wait here," Asher demanded. "Jeff, you'll get fifty years or more if you don't take the deal. You can't take this to trial. You'll get . . ."

He stopped arguing when Jeff put his hand up. "I'm not taking any deals, and you're no longer my attorney."

Grayson could see the panic in Asher's eyes. The attorney had gotten past his surprise and now was letting his anger control him. His body was rigid and his hands were fisted at his sides.

"Jeff, it's time to go back to your cell," Grayson said as he motioned to the jailer.

"Wait," Asher demanded. "Just wait a minute. We're not finished here."

"Yes, we are finished," Olivia stated emphatically.

Asher turned to her and took a threatening step forward. Grayson pulled Olivia to his side.

"Listen, you," Asher muttered, "go back to your boss and tell him we've already made the deal and it's solid. It's done. Kaplan will just have to step back."

Olivia had had it. She took a step toward Asher and said, "No, you listen. There isn't any deal. Got that? No deal. And, by the way, I don't work for Mitchell Kaplan."

Asher was obviously scrambling to keep his sinking ship afloat. His eyes darted back and forth between Jeff and Olivia while he tried to think of a way to stop what was happening.

The jailer escorted Jeff out of the interrogation room. Asher didn't move. He seemed rooted to the floor, he was so livid. "I don't know what you think you're doing here, but you're messing with the wrong people," he hissed. "Powerful people."

"Oh, I think I know exactly who I'm messing with," she replied. Her voice was as smooth as a summer breeze. "Allow me to introduce myself. My name is Olivia MacKenzie."

She picked up her briefcase and walked to the door. Grayson pulled it open for her. She looked back over her shoulder and said, "Tell my father I'll see him in court."

TWENTY-ONE

Grayson arrived at the Morgan Hotel a little after nine o'clock. He noticed all the security as soon as he walked inside. Because he'd worn a gun—he never left home without it—he had to show his credentials three separate times before he reached the guarded ballroom doors.

Ronan caught up with him as he was going in.

"Wait up," he called. He showed his identification to another guard and started to walk past. The guard reached out and put his hand on Ronan's arm. "Do you have an invitation? I don't see one. You can't go inside without an invitation. There're some very important people in there."

One glacial look from Ronan, and the guard immediately pulled his hand back. The antagonism in his voice irritated Ronan. "I'm FBI. I can go wherever the hell I want to go. Got that?"

"Yes, sir." The guard hastily opened the door and stepped away.

"What are you doing here?" Grayson asked.

"I didn't want to miss the show."

"You've met MacKenzie," he reminded. "You interviewed him, remember?"

Ronan grinned. "Of course I remember, but that was

one-on-one, and I want to see what he's like in a crowd. I'm betting he's as humble as he was with me. He's a real nice guy," he added. "Just ask anyone."

His sarcasm wasn't lost on Grayson. "Yeah, right. Nice guy. Olivia's worried I'll like him."

Ronan shook his head. "Did you tell her we put a lot of nice guys in prison every damn day?"

"Sure I did."

The two agents moved to the back of the room and tried not to draw any attention as they watched the guests.

Four bars were set up, one in each corner, and people thronged around them as the bartenders rushed to fill their drink orders. Waiters passed among the crowd, offering dainty canapés or glasses of wine from their silver trays. The double doors to the adjacent ballroom were open, and there were stations with every kind of delicacy to eat. The best of everything. Guests were encouraged to help themselves to whatever they wanted.

A man walked past carrying a heaping plate piled with oysters, crackers, and a mound of caviar. The glutton was practically drooling in anticipation of his feast.

"I wonder how these people would react if they knew they were paying for this," Grayson said.

"I think they're going to be real pissed when they find out they paid for his mansion on the beach."

"You're right. No expense spared tonight. Do you know how much a bottle of that champagne costs?" he asked when a waiter offered fluted glasses to a couple in front of them.

"I drink beer, not champagne, but I'm guessing a whole lot."

Grayson laughed. "Yes, a whole lot. It tastes like seawater, too."

Grayson spotted Olivia's brother-in-law, George, and

pointed him out. There was a woman next to him, smiling and sipping champagne. She didn't look anything like Olivia, but Grayson was sure she was her sister because she was holding George's hand and occasionally smiling at him. Grayson thought the affection looked forced. George appeared to be miserable.

"I wonder if he paid the loan shark back," Ronan remarked.

"It's easy to check."

"From the look on his face, I'm guessing, no. Is that his wife with him? She's pretty. There's a small resemblance to Olivia."

"I don't see it." But then he knew what a witch Natalie was to her sister.

It took a lot to surprise Grayson, but he nearly did a double take when he saw who walked in the door.

"Olivia and I went to see one of MacKenzie's victims today," he told Ronan. He then explained everything that had happened with Jeff Wilcox.

Ronan was impressed that Mitchell Kaplan had taken the case. "The prosecutor won't like that."

Grayson shrugged. "Asher's reaction was telling. He went into a panic."

"His reaction to getting fired? From what I know about him, he's got to be used to it. I've heard he's a terrible attorney."

"I'm going to look into his finances. I think he was paid to make the deal and put Wilcox away. The last thing Robert MacKenzie wants is a trial."

"Are you thinking MacKenzie paid Asher?"

"That's what I'm thinking. Not directly, of course. The guy's one shrewd son of a bitch."

"It's going to be tough to prove that Asher even knows MacKenzie," Ronan said.

Grayson smiled. "Not that tough. Asher just walked in the door."

"Are you kidding me? Showing up here . . . not real bright. I'll get some pictures of him with MacKenzie. I'm gonna have to use my cell phone," he said. "And I can't let MacKenzie see me do it. Where's Asher now?"

"At the bar on the left. He's gulping down whiskey."

"From what you've told me, Asher has had one hell of a day. He must need courage before he talks to MacKenzie. Real stupid to talk to him here, though. Speaking of the devil, there he is. The birthday boy. I'll see what I can do about pictures."

The crowd had parted, and Grayson had a clear view of Robert MacKenzie. He was standing by the French doors to the terrace, surrounded by well-wishers. His wife stood just behind him. There was no doubt who the stunning woman was, for Olivia was her spitting image.

Grayson dismissed her and focused on MacKenzie. The man was quite the showman. He had an easy smile and a charming way about him. Self-confidence oozed from his pores. Grayson watched him closely and decided that what made him so charismatic wasn't just his handsome looks or his personality but the way he interacted with other people. It was a talent really. His gaze never left the person he was talking to. He didn't once glance to the left or the right. His concentration couldn't be broken. If he were talking or listening to a woman, he added touch to his repertoire. He would pat her arm or clasp her hand, nodding sagely when the woman paused for a response, and all the while his eyes would be locked on hers. He appeared to be fascinated by whatever his companion was saying. His intelligent eyes reeked sincerity.

MacKenzie reminded Grayson of a sorcerer. He could

be all things to all people. He made them feel as though they could whisper their secrets, and he alone would keep them safe. He didn't pretend to be God, just one of His agents.

How could they not trust him? Grayson was impressed. He was watching a master work the crowd, and because MacKenzie's guests were all so spellbound, they couldn't see what he really was.

MacKenzie used their greed to lure them in. He didn't go after all the wealthy people, just the ones who coveted more. There were plenty of rich, successful people who were prudent with their money, who used their wealth wisely and generously, but Robert MacKenzie knew how to weed them out. He went after those who were never satisfied. He understood their twisted and pathetic insecurity, and he pounced on it. He knew exactly how to snare them: You're a rich man now, but is it enough? And will it last? With your well-deserved, though admittedly lavish, lifestyle and with rampant inflation? No, of course it won't last. How could it? Can you envision what your life will be like when it's all gone? Do not worry, my friends. Give me your millions, and like a modern-day Midas, I'll double it . . . triple it . . . quadruple it.

He made them believers.

And because they were the superrich, others wanted to emulate them. People who aspired to such wealth looked to these paragons of affluence for examples of what to do. The hopefuls believed the rich had an in, that they were in the know and understood the fluctuating market. If the man who signed their checks invested with MacKenzie's Trinity Fund, shouldn't they take their meager life savings and invest, too?

It was the domino effect, Grayson thought. From the top to the bottom, from the first to the last, they would all fall.

Drink in hand, Asher was weaving his way through the crowd to get to MacKenzie. When he reached him, he motioned to MacKenzie's wife and waited a few feet away. MacKenzie ignored him and everyone else until he finished his conversation; then, with a whispered word from his wife, he excused himself and joined Asher.

The attorney's forehead was beaded with sweat, and as he pulled a handkerchief from his pocket and wiped the sweat away, he talked fast and furiously. Grayson waited to see how MacKenzie would react to Asher's bad news.

Had he not been watching so closely, he would have missed it. For a second or two, but certainly no longer, MacKenzie's expression cracked. Grayson saw real, raw anger. Then—wham bam—Mr. Nice Guy was back. Smiling broadly, he put his arm around Asher's shoulders. He looked like a man who couldn't have been happier to see an old friend and hear the latest news. MacKenzie was good, all right, a pro playing his role.

Grayson thought about Olivia and the hell she'd endured from the time she was just a little older than Henry, and he suddenly wanted to smash his fist into MacKenzie's sparkling white teeth.

Ronan came back carrying a stemmed glass of ice water and a small digital camera. "I got some great photos with this camera and my phone. I've already sent a couple of them on to our computers."

"Where'd you get the camera?"

"I confiscated it." He slipped the camera into his pocket and said, "Hey, isn't that Senator What's His Name?"

Grayson nodded. "Yeah."

"What a schmuck."

"Yeah, he is." He lost sight of Asher and asked Ronan if he knew where he was.

They both spotted him at the same time. Asher was standing by the entrance, guzzling one last drink. He put the glass down and headed for the door.

"Who's that calling out to Asher?" Ronan asked. "I can't see his face."

"Neither can I," Grayson said.

They watched Asher drag his feet as he crossed the ballroom. The man demanding his attention finally separated himself from the crowd.

"Carl Simmons," Ronan said. "Wonder what MacKenzie's top attorney wants to chat with Asher about." He was grinning as he asked the foolish question. "Talk about a schmuck."

"No, Simmons is much worse than a schmuck."

"He's got an alibi for the night of the shooting. While Olivia was taking three bullets, Simmons was with a woman. According to her, they were supposed to attend a party but decided to spend the night in bed instead. Of course, Simmons could have paid someone to shoot Olivia, so, yes, you're right."

"Right about what?"

"He stays on the list." He pulled out the camera he'd lifted and said, "I think I'll get some shots of Asher with Simmons. Look how scared Asher is. Maybe I can capture that expression and show it to him when we pull him in."

Ronan left on his errand, but Grayson stayed where he was and kept his eyes on Simmons. The longer Asher talked to him, the more Simmons's outrage grew.

Olivia was going to get her security guard back whether she wanted it or not. Simmons's expression went way beyond anger, and Grayson knew his hate would be directed at her.

If Simmons was going to do something, it would be soon, and with that possibility in mind, Grayson called two bodyguards on his list and sent both of them to Olivia's apartment. One would stay outside her door, the other in the lobby.

He then phoned Olivia. Hell, what if she wasn't home? He took a breath when she answered.

"Is your door locked?"

"Grayson, where are you? I can barely hear you."

He walked into a back hallway. "Is this better?"

"Much better," she said. "Where are you? I thought you were going to the birthday party."

"I'm at the party . . ."

"Have you seen him?"

He could hear the anxiety. "I'll tell you all about it. You're staying in tonight, right?"

"No, I was just leaving. Jane's back in the hospital, and I thought I'd sit with her for a while."

"Does she know you're coming?"

"No."

"Good. Then you won't have to call and tell her you're staying home." He told her about Asher and Simmons. "I've got a feeling Simmons is going to do something. The look on his face . . . He's going to come after you. Could be as soon as tonight. You have to stay home. Check your door and make sure the dead bolt is in place. I'm sending over a couple of bodyguards, and I'm going to come by as soon as I'm finished here."

"Yes, all right."

"I mean it. Promise me."

"I promise," she said without hesitation.

"Don't let anyone in, no matter who it is. If your sister or your mother knocks on the door, don't answer."

"I understand," she insisted. "Stop worrying. I won't let anyone but you in."

"One more thing," he said. "If one of your kids calls, you don't leave. You call me. I'll leave here in five and be at your apartment in fifteen. If you need to go, I'll drive you."

"Okay."

Her quick agreement pleased him. He checked the time, then went to find Ronan. He spotted Asher leaving the ballroom. The guy was practically jogging, he was in such a hurry to get away. Simmons was on his cell phone and followed Asher at a much slower pace. He wasn't paying any attention to where he was going and nearly knocked a waiter over.

Ronan came up behind Grayson. "Want to say hello to the birthday boy?"

Grayson smiled. "Yeah, I'd like that. Got to make it quick, though. I'm going to stay with Olivia tonight. I've got an uneasy feeling . . . probably nothing, but I want to hang around."

MacKenzie saw them coming. He had just blown out candles on a gigantic birthday cake amid cheers.

"What's the wife's name?" Grayson asked.

"Deborah."

"Olivia looks like her."

"Wait until you get a close look at her father. Same color eyes."

"Ronan." MacKenzie said his name and extended his hand. "Good to see you again. How is your investigation going? Have you arrested the man responsible for shooting my daughter?"

"Not yet," Ronan answered.

"Then what brings you here?" MacKenzie asked pleasantly. He looked at Grayson and then back to Ronan.

"I heard it was your birthday, and I wanted to give my congratulations," Ronan responded.

Without so much as a blink, MacKenzie smiled broadly and said, "I appreciate that. Please . . . have a drink and something to eat. Enjoy yourself." He paused and then turned to his wife. "Where are my manners. Deborah, this is Agent Ronan Conrad. He was assigned to our daughter's investigation."

She greeted Ronan with a warm smile. "Such a terrible ordeal, to get a phone call telling us our daughter had been shot."

"Did you rush to her side?" Grayson asked the question.

Deborah looked at her husband, no doubt hoping he would answer.

"It wasn't possible to go to our daughter," Robert answered. "We were in Florida at the time, and our schedule wouldn't permit deviation."

"She's put us through such worry over the years," Deborah said. "She's been ill most of her life. Hasn't she, Robert?"

"How inconsiderate of her," Ronan drawled.

Grayson didn't show any outward reaction to Deborah's comments, though he was seething inside.

"Allow me to introduce myself. I'm Agent Grayson Kincaid."

"FBI," Robert told his wife.

Deborah's hand went to her throat. It was impossible not to notice the huge diamond ring she wore. "Is there a problem?"

"Are you working on the investigation with Ronan?" Robert asked.

"Yes, but I'm also a friend of Olivia's."

"Then you know . . ." Deborah began.

"Know what?" Grayson asked when she hesitated and looked to her husband again.

Robert answered. "How fragile our daughter is." He suddenly looked quite sad. "Mentally fragile. She's been through so much . . ."

"And put you through so much, Robert," Deborah reminded him.

He showed a flash of impatience for being interrupted and then a quick nod. "Yes, she has."

Grayson couldn't be quiet any longer. "Do you mean when she was in the chemotherapy unit? Was that when she put you two through so much?"

"I see she's talked to you about her past," Deborah said. Her voice had taken on a hard edge.

"She had you to comfort her when she was going through that hell, didn't she?"

Once again Deborah deferred to her husband, who said, "The poor thing. She does tend to exaggerate."

"Exaggerate what? The side effects?" Grayson asked.

"It wasn't as bad as she tells people," Deborah explained. "She's got quite the active imagination."

"Then you did stay with her while she was going through the chemo? She was just a child, wasn't she?"

"No, neither one of us stayed with her. It just wasn't possible," Deborah explained.

"Then how do you know that Olivia exaggerated?" Ronan asked the question.

"I don't believe this is the time or the place for this conversation," Deborah said. She was angry and opened her mouth to say something more, but her husband stopped her by putting his hand on her arm.

"You're right. This isn't the time," Grayson agreed.

"You were explaining that Olivia has become mentally fragile," Ronan reminded Robert.

"Yes, indeed she has. It's not her fault," he insisted. "We love her dearly. Don't we, Deborah?"

"Oh yes, of course we do. We would have loved to have had her here tonight to celebrate with us, but we couldn't dare include her. She's so unpredictable, we couldn't risk a scene and watch her embarrass herself."

Robert looked almost sympathetic. "It's all those poisonous drugs she's taken over the years. They've made her paranoid. She really can't help how she is."

"How exactly is she?" Grayson asked.

"She makes up the most bizarre stories," Robert said. "And no matter how outrageous they are, she can't let them go. Olivia needs medical attention and a safe environment. As her parent it's my responsibility to see that she gets it."

Grayson smiled. "You'd better not let Olivia hear you talk about her like that, or she'll never come see you in prison."

With those parting words Grayson and Ronan left the ballroom.

"He pretty much spelled it out, didn't he?" Ronan said.

"Yeah, he's laying the groundwork."

"How soon do you think they'll come for her?"

"Soon. Maybe tonight."

"That son of a bitch is gonna lock her away somewhere, keep her drugged so she can't make trouble."

"Know what's worse? That son of a bitch is her father."

TWENTY-TWO

Grayson arrived at Olivia's apartment with his gym bag in hand and announced that he was staying over.

"You went home and packed?" she asked.

"I always keep clean clothes and a shaving kit in the trunk of my car."

Frowning, she followed him into the living room. "For sleepovers?"

"No, for the gym," he patiently explained. He dropped the bag on the chair.

He wanted to pull her into his arms, but he wouldn't let himself. It took all the willpower he could muster not to kiss her sweet lips.

"You're sleeping here tonight?" she asked.

"Yes. I'll take the sofa," he answered.

"Why?" she asked, bewildered. "I think you'd better explain what happened at the birthday party, and if you tell me my father's your new golf buddy, you're sleeping on the floor."

"Olivia, sweetheart . . . ?"

"Yes?" she asked, trying not to be worried. Grayson couldn't be fooled. Her father couldn't charm him.

Grayson looked into her eyes for several seconds, then said, "Your parents are god-awful people."

She was thrilled. She threw her arms around him and kissed him on the cheek. "Thank you. That's about the nicest thing you've ever said to me."

The doorbell rang. He took her hand and led her into her bedroom.

"Stay here," he said. He was reaching for his gun as he left the room and pulled the door closed behind him.

She didn't have to wait long. A minute later Grayson told her she could come out, and she emerged to find Ronan removing his coat. He tossed it on the back of a chair near the door, lifted a gun out of the back of his waistband, and handed it to Grayson. "I thought you might need some extra firepower. Never know. There are more clips in my coat pockets."

Grayson turned to Olivia. "Ronan's going to hang out for a while."

Instead of asking why, she simply said, "Okay," and waited for one of them to start talking. Her patience quickly ran out when neither of them spoke. Hands on her hips, she said, "Exactly what are you boys expecting to happen here? A shoot-out on the third floor? I'll tell you right now, Mrs. Delaney won't like that."

Ronan smiled. "Mrs. Delaney?"

"The tyrant in three-ten," Grayson answered. "She makes Olivia do her grocery shopping for her."

"She does not make me grocery shop. I just pick up a few things for her now and then . . . That isn't important now. What's going on?"

"You didn't tell her?" Ronan asked Grayson.

"I haven't had time."

"Tell me now," she demanded.

Grayson told her about the party and his conversation with her parents. By the time he'd finished, Olivia had dropped down on the sofa and was speechless.

"She seems to be taking this pretty well," Ronan remarked.

"Yeah, right," Grayson said. Then he started counting. "Five, four, three, two . . ."

She bounded to her feet with a roar. Grayson smiled. "There it is," he told Ronan.

"How dare he! If Carl Simmons comes through my door and invades my home, I want you to shoot him, Grayson. You can shoot him, too, Ronan. No, I'll do it. Ronan, give me a gun, and I'll shoot him. I'll be doing the world a favor. That snake, that creepy slimeball, that . . ." She stopped sputtering for a second, searching for more names. "That no-good . . ."

"Take a breath, sweetheart," Grayson suggested. She was starting to wheeze as she paced back and forth.

"Yes, you're right. I need to calm down so I can think. That's what I need to do. That son of a . . . When do you think this will happen?"

"Soon." Grayson took off his jacket and began to unbutton his shirtsleeves.

Olivia stopped in the middle of the room. It was really beginning to sink in, the lengths her adversaries would go to. "You really believe Simmons will bring men here to take me?"

"Yes, that's what I believe. If you'd seen the look on his face when Asher was talking to him, you'd be a believer, too."

"Your father's in this, as well, Olivia," Ronan said. "You need to know that."

"Oh, I know."

"I'm going to get out of these clothes," Grayson said.

Olivia widened her pacing trail from the sofa to the kitchen and back. On one of her trips she noticed another FBI gym bag on the floor outside her office. "Are you staying over, too?" she asked Ronan.

"Maybe."

Olivia walked into her kitchen. It was dark, and she stood in the shadows looking out the window, trying desperately to understand how it had come to this and how her father could justify what he was doing. She was suddenly overwhelmed with sadness. How could she miss what she never had?

Oh, snap out of it, she scolded. Feeling sorry for herself wouldn't accomplish anything. Besides, she had a family. She had Jane and Collins and Sam. They were her sisters. But as loving and supportive as they were, she had to admit she needed more. God help her, she needed Grayson in her life.

She took a deep breath and closed her eyes. Concentrate on now. Don't worry about the future; just focus on tonight. Stop thinking like an outcast daughter and start thinking like a smart, strong, independent woman.

Pep talk over, she went back into the living room. Who would come to get her? How many would there be? And where did they think they would take her?

"Wait a minute," she said.

"Yes?" Ronan was carrying his bag into the guest bathroom. He turned back and waited.

"Simmons has to know I would never let him in my apartment."

"Okay."

"Wait . . ."

"Yes?" he asked, trying not to smile. She was so earnest.

"That's it, isn't it? Simmons knows I'll be cautious, and I won't let just anyone in. He'll send someone I know, someone I'll open the door for. That no-good . . ."

And she was off on another tirade. Grayson came out of the bedroom just as she was winding down. He'd changed into jeans and a shirt and had his gun and holster back on his hip. He was on his cell phone.

"Yes, I'll tell her." He ended the call and said, "That was Agent Huntsman. He's helping us out with Jeff Wilcox's old attorney, Asher. He said to tell you that you owe him one, Olivia."

"I do? Okay."

Before she could ask what Huntsman was doing to help, Grayson said, "You were right, Ronan. Asher was going to try to disappear. He was getting in his car with a suitcase and files when they picked him up."

"Is he being arrested, and if so, on what charges?" Olivia asked.

"He was taken in for questioning. No charges yet," Grayson said. "He's going to explain where the twenty-thousand-dollar deposit came from."

"What twenty thousand?"

"That was the amount of cash deposited in Asher's account the day before he offered his services to Wilcox."

"How did you get that information so quickly?" Olivia asked.

"Our resources are extensive," Ronan explained.

"Didn't you need a court order or a . . ." She stopped when Grayson gave her the look. She was getting used to seeing that expression, the did-you-really-just-ask-that-question look.

"Never mind." She went into the kitchen and got a grape Popsicle from the freezer. She was about to tear the wrapper off when Grayson grabbed it from her.

"Oh no, you don't. I'm not going to be distracted tonight." He put the Popsicle back in the freezer.

She followed him. "I wasn't going to . . ." she whispered. "You know."

"Do you mean drive me nuts like you did with the last Popsicle?"

She smiled. "I drove you nuts?"

"You know you did."

She laughed. "Yes, but it's good to hear you admit it."

Olivia realized there was nothing she could do now but wait. Grayson had taken his laptop into her office to write a report, and Ronan had turned on the television. She sat next to him and watched him channel surf. He settled on a station and leaned back when the news came on.

"Does Agent Huntsman know why you're here?" she asked.

"Yes, he does. I told him."

"Is he your superior?"

He flashed a smile. "No, we just help each other out every once in a while."

"What happens if Grayson's wrong?"

"He isn't wrong. He's got this way of reading people. I don't know how else to explain it. It's something he sees in their eyes maybe. He's saved our lives more than once. A couple of years ago we were called in to help on a case with Huntsman. There were five of us and an informant who had worked with Huntsman for over a year. Very trustworthy," he added. "We knew there was a deal going down, and we were waiting for the suspect to show up with his crew. We got there real early and had time to set up the ambush. We had a good two hours to wait. Anyway, Grayson's watching the informant talk to Huntsman, and he goes over to the two of them and chats for a minute, surely no longer. The informant's supposed to leave, but Grayson grabs him and puts him in cuffs. Then he tells all of us we have to get out."

"Why? What happened?" she asked when he hesitated.

"He won't even take the time to explain, so we all hightail it out of that house. We're all in our cars down the street, parked behind an abandoned building, and we're waiting there for maybe ten minutes. No one's saying anything to Grayson, but I know Huntsman and the other agents are thinking, what the . . . has Grayson lost it? We've got a major bust about to happen, and he's screwing it up."

"But you weren't thinking that."

"No, I trusted his instinct. And about five minutes later the house blows up. And I mean blows. It was like a nuclear bomb went off. Even tore out the foundation. From that night on, Huntsman doesn't question Grayson. If he says he's got a feeling or he's read something in the guy's eyes or in the way he's behaving that none of us notice, we listen. Grayson would make a hell of a profiler," he added. "But that doesn't interest him."

"And tonight he saw Simmons's reaction to Asher's news."

"Yeah, but that was easy. Grayson said anyone with half a brain would know Simmons was going to do something crazy. You know those cartoon characters that have fire coming out of their eyes and ears when they get mad? According to Grayson, Simmons looked like that."

"He compared him to a cartoon character?"

He nodded. "He won't admit it, but I'm pretty sure he watches cartoons with Henry."

Olivia imagined Grayson kicking back with his nephew and laughing at some juvenile TV show, and she got a warm feeling. No wonder she loved him.

"Anyway, he knew Simmons was going to do something because you . . ."

"I what?"

He grinned. "You really pissed him off."

She laughed. "Oh, I hope so."

"After we chatted with your father, we knew what the plan was, especially after he said he was going to see that you were put somewhere safe. Grayson's convinced it'll happen tonight."

"Was my mother with him?" she asked. She didn't wait for a response. "Of course she was. She never leaves his side if she can help it."

Grayson joined them. "Huntsman's here with Larson. One will stay in the security room off the lobby watching the garage and the front entrance, and the other will watch the back steps. They won't be seen."

"All the floors are on closed-circuit," Olivia said. "I hope Simmons comes. I'd love to sit down and have a chat."

Grayson shook his head. "He'll stay away and wait to hear."

"What if they're coming here to kill me? Have you considered that possibility? Hide my body where it won't be found. Simmons would like that."

She saw the look on Grayson's face and went to him. She didn't care that Ronan was watching as she moved into his arms. "I'm just saying—"

"No one's going to hurt you ever again," Grayson stated with an unflinching resolve.

Olivia had just looked at the time on Grayson's watch—it was straight-up midnight—when a knock sounded at her door. Then the doorbell rang.

Grayson motioned for Olivia to go into the kitchen. Both he and Ronan had their guns drawn. Ronan looked through the peephole. The only man visible was George Anderson, Olivia's brother-in-law.

The banging got louder. George shouted her name. "Come on, Olivia. Open the door. I've got to talk to you. It's important."

It got quiet for a minute while George conferred with the men accompanying him, and then he started banging on the door again. "There's been an accident. Open the door."

Olivia could hear him, of course. She came out of the kitchen and shouted, "All right. I'm opening the door. Hold on." She'd tried to sound sleepy and thought she'd done a good job. She stood there smiling over her performance until Grayson tilted his head toward the kitchen. Nodding, she went back to hide.

Ronan waited just inside the entrance to Olivia's study. Grayson opened the door and moved out of the line of sight.

There were two men with George. They knocked him to his knees as they pushed their way inside. They were in such a hurry they got halfway into the living room before they realized their target wasn't there.

George didn't wait around. He staggered to his feet and ran down the hall to the elevator, frantically hitting the button.

The men Simmons had sent were big and looked like bodybuilders. Dressed alike in black pants and white shirts with identification cards clipped to their pockets, they were obviously trying to look like hospital orderlies. Damned scary orderlies who would give patients nightmares. One was bald and had an eagle tattoo on the back of his head; the other had a scar that cut into his chin. Tattoo held a gun, and Scar carried a small black bag.

Disarming the man with the gun came first. Grayson didn't waste time. He came up behind him and clipped him hard on the back of his neck. The hit didn't seem to faze him, but the barrel of Grayson's gun pressed against the face of the eagle got his attention.

"Drop the gun," Grayson ordered.

"Hey, we're just here to—"

"Drop the gun."

Ronan had his weapon pointed at Scar. "Shoot him," he told Grayson. "We only need to interrogate one."

"Yeah, okay."

Tattoo heard the click of the weapon and quickly dropped his gun. "Don't shoot," he cried out.

Thirty seconds later, both men were handcuffed and sitting side by side at the kitchen table. They'd been read their rights but thus far hadn't asked for a lawyer.

"You've got this all wrong," Tattoo said.

They had been searched and their wallets were now on the table. Grayson found their drivers' licenses, read their names, and said to the tattooed man, "Where did we go wrong, Kline?"

"We were sent here to get Miss MacKenzie and take her to Marydale Hospital, where she can get the treatment she needs."

"Marydale is at least a hundred and fifty miles from here," Ronan pointed out.

Kline shrugged. "It's where we were told to take her."

"Who told you to take her?"

The two men looked at each other. Then Kline said, "I guess her doctor."

"You guess?" Ronan asked.

Grayson opened the black bag and held up two vials of a milky substance. "What were you planning to do with these?"

The other man, whose name was Vogel, answered. "We were going to sedate her because we were told she was violent."

Grayson found a third vial in the bag. "There's enough here to put down a horse."

"Did you know how much to give, or were you just going to guess?" Ronan asked.

"I knew about how much." Vogel was becoming defensive. "And it was going to be a long drive. I didn't want her to wake up."

"*About* how much? You could have killed her." Grayson was trying to keep his temper under control. He was so furious, he wanted to throw both of them out the window.

"I would have been careful," Vogel insisted.

"Oh, then that's all right."

Vogel perked up. He obviously didn't understand sarcasm. "I didn't want to hurt her, but . . . you know . . . she's . . ." The way Grayson was looking at him broke his concentration. He looked at Kline for help.

"Violent," Kline whispered.

"Right. Violent."

They were following a script, and any deviation rattled them.

"Were you just going to drop her off at the door?" Grayson asked.

"No, we were going to take her in and then . . . you know . . . leave her because . . ." Vogel answered.

"She's violent?" Grayson supplied. He glanced over at Olivia. Had he not known better, he might have given some credence to their claim. She was standing behind Vogel with her lips clinched tightly, looking as though she could strangle the man with her bare hands.

"How come you're dressed like orderlies?" Ronan asked.

"We wanted to look professional," Vogel explained.

"Yes, professional," Kline agreed.

"Cut the BS." Ronan shouted the order. Olivia flinched in reaction.

"I'm going to go get George. I'll be right back," Grayson said.

Olivia couldn't believe he was leaving now. They

hadn't gotten Kline and Vogel to tell them anything yet. She followed him into the living room. "You're leaving now? George is long gone. Don't leave." He gave her the look again. "Oh . . ." she said, suddenly understanding. "George isn't gone. Where is he?"

"I imagine he's beating the hell out of the elevator button about now. The elevator is locked on the ground floor."

"He could have taken the steps."

"One of the bodyguards blocked it. George can't open the door."

"Oh. Okay, then. Go get him."

There was a warm glint in his eyes. "You're gonna have to let go of me first."

She had a death grip on his hand. She let go, and turning on her heels, she hurried back into the kitchen.

Grayson was marching down the hallway toward George when the medallion above the elevator doors lit up. George spotted Grayson coming and, in a panic, pounded on the doors, chanting, "Come on, come on . . ."

The doors opened, and for a second George thought he was going to get away. He tried to run inside, but Agent Huntsman stopped him. Without breaking stride, Huntsman grasped George by the back of his neck and dragged him down the hall.

Grayson led the way to Olivia's apartment as Huntsman shoved the blubbering George inside.

"Shut the hell up," Huntsman ordered.

Grayson grabbed George and dropped him into a chair adjacent to Kline and Vogel. With his head in his hands, George began to cry. "I'm sorry, Olivia. I didn't want to be a part of this, but I didn't have a choice."

"The hell you didn't," Grayson snapped.

Ronan caught Huntsman up on what they had learned.

"We'll take these two in," Huntsman said, pointing to Vogel and Kline.

"Where's Larson?"

"He's babysitting the driver. He was sitting in his van in front of the building with a loaded .45 in his lap."

"You can take them just as soon as they tell me who hired them," Grayson said.

Kline responded with a defiant smirk on his face. "You can't make us tell you anything. You can talk to our lawyer. Right, Vogel?"

"Right."

Grayson conceded. "You don't want to talk to us, then don't. We've got you for attempted kidnapping, and I'm going to add attempted murder. I'll make it stick, too."

"Attempted murder? We weren't going to murder her," Vogel protested.

Grayson pointed to the vials. "Sure you were."

"You're part of this, too, George," Ronan interjected. "Attempted kidnapping and—"

In a panic, George began to stammer. "No, no, that's not right. I . . . I was told she was mentally ill, and I was only trying to help."

Ronan grinned. "That's pretty good, George. You got that lie out without blinking."

"I'm telling the truth. I didn't mean any harm."

Huntsman stood behind George while he recited his rights. "We need another pair of handcuffs."

"Hey, George, did you ever pay that loan off? It must have tripled by now. If you didn't pay it back, you'll probably be safe in prison," Grayson said.

"And you will be going to prison," Ronan assured him.

"Did you pay the loan off?" Grayson asked again.

George's face was turning white. "Not yet. No."

"Who hired you?" Grayson asked Kline.

He wouldn't answer. Neither would Vogel. George was the weakest link, so Grayson concentrated on him again.

"How did you end up with these two? I know you don't run in the same circles. So how do you know them?"

"They work for Carl Simmons."

"Shut your mouth," Kline demanded.

"You do work for him. Everyone knows it."

"We said shut up," Vogel yelled this time.

"Olivia, do you have any duct tape?" Grayson asked.

"Yes. In the cabinet by the pantry."

Grayson found it. He ripped off a long strip.

"I know my rights. You can't—" The first strip covered Vogel's mouth.

"That might not stick," Grayson said. "I'd better reinforce it." And with that, he taped over Vogel's nostrils, making breathing impossible. "That should do it."

He crossed to the other side of the table, winked at Olivia as he passed her, then pulled out a chair and straddled it. Stacking his arms across the back, he stared at George, completely ignoring the wide-eyed Vogel.

"You were telling us that these two work for Simmons. What do they do for him?"

Vogel's face was turning beet red.

George was gaping at him. "He can't breathe."

"Yes, I know," Grayson said. "What do Kline and Vogel do for Simmons?"

"You're killing him."

"What do Kline and Vogel—"

"I'll tell you. Just get that tape off him and let him breathe."

Grayson reached across the table and ripped the tape off. Vogel gasped for air.

"You keep your mouth shut, George," Kline blurted.

"Hand me the tape," Huntsman said.

"Okay, I'll be quiet. No tape. This isn't right," Kline said. "You can't treat us this way."

"No, it isn't right." Grayson nodded to Huntsman, who immediately covered Kline's mouth with the tape. "Know what else isn't right?" he continued. "Kidnapping and attempted murder."

George looked as though, at any moment, he could burst into tears. "Oh God, how did this all get so messed up?"

"This is the last time I'm going to ask . . ."

"All I know is that Kline and Vogel have been working for Carl Simmons for at least a year. He tells people they're his bodyguards. I heard him offer them a big bonus if they could get it done fast."

Kline grunted and shook his head. Grayson raised his hand, and Kline immediately stopped making noise. It was almost a Pavlovian response.

"It?" he asked George.

"Olivia. If they could take care of Olivia fast."

"How did you end up with them tonight?" Ronan asked.

George's shoulders slumped. He looked completely defeated now.

Ronan got down in his face and shouted, "Answer the question."

George flinched. "Something happened during the party. I don't know what set Carl off, but I swear he was shaking. I've never seen him so angry. He dragged me out to the lobby, and when he couldn't see Kline right away, he called him on his cell phone. I heard him tell him what to do."

"And?" Ronan prodded.

"He told me I had to go with them because Olivia wouldn't open her door to two strangers, but she would if she saw me through the peephole. I told him about the doorman, that he could call Olivia and tell her there were three of us and she'd never let us come up."

"What did he say?" Ronan asked.

"He told me not to worry about it, that Kline would take care of the doorman."

"Did he tell you how Kline would take care of him?"

George shook his head. "No, and I didn't ask. I didn't want to know."

"What a weasel," Grayson said under his breath.

"As it turned out," George continued, "the lobby was empty and the door was unlocked. He must have been on a break. . . . No, he wasn't," he said, finally figuring it out. "You wanted us to come inside. You were waiting for us. How did you know we were coming?"

"What else did Simmons say?" Grayson asked, ignoring the question.

George couldn't look Olivia in the eye. Staring at the table, he said, "The place they were taking her would keep her locked away where she couldn't make any more trouble. She'd be let out in three days. Carl said that was all the time Robert needed."

"Three days?" Ronan asked.

"What's MacKenzie going to get done in three days?" Grayson asked.

"He told Carl he'd have it all cleared out by then."

"You heard him say that?" Ronan asked.

"Yes, I did. Robert came out in the lobby and pulled Simmons over behind some potted plants. Both of them were hopping mad. I don't think my father-in-law cared at that point if I heard him. He was in a rage about some attorney—Mitchell Kaplan—and Olivia hiring him."

Olivia smiled. "He's afraid of Jeff Wilcox's attorney because he knows he'll have to open up his files." She looked at her brother-in-law. "George, tell me what you think 'clearing it out' means." She wanted him to acknowledge what her father was going to do.

"You know . . ."

"Tell me, George."

"The money, the stocks . . . he's going to close it all down."

"He'll hide money," Ronan predicted.

"What were you promised?" Grayson asked. "No, let me guess. Simmons found out about your gambling debts and was going to see that you got enough money to pay them off without Natalie finding out. I'm right, aren't I?"

"Yes. Simmons told me nobody else knew about the loans, and he'd help me out. He said there was no way I could get money out of the fund without the family suspecting."

Olivia couldn't understand George's stupidity. When was he going to pull his head out of the sand? "Aren't you beginning to figure it out?" she said to him. "Simmons wasn't going to give you any money. You have to know."

He looked up at her with weary eyes. "Know what?"

"That it's gone, George. You're never going to get it back."

TWENTY-THREE

P robable cause. The legal term would be a game
changer.

Grayson contacted the New York office, which
would continue the investigation. Since there was now
probable cause, he anticipated it wouldn't take long to
get a signed order to stop Robert MacKenzie and Carl
Simmons from clearing out any accounts.

Once Kline and Vogel had been removed from the
apartment, George became more talkative. To Olivia, he
seemed genuinely contrite, but neither Grayson nor
Ronan was buying his remorse.

Olivia fixed George a cup of coffee, ignoring Grayson's
frowns, and sat with him while he talked about all the
mistakes he had made. He was certain Natalie would divorce him, and before Olivia realized what was happening, she became his counselor, even suggesting ways she
might discuss his problems with her sister.

"I should have told her about the loan, and he's right,"
George said, tilting his head toward Grayson. "I did borrow the money from a loan shark. I should get it all out
in the open, shouldn't I? How will Natalie ever forgive
me if I keep secrets? Could I text Natalie?" he asked
Ronan, who had taken his cell phone. "I'll tell her now."

"No," Ronan answered.

"George, you can't text that information or e-mail her. You have to sit down with her and explain." Olivia couldn't believe he thought it was okay to drop that bomb in a text. How would he phrase it? Oh, by the way, I owe around five hundred thousand to a man who will break my legs if I don't pay up soon? "She might understand," she told him. If she had a lobotomy first, she thought. "I'll help you tell her if you want."

"You would do that?"

She nodded. "Yes."

Grayson was about to drag Olivia into the living room and ask her what the hell she was doing when George whispered, "I can help you, too."

She wanted to nudge Grayson and say, "Aha! See what happens when you're patient?" She didn't, though. She kept her attention on George and asked, "How can you help?"

"He keeps files." His voice gained strength, now that he'd made up his mind to share the information. "Your father keeps files hidden."

"Where?" Grayson demanded, his tone surly.

George immediately shut down. Olivia shook her head at Grayson. "Have you seen the files?" she asked softly.

"I shouldn't . . . He's my father-in-law, and every dollar Natalie and I have is tied up in investments he's made for us."

Grayson and Ronan looked as though they wanted to grab George by the throat. Olivia remained calm and refused to give up.

"It's time for you to get a backbone, George." She put her hand on his and with sincere compassion said, "Do the right thing."

He rubbed his brow and kept silent for another minute. "They're in the wall in his study."

"The New York apartment study?" Ronan asked. "Or are they in San Francisco or Miami?"

"New York. I swear you'd never know the wall moved. There aren't any panels. It looks just like . . . a wall. He doesn't know I saw him, thank God. None of us are allowed to go into his study, even when he's there, and he always keeps the door locked. I made a joke about it once. I think I called it Fort Knox or something, and he exploded. I was in shock. It's the first time I'd ever seen him lose his temper like that. I saw that ugly side of him again tonight."

"When did you see the files?" Olivia asked.

"About a month ago. Natalie and your mother were in the dining room, and I went down the hall to knock on the study door to tell him dinner was ready. The door was open a crack. I was surprised because that never happened. I almost didn't look in, but . . . you know . . . curiosity."

"And what did you see?" she asked.

"Your father had his back to me, and he was putting a file folder away. I swear the entire wall moved. I got away from the door as fast as I could because I knew he'd kill me if he saw me watching."

Grayson took a call and left the room. Ronan leaned against the wall, going through George's cell phone messages while Olivia and George continued to talk.

"Did my mother know men were coming here tonight?" Olivia asked.

"I don't think so. She usually just repeats whatever your father says. She thinks she's being a supportive wife."

"What about Natalie? Did she know?"

"No. This was all Carl Simmons and your father. Start to finish."

Ronan had just read one of many angry texts from

Natalie demanding to know where George was when another text appeared. After he read it, he said, "The son of a bitch is going to try to shred those files."

Grayson had just returned to the kitchen, and Ronan tossed him the phone. He quickly read it, cursed, and said, "Yes, that's exactly what he's going to do."

"What happened?" Olivia asked.

"Natalie sent George a text. Your father has decided to fly back to New York right away. He's on his way to the airport, and you, George, are an ingrate because you bailed on the party. I guess that's still going on."

"He's going home now?" George asked. "He left his own party to go home? He's got his own jet, so he can get back to his apartment in a couple of hours."

"McGraw's the lead on this in New York," Grayson said. "He just called, and I told him about the files in the wall. He's putting an agent on MacKenzie's door just in case he slips past the others."

"What about Simmons?" Ronan asked.

"He left the party right after Olivia's father. We'll find him."

"Are you taking me in?" George asked. He looked frantic.

"Yes," Ronan answered. "In fact, we're leaving now."

"Wait, please," Olivia called. "I'd like to ask George another question."

"Go ahead," Ronan said.

She looked George in the eye and asked, "Do you think Simmons hired someone to shoot me?"

He hesitated several seconds and then nodded. "He's capable of it. I wouldn't have thought that a year ago, but now . . . yes. In fact, I wouldn't be surprised if he tried to shoot you himself. I don't have proof that he's involved, though."

Olivia nodded. "That's okay."

"Except . . ."

"Yes?"

"When Carl was talking to Kline in the lobby, I heard him say he wouldn't be upset if something happened on the drive to Marydale tonight. I thought he was joking because he was smiling, but then he told Kline not to mess up again."

"You left that part out before, didn't you?" Ronan said.

George nodded but insisted it hadn't been on purpose. "That could mean anything, couldn't it?"

Grayson towered over him. "What do you think it meant?" he asked.

George seemed to shrink before their eyes. "I guess it could mean that Simmons had hired Kline to shoot Olivia, and he messed up because . . ."

"I didn't die," Olivia finished.

"Yes, but it could have meant something altogether different, and that's why I didn't mention it." He put both hands up. "I know, I know. I should have told you everything."

He looked at Olivia then. "That's why I was going to ride all the way to the mental facility with you. I wanted to make sure Kline didn't hurt you. I was going to protect you."

"By hurt her you mean kill her," Ronan stated.

"Yes."

"If you were going to protect her, why did you run the second she opened the door?"

He bowed his head. "I got scared, but I was going to wait in the van. I didn't want to watch them drug her. I didn't want to be a part of that."

"Yeah, right," Ronan said.

"You are part of it," Grayson said.

Olivia could see his anger building and sought to diffuse it before he punched George. She got up from the table and went to Grayson.

"Could I please be there when you question Simmons? I can't wait to hear the spin he puts on this."

Her smile calmed him. "I'll see what I can do."

Grayson suddenly needed to be alone with her, to hold her, to love her. With that thought in mind, he vigorously helped George to his feet. Ronan then gripped his arm and shoved him toward the front door. A minute later, as Grayson was sliding the dead bolt into place behind them, he could hear George blubbering once again that his life sucked. Grayson had to agree.

He returned to Olivia. "I want to go to bed," he said, reaching for her.

She pulled away. "No, Grayson. We can't. You said yourself we have to stay away from each other."

"I know what I said. But damn it, Olivia, staying away is killing me."

She stepped back. "What about Henry?"

"He's already in bed."

"You should go home and be there when he wakes up."

He put his hand on her neck and gently pulled her closer. "I ate dinner with him last night, and he almost fell asleep at the table. He and Patrick go back to basketball camp tomorrow. They'll leave around seven thirty, so it doesn't matter if I'm there or not. He'll tell me all about it tomorrow night."

"I don't want you to ignore him," she said, trying to catch her breath. His body was pressed against hers.

"I don't ignore him." His mouth was now hovering over hers, his warm breath tickling her lips. "It's sweet the way you worry about Henry."

"I don't really worry about him," she whispered. "He has you."

He tilted her chin up so he could look into her eyes and said, "So do you, sweetheart. Like it or not, you've got me."

He didn't give her time to reason or to argue. He sealed his promise with a kiss that let her know how much he wanted her.

Backing her into the living room, he pulled her T-shirt over her head. His hands quickly went to work on the zipper to her jeans, as she struggled to unbutton his shirt and pull it off his shoulders.

She pushed away and gazed up at him for a second. His eyes were filled with such passion. She took his hand and led him toward her bedroom. "Just this once," she said.

"Yes," he agreed. "Just this once."

TWENTY-FOUR

Sunday morning with Grayson was wonderful. And enlightening. He woke Olivia, caressing her as he nuzzled the side of her neck. He was making love to her.

"Shouldn't I be awake for this?" she asked, her voice a sleepy whisper.

"It's not necessary. You can go back to sleep."

As if that were possible. His mouth and his hands were everywhere, and oh, did he know how to drive her out of her mind. She was soon writhing in his arms, demanding that he come to her.

She climaxed twice before he did. He held her close for several minutes until his breathing calmed and his heart stopped racing. "Each time it's more intense, isn't it? More amazing."

Olivia started to tremble. "Grayson, we need to talk. I . . ."

He wouldn't let her say another word. He kissed her hard, then got out of bed. "We'll talk later. I'm getting in the shower now, and then I'm making breakfast."

"I don't eat breakfast."

He was heading into the bathroom when he said, "Sure you do."

She'd already lost her train of thought because she'd

watched him walk away, and all she could think about was how sexy he was. She knew for a fact that he was all muscle because she'd touched every inch of him. That thought led to another, and she was suddenly replaying the different ways they'd made love during the night. Had she really been that uninhibited, that wild?

With an audible sigh, she got out of bed and put on her robe. She should have been exhausted, but she wasn't. Fact was, she'd slept better than she had in years. She'd felt so safe and protected in his arms.

As it turned out, she did eat breakfast, and Grayson didn't even have to coax her. He made an omelet with peppers and chives and mushrooms. It was delicious.

She was sipping hot tea while she watched him clear the table and stack the dishes in the dishwasher.

"I'll clean up," she promised. "You cooked."

"It's done."

She smiled. "I know. That's why I offered." She tapped her forehead. "Always thinking."

She put her teacup in the sink and followed him into the living room. He took his laptop out of his bag and sat on the floor. Leaning against the sofa, he stretched out his legs, opened the computer, and pulled up *The Washington Post*.

"The newspapers are in the hall," she told him. "I'll get them."

After she looked through the peephole, she opened the door, scooped up the papers, and locked the door again.

"I like reading the actual paper," she explained. "I stare at a computer screen all week. It's a nice change."

Grayson took *The Washington Post*, and she started reading *The New York Times*.

She noticed he read the financial section first, then the sports section.

"Grayson, may I ask—"

"Not yet, sweetheart." He moved the paper so that he could check the time. "We're having a normal, leisurely Sunday morning. At noon you may ask questions."

"But—"

"Noon."

She understood, and she was happy to wait. The world and all the ugly problems could return at noon. Until then, Grayson wanted time for just the two of them.

And it was lovely. Curled up against his side, she read most of the *Times*. There was a particularly interesting article about a renowned Broadway producer she thoroughly enjoyed. She even read the entire editorial page and checked out the new fashions in the style section. At one point she glanced over at Grayson, who was immersed in a story about a new construction project, and she marveled at how comfortable they were in their silence.

At twelve o'clock, Grayson reluctantly let reality intrude. He stacked the papers on the table and tensed in anticipation of what he was pretty sure was coming. Olivia would ask him about the future. His future. She would tell him that he needed to move on, that there could never be a future with her. She'd hinted at it several times already. It didn't matter how she phrased it. Whatever she told him would lead to a quarrel, and as stubborn as she was, it would be a long one. He was stubborn, too, and this was one argument he was determined to win. He wasn't going anywhere, and he wondered how many times he would have to say those words before she believed him.

"Okay, what's the question?" he asked.

She surprised him. She straddled his hips and put her hands on his shoulders. Sighing, she said, "I was going to ask if you wanted to go back to bed. You know, for sex."

She leaned forward and ran the tip of her tongue across his lower lip; then she shrugged her shoulders and looked at him with sad, innocent eyes. "But you wouldn't let me ask any questions . . . and now it's too late."

He was laughing as she got up and headed to the kitchen to get them something to drink. A knock on the door changed her direction.

"Ronan's here," she announced as she swung the door open. Please don't let it be more bad news, she prayed.

"It's bad news, isn't it?" she asked before Ronan could step inside. "It's Sunday, and you're here, so it's bad news." So much for taking a stab at optimism.

Ronan smiled at her. "No, it isn't bad news."

"Oh, okay then."

"We're going to New York," Ronan told Grayson, who was already heading to the closet to get his coat.

"Why?" Olivia asked.

Ronan answered. "We want to see what's in that wall."

"They're going to let you?" she asked.

He gave her the look, just like Grayson did, the how-could-you-ask-such-a-dumb-question look.

She found his arrogance amusing. "Of course, you're going in. Why haven't they opened the wall?"

"They're waiting for McGraw, so no one's been inside the apartment yet."

"What about my father?"

"They've been holding him, and he's not too happy about it. He was picked up when he landed in New York. He can't be held much longer. We have to get moving or we'll miss our flight."

Grayson followed Ronan to the door. He stopped, pulled Olivia into his arms, and kissed her passionately. "I'll call," he promised. "Don't go anywhere without—"

"Calling one of the bodyguards," she recited as though she'd memorized the rule.

"Call Carpenter," he suggested. "His wife's pregnant. He can use the extra money."

And he was gone.

TWENTY-FIVE

obert MacKenzie's apartment reeked of wealth. Original artwork hung on every wall, rare antiques blended in with the elegant furnishings, and beautiful rugs covered the gleaming hardwood floors. Grayson walked by a table with a vase he knew cost more than ten thousand dollars. He wondered whose pension paid for that.

A locksmith was working on the door to the study. One of the agents told Grayson he'd been at it for twenty minutes.

The locksmith heard him. "I haven't seen a lock like this before. It's tricky."

Grayson motioned to Ronan. "You want to get this?"

Ronan stepped forward. "Yeah, I've got it."

The locksmith moved out of the way. "I'm telling you, it's tricky."

"Yeah, okay," Ronan said as he reached for the tool the man was holding. He squatted down eye level to the lock and, after a couple of maneuvers, turned the door handle, and the door opened wide.

The locksmith's mouth dropped open. "How did you do that?"

How? Ronan had grown up in the inner city and had learned all sorts of tricks, most of them illegal. That's how. But he wasn't going to talk about his past with a stranger or boast that he could pretty much open any lock by the age of ten. Instead, he said, "Just lucky."

Agents rushed into the study with cameras. While everything was being documented and recorded, Grayson and Ronan turned their attention to the walls. They examined each one carefully and finally agreed on the one that would move. It took them a while to figure out how it worked, but once they pinpointed the correct spot and gave it a firm push, a section of the wall, about four feet wide, swung open, revealing a small room. File cabinets lined one wall, and a stack of file folders sat on an immaculate desk in the center.

Grayson and Ronan were the first to have a look. They sifted through some of the files and called in a couple of investigators who, after several hours of inspection, verified what the two agents had concluded: Robert MacKenzie was running one of the most elaborate Ponzi schemes they had ever seen.

It was all there. His meticulous record keeping was impressive. There were statements for every investor and every deposit. Transaction records showed that he made purchases of stocks, bonds, and other funds, but when these were cross-referenced with the statements the investors got, it was apparent that he had bought only a fraction of the amount he had reported to them. Buying ten shares of a stock and then showing a hundred shares on the investor's statement, he was able to pocket the difference, and the investor never knew. The number of transactions he showed in one month alone was mind-boggling, making it almost impossible for his clients to keep up. The inspectors surmised that some of the companies and funds that appeared didn't actually exist. There were lists of handwritten names crossed off in a ledger book, and these names appeared on statements as a buy, and the very next month they were listed as a sell. If an investor were to ask about any particular security, it would already have disappeared. Like a Ping-Pong ball, MacKenzie had bounced from one to the next, never landing for long in one place.

Investors were sent reports that showed how much money they were making, and even with those, MacKenzie was clever. One month the profit would be slight; the next it would be bigger. He even showed a couple of minor downturns, just to make it realistic.

There were records that indicated some investors had cashed in and taken profits, but these were few and far between. With his charisma and powers of persuasion, Robert MacKenzie had most likely convinced his clients to wait for a bigger payout. How long he could have held on to his deception was the question. The only way he could keep going was to take in more than he returned . . . or spent on his lavish lifestyle.

Without a doubt, it was the most convoluted scam Grayson had ever seen. It was also brilliant. No wonder Olivia was having such trouble finding proof. It was a maze of lies.

A particularly thick file caught Grayson's attention. It had Eric Jorguson's name on it.

He picked it up and thumbed through the papers. Some of the pages showed names of other people whose investments appeared to be linked with Jorguson's. One was Gretta Keene. It didn't take much scrutiny to discover that funds were being moved from one to the other through the account. Grayson could tell that it would take some time to unravel all these figures, but he knew Huntsman was going to be ecstatic when he got his hands on this information.

Jeff Wilcox's file was there, as well. Inside were several signed documents.

Grayson looked through them and held up a couple of pages, comparing them to two pages he had laid on the desk. He called to Ronan. "Look at this."

"What have you found?" Ronan asked.

"Contradictory documents," Grayson said. "And they all have Jeff Wilcox's signature on them."

"Why would MacKenzie keep them?" he asked. "These alone will put him away for years."

"For his signature," Grayson answered. He pulled out a sheet with Jeff Wilcox's name signed at least a dozen times. "When MacKenzie forged his name, he wanted it to look authentic."

"What about the money from the charity Wilcox gave him?"

Grayson gathered the papers and slipped them back in the file. "Looks as though Wilcox gave it to him in good faith, and MacKenzie lost a good deal of it in a risky scheme and kept the rest for himself."

"What a guy," Ronan said, shaking his head.

"Yeah, a real peach," Grayson agreed.

"I'll bet Olivia will be happy, knowing that her suspicions were true. She was right all along."

Grayson thought for a second. "I don't think she'll be celebrating."

"Why? She's been vindicated. Her father won't be able to scam innocent people anymore."

"That's true," Grayson said. "But now all those people who trusted in Robert MacKenzie, the innocent clients who gave him their life savings, are going to find out the truth: They've lost it all."

TWENTY-SIX

Monday was a nightmare. The sins of Olivia's father were being broadcast all over the news channels and the Internet. It was the story of the day. Investors were in shock and disbelief. They awakened to find that they had been duped and that all of their money was gone. Those who had lost their life savings felt helpless. They had no one to turn to, nowhere to go to get back their hard-earned money. Such deceit was simply inconceivable.

Once the initial shock wore off, they were out for blood, and who could blame them? They couldn't get to Robert MacKenzie—he was safe behind bars with guards protecting him—and so they took their anger out on the other members of his family. Olivia had anticipated what was coming once the news broke, and she knew it would be bad. She still wasn't prepared.

Officer Carpenter drove her to work, but instead of leaving and returning for her at the end of the day, he stayed. He pulled up a chair and sat right outside her office door—Grayson's instructions, no doubt.

Working at her desk, she received a multitude of hateful phone calls. She listened to the comments of the first few callers, and from then on, she simply hung up as soon as the irate words began to fly. If she took the time to respond to each one, she'd never get anything done. Mr. Thurman stopped by a couple of times to check on her.

"Are you worried about me?" she asked.

"Just a little," he admitted. "There are some terribly angry people out there calling and threatening you."

"Sir, I work for the IRS. I'm used to it."

He smiled over her joke and said, "All right, I'll let you get back to work, but I insist you take half the day. Go home at noon, and if you must, work from there."

Olivia didn't argue. She intended to leave at noon as Mr. Thurman had ordered, but it took her longer than expected to finish working on one particularly challenging file. It was after two when Officer Carpenter dropped her at her apartment door.

Safe and sound, she thought and sighed with relief. She actually believed that, once she was inside her apartment, she would have a little peace and quiet.

There were forty-eight extremely hostile messages waiting for her on her home phone and half that many on her cell phone. Both numbers were unlisted and Olivia was surprised that so many people had been able to get hold of them. She wanted to hit the DELETE button, but she made herself listen to each and every message. By the time the last one played, she felt completely drained.

She was just about to change out of her black wool skirt and silk blouse when another call came in. The second she heard the voice, she picked up.

"Olivia, it's me, Henry Kincaid. Can you come to school?" The little boy's voice trembled.

"Of course I'll come to your school."

"Now? Can you come to Pinebrook now? 'Cause I need a lawyer and you're my lawyer, right?"

"Yes, now," she promised, hoping her quick agreement would calm him. "Henry, can you tell me what's wrong?"

"We have to go to the principal's office 'cause I got into trouble," he whispered. "It's because of soccer. Bobby told me not to try out or I'd be sorry, but I told him I was going to try out anyway. Ralph is going to try out, too."

Olivia checked the time. Two thirty. "Where are you? Shouldn't you be in the classroom?"

"I'm in the nurse's office. Miss Cavit wants to talk to you. Okay? And after we talk to the principal, will you take me home?"

"Henry, I'm not authorized to take you out of the school—"

"But I—"

"I'll sit with you until your grandfather or Patrick gets there."

"You won't leave me alone?"

"No, I'll stay with you. I promise."

The nurse came on the line a second later. She introduced herself and said, "Henry had a little accident. He tripped into a locker and struck his forehead, his nose, and his eye. The nosebleed has stopped, but I'll keep him here until school dismisses at three fifteen. He's resting on a cot," she explained. "The poor lamb's got a bump on his forehead. I've got an ice pack on it now."

"Have you notified his family?"

"I left a message for Grayson Kincaid. Henry told me his uncle is in New York on business. I also left a message for Henry's grandfather, and I just spoke to Patrick, Henry's housekeeper. He was at the dentist and couldn't leave yet. He'll be here at the regular dismissal time, but Henry seems insistent that you come, too."

"May I speak to Henry again?"

"Olivia," Henry whispered, "Miss Cavit says you should come when school is over."

"Henry, let her think that's what I'll do, but I'm really

leaving now and should get there in fifteen minutes or less. All right?"

She could hear the anxiety leave his voice. "Okay."

Olivia was out the door minutes later. She said a prayer there wouldn't be any angry people in the garage waiting for her, and blessedly there weren't. Once she was in her car with the key in the ignition, she used her iPhone to get directions to Pinebrook School. It was a cold, rainy day, which worked to her advantage. Few reporters liked waiting outside in the raw elements. There were several cars parked along the street with their motors running. She spotted them before she turned in their direction and quickly drove the other way, even going so far as to drive down an alley on the off chance she was being followed.

She thought about calling Grayson to let him know she was going to the school, then decided to wait until she had the full story from Henry.

The private school was all red brick and ivy vines. Very Georgetown, she thought to herself. She pulled in to one of the visitor's slots and went up the stone steps.

A security guard opened the door for her. He was a man in his late sixties and wore a brown uniform. He had a sincere smile and a wealth of information to impart. "You're here for the Kincaid boy?"

"Yes, sir, I am," she answered. "My name is Olivia MacKenzie."

She put her hand out, and he quickly shook it and introduced himself. His name was Arthur. He motioned to a corner, and she followed. "I didn't see it myself, but I have no doubt what happened," he stated with a nod. "That Deckman boy is a bully, and he's been after Henry and his friend Ralph because they're younger and smaller. I used to be just like those little boys. I was small for my age, and I got picked on. I know what it feels like. I wish Principal Higgins would take a firmer hand."

"Is the Deckman boy's first name Bobby? Henry mentioned that name to me."

"That's right. Bobby Deckman. He's been in trouble before, several times, as a matter of fact, but his father does some fast talking and makes a hefty donation, and bam, the problem goes away. I know I shouldn't be saying this, but I figure, what the heck. I'm retiring in a couple of months, and it's time someone said something."

"Tell me what you suspect."

"The Deckman boy attacked Henry. He smashed his face into the locker. If the custodian hasn't gotten to it, there's blood still on the locker. Poor little Henry's blood."

"Are there cameras in the hallways?"

"Oh my, yes." His eyes widened. "I could make you a disc, but I'd have to hurry. As soon as Bobby's father gets here, I'm afraid the disc will accidentally get wiped."

She smiled. "Could you make me two?"

He nodded and ducked into the security office next to the school's entrance.

Olivia didn't have to stand there long. Arthur reappeared, grinning and waving two discs, just as another security guard rushed down the hall toward them. He explained he had gotten Arthur's page and would take over front door duty.

"Come with me," Arthur told her.

He led her up some stairs to a computer lab. Fortunately it was empty. Arthur used his security code to access the Internet, then stepped back so that Olivia could insert the disc. She quickly sent the file to her e-mail account, and she sent another to Grayson. With Arthur hovering over her, she watched the video. The encounter between the two boys lasted less than a minute, but the video left no doubt who the aggressor was. Olivia felt heartsick. Bobby was twice the size and weight of Henry.

Olivia played it one more time. "What grade is the Deckman boy in? He looks like a senior in high school."

"Fifth. He's quite big for his age," Arthur said. "And mean," he added in a whisper. "Look at his expression as he grabs Henry. He's enjoying himself. It's downright evil, if you ask me. I tell you, there's something missing in that boy's head."

She silently agreed. There wasn't any provocation. Bobby came up behind Henry, half lifted him, and threw him into the locker.

Olivia could feel her anger building. Arthur fueled it when he said, "Do you see? That's what the Deckman boy does. He chooses a kid and goes after him. Then, when he gets bored, he chooses another kid. Always younger so they can't fight back."

"And Principal Higgins?"

"He's never had any concrete proof until now," Arthur said. "The kids Bobby goes after won't tell what happened. They're afraid. Bobby's a bully, all right. The school needs to get rid of him."

Olivia was in wholehearted agreement. She grabbed her phone and called Officer Carpenter, quickly filled him in, and after he gave her his e-mail address, she sent the video to him.

"I'll take care of it," he told her.

After making the promise, Carpenter demanded to know why she had left her apartment without a bodyguard. The man was almost as bossy as Grayson, she thought. She had to listen to a lecture and vow to wait for him to come to her.

Arthur walked her to the nurse's office. "You'll like Miss Cavit. She worked in a hospital for twenty years before she retired from the long hours and took this job. She's real good with kids."

The nurse was sitting at her desk in a tiny room. Beyond was another little room with two cots side by side. Henry was resting on one of them. He lit up when he saw Olivia in the doorway.

Miss Cavit said, "There's a meeting with Bobby Deckman's parents after school. Three forty-five. Henry tells me you're his lawyer."

She smiled. "Yes, that's right."

"I imagine you'll want to be at the meeting, too."

"Oh yes, I will." Olivia walked to the cot and sat down beside Henry. "How are you feeling?"

"Good," he said. "I knew you'd come here 'cause you said you would."

She turned to Miss Cavit. "Could you give us a moment while I confer with my client?"

"I'll be at my desk if you need me," she answered.

When she'd pulled the door closed, Olivia turned to Henry. "Okay, tell me what happened."

He took hold of her hand, surprising her. His expression was so earnest. "Bobby decided Ralph and I couldn't try out for soccer."

"Did he tell you why he didn't want you to try out?"

"He was just being mean 'cause he can. He's like that with other kids, too. Honest," he insisted.

"I believe you, Henry." She reached into her purse and pulled out a small notepad and pen. "Tell me about the other kids he's bullied."

Olivia took copious notes, and when she was finished with her questions and had deciphered Henry's convoluted stories, she asked, "Why didn't you tell your uncle Grayson about Bobby Deckman?"

" 'Cause Ralph and me were going to stand up to Bobby together."

"Ralph and I," she automatically corrected.

He grinned. "You're just like my uncle and Patrick. They're always telling me the right way to talk. How come you do it?"

"It's how I roll." She laughed after using the silly expression she and the other Pips had often used when they were in the unit together. The nonanswer always baffled the nurses.

Patrick arrived a few minutes before three fifteen. He sat on the empty cot next to Henry's and his tall frame dwarfed the tiny room. Olivia pulled up the video on her phone and let Patrick watch Bobby throw Henry into the locker.

"Oh man," he whispered. "Has Grayson seen this? He's going to go ballistic."

"Not yet," she answered. "I think we should go to the principal's office now. It's almost three forty-five."

Henry clasped Olivia's hand and walked by her side down the hall until he spotted some of his friends. He let go then and walked behind her with Patrick, imitating his swagger.

The Deckmans were waiting in the reception area. Mr. Deckman looked like an uptight banker with his conservative suit and tie and his rigid stance. His wife looked like one of those reality show housewives of Washington, D.C. She was unattractive, painfully thin, and had had way too much face work. *Brittle* was the word that came to mind. Olivia feared that if she shook her hand a little too vigorously, the woman would crumble into a thousand pieces.

Mr. Deckman didn't acknowledge them, and his wife kept giving them covert glances but didn't speak.

Bobby was waiting in the principal's office. When they were all ushered in by the receptionist, Olivia was taken aback by the hostility in the boy's eyes. He wasn't looking at her, though. His anger was directed at his father.

Extra chairs were dragged in. On the left of the principal's desk sat Brittle, Uptight, and Bobby. On the opposite side, Henry and she sat in straight-backed chairs. There was a chair for Patrick, but he preferred to stand behind Henry. She could tell he was still hopping mad.

Principal Higgins was a young man, probably in his early to middle thirties, Olivia estimated. There were stress lines around his mouth and dark circles under his eyes. Running the all-boys school had taken its toll.

Higgins rubbed his jaw. "This is a difficult situation. We know Henry and Bobby were in an altercation, but the boys have given different interpretations of what happened."

"Boys like to fight," Mr. Deckman said.

Had he not shrugged and acted so indifferent, Olivia might have softened her response.

"Your son is a bully."

"He is not," Mrs. Deckman snapped. "He's a normal fifth grader."

"He's a bully," she repeated. "And that won't stand. Principal Higgins, this isn't the first time Bobby's been accused of attacking a student, is it?"

"Now, see here. That's confidential information," Bobby's mother said.

"No, it isn't," Olivia replied. "Your son punched Tom Capshaw. Split open his lip."

"There is absolutely no proof that it was our son who struck Capshaw," Mr. Deckman argued.

Olivia opened her notepad and glanced at it. "What about Will Kaufman or Matt Farrell?"

"Those altercations happened last year," Mrs. Deckman said. "It was all hearsay, one boy's word against an-

other's, and then both Will and Matt changed their
stories." She turned to her husband. "They were just
roughhousing, weren't they, Sean?"

Her husband nodded. "That's exactly right. No proof
of any wrongdoing."

"This time there is proof," Olivia said. She handed the
principal one of the discs.

"What is that?" Mr. Deckman asked.

"A security tape," Olivia answered.

Principal Higgins looked surprised. "I don't know
how you got this, Miss MacKenzie, but I'm not sure we
can . . ."

Olivia turned to Bobby's parents. "You do want to
know the truth, don't you? If it was just two boys roughhousing, this will prove it."

Mr. Deckman stammered, "Well, of course I—"

"Good," Olivia said. She nodded to Principal Higgins,
who slipped the disc into the computer slot. He adjusted
the monitor so they could see it, then came around the
desk to watch the video with them.

Not a word was spoken as the event played out on the
screen. Mrs. Deckman's face turned white, and she winced
when she saw Bobby throw Henry into the locker. Mr.
Deckman's face turned red. When Olivia turned to look
at Bobby, he was smiling. What was he? A sociopath in
the making?

Principal Higgins was appalled, but Olivia could de-
tect a hint of relief as he returned to his chair and removed the disc.

Mr. Deckman grabbed the disc from his hand, slipped
it into his pocket, and said, "I'd like to look at this again
at home."

Mrs. Deckman smiled at her husband's quick response. Did she think the problem had just gone away?

"That's fine," Olivia said. "I've sent the video to Henry's uncle and to others as well. This isn't going away."

Mr. Deckman sprang to his feet and was all bluster when he said, "That's illegal. I'll sue. You can't confiscate private property. It's an invasion of privacy. It's . . ." He turned his outrage on the principal. "Do something, Higgins. If you want to keep your job, fix this."

Principal Higgins was not intimidated. He looked directly at Deckman and stated, "We do not tolerate violence or bullies in this school."

Mrs. Deckman's smile had disappeared and she now looked worried. "Yes, we understand, but he's just a child. We could get him counseling. We'll do it right away."

"I don't know . . ." Higgins began. "We simply can't have this behavior . . ."

"If we bring charges," Olivia told the principal, "the decision would be out of your hands. This is clearly a case of assault, and I'm confident that any court would see it our way."

Principal Higgins was the one who looked worried now. "I understand your point of view, Miss MacKenzie, but for the sake of our school and its reputation, I hope we can find a way to settle this without a legal battle."

Olivia appeared to consider his concerns and then said, "We suggest that Bobby be expelled from Pinebrook immediately. He should not be allowed to return here or attend any other school until he's gotten the help he needs. He could have broken Henry's neck. Surely, you wouldn't wait until something that serious happened before taking action, Principal Higgins?"

The Deckmans erupted, but Olivia stood her ground. Any threats that the parents hurled at her were met with the sound and logical details she would use in a suit against them and their son.

Until now, Bobby had sat quietly with a smug grin on his face, but he was beginning to see the handwriting on the wall. He rushed to his father, poked him in the chest, and screamed, "Don't you dare let them kick me out. You'll be sorry if you do."

There was no calming the boy. A minute later, as he was being dragged from the office by his mother and father, everyone could hear Mrs. Deckman trying to comfort him with the promise of a new iPad as soon as this mistake was sorted out. Mr. Deckman paused at the door to give Olivia a contemptuous glare before he left.

Olivia spent a few more minutes talking to the principal, and Patrick and Henry waited for her in the reception area. When she came out, Henry hugged her. "Thank you, Olivia," he said.

She leaned down, smiled, and kissed his cheek. "You're very welcome, Henry."

Officer Carpenter was standing by the front door to the school when she walked outside. He held out his hand to take her car keys, but after her protest, he agreed to follow her in his car if she promised to be cautious. Just to make him happy, she drove under the speed limit the whole way home.

He was just about to say good-bye to her at her apartment door when Mrs. Delaney, who must have been listening for Olivia to return, stuck her head out and announced she needed milk. Carpenter waited while Olivia went into her apartment and came back with a quart. The grumpy woman made her stand there while she found her reading glasses and checked the expiration date; then she thanked Olivia and went back inside.

After Carpenter wagged his finger in Olivia's face and told her to stay home, he left. Olivia locked her door and leaned against it. She suddenly felt very tired. She changed into snug jeans and a blouse, put her hair up in a ponytail, and went into the kitchen to find something she could microwave for dinner. Determined to eat something healthy first, she made a salad and ate every bit of it. She thought about what had happened at Henry's school and realized how lucky she'd been that no one had recognized her. Maybe they hadn't seen the news yet or hadn't associated her name with the family. Regardless, she was thankful. She even had the thought that maybe it wasn't going to be as bad as she'd anticipated. Maybe it would go away sooner rather than later.

In her dreams perhaps. Just as she was going to put her frozen dinner in the microwave, another call came in. It was so grossly disturbing, she lost her appetite. She put the dinner back in the refrigerator and curled up on the sofa to watch television.

Her father's face was plastered on all the major channels. The broadcaster on one news network was interviewing a tearful woman who kept saying she'd been promised a triple return on her money. Olivia pushed the button on the remote and turned the television off. The silence brought a few welcome moments of peace.

She decided a Popsicle sounded good so she got one from the freezer, put it on a plate, and went back to the television. Maybe she could find an old classic movie to take her mind off her worries. A knock on the door startled her, and an instant of panic gripped her stomach. Had one of the angry investors gotten inside the building? She walked over and peered through the peephole. When she saw Grayson standing there, she threw the door open and fell into his arms. He looked tired, she thought.

"What are you doing here? It's almost ten. Did you just get back from New York? Shouldn't you be—"

His mouth stopped her. He tightened his hold and kissed the breath out of her. She didn't resist him. She wrapped her arms around his neck and kissed him back passionately. It had been such an awful day, but he was here now, and everything was better.

"I missed you, too." He took off his coat, hung it in the closet, and draping his arm around her, pulled her along to the sofa.

"How's Henry?"

"Fully recovered," he replied. "When I opened the file you sent and saw Henry being slammed into his locker, I wanted to lock that Deckman kid up in solitary for the rest of his life."

"That's a little extreme, don't you think?" she teased.

"Henry and Patrick are singing your praises. Thank you, by the way."

He kissed her on her forehead and pulled her down next to him. They talked about the school for a few more minutes, and then Olivia said, "I want to hear about the files again. Tell me everything. Start at the beginning when you entered the apartment."

She took a bite of the Popsicle and waited. Grayson, she noticed, was staring at her mouth.

"I can't concentrate while you're eating that," he said.

A little bit of the devil in her came out. She put the Popsicle in her mouth and sucked the sweet cherry juice. "How come?" she asked innocently.

His eyes narrowed. "Olivia," he warned, "want to find out how fast I can get your clothes off?"

Smiling sweetly, she stopped tormenting him and took the Popsicle to the sink. Her mood changed immediately when she heard her phone ring.

Grayson went to the door of her study to listen to the incoming call. He obviously didn't like what he heard. "Son of a bitch," he growled. "Did you hear that?" he asked when she came back into the living room.

She shook her head. "Come sit and tell me—"

"How many others are there?" he demanded.

"I'm up to fifty-some now."

"Son of a . . ."

"Grayson, you knew this was coming."

"Did you listen to all of them?" His voice shook, he was so angry.

"Yes," she said. "Trust me. You don't want to. Some of them are sick."

"How many were death threats?"

"Stop snapping at me. I didn't make the calls."

Her retort eased some of the tension, and he gave her a slight smile.

"I should have erased them and turned the phone off," she admitted.

"No, absolutely not. I'm going to have every damned call traced."

"You can't arrest people for saying mean things."

"Death threats? Hell yes, I can arrest them."

"When did you get back from New York?" she asked to keep him from getting worked up again.

"Around five today. I didn't see the video until I got home." He was still glaring as he followed her.

"Did you get to see any Broadway shows?" she asked with a straight face.

The question jarred him; then he laughed. He dropped down next to her and swung his feet up on the ottoman. "I was in your father's study until after two. Then I went back around nine this morning. Spent most of the day there."

"I've never been to the apartment," she said.

He described the layout but didn't mention the fact that there wasn't a single photo of her anywhere. He went into detail about the secret room and what he had seen in the files.

"Ronan talked to Wilcox's attorney, told him what we found," he said.

"That's wonderful," she said. "Emma will be so relieved."

"There's more," he continued. "And I think you'll really like this."

"What?" she asked.

"You know that Eric Jorguson invested with your father."

"Yes."

"It appears that not all the money Jorguson had flowing through the fund was going into his retirement nest egg. When the auditors sort it all out, I'm pretty sure they'll be able to prove this was one of his money-laundering accounts."

"Wouldn't that be something?" Olivia shook her head. She'd listened intently to all the evidence that was piling up against her father, and the cold reality of the situation was setting in. "This is going to go on for a long while, isn't it?" she asked. "The phone calls and the threats?"

"Depends on the next big story." Grayson could see her wilting before his eyes, so he changed the subject. "Want to know what I did when I got home this evening?"

"What?" she asked, wondering why he suddenly sounded exasperated. "Did you eat dinner with Henry and Patrick?"

"Yes," he replied. "Henry met me at the door and went into a long narration of what happened at school. Then Patrick gave me his summary. Then Henry started over again," he said, smiling. "You impressed the socks off him, Olivia. He's now quoting you."

"He's sweet," she said. "And so is Patrick."

"Uh-huh, sweet. We sat down for dinner when sweet Henry remembered he had another assignment due tomorrow."

She bit her lower lip to keep from laughing. "What was it?"

"He had to memorize all the states in alphabetical order and all the capitals. He was supposed to have been working on it for a couple of weeks, but he just remembered tonight." He shook his head as he added, "When he told me, I swear I was speechless."

"What did you do?"

"It wasn't as bad as I thought. He knew some of them, and Patrick came up with a rap tune. It made it easier for Henry."

"Did you memorize them along with him?"

"Yes . . . and, no, I'm not singing for you."

"Children learn quickly. I'm sure you got through the assignment in no time."

"I haven't told you about the math yet."

The lighthearted conversation ended with the doorbell. Then the banging on the door started. Olivia reluctantly went to answer it. She looked through the peephole and groaned.

"Who is it?" he asked, coming up behind her.

"World War Three," she said. "Natalie and my mother."

"You don't have to let them in."

"Oh yes, I do. Natalie will stand there hitting the door and shouting until tomorrow if she has to. I might as well get it over with now."

Grayson made her step back into the living room before he opened the door. Natalie couldn't storm inside because he blocked her.

"Where is my sister?" she demanded. She pushed against his chest.

"You don't want to do that."

"I know she's here. Let me in," she shouted.

Since she was acting like a child, he decided to treat her like one. "You will behave yourself, or you will leave."

The second he stepped back, Natalie rushed in. Her mother, Deborah, showed more decorum. She nodded to Grayson as she walked past.

Natalie saw Olivia and screamed, "Do you know what you've done?"

Ignoring her sister, Olivia said, "Hello, Mother."

Deborah MacKenzie looked exhausted. Grayson noticed her hands were shaking as she struggled to remove her coat. He took it from her.

She was a beautiful woman. Except for the color of their eyes—Olivia's were blue; Deborah's were brown—Olivia looked just like her.

"Hello, Olivia. How are you feeling?"

"I'm fine. How are you?"

"I'm very distressed," she said. "I don't understand what's happening. Your father's in jail, and he's been accused of stealing money. It's outrageous to think that my husband would do such a thing. It's all a misunderstanding," she whispered. "It has to be."

"No, Mother, it isn't a misunderstanding. This is what I've been trying to tell you, but you wouldn't listen."

"This is all your fault," Natalie yelled. She was pacing around the room with her arms crossed.

Olivia turned to her. "Sit down and wait your turn. I'm talking to Mother. When I'm finished, I'll listen to you."

"You selfish—"

"Don't say it. If you call me names, you're out of here."

Grayson smiled. He was impressed with the way Olivia had taken the upper hand.

"Mother, I know this is a shock."

Olivia could see the anger washing over her mother.

She straightened up, her spine rigid. Her voice turned to ice when she said, "A shock? My husband is in jail. It's all a mistake," she insisted. "Because of you, young lady. You started all those rumors. You've ruined your father with your foolish accusations."

Rumors? Olivia didn't know where to start. She looked at Grayson and lifted her shoulders.

"You must fix this," her mother implored. "Show your father the support he needs now. He's all alone in New York, without any family to help him through this humiliation. I wanted to go and stand by his side, but he's been denied bail."

For good cause, Olivia knew. They were sure he would try to run.

"I'm going home with Natalie," she said then. "I'll stay with her until this is resolved."

Hopeless. Her mother was completely hopeless. Still drinking Robert MacKenzie's poisoned water, Olivia realized. Eventually she would be forced to face reality. And so would Natalie. It wouldn't do any good to try to reason with either of them now. She actually felt sorry for them. Acknowledging the truth was going to be painful.

"Okay, Natalie, it's your turn," Olivia said.

"Did you know George is sitting in a cell? He's been accused of the most heinous crimes."

"Yes, I do know," she replied calmly. She crossed the room to Grayson and leaned against him. She needed comfort.

"This is all such a mess," Natalie railed.

"The time is getting away from us, Natalie. Get out the papers," her mother ordered.

Uh-oh. Olivia didn't like the sound of that.

Natalie opened her purse and pulled out a stack of papers. She unfolded them and was searching for a pen.

"What are you doing?" Olivia asked.

Natalie finally explained. "Mother and Father's assets have been frozen, and most of my money is unavailable. I have a small account that will get us through, but there isn't enough to pay for George's defense. So, you're going to sign over your trust. I know you don't get the money for another year, but if you sign it over to us now, we can borrow against it and hire the best attorney we can find to clear this up. You got him into this mess. You can damn well help to get him out."

"You must help your father, too," her mother said firmly. She put her purse over her arm and reached for her coat. "You simply must call your aunt Emma and insist that she support your father."

"And by support, Mother, do you mean you want me to ask her to give Father all of her money?"

Her mother's chin came up. "Yes, that's exactly what I mean. His defense will be expensive, and Emma is a member of this family. She must do her part."

"You need to sign these papers," Natalie reminded, shoving them at her. "And we aren't leaving until you do."

Olivia pushed them away. "I'm not signing anything."

"Yes, you are," Natalie cried. "You owe us."

For Olivia, that was the final straw. As she calmly walked out of the room, she turned back and said, "Grayson, please get the door."

TWENTY-SEVEN

Olivia was sitting with Jane and Collins in Jane's hospital room, catching them up on the latest events. The news about her father was still a hot topic on TV, but now the how-could-this-have-happened-again questions had started. Fingers were pointed; and if history were to repeat itself, no one was going to step up and take responsibility for not doing his job.

Olivia wondered how many had ignored all the signs and all the complaints and had simply turned a blind eye.

Collins couldn't understand how Natalie could blame Olivia.

"It's easier to blame me than to admit that she was horribly deceived by her father," Olivia explained. "Natalie trusted him."

"Natalie knows what a Ponzi scheme is, doesn't she?"

"Of course she does," Olivia said.

"What do you think she'll do when she finds out about George's debt to that loan shark?" Jane asked.

"She won't be happy," Collins predicted.

Olivia laughed. "You think?"

"What about your mother?" Collins asked. "Do you think she'll ever figure it out?"

"I doubt it. She's a lost cause."

"No, she's just loyal to a fault," Jane said. "No one's a

lost cause. Look at my brother. Logan's completely turned his life around."

Olivia smiled. Jane always looked for the good in people. She wished she could be more like her friend. She had such a sweet disposition and a gentle soul.

"If convicted on all counts, your father will never get out of prison," Collins predicted.

"How do you feel about that?" Jane asked. She sounded like a therapist now. She was sitting up in bed, trying to ignore Collins, who was fluffing her pillows.

"It's for the best," Olivia said. "If he got out, he'd just do it again. He really can't help the way he is."

Collins disagreed. "Your father knows the difference between right and wrong. He set out to steal."

Jane pulled a pillow from behind her and whacked Collins with it. "Go sit down and stop fussing over me."

Laughing, Collins dodged the attack and sat on the edge of the bed. Olivia took the pillow and put it on a chair. She noticed a couple of long strands of Jane's hair. Oh God, it was falling out again. Was she doing chemo and not telling them? She turned the pillow over so Jane wouldn't notice, then went to the window ledge and leaned against it.

"What's the matter?" Collins asked when she noticed Olivia's stark complexion.

Olivia wasn't going to talk about Jane's illness now, and so she said, "I don't want to talk about family any longer. I'm sick of it. Let's talk about something else."

"Okay," Collins agreed. "Tell us about Grayson."

"Olivia can't keep her hands off him," Jane announced.

Both of her friends had a good laugh. Olivia didn't take exception because it was true. She couldn't keep her hands off him. Jane was simply repeating what she'd told her.

"I don't understand it. I really don't," Olivia said, perplexed. "I make all these resolutions, and the second I see him, I want to . . . you know."

"You're in love with him." Collins stated the obvious.

"Of course I'm in love with him. I wouldn't be so miserable if I weren't. But I'm not going to marry him."

"Has he asked?" Jane wanted to know.

"No."

"Has he told you he loves you?" Collins asked.

"No," she answered. "But I know he cares about me. It's all the little things he does . . ." Her voice trailed off as she thought about him.

"Like?" Collins asked. "Give us an example."

"He carries an extra inhaler for me because he knows I'll forget to put one in my purse," she said. "And he does so many sweet, loving things for me." Tears came into her eyes. "When I first met him, I thought of him as the James Bond type. He was so sophisticated and sexy and . . ."

When she didn't go on, Collins said, "Love 'em and leave 'em, like Bond?"

"Exactly. He isn't like that, though. He's responsible and solid." She thought of him with Henry. Grayson was patient and loving, and she knew he would always be there for his nephew. Henry knew it, too.

"I sometimes think about a future with him, and then I remember what your parents went through, Collins, and your mother, Jane. Sam's family, too. I saw their fear, and I heard them crying. For a while there, when everyone but Dr. Pardieu thought we were dying, your families came and kept vigil. It was awful for them."

Collins nodded. "We all remember, Olivia."

"How can I put Grayson through that?" She shook her head. "I can't do that to him. I won't."

Collins didn't try to convince her that she was wrong. How could she with Jane so ill now?

"You can't live your life waiting for it to come back."
Jane made the statement. "What a fatalistic attitude. Olivia, you need to stop being afraid."

"What about you, Jane?" Olivia asked. "What's going on?"

"And don't tell us it's the flu again," Collins warned.

"I'm feeling better again. It's the weirdest thing. I get so sick, and then I bounce back. Since Dr. Pardieu has been away, another doctor has been seeing me. By the way, Logan's going to be here any minute. Please don't talk about my illness in front of him. Okay? He gets so upset. I know he's scared, so keep it upbeat."

They quickly agreed. Then it was Collins's turn to catch her friends up. She told them she was still waiting to hear when she would start at the academy. She couldn't understand why it was taking so long, but she thought it might have something to do with her medical history.

Exasperated, Jane said, "You're just like Olivia. The two of you need an attitude adjustment."

An argument ensued, and Jane deflected it by changing the topic. "I can't believe everything that's happened to you in the last few months, Olivia. You were attacked by the CEO of a major corporation and his goon, and you were rescued by the FBI. You were shot three times, and then you were almost kidnapped and taken to a mental hospital."

"I hope that's the end of it, and I really hope and pray they find whoever shot you," Collins said.

Logan walked in and heard what she'd said. "Jane told me that Martin guy was the shooter."

His eyes were red, and it was obvious he'd been crying. No one mentioned his condition.

"I thought so, too," Olivia said. "But until there's absolute proof, Grayson is going to continue to provide protection for me. He doesn't care if I want a bodyguard following me around or not. He's extremely stubborn."

"What's absolute proof?" Logan asked. He walked to the side of the bed and kissed Jane's forehead.

"A confession would seal it," Jane suggested. "But he obviously isn't talking."

"Finding the weapon would also do it. If they could trace it to Martin, Grayson would be convinced," Olivia said.

"When do you get to go home?" Collins asked Jane.

"Hopefully tomorrow," she answered. "Olivia, will you be around in a couple of weeks?"

"For the Dracula room? Absolutely."

"Why is the doctor waiting so long?" Collins wondered.

"He wants me to finish some meds first."

Olivia yawned again. "I'm exhausted. I'm going home. Come on, Collins. Let Jane visit with her brother."

Olivia waited until she and Collins were in the elevator before talking about Jane's condition. "She's losing her hair."

"I saw it on the pillow," Collins said.

"She doesn't want us to know."

"We could try to talk to the doctor who's covering for Dr. Pardieu, but he has to hold her confidence, and if she wants to keep it secret, he can't tell us anything."

Several heartbeats later, Collins took Olivia's hand and whispered, "It's back, isn't it?"

"Maybe," Olivia allowed. Determined to be more positive, she added, "And maybe not."

TWENTY-EIGHT

Olivia had suffered a week from hell. The phones never stopped ringing, the threats never subsided, and because of the disruption she was inadvertently causing at the office, she'd been forced to work at home. By Friday, she was feeling like a caged orangutan.

She pretty much looked like one, too. She continued to shower and brush her teeth every day, but getting dressed didn't seem all that necessary. Her new uniform was a pair of baggy sweats and an old faded T-shirt. She didn't bother with a bra or shoes and didn't do much of anything with her hair. Every morning she put it up in a ponytail, but by nightfall, most of it was hanging around her face. Her eating habits weren't much better. She walked around with a bag of chips—the unhealthy kind—and a Diet Coke.

She was sitting cross-legged on the floor with her laptop balanced on her knees and a pencil clutched in her teeth. She had just reached for a potato chip when there was an unexpected knock at the door. She stuck the pencil in her hair, popped the chip in her mouth, and went to answer it.

When the door opened, Grayson took one look at her and started laughing.

She dared him to criticize her. "What's so funny?"

He wasn't about to tell her. In her present frame of mind, she wouldn't believe him if he told her that, no matter how she dressed, she was beautiful to him. Her face scrubbed clean and dressed in clothes that could pass for bag lady rejects, Olivia could still grace the cover of any glamour magazine.

The phone was ringing as he shut the door behind him and locked it. Another caller was leaving a threatening message.

"How many . . ." Grayson began.

She shoved the bag of chips into his hand. "Hold that thought," she said as she rushed into the study to listen to the rest of the message.

The voice was an angry growl. "You got that, bitch? Bill and me are gonna hurt you because you took all that money. We're gonna . . ."

Olivia picked up the phone before Grayson could get to her and yelled, "It's not 'Bill and *me*'—it's 'Bill and *I* are going to hurt you'—dumb ass." She slammed the phone down.

"Okay, sweetheart. I think it's time for you to get out for a little while," Grayson said calmly. He put his hands on her shoulders and guided her out of the study. She was as stiff as an ironing board.

"How can you want to be seen with me?" She sounded pitiful. She realized she was feeling sorry for herself, but the phone calls were getting to her, and so was the isolation. She hadn't stepped outside her apartment since Monday.

"I'm hoping you'll change your clothes and put on shoes," he answered drily, as he pushed her along into her bedroom.

"I'm going to have to change my name," she said, "and move to Europe where no one knows me. That's what I have to do."

"It will get better," he promised.

She scoffed at his prediction. Grayson turned her around and tilted her chin up. "Snorting isn't ladylike, sweetheart."

Ignoring his comment, she said, "Do you know what's really ironic? Natalie and my mother haven't gotten all these hostile calls."

"Have you talked to them?"

"Only once. Natalie's been leaving her own horrible messages for me. I picked up yesterday when she called, and it was more of the same. She and Mother have gone into hiding, so these threatening calls aren't reaching them."

"Do you want them to get the threatening calls?"

"No, of course not. I'm just saying . . ."

The tenderness in his eyes warmed her heart, and suddenly the whining and complaining weren't all that satisfying.

"Why are you here?" she asked.

"I'm taking you out to dinner."

"Do you have your gun with you?"

He smiled. "Yes."

"Okay. If you want to risk it, we'll go to dinner."

The lopsided ponytail was driving him to distraction. He pulled the elastic band free and handed it to her. "That's better," he said. He traced the side of her jaw with his fingers, leaned down, and kissed her.

"Sometimes you overwhelm me," she whispered. How could this gorgeous, sexy man want to be with her? He could have any woman in the world, and yet here he was.

"Overwhelm, huh? I like that."

He looked a little too arrogantly pleased with himself. "Only sometimes, Grayson."

"We have a reservation at Veronique's in ninety minutes. You're wasting time."

She was astounded. Veronique's was the hottest restaurant in D.C. It had received rave reviews and had been booked solid every night since it opened.

"It takes six months to get a reservation there. How did you—"

"Olivia?"

"Yes?"

"Wear the white dress."

She gasped. "But that means—"

"I'll explain everything in the car. Get moving."

He didn't have to tell her again. She was already stripping out of her clothes in the bathroom before he pulled the bedroom door closed behind him. She showered and washed and dried her hair in record time. It took her longer to do her makeup. She was going for the pouty, sultry look. Her dark, smoky eye makeup made the color of her eyes more intense. After applying her red lipstick, she dropped her robe, sprayed perfume, and slipped into her lacy undergarments. Next came the dress. It was probably sinful to love a piece of clothing as much as she loved this dress, but it was so perfect. It was made in 1960, but it had never been worn . . . until tonight. She'd paid a fortune for it at a vintage shop, and it was worth every dollar. It had a low-cut square neckline and long tapered sleeves that came just below her wrist. The straight skirt was short, just to her knees, and the fabric clung to every curve of her body. This dress was so spectacular, it would make any woman look and feel like a temptress.

And she was ready. After one last inspection in the full-length mirror, Olivia took a deep breath and opened the door without making a sound.

Grayson was standing by the window. His head was bent, and he was going through his text messages. He glanced up and saw her, and his reaction was instantaneous. His mouth suddenly went dry. He couldn't swallow, and breathing was impossible. She was stunning. He was so aroused, he would have sworn his blood was on fire coursing through his veins.

Olivia didn't need to hear any compliments. His smoldering eyes said it all.

A minute passed and then another, and he still hadn't said a word. He slowly began to walk toward her. The way he was looking at her made her heart race. If he were a panther, she was his prey, and every nerve in her body tensed in anticipation.

For Grayson, the primal need to touch her overrode caution. He stood in front of her, one hand on the small of her back, the other at her neck. He roughly twisted her hair around his fist, forced her head back, and growled, "Open your mouth for me," a scant second before his mouth covered hers. His tongue thrust inside, stroking hers, forcing her to respond. He savored the taste of her. For this moment in time she was completely his. No one else could have her. She belonged to him.

The scorching kiss ended. He lifted his head, and staring into her eyes, he slowly rubbed his thumb across her lips. He took a deep, shuddering breath. "I'll get your coat."

Olivia could barely get her wits about her. She hurried back into the bedroom to collect her evening bag. The kiss so rattled her, she'd almost forgotten it. She caught a glimpse at her reflection in the mirror. Her lipstick had stayed on her lips. Impressive, she thought. Especially considering the way Grayson had tried to devour her. Just thinking about that kiss made her heartbeat quicken.

Grayson helped her with her coat and locked the door for her. He still hadn't said a word about her appearance, and for some reason she was inordinately pleased by that fact.

He had parked illegally in front of her building again. John was standing behind the counter talking to a policeman at the door. She slowed to greet them, but Grayson had her elbow and was in a hurry to get her in the car. Were there angry people outside waiting for her? Sleet was spitting across the windshield. Who would stand outside in this weather? She could feel a dark cloud closing in on her mood and rebelled against it. Not tonight. She was not going to be pessimistic and worry about anything. She was going to have the most wonderful evening with Grayson. No worries. No complications.

Once they were on their way, he finally spoke. "I'm gonna want you to keep your coat on during dinner."

She laughed. He didn't join in. "Oh my . . . you're serious? I am not keeping my coat on while I eat." She laughed again. "So, you like the dress?"

"How about I tell you what I wanted to do to you when I saw you standing in the doorway?"

Her face felt warm, and she knew she was blushing. "The dress isn't inappropriate . . . is it?"

His slow smile caught her by surprise. "No, the dress is beautiful."

"Then what's the problem?"

He decided he might as well tell her the truth. "It's you. You're the problem."

Turning toward him, she folded her arms defensively. "Would you care to explain?"

"It's the way you fill out the dress. It hugs your perfect, voluptuous body, and the sensual way you move in it . . . hell, it should be illegal." His voice was becoming more intense. "You're the sexiest woman I've ever known, and in that dress . . ." He shook his head. "Just keep the coat on."

He thought her body was voluptuous? She fought the urge to look down at her chest. Wait a minute. . . . Was *voluptuous* a code word for "fat"? No, it couldn't be. Grayson wouldn't be looking at her that way if that's what he meant. He was telling her she looked hot. She smiled at him to let him know she appreciated the compliment, but he returned her smile with a frown.

"Now what?" she asked.

"How many other men have seen you in that dress?"

"This dress is a 1960 vintage—"

"How many?"

"None. This is the first time I've worn it. I was waiting for a special occasion, and you did tell me to wear it."

"Yes, I did."

"Remember the promise? As soon as you were convinced you had the right man behind bars for trying to kill me, you'd pull the bodyguards and we'd celebrate."

"We've got the gun—"

She interrupted. "The gun used to shoot me?"

"Yes," he said, smiling. "That gun."

"Where did you find it?"

Grayson promised to tell her everything later. He pulled up to the restaurant entrance. A valet rushed forward to open Olivia's door while another attendant came around to give Grayson a claim ticket. He told the man to keep his car close.

Veronique's was a small bistro with a European flair. Grayson was watching the crowd as they entered. He thought every man there was staring at Olivia, and he didn't like that one little bit. She hadn't taken off her coat yet, but the second she'd walked in, she had their attention.

"Would you like to check your coat?" the maître d' asked her when they stepped up to his lectern.

She looked at Grayson. "Would I?"

He muttered something she couldn't quite catch before he helped her remove her coat. He took her hand and headed to the bar. Like the sea parting, men stepped back on either side, making a path for her. It was actually comical, and had he not been feeling so possessive of her, Grayson might have laughed. Instead, he decided a little intimidation was called for, and he unbuttoned his suit jacket so that his badge and gun were visible.

Olivia also noticed the stares. Her reaction was panic. Ever since the scandal with her father had hit the news, various photos of the MacKenzies had been plastered on all the media. There were quite a few pictures of her parents and her sister attending parties, and since Olivia was never with them, she hadn't expected she'd be so easily recognized.

She turned back to Grayson and whispered into his ear. "I'm not so sure this was a good idea. I think some of these people might know who I am. They're staring. Maybe we should leave."

He put his arm around her waist and pulled her close. "It's the dress they're staring at." It wasn't just the dress, of course. They were staring at a beautiful woman.

The maître d' appeared and told them their table was ready. Grayson didn't like the first choice—the table was in the middle of the room—but another was available against the wall near the back. It was more intimate.

Once Olivia was seated with a menu in front of her, she began to relax. Her back was to the other diners, and she decided she would let Grayson handle any problems tonight. If anyone wanted to get in her face and yell at her because of what her father had done, she would let Grayson shoo him away. She was not going to let anyone or anything mar her evening.

She tried to ask Grayson for the details about the gun,

but he shook his head and said, "We'll talk after dinner. Every time I think about you getting shot, I get angry, real angry. I don't want to ruin my appetite."

She turned her attention to the menu. Each selection was written in French with the English translation below. Everything sounded wonderful.

"I'm starving," she admitted.

"Potato chips didn't do it for you?"

A waiter placed a silver basket filled with freshly baked bread and a small silver disk with sweet, creamy butter on the table.

"Dr. Pardieu would like this restaurant," she remarked.

Grayson's cell phone vibrated. He pulled it out of his pocket to see who was calling, then quickly got up from the table. "I'll be right back. I've got to take this."

He wasn't gone long. "I'm sorry, Olivia, but we have to leave. Henry's on his way to the emergency room to get stitches. It doesn't sound too bad," he rushed to add when the color left Olivia's face.

She didn't ask questions until they were in the car. "What happened to him?"

"He went to a birthday party at one of those indoor playgrounds. I guess he tried to do a somersault into some kind of ball pit and didn't quite make it. Ralph's father thinks Henry will need about six stitches in his forehead. Ralph is Henry's best friend, and he doesn't have a brain in his head either."

"Henry's a smart little boy."

"Yes, he is," he agreed. "But he also just turned nine, and at that age, *caution* isn't a word he's familiar with."

A few minutes later, they were walking into the emergency room lobby. Ralph and his father were in the waiting area. As soon as they saw Grayson, they hurried over.

"Henry's getting an X-ray to make sure he doesn't have a concussion. Who's this?" the father asked, thrusting his hand out to Olivia.

Grayson made the introductions. "Olivia, this is Dr. Ralph Jones."

The doctor wasn't letting go of Olivia's hand. Staring intently at her, he said, "I'm an ophthalmologist. A divorced ophthalmologist. Would you like to sit with Ralph Junior and me while Grayson checks on Henry?"

What the hell? Grayson thought. Ralph was hitting on her. Grayson put his arm around her shoulder and said, "She works for the IRS."

A pallor came over the doctor, but he quickly recovered. "Someone's got to, I suppose. Why don't you tell me all about your job?"

"She's coming with me," Grayson said. "Let go of her, Jones. You don't need to stay now that I'm here."

Olivia softened the harshness of his command. "I'd like to sit with Henry."

She noticed a nurse waving to her. It was Kathleen from the chemo ward. Olivia excused herself and went to say hello. "What are you doing in the ER?"

"They were short staffed, so I'm filling in," she said. "How are you doing, sweetie?"

"I'm good."

"Yes, you certainly are," she replied, looking past Olivia to Grayson. "That's one fine man you've got there."

Olivia agreed. Grayson was one fine man.

"Has Jane been admitted again?" Kathleen asked. She knew everything that went on inside the hospital, and she'd made it a point to keep up with all the Pips. "Is that why you're here?"

"No," Olivia answered, "not this time."

"Jane certainly has had a rough go of it," Kathleen said.

"She says she's doing better, but I don't believe her. Neither does Collins or Sam."

"Dr. Pardieu is back from his medical conference, and you know what a miracle worker he is. He'll sort it all out. Why are you here then?"

After Olivia quickly explained, Kathleen called radiology to see how much longer Henry would be. "He's on his way up now. Did you have a big evening planned? You're all dressed up."

"Dinner at Veronique's," she answered.

"Oh, that's fancy," Kathleen said. "I don't believe I've ever seen you with makeup on. You look lovely. Let's see what you're wearing."

Smiling, Olivia unbuttoned her coat and held it open. "Gorgeous," Kathleen raved. "The fabric is divine."

Grayson had finished the paperwork and came up behind Olivia. Kathleen introduced herself and asked, "Have you and Olivia been dating long?"

"We're not—" Olivia began. She'd seen the speculative look in Kathleen's eyes and thought she should explain that they weren't actually dating, that the evening was more of an obligation for Grayson because of the investigation.

Grayson cut her off. "For a while now," he said.

"Then you know Olivia's a hellion, don't you?" the nurse said, smiling. "She gave us such trouble when she was about your nephew's age. Made all of us love coming to work just to see what she'd do next."

"Kathleen's being polite," she said. "I was a holy terror back then."

Grayson leaned down and whispered, "Back then?"

"My break's over," Kathleen said. She hugged Olivia. "They'll put Henry back in bay four. It's the second curtain on your left. Why don't you wait in there?"

As soon as Kathleen hurried away, Olivia said, "I should stay out here. Have Ralph and Ralph left?"

"Yes," he replied. "But you're coming with me. Henry will be happy to see you. He asks about you all the time."

"He does?" she asked, smiling.

"Yeah, he does. I have to make up all sorts of terrible stories about you."

They walked to the curtained-off bay Kathleen had pointed out. Henry's shoes were on a chair in the corner with his coat. There was another chair on the opposite side of the bed.

"Why don't you sit here while I go see what's taking so long," Grayson said.

He was on his way to the elevators when the doors opened, and Henry was wheeled out by an orderly. The child had blood all over his face. There was a jagged cut that started at the top of his hairline above his right temple and ended at the tip of his eyebrow. He also had a bloody nose.

Grayson's breath caught when he saw all the blood, but he concealed his appalled reaction because Henry was watching him. "How are you doing, Henry?" he asked, his voice filled with sympathy.

The child was trying hard not to cry. "It hurts," he whispered as he was wheeled past. "Ralph said they're going to put a needle in my head. A big one," he added worriedly.

Henry spotted Olivia just as the orderly stopped the wheelchair. He was so happy to see her, he bolted out of the wheelchair and ran to her. She was getting up when he threw himself into her arms, nearly knocking her off her feet.

"Don't . . ." Grayson called. But it was too late. Henry had his arms around Olivia's waist, and his bloody face was pressed against her chest.

"I'm glad you came to see me," he said.

"You certainly have had more than your share of injuries lately, haven't you?" she said sympathetically. "Let's see what you've done to your face."

He stepped back and looked up at her. "The nurse cleaned it, but it started bleeding again."

"Does it hurt?"

He nodded. "A lot," he admitted. He noticed the front of Olivia's dress was covered in his blood, and he became teary eyed again. "I ruined your pretty dress."

Her smile was filled with tenderness. She brushed his hair out of his eyes and said, "That's okay. It's old."

Henry moved on to his major concern. "They're going to put a needle in my head."

Grayson stood there watching her as she listened to Henry's worries. She couldn't have cared less about the dress now. All she wanted to do was comfort the child.

Grayson's heart swelled with his love for her. He probably should tell her how he felt, he supposed, but he knew what would happen. She would panic and bolt. He understood how her mind worked now. She'd run, all right. She wouldn't get far, though, because he was determined to spend the rest of his life with her. Getting her to agree was going to be a challenge.

Grayson filed the problem away for another time and went to his nephew. He picked him up and placed him on the bed, then tilted his head to the side so he could get a better look at the damage.

"Did you break your nose?"

"No, he didn't, and he doesn't have a concussion." The emergency-room physician gave the news. "He just banged his head. The plastic surgeon on call is already here finishing up with another patient. I thought, because of where the cut is, a plastic surgeon should do the repair. He wants me to go ahead and numb the area and clean it."

A nurse placed a metal tray on the counter. Henry

spotted the needle and grabbed his uncle's arm. Grayson calmly assured him that the needle would take away the hurt, and as soon as the area was numbed, Henry relaxed. By the time the plastic surgeon arrived, Henry was laughing at a story Olivia had told him.

They didn't leave the hospital until after ten, and Henry was sound asleep in the back of Grayson's car before they pulled out of the hospital drive.

"Thank you," Grayson said to Olivia as he checked on his nephew in his rearview mirror. "Having you there made it easier on Henry."

"I'm just glad he's okay," she answered. "Henry's a great little boy."

"I'm really sorry about tonight," he continued. "The evening didn't exactly turn out the way I'd planned."

"There are more important things than dinner at a swanky restaurant," she said.

"We'll celebrate another time," he promised.

"You haven't told me about the gun," she reminded him. "Are you sure they've found the gun that shot me?"

"Yes, ballistics confirmed it. It's a match. No question."

"And?"

"Ray Martin's house. They found it inside Martin's house. No fingerprints, though. The weapon had been wiped clean."

"But the police had already gone through that house from top to bottom. How could they have missed anything? And how did they know to search again?"

"A guy called. He didn't give a name, just identified himself as a neighbor. He said his son and some of his friends had gone into the abandoned house and found it."

"So, it was Martin after all. A simple motive: revenge," she said. "I was sort of hoping Simmons had done it. He could have found out about Jorguson and Martin and planted the gun. I was hoping my father's sleazy partner would never see the light of day again."

"Your wish may come true anyway," he told her. "We picked him up at his D.C. office. He was just beginning to shred documents when we got there. We'll not only indict him for his part in your attempted kidnapping, but if we find what we think we'll find in those files, we'll be able to get him for his part in your father's Ponzi scheme as well. Unfortunately, he's already posted bail so he's free for now, but he's got a lot of prison time ahead of him."

"You didn't think it was Martin who shot me, did you?"

"No, I didn't," he admitted. "But finding the weapon . . ." The sentence trailed off, and he shook his head.

"Do you know what this means? With Martin locked up, the case is closed. My case anyway. No more bodyguards."

She was smiling until he reminded, "And all the death threats on your phone?"

"Oh." The burst of optimism was gone. How could she have forgotten the calls?

"That's right," he said. "The bodyguards stay."

"Maybe for a few more days," she conceded. "Surely, all the anger about my father will die down soon."

"It's going to take longer than a few days."

She knew he was right. "I'm paying the bodyguards."

"No, you're not."

She counted to ten. It didn't help. "I'm going to insist."

The set of his jaw told her he was going to be stubborn. "Insist all you want."

She decided to table the discussion since she wasn't winning. Besides, her asthma was kicking up. The cold night air had triggered the wheezing. She opened her purse and only then realized she didn't have her inhaler.

"Grayson . . ."

He reached into his coat pocket and pulled out an inhaler. "Here you go."

She used it and, without thinking, handed it back to him. It wasn't until he drove into his garage that she realized where he was taking her.

"You should have dropped me at my building. There's a guard right inside the door."

"I can't take you home yet. We haven't had dinner."

He parked the car and came around to open her door. "McDonald's is open," she said.

"I'm going to prepare a gourmet dinner for you."

"Really?"

"How do you feel about hot dogs?"

TWENTY-NINE

Olivia tried to say good night to Grayson at her door, but he was having none of it. He backed her into her apartment, kicked the door shut, and jerked her into his arms.

"I want you."

From gentleman to caveman, she thought. The transformation was extremely arousing. She tried to remember why she shouldn't go to bed with him. Oh yes, they needed to talk. "Grayson, I need to tell you—"

"Now. I want you now."

He didn't give her time to argue. He kissed her hard and then proceeded to tell her in the most graphic detail exactly how he was going to make love to her. By the time he finished, her legs had turned to Jell-O.

He was waiting for her permission. She wrapped her arms around his neck and spread her fingers up into his hair. "You do have a way with words," she whispered.

Just tonight, she promised herself. Just one more night. Then she would make him leave.

Their need for each other was fierce, and their love-making was wild. Grayson wasn't gentle, nor was she. Her lips were swollen from his kisses, and his shoulders wore scratches from her demanding touch. When Grayson finally summoned enough strength to move away from her, he was panting for breath, and his body was covered with a fine sheen of perspiration. Her scent mingled with his, clinging to the air around them.

"Oh my." Olivia sighed.

"Your voice is hoarse," Grayson told her.

"I might have screamed."

"Might have?" he asked, grinning. "You were ... demanding. I got a little rough, didn't I?"

"I got a little rough, too."

Now or never, he thought to himself. It may not be the best timing, but he was going for it regardless, while she was still recovering. He moved so quickly, she didn't have time to react. Pinning her to the bed, he said, "I have something to tell you." He cupped the sides of her face with his hands, holding her captive.

She looked wary. "Yes?"

"I love you."

Tears came into her eyes. "No. You can't love me. I should have—"

"I love you," he repeated firmly.

"Grayson . . ."

He kissed her forehead. "You love me, too."

She pushed against him. "That doesn't matter," she cried out.

"I sure as hell think it does."

He rolled onto his back and stared at the ceiling. She tried to get up, but he grabbed her hand and pulled her back down. She landed on top of him. Holding her prisoner with his arm wrapped around her, he forced her head down on his shoulder and said, "Calm down, sweetheart. It's going to be all right."

The irony in the situation wasn't lost on him. He was having to soothe her because he'd told her he loved her.

Olivia was desperately trying not to cry. "I let this go too far," she whispered against the side of his neck. "I shouldn't have. I knew better. I really did, but you're so irresistible, and I'm weak when I'm with you."

He decided to ignore her ramblings. "I want you in my bed every night," he said gruffly. "I want to wake up with you beside me."

"No, I can't . . ."

"I love you," he repeated. "Will you marry me?"

Her reaction wasn't what he would consider an encouraging one. She bolted upright and in a near shout said, "Oh God, no."

At the very least he should have been insulted. The appalled look on her face did smack at his ego. He didn't get upset, though, because he was pretty sure he knew what was going on inside that wonderful, but decidedly warped, mind of hers.

"Tell me you love me," he demanded. His hand moved to the nape of her neck, and he tugged on her hair, forcing her to look at him. "Tell me. I know you do. I want to hear you say the words."

"It won't matter," she said. A single tear escaped and slowly trailed down her cheek. "I don't understand why you want—"

"I just do," he snapped. "Tell me."

"I love you."

The tightness in his chest immediately eased. Although he already knew how she felt, he needed her to acknowledge it. The rest was up to him.

"I won't marry you, Grayson. I can't marry you. You need to move on without me."

"What about Collins and Jane and Samantha? Can they ever get married? Will they?"

"What do my friends have to do with this conversation?"

"Everything," he answered. "They have everything to do with this. And so does Dr. Andre Pardieu. Your friends were in the same experimental program under his supervision."

She couldn't look at him. She dropped down beside him. "Yes."

He began to stroke her back and could feel how tense she was. "Your aunt told me a little about that period in your life. You were in the hospital a long time, weren't you?" She refused to answer. He wasn't deterred. "I know your family didn't come to see you. You were all alone."

"I was glad of it," she blurted. "I saw what my friends' families went through. It was horrible for them. I can still see their faces, their anguish."

She remembered what Sam had once said after her family had visited. They'd all been crying, and Sam told her that maybe it would be better if she died because then they would be at peace.

"You think it's going to come back," he said very matter-of-factly. "And you don't want anyone you love to go through that agony. Right?"

She kept silent.

"Do your friends share your fatalistic attitude?"

"They're realists like I am."

"I see." His fingers gently trailed down her spine. "So you are willing to live your life waiting for death? What the hell, Olivia? Do you not see how crazy that is?"

She was suddenly furious. She pushed away from him and got out of bed.

"I don't care if you understand or not," she cried. She grabbed her silk robe and put it on. Her hands were shaking so, she could barely get the sash tied. "Fatalist? Ask Jane how she's feeling these days." She threaded her fingers through her hair in agitation. "Of the four of us, she's the most optimistic, but what good does that do? It's come back. I know it has, and oh God, poor Logan. He's only just become her brother again, and now he's going to go through hell. All those years he drank and used drugs, he was so horrible to her, and he's desperately trying to make up for the past, but it's too late. I don't know what will happen to him when she dies." Tears streamed down her face. "And Henry. What about him, Grayson? He's already lost his mother. Do you want him to watch me die?" She put her hands up. "I'm done talking about this."

Grayson wanted to go to her, to comfort her, but in her nearly hysterical state, he knew she'd fight him. He sat up, casually leaned against the headboard, and said, "Okay. My mistake. Never mind."

His blasé tone confused her. She took a step toward him. "Never mind what?"

"The proposal. Never mind. Forget I mentioned it."

"Oh."

"Come sit with me. I have a favor to ask."

She slowly walked over to the side of the bed. He put his hands on her hips and pulled her onto his lap. With a wary look in her eyes, she faced him with her hands on his shoulders.

"I want you to give Dr. Pardieu permission to talk to me," he said.

Her grip on his shoulders tightened. "Why? I thought you understood what I just said. Now that you have the right man locked up, my case is closed. You must move on."

"Yeah, right. I'm moving on," he agreed a bit quickly. "I still want to talk to the doctor, and he can't tell me anything unless you give permission."

"I don't know why you need—"

"You're going to do this, Olivia. First thing in the morning," he ordered, leaving no room for negotiation.

She glared at him.

"Are you going to call me a dumb ass?" he asked.

"No, but I'm thinking it," she muttered. "Why are you smiling?"

"Because we had our talk, and I understand. You aren't going to marry me, and you hope that I'll get on with my life . . . my life without you."

"Yes," she said defiantly. "When you leave here, that's exactly what I want you to do."

"Okay. You give Pardieu permission to talk to me about you, and after that conversation, you'll never see me again. That's my condition."

Never see him again. The thought made her sick.

"Yes, all right."

Grayson untied her belt and opened her robe, uncovering her beautiful breasts. She was so lovely. His fingers caressed her soft, flawless skin.

Olivia was confused. She didn't want him to stop touching her, and yet she wanted him to go.

"Everything will change when I leave here. I know that's what you want," he told her. He pushed the robe off her shoulders. "But I haven't left yet."

THIRTY

Grayson had been up half the night working at his computer. It was amazing how much confidential information was available when one had the right credentials and knew where to look.

Olivia had said that it would have been easy for Simmons to find out about her connection to Jorguson and Martin, and that was true. Her entire life was there with a push of a button, including the names of her employers. Simmons had obviously gained access to that information because he'd called them to try to discredit her.

Yes, it would have been easy for Simmons to plant the gun in Martin's house. Grayson considered the possibility while he showered and got dressed. It was Sunday morning, and he was getting ready to leave for the office. He knew Ronan was already there, catching up on his own reports.

In the kitchen, Henry was having breakfast with his grandfather and Patrick. The two men were getting a blow-by-blow of what had happened the night before. Grayson heard Henry boast that Olivia had come to the hospital and had insisted on holding his hand while he got stitches. He also mentioned once again that she was his very own attorney, which the men knew was his segue into the story of what had happened in the principal's office.

Grayson poured himself a glass of orange juice and pulled out a chair across from his nephew. "Has there been any change in plans?" he asked.

Henry nodded. "Grandfather is going to take Ralph and me to the movie, but Ralph has to go home after because"—he glanced at his grandfather before continuing—"because he can only take so much of Ralph."

"I get that," Patrick said, smiling.

Grayson nodded. Ralph was a little on the wild and loud side, but then, so was Henry. Together they sometimes sounded like a tornado.

"Henry, how would you feel about me marrying Olivia?" Grayson asked.

Henry's eyes clouded with worry. "Will you move away?"

"No, she would move in here with us."

"With me and Patrick?"

"Yes, and with me," he said.

"Will you have a wedding?"

"Yes."

He shook his head. "No, I don't want you to marry her." He bowed his head and stared at his cereal bowl.

"We know you like Olivia," his grandfather said. "You talk about her all the time."

Henry wouldn't look up. "I do like her. I just don't want Grayson to marry her."

"Tell us why," Patrick insisted. "We want to understand."

Henry glanced at his grandfather, received his encouraging nod, and turned to Grayson. "Because if you have a wedding, you have to ask my father, and he'll come back here and take me away."

Grayson was surprised by Henry's response. The child's anxiety was almost palpable. He shouldn't have such a worry, Grayson thought. He sat quietly while his father tried to calm the boy's fears. "We would never let that happen. Never."

Grayson explained that he had full custody, but that didn't make much difference to Henry.

It was Patrick who finally convinced him. "Don't you have your own attorney?"

Henry nodded. "You know I do. It's Olivia."

"Do you think she'll let your father take you away?"

Henry didn't have to think about it long. "No." He smiled then. He looked at Grayson and added, "If I tell her, she won't let you invite my father."

Grayson laughed. "I think you're right."

"Are congratulations in order?" his father asked. "You do know I've yet to meet this woman."

"You will," Grayson said. "And, no, congratulations aren't in order. She's being difficult."

"Do you want me to ask her?" Henry offered.

Patrick gave his opinion. "You might have a better chance with the kid."

It was the last time Grayson smiled the rest of the day. When he got to the office, he told Ronan about Olivia's hope regarding Simmons, and after tossing the football for a few minutes, the two decided on a plan of action.

"It can't hurt," Ronan said.

"Right. Just to be sure," Grayson replied.

For the next several hours, both he and Ronan caught up on their case files. It was late afternoon before Grayson finished his last report. He had just logged off his computer when his cell phone rang.

"Grayson Kincaid?" The voice had a thick French accent.

"Yes."

"This is Dr. Andre Pardieu. Olivia MacKenzie asked that I give you a call. She has authorized me to discuss her medical history and her prognosis with you. What would you like to know?"

"Thank you for calling, Doctor. I know you're a busy man, so I'll get right to the point. I'm in love with Olivia and I want to marry her, but she's a very stubborn woman."

Dr. Pardieu laughed. "Yes, I've known that for quite some time."

"Olivia is afraid to commit. She fears that her cancer will return. She sees her friend Jane so ill, and that has convinced her she can't make plans for the future. I don't know how I'm going to persuade her, but I figure if I got some assurance from you, I'd have a better chance."

"I can't discuss Jane's case specifically, but I can tell you that Olivia should not be concerned. I've been away from the hospital and haven't been able to give this latest development my full attention, but now that I'm back, I'm going to get to the bottom of it. Let me assure you, Olivia has not shown any symptoms of toxemia, so, from what I've seen, she has nothing to worry about."

"Thank you, Doctor," Grayson said.

"Good luck," Dr. Pardieu said. "Olivia deserves some happiness, and I hope she'll find it with you."

"Yes, sir. That's my plan," Grayson assured him before he ended the call.

Grayson sat back in his chair and thought about what the doctor had said. Something stuck in his mind. Toxemia was a general term for blood poisoning, wasn't it? He booted up his computer again. He began feeding in data, and that only created more questions. When he ended his search, he told Ronan what he had discovered. They knew whom they had to talk to and what information they needed to gather. By late afternoon, their questions had been answered, and he phoned Dr. Pardieu right away. If the doctor confirmed his suspicions—and

Grayson was certain he would—he needed to act immediately. Time was critical.

Olivia tried to keep busy so she wouldn't think about Grayson, but that was impossible. Sam called, and even with a horrible connection, she knew something was wrong. She heard it in Olivia's voice. The questions came, one after another, until Olivia was close to tears.

"I can't talk about him," Olivia said. "Tell me the story again, Sam. It will take my mind off my miserable life."

"No, you've heard that stupid—though amazingly incredible—story at least five times."

"More like twenty, but tell me again. It makes me laugh every time I hear it."

Sam's sigh was loud and clear even with the static. "There I was, minding my own business in seat twenty-eight A on flight—"

"Twenty-seven forty-three," Olivia supplied.

"The plane was packed, and it was noisy, but I'd blocked it all out because I was frantically studying for a final I had to take the next morning at zero eight hundred. The flight was making good time and I, along with everyone else, thought everything was just fine, when a flight attendant tapped me on the shoulder and asked me to come with her."

Olivia added the details she remembered. "You shoved your notebook into your flight bag and dragged it with you. You thought you were being upgraded to first class for some bizarre reason."

"Yes, that's what I thought. Clever deduction."

"You told me."

"Should I go on?" Sam asked.

"You want to, don't you?"

"Okay, yes," she said, her voice eager. "You and Collins and Jane are the only ones I can brag to. My brothers are so sick of hearing this story, they groan whenever I bring it up."

"I'm not groaning," Olivia assured her.

"It was a beautiful plane," she continued. "A jet, of course, with—"

"Don't get technical again. Suffice it to say it was pretty."

Sam laughed and continued, "It wasn't a jumbo jet, but it was still pretty, I suppose. Anyway, I followed the perky flight attendant past first class, noticing that all the seats were occupied. I started to get a bad feeling, but the flight attendant was smiling and acting like nothing was out of the ordinary. She said that she'd heard me tell another passenger that I'd gone through the Air Force Academy. I hadn't said anything to any of the passengers, and I was about to correct her when she said in a rather loud voice that the captain had also gone through the academy and wanted to say hello. That didn't make any sense, and she could tell I was going to argue. She knew the cockpit door was locked while the flight—"

"I know. Don't cite regulations. Get to the good part."

"The attendant whispered 'please,' then tapped on the door—that crazy smile on her face all the while—and the door opened, and she pushed me inside. And I mean pushed me," she reiterated.

"You don't have to go into a long description of this part," Olivia pleaded.

"Oh, I want to. The whole crew was throwing up into these plastic bags, and it began to dawn on me: they must have gone through their passenger list looking for a pilot. It smelled so vile in the cockpit, the attendant gagged. I didn't, of course. I grew up with such gross brothers. That, plus going through chemo . . . nothing really gets to me.

"Anyway, their complexions were lime green and they were throwing up what looked like chunks of bile."

"Oh God, Sam. Don't be so . . . visual."

Sam laughed. "I naturally thought the worst, that they had been poisoned, but the captain told me they had just been on a flight where several passengers became quite ill. It took two of us to get the copilot out of his seat and move him. You know the rest."

"Oh no, you have to tell it."

"In the midst of dry heaving, the captain gave me instructions. As you know, I've flown just about everything with wings," she boasted. "This plane wasn't a challenge. I told him to relax; I'd take over. The attendant came back in with a napkin over her mouth and nose because of the awful smell that I'd kind of gotten used to, and she told me some of the passengers knew something was wrong and were getting nervous. The captain flipped on the intercom to calm them down. He still thought he was going to land the plane."

"But you didn't know the intercom was left on," Olivia interjected.

"No, of course I didn't. I wouldn't have argued with the captain if I'd known passengers were listening, and he was so sick, he forgot. He looked like he was going to pass out any second. I told him to relax, that I could handle it, and I began to familiarize myself with the control panel and do a couple of maneuvers to get the feel of the plane.

"The poor captain's eyes kept closing, and he was struggling to stay conscious. He said that, on final approach to the runway, I must instruct the passengers to get into a crash position. I tried not to take insult, and I asked him why would I want to do that, and we got into a bit of an argument."

Olivia laughed. "A bit of an argument? I heard the recording. It was more than a bit."

"Can you believe passengers recorded the conversation? You can't do anything these days without someone documenting it. I swear, our privacy—"

"You're getting off track, Sam," Olivia reminded.

"Yes, okay. So even though I tried not to take insult, I was insulted. I mean, how could I not be? I tried to explain my position, and I listed all the different planes I'd flown, and I ended my litany by saying that I am a pilot in the United States Air Force, and I have been trained by the finest. Air Force fighter pilots don't crash planes. I also told him I could understand his reticence if I were a crop duster or even a Navy pilot, but come on . . . I'm Air Force. Didn't he realize how superior we are?"

"You also said—and I'm quoting—'We are the best pilots in the world.'"

"We are," she countered, and Olivia could picture her friend shrugging. "So I might have said something like that. Yes, it was ego, but the passengers calmed down. At least, that's what the attendant told me. She also said there were three passengers in the back of the cabin throwing up. Whatever that virus was, it was quick and powerful."

"But you did instruct all of them to get into crash position?"

"Only because the captain insisted."

"Tell me what you said, your exact words."

"Don't make me. It was all over the news."

"Tell me."

"I just explained that the captain and the copilot were under the weather and that I would be landing the plane. I also said that, even though I personally did not believe it was necessary, they all should get into crash position, and I only hoped they were as insulted as I was."

"And?"

"And on approach I saw all the fire trucks and the

ambulances, and I might have said something to the tower about getting them the hell off my runway."

"Might have."

"I also told the passengers that the landing would be the smoothest they'd ever experienced. It was, too," she asserted. "Not a single bump."

"That's what I heard on the news," Olivia said.

"The tower thought we should use the chute, but I got them to let us park at the gate because it would be much easier to get all of the sick off the plane that way. Once we opened the door, I got out of the way so the paramedics could get into the cockpit. I waited a long time in the galley while all the passengers filed off, but then I saw what time it was, and I knew my ride was waiting for me at baggage claim. I put on my baseball cap and my jacket, grabbed my flight bag, and headed into the terminal. I was relieved no one stopped me because I had to get back to base before curfew."

"You just left."

"You know I did. I had to," she explained. "Randy was driving three of us back. He'd already picked up the others, and I didn't want them to be late, too."

She sighed before she continued. "I had this stupid hope it would blow over. You know, no big deal, right? Unfortunately, it was all over the news. I got back in plenty of time, and after I dropped my bag in my room, I went to report to my commander. That was mortifying. He was in a bar with some other officers—a sports bar—and there were jumbo screens all over the place. I asked him for a moment alone and quickly explained what had happened. I also told him I thought the newsmen would try to get on base, and if they wanted any interviews, I was going to assume he'd handle them. He didn't like me dumping it in his lap, but I argued I had an exam the next morning, and I needed to concentrate on that. The com-

mander is never in a good mood, but he was that evening, and it was only later that I found out why. He'd
heard what I'd said about being superior to the Navy. He
liked that."

"Ego," Olivia said. "All of you pilots have major egos."
Olivia heard a beep on the line, indicating there was a
call waiting. "I've got to go," she said after she looked at
the screen.

"Wait. Don't you want to hear about the press conference? It was really hilarious."

"I'm sure it was," she agreed. "Sorry. I can't hear more.
Jane's beeping in."

"E-mail me after you talk to her," Sam said, "and tell
her I'll call her this week."

Olivia said good-bye and switched to Jane's call. Her
friend was phoning to invite Olivia to dinner. She insisted that she come because Logan was making a special roast with fresh herbs. Although Olivia really didn't
want to go out—the weather had turned nasty and it was
beginning to sleet—she did want to see Jane and make
sure she was all right. She would pretend that everything
was fine, but Olivia would know the truth as soon as she
looked at her face. She told Jane she'd be there in an
hour.

The nasty phone calls about her father had subsided—there were only two that morning—and, at Olivia's insistence, Grayson had canceled the guard at her
door as long as she promised to call one of them if she
chose to leave. Since Jane lived just a short distance
away, Olivia decided she'd be safe if she took extra pre-
cautions. John, the doorman, kept her informed about
the number of reporters trying to get in the building to
interview her. He had warned her that some of them sat
in their cars, waiting, so, before leaving her apartment,
she called down to John. The sleet was working to her

advantage, he told her. There weren't any cars on the street tonight.

John escorted her to her car in the parking garage and watched her pull out onto the street. Olivia drove around in circles until she was convinced she wasn't being followed, then headed over to Dupont Circle where Jane lived.

Jane's three-story town house was quite small, but there was an art studio on the top floor. The converted attic was the reason Jane had purchased the space because the light coming in through the windows was perfect for her work.

Logan opened the door. He looked surprised to see her.

"Jane didn't tell you she invited me?" Olivia asked.

Logan stepped back to let her inside. "I'm sure she did. I just forgot. Don't worry. There's plenty of roast."

Olivia followed him into the living room. The room was dark except for the glow from the fire he'd started in the hearth. He switched on a lamp, and she could see how haggard he looked.

"Jane's upstairs resting," he said. "I'll go get her."

"How is she doing?"

"Not good," he replied. He was looking everywhere but at her. "I'm scared," he said.

"Let her rest awhile longer," Olivia said. She nodded toward the kitchen. "Something smells wonderful. Can I help?"

He smiled. "Thanks, but I've got it under control."

"Then don't let me keep you. I'll occupy myself until Jane comes down." She pointed to a stack of magazines on the coffee table. "I can do some reading."

As soon as Logan went into the kitchen, Olivia picked up the magazine on top of the pile and sat down on the sofa. She flipped through the pages. Nothing caught her attention, so she placed it back on the table. She then spotted a laptop sitting on the floor next to an easy chair. She hadn't read the newspaper, and she thought she'd pull up the *Times* and catch up on the latest happenings. She knew Jane wouldn't mind if she used her computer for a few minutes.

Olivia reached for the computer and lifted the lid. The dark screen came to life, and an open page appeared. The title at the top caught her attention: "The Pathological Effects of Arsenic Ingestion." What an odd subject to be reading about, Olivia thought. She hit the key to return to the previous page, and then the page before that. It didn't take long for her to realize she wasn't holding Jane's computer at all. It was Logan's.

Logan's voice called from the kitchen. "When do you give her blood again, Olivia?"

Olivia quickly closed the computer and placed it on the floor where she'd found it.

"I'm not sure," she answered.

Logan walked into the living room, drying his hands on a dish towel. He glanced at the stairs, making sure Jane wasn't there, and lowered his voice. "She's talking crazy. She won't tell you, but she's in a lot of pain." He walked closer and in a whisper said, "I think she might kill herself. That's how depressed she is."

Olivia moved to the side so that Logan would turn his head toward the light and she could see his eyes more clearly. She took a step back. She was so rattled, she couldn't think what to say. Her hand went to her throat. "Oh God," she gasped. His pupils were dilated as big as saucers.

Logan patted her shoulder. "I've moved into the guest room so I can watch her. It will actually work out for the best. My meetings are a few blocks away, and I can go more often. Next to Jane, of course, my sobriety is the most important thing to me."

"Good," she said, trying to stay calm. "And you've been cooking for her so she'll keep her strength. You're doing everything you can."

"I'll go get Jane. Please don't tell her what I said. It will only upset her, and she won't confide in me anymore."

"Of course," she agreed.

He stopped at the bottom of the stairs. "Do you mind if we eat right away? I've got a meeting to get to. They help me stay sober," he explained.

"I don't mind. I'm hungry."

She wanted to call Grayson, but by the time she dug her cell phone out of her purse, Jane and Logan were joining her.

"Go sit at the table," Logan told his sister. "The roast will dry up if I don't get it out of the oven. I'll go ahead and scoop it out on the plates." He disappeared into the kitchen.

"Have you talked to Grayson today?" Jane asked.

"I'm going to call him now," Olivia answered.

Jane smiled. "Good."

Olivia wanted to cry. Jane looked like hell, and she'd lost so much weight. She waited until her friend took a seat at the table, then walked into the living room and called Grayson. He answered on the second ring. His greeting wasn't polite.

"Where the hell are you? I just left your apartment. You were supposed to—"

"I'm at Jane's, Grayson," she said. "Logan's here." She was just about to tell him about her suspicions, but Logan came into the living room. She quickly said, "Grayson, I'll call you back. It shouldn't be long, Grayson." She ended the call quickly. Logan was standing there, listening. Plastering a smile on her face, she went to join her dearest friend and her psychopath brother.

The plates were already on the table. Logan had prepared them, and they all looked the same, except for one thing. Olivia noticed that Jane's plate had a sprig of parsley on the side. Logan's didn't, and neither did hers.

She went to Jane, kissed her on the cheek, and hugged her. She took her place at one end of the table. Logan took the other.

"Logan, do you have any pepper?" she asked.

"Sure. I'll get it for you."

The second he disappeared into the kitchen, Olivia grabbed Jane's plate and switched it with Logan's. She switched the parsley, too.

"What are you doing?" Jane asked.

Olivia put her finger to her lips, a sign to keep silent. Jane nodded but continued to frown.

"What's this orange stuff?" Olivia asked Logan when he returned.

"Mashed sweet potatoes. Jane loves them. Some nights, that's all she eats."

Logan ate his dinner quickly. "I don't want to be late for the meeting," he explained.

Olivia moved the food around on her plate, but didn't eat any of it.

"Not hungry?" Logan asked.

"I thought I was, but I guess I'm not feeling very well. Grayson and I had a fight," she explained.

Olivia didn't know how much longer she could keep silent. Jane was repeating a story Collins had told her, and Olivia noticed she had eaten every bit of the mashed sweet potatoes, and so had Logan.

She dragged dinner out as long as she could, telling two stories about Jane, praying that Grayson would get there soon. She hoped she'd said his name enough times for him to figure out that she was in trouble. Jane's home wasn't far from Olivia's apartment. She had just finished her second story and was frantically trying to think of a third when Jane said, "Okay, Olivia, dinner's over. Tell me why."

"Why what?"

"Why you switched my plate with my brother's."

If Olivia had any doubts, they were all erased in that second. Logan leapt to his feet, overturning his chair.

"You what?" he screamed.

Jane looked thunderstruck by his behavior. "What's going on?"

Olivia kept her attention on Logan. Oh, this was going to be bad, she thought . . . really bad . . . for she could see the rage coming over him.

"Olivia?" Jane asked.

"Logan's been poisoning you."

"That's absolutely ridiculous," he roared. "Why would you tell such a lie?"

"Your eyes are dilated, which tells me you're using again," she began. "You have a very interesting Web site on your computer, all about arsenic."

"Oh my God . . ." Jane whispered.

"He told me he was worried you would kill yourself, Jane. Laying the groundwork, I suppose. I guess you were taking too long to die."

"Shut up," Logan shouted.

Olivia continued to address Jane. "That's why you've been so sick. He's been giving you the poison, and he's been clever about it. He makes sure it's no longer in your blood by the time you go to the hospital. I'm guessing he's been giving it to you for a long time. After a few days, arsenic doesn't show up in the blood, but it's everywhere else. Now that we know what to look for, we'll have all the proof we need."

Logan was frantically trying to search for a way out. He grasped his head in his hands. "I can't think," he muttered.

"That's because you're high," Olivia pointed out. "You can't lie as well when you're drugged, can you?"

"You're crazy. You can't prove anything." His agitation was beginning to take over.

"Yes, I can," she said. "You're not as clever as you think."

He turned to his sister. He couldn't seem to control the twitch in his neck that had suddenly appeared. "That's my money sitting in your account. Mother meant it for me, but you convinced her to leave it all to you. I want what's rightfully mine."

"You wouldn't have gotten away with it," Olivia said. "An autopsy would have shown the poison."

"I'm smarter than you think," he boasted. "The arsenic was just supposed to weaken her a little. I figured the cancer or something else would kill her, but she wasn't sick enough, so I decided to speed things up. Since she's been feeling so ill, no one would blame her for wanting to end it all with a bottle of sleeping pills."

Olivia went to Jane and put her hand on her shoulder to keep her in her chair. When she looked up, Grayson was standing in the doorway, his gun trained on Jane's brother. He didn't make a sound. She knew he wanted her to move away from Logan, but she was afraid to leave Jane's side.

"You think that's clever, Logan?" she taunted. She wanted him to continue to look at her until Grayson grabbed him. "I don't believe you've ever done anything clever in your life. You're too stupid." She could tell he was losing control. She could see it in his eyes.

Logan lunged for her and grabbed her around the neck, choking her. Grayson moved like lightning and tore him off her.

"What the hell, Olivia," he shouted as he slammed Logan against the wall. "Why didn't you move away from him?"

She coughed the words, "I should have." She rubbed her neck and said, "I wanted him to keep talking."

She looked at Jane, who appeared to be so stunned she couldn't move. Olivia took her hand and pulled her to her feet. She put her arm around her friend's shoulders and said, "Come on. You're going to the hospital."

THIRTY-ONE

It was almost nine before Olivia arrived home from the hospital. Grayson had followed her in his car and waited until they were inside her apartment to give her hell again.

"If he had a knife . . ."

"He didn't."

"If he . . ."

She went into the kitchen to get something to drink. "You had your gun on him. What could he do?" Too late, she realized it was a dumb question.

"How about use you as a shield? He could have snapped your neck. He could have—"

"But he didn't."

Ronan arrived, interrupting the lecture Olivia knew Grayson was about to launch into.

Olivia told him to help himself to whatever he wanted to eat or drink. He grabbed a Coke and sat facing her.

Grayson wanted to pace. "Should have checked sooner," he told Ronan. "When Olivia mentioned that Logan was an addict, I should have checked to make sure he was still clean . . . do my damned job. I wasn't paying attention. She could have been killed."

"Jane's going to be okay," Olivia reassured.

Ronan smiled. "He was talking about *you*."

"Oh."

"Nothing more impulsive than a devout cokehead," Ronan remarked. "Where is Logan now?"

"He was taken to the hospital to have his stomach pumped and then to jail," Grayson answered. He shook his head. "Everything that came out of that bastard's mouth was a lie. He didn't live in a halfway house, and he only worked for the car rental agency a couple of months." He came around the sofa as he said, "And he sure as hell didn't go to any meetings. I'll bet he was getting high every night."

Olivia turned to Grayson. "Did you know he was poisoning Jane?"

"Once I found out everything out of his mouth was a lie, I called Dr. Pardieu and told him my suspicions. He confirmed that it all added up. I told him we'd bring Jane in. I wanted to make sure you were safe, and I'd stopped to warn you when I got your call."

"We went to Logan's apartment," Ronan said. "It was a real dump. We found the arsenic there."

"The poison only stays in the blood a couple of days," Grayson said. "Logan timed it so that when she went back into the hospital, it wouldn't show up. He was giving her small doses, just enough to weaken her. I think he was hoping it would make her cancer come back."

The doorbell rang, and he went to answer it. A lovely blond, blue-eyed young woman with a bewitching smile was standing there, waiting for him to let her in.

"Collins," he said.

Her smile widened. "Grayson."

Introductions over, she rushed past him. She was yelling before she reached Olivia. "I told you Logan was a sleazebag. Didn't I tell you?"

"You might have mentioned—"

"If I had a gun . . ."

"Don't finish that," Olivia blurted. "There are two FBI agents here."

Collins whirled around. "Two?"

Ronan was standing right behind her. They stared at each other for several seconds, neither saying a word. Olivia watched, fascinated. She could almost see the electricity flowing between them.

Grayson introduced them. Collins smiled up at Ronan, then turned around and continued her rant.

"I called Sam and told her. She didn't believe Logan had changed either." Hands on hips, she faced Grayson. "How did you finally figure it out?"

Olivia groaned. Collins had inadvertently gotten him worked up again. He went through the process, and by the time he was finished, he was furious once more.

"Don't ask any more questions, Collins," she pleaded.

"Just one," she countered. "How did you find his apartment?"

"He put his address on the application at the rental agency."

Ronan was having trouble paying attention to the conversation. He couldn't seem to make himself stop staring at Collins.

"I'm getting a Popsicle. Want one?" she asked Olivia.

"Sure. Grape."

Five minutes later, Grayson and Ronan stood side by side watching the two women.

"Why do you like Popsicles?" Ronan asked.

"We got hooked on them when we were going through chemo," Collins answered matter-of-factly. "The cold soothed the blisters in our mouths."

Both women put the Popsicles in their mouths at the same time. Grayson moaned, "Ah, come on."

Olivia knew what he was thinking. Her tongue swirled

around the tip of the Popsicle, her gaze locked on his. "Want some?" she innocently asked.

"Jeez," Ronan muttered.

"I've got to get out of here," Grayson said, glaring at Olivia.

Ronan gave him an understanding slap on the back. "I'm right behind you."

THIRTY-TWO

Ray Martin was sitting in jail, charged with the attempted murder of Olivia MacKenzie. Grayson and Ronan still weren't convinced they had the right man. They needed to be sure.

They brought Carl Simmons's alibi in for another interrogation. Her name was Vicky Hyde Clark, and she was a paid escort. Simmons was one of her best clients. He always overpaid her for her services, and he didn't mind being seen in public with her. She considered him a good friend.

Vicky was tall, thin, and wore a dress that was a little too tight. She wasn't pretty, by any means, and there was a hardness about her and a look that suggested she'd been through a couple of wars.

She sat at a table across from Ronan, who had a file open in front of him. Grayson leaned against the wall behind the agent and stared at Vicky. He had yet to say a word to her.

He was an expert at intimidation, and he knew he was scaring her, all without moving a muscle or uttering a sound.

"I've told you everything I know," Vicky whined. "Carl's one of my dearest friends ... He used to be, anyway, but now that he's going to prison for all that fraud business, I don't see how I can help you. I understand . . . Carl's innocent until proven guilty in a court of law, but we all know . . ." She took a breath and said, "I told you the truth. Carl was with me that night you asked about . . . you know, when that girl got shot. Carl was in my bed all night."

She kept nervously glancing at Grayson, then back to Ronan. "I don't know what you want from me," she cried. "I haven't done anything wrong."

"Just a couple of questions, Vicky. Then it will be over and we'll take you to lockup," Ronan said smoothly.

"What's this?" she gasped. "Lockup? Why?"

Grayson finally spoke. "You lied to us."

"No, I . . ." She couldn't hold his stare.

"Like I said, Vicky, just a few questions and we'll be done," Ronan repeated. "Where did the ten thousand dollars come from? You made a five-thousand-dollar deposit in your savings account and a five-thousand-dollar deposit in your checking account. You made those deposits on the same day, exactly one week after Olivia MacKenzie was shot."

She was so rattled she had to think about the question a minute before blurting, "It was money I saved."

"That's another lie," Ronan said. He tried to sound disappointed.

"I don't know what you're talking about. I really don't."

Ronan's voice hardened. "We traced it, Vicky. The money came from Carl Simmons's account."

"No, no, it didn't. I saved all that money."

"Carl withdrew that precise amount," he said. He didn't have proof that Carl had done any such thing, but he was going to see if Vicky would take the bait. "And you deposited that amount. There's only one conclusion we can draw. Carl gave you the money. So now I have to ask, why? Could it be for the alibi you gave him?"

She hadn't asked for an attorney, so Ronan kept at her, question after question, trying to wear her down.

Grayson spoke again. "You're going to prison for a long time if you lie to us. You're as much responsible for shooting Olivia MacKenzie as Carl is."

"No. Why would you think—"

"You're lying for him to give him an alibi, so you're in it with him," Ronan said. He slapped his hand down on the table, and the sound reverberated around the small room. Vicky jumped.

"Tell her about the proof we have that she's lying," Grayson told Ronan. "The other proof."

What the hell? Ronan had no idea what Grayson was talking about, but he nodded and said, "I will. I'm getting to it."

"There's more proof?" Vicky was scared and unsure now.

"I don't understand," Ronan said, shaking his head. "Carl's going to go to prison for his other crimes. Why are you protecting him? You certainly don't have to worry about giving the money back to him."

Grayson knew they were going to have to let her go. Aside from the fact that Vicky had deposited ten thousand dollars, everything they claimed to know about her was fabricated. He wasn't through messing with Ronan, though. "Go ahead, Agent Conrad. Tell her about the other proof."

Ronan was going to have to come up with something, and Grayson couldn't wait to hear what he would say. He knew his friend's mind was scrambling.

Vicky panicked. "I want a deal."

"You what?" Ronan asked. He'd also been thinking they were going to have to cut her loose.

Grayson stepped forward and leaned on the table. "What kind of deal?"

"I'll tell you what really happened, and you don't put me in lockup. You let me go for good. No charges . . . ever."

They nodded, but before they spoke their agreement or disagreement, she blurted, "Yes, I lied. He made me. He was with me that night, but only for a little while. He left early. He seemed to be in a real hurry."

"Did you see what he was driving?" Grayson asked.

"I did. I'd never seen it before, so I asked him about it. It was a brand-new SUV. One of those big fancy ones. He said it belonged to the fleet that they used whenever lawyers from other branches were in town."

"What color?" Ronan asked.

"Black. Real shiny black."

Grayson walked out into the hall. Ronan followed him. "A black SUV doesn't prove anything."

"Unless we can show where it's been," Grayson said, and then added, "GPS."

Ronan smiled. "Of course. Simmons spends most of his time in New York. He can't be that familiar with D.C. He might have needed directions to Olivia's apartment."

"Or maybe even Martin's house to plant a gun. If he programmed an address into the GPS, there would be a record."

"It's worth a shot."

"Let's go find that SUV."

Carl Simmons's misery started and ended with Olivia MacKenzie. She had set out to destroy her father and him, and she had succeeded. He'd tried, but he hadn't been able to shut her up or stop her relentless quest.

Carl had estimated he had at least another good year to draw more and more rich investors into the Trinity Fund. He'd tucked away a little bit in foreign banks, but he simply hadn't had enough time to hide what he'd need to live on. It was too late now. He had to figure out a way to get out of the country.

He'd made sure there weren't any papers to prove he was a silent partner in the fund. Nothing in writing to damn him. That was only slowing the Feds down, though. Eventually they'd have enough to fry him.

Yes, it started and ended with her. He'd tried to stop the woman by threatening her, but she didn't scare that easily, so he took it to the next step and went to her employers to discredit her. That didn't work either. Killing her seemed the most logical solution.

Kline needed money and agreed to do it, but he backed out at the last minute. Simmons decided that he would have to pull the trigger himself. Three bullets and he still couldn't get rid of her.

He felt confident he'd covered his tracks pretty well, but then finding out about Ray Martin was a lucky break. His arrest was covered in all the papers, so Carl took advantage of his good fortune and decided to hide his gun at Martin's house. Simple as could be. Martin would go down, and maybe Olivia would be so shaken she'd worry about the shooting and back off her persistent prying. He actually thought it was a possibility—that is, until she started messing with Robert's deal with Jeff Wilcox. She brought in the lawyer, Mitchell Kaplan, and Carl knew that pit bull wouldn't stop until their whole operation was exposed.

All they'd needed was a little time, a few days for them to clean out their accounts and hide what was left of the money before they took off and disappeared, but when he learned about her visit to Jeff Wilcox, he could almost hear the clock ticking down the minutes before he and Robert MacKenzie were destroyed. Carl should have killed Olivia then, but he had to act quickly, so he'd tried to use the mental illness ploy to get her hauled away to an institution for a few days. He never should have trusted those idiots, Kline and Vogel. They screwed up everything, and if he'd just been a little quicker, he would have gotten away before the Feds showed up.

Carl refused to be defeated. They may have arrested him, but he was smart enough to convince the judge to release him on bail. Obviously they'd underestimated him. He had a plan. He was going to leave in the middle of the night, drive one of the fleet cars that wouldn't be recognized, and hightail it to Miami. He had connections there, people who could get him out of the United States.

Everything was in place. He was all set to leave that night, but then he got the phone call that changed everything. An inside source, an attorney who had a contentious relationship with the FBI and who owed Simmons a favor, called to let him know his bail was going to be revoked. The Feds were on their way to his house to take him in. He was being charged with attempted murder. The source told him about the evidence. The GPS had damned him, and Carl knew there wasn't any way out of this now. Even if he tried, he couldn't get away.

When he'd been arrested for his white-collar crimes, he hadn't panicked. Even if he didn't make it out of the country, at the very worst, he'd be sent to a minimum-security prison, or as the media liked to call these facilities, a country club. Now that he was going down for attempted murder, minimum security was off the table. The judge would put him in a hard-core federal prison, and Carl knew he couldn't handle that. Just thinking about it terrified him.

He'd rather die.

The more he thought about it, the more sense it made. He would die. It would be quick and over. No long years of terror in prison. He'd go out on his own terms. And he wouldn't go alone. Yes, he'd take her with him. It was fitting, wasn't it? She'd caused all this pain in his life. She had been his ruination. Now he would be hers.

He already had the fleet car waiting, a dark blue Honda. It was parked on a street a couple of blocks away. He'd removed the license plate and swapped it with one he found on another Honda in a parking lot.

He had to act fast. Once the Feds discovered he wasn't at his small D.C. apartment, they'd put out a search for him. He knew he couldn't evade them long. He took the gun he kept in his safe and hurried down the street to the waiting car. He drove to Olivia's apartment building, pulled into the garage across the street, and waited. Darkness was descending. It was Saturday, and he hoped she'd go out. He'd follow her and ambush her. It wasn't much of a plan, but he hadn't had time to figure out something more elaborate.

There were other cars parked on the street across from the entrance to her building. People were sitting inside them. Newspeople, he knew, waiting for a chance to talk to her about her father. He might just get lucky and shoot a couple of them, as well. They certainly hadn't been kind to him. Why should he care about them?

Carl decided he'd have a better vantage if he joined the other vans and cars. An Acura left, and he pulled into its slot behind a white van. It was a great spot. A red SUV honked at him because he'd gotten to the space first. Like the other vans and SUVs and sedans, he kept his motor running. Slinking down in his seat, he waited. Condensation quickly covered the windshield and windows, making it difficult for anyone walking by to see inside.

Carl had brought a flask of whiskey with him. He took a long swallow and felt the liquid burn his insides. The whiskey gave him courage. Before he killed himself, he hoped he could watch Olivia die. He smiled thinking about it and took another swig. It would all be over soon.

Grayson paced in Olivia's apartment while he waited to hear that Simmons had been picked up. Agents were on their way to Simmons's apartment now, and it shouldn't be much longer before Grayson got the call that the bastard was in handcuffs. Only when Simmons was in lockup would Grayson stop worrying.

Olivia was getting ready to go out. Grayson was taking her to a dinner party honoring Dr. Pardieu.

She had taken the news about Carl Simmons well and admitted she was actually more relieved than surprised.

"The GPS was his big mistake. He left a clear record that he'd driven to Martin's house to plant the gun," Grayson told her. "Are you happy now that you know it was indeed Simmons who tried to kill you?" he asked.

She laughed. "Happy? This will put him away forever, so yes, I guess I am."

Grayson had told her that as soon as Simmons was picked up they could leave.

The bedroom door opened, and there she stood. She wore a black dress with a V-neck that showed just enough cleavage to make Grayson nuts.

"You look beautiful," he told her as he pulled her into his arms and kissed the side of her neck. "Every time I get near you, I want to take you to bed."

She felt the same way. She kissed him on his cheek and pulled away. "We're going to be late if we don't leave now. It's a thirty-minute drive to the restaurant."

"I haven't heard about Simmons yet. We're going to wait—"

"Couldn't we get in the car and start driving?"

"Olivia . . ."

The warning in his voice didn't deter her. "If we get to the restaurant and Simmons still hasn't been taken into custody, we'll turn around and come back. I don't want to wait here, then drive like crazy to get there before it's over. It's Dr. Pardieu," she said. "I can't miss it. He's like a father to me."

He relented. "Okay, we'll leave now, but you have to promise you'll stay in the car and not balk if we have to turn around."

She smiled. "I'm not sure about the balking, Grayson. I'll stay in the car, but I feel I'm entitled to a little balking."

He helped her with her coat, kissed her neck again, and buttoned his suit jacket. "Ready to walk the gauntlet?"

"How many reporters did you see?"

"Three vans, a couple of SUVs. They'll try to swarm as soon as you step outside. Keep your head down," he told her. "I'll get you out of here as fast as I can."

"You should park in the garage from now on," she suggested.

"They're down there, too," he replied. "More than are on the street. When we get back, I'll talk to the doorman about sweeping the garage."

He pulled up her collar as the elevator door opened in the lobby. "Ready?"

She nodded. Grayson took her hand and strode past John. She waved to him as she was being pulled through the door.

A door opened on every car that was parked across the street, and cameramen and reporters came running. Grayson noticed a blue Honda opposite the apartment entrance. It hadn't been there when he'd arrived. The sedan was squeezed in between two vans. As Grayson hurried Olivia around his car to get to the passenger side, out of the corner of his eye he saw the door of the Honda open and Carl Simmons step out into the street.

Olivia was blinded by camera lights. She put her hand up to shield her eyes, unaware of the danger.

Simmons swung his right arm up, and Grayson saw the glint of steel. He moved so quickly, Olivia didn't have time to brace herself or react. He threw her behind him, and she fell to her knees before he flattened her with his body. In one fluid motion, he covered her and trained his gun on Simmons.

He shouted to the reporters, "Get down, get down . . ."

"What—" was all that Olivia could utter. Grayson had knocked the wind out of her. Gunshots stopped her from asking questions. She squeezed her eyes shut and prayed Grayson wouldn't get hit. Protecting her, he'd made himself a target.

Camera lights illuminated the scene that was unfolding. Simmons ran toward them, shooting again and again, trying desperately to get Olivia. Grayson fired only one shot. That was all he needed. The bullet sliced into Simmons's black heart. His arms flailed, his legs buckled, and he crashed spread-eagle to the ground, face-first.

The noise was ear-piercing. People were screaming and running every which way. Olivia's heart pounded in her chest, and she couldn't catch her breath. Grayson lifted her, checking to make certain she hadn't been hit by one of Simmons's bullets. Her dress was ripped all the way up to the top of her thigh, her elbow was scraped, and she was shaking from head to toe.

Grayson's eyes showed fear mixed with his rage. "Are you all right? Did he—"

"I'm okay," she whispered, surprised by how weak her voice sounded. "What happened?"

"Carl Simmons."

Stunned, she asked, "He's here?"

"He's dead. Can you walk? I want you to get inside. Tell John to lock the door. Don't talk to anyone. Just sit and wait for me. I need to get to Simmons's gun—"

"Go," she said.

John held the door for her, blocking two eager reporters from entering. He bolted the door behind her and led her to the security room behind the desk. "No one will bother you here, and you can watch the street, see what Agent Kincaid is doing."

Grayson ran across the street. Pushing reporters out of his way, he knelt beside Carl to check for a pulse while he called it in.

Others had called 911 already. Within bare minutes, police and agents filled the street. Olivia waited patiently, but her chest was getting tight, and she knew she was going to be in trouble if she didn't use her inhaler. She then realized she didn't have her purse. She must have dropped it when Grayson pushed her. John found it under the car and brought it to her, and once she'd used her inhaler, she felt immediate relief. She put her head back, closed her eyes, and tried to calm her racing heartbeat.

She thought about Grayson and how calm he'd been while that maniac was shooting at them. He was completely in control, until it was over. Then his composure turned into fury that Simmons had tried to hurt her. He had put his life on the line to save hers, she realized, and her eyes filled with tears at the thought of what could have happened to him.

Knowing it would be some time before Grayson was finished, she went back upstairs. She stripped out of her clothes, washed her hands, and cleaned the cut on her elbow. She slipped into her silk robe and curled up on the sofa to wait for him.

He arrived a half hour later and found her standing at the kitchen window, looking down at the street.

"Is he really dead?" she asked.

"Yes."

"What was he thinking to come here? With all the reporters . . . He couldn't have thought he'd get away with it."

"He wanted to die, but he wanted to kill you first."

"He really hated me, didn't he?"

"Yes, he did. You stopped him from destroying more innocent people's lives. The world's a better place without him." Grayson tossed his tie on the table. "You took your clothes off," he commented.

"Yes."

He took a step toward her and stopped. "It's not too late. We could catch the end of the party, I guess."

She took a step toward him. "I don't want to go out. I could fix dinner . . . microwave something. Are you hungry?"

He slowly looked her up and down, smiled, and said, "Yeah, I'm hungry."

Lifting her into his arms, he walked into the bedroom and kicked the door shut behind him.

THIRTY-THREE

Grayson wouldn't leave Olivia alone. He was determined to marry her, and nothing she could do or say would change his mind. He had listened to her protests for two months, but he was persistent.

"If I were to get sick again, you'd have to suffer with me," she argued. "Are you ready for that?"

"How about I toss you out if you get so much as a cold?"

"I'm serious."

"What happens if I get sick?" he countered.

The question gave her pause. "I'd take care of you."

"Marry me." He was backing her into her bedroom while he made his demand. "I'm not asking. I'm telling you. You're going to marry me."

She promised to think about it. He knew what that meant. She'd be thinking about it six months from now.

"When you wake up, you'll have a ring on your finger. I'm done waiting." He pulled her to him and began to undress her.

"You think I'll sleep through you putting a ring on my finger? I'm a very light sleeper, Grayson."

"When I'm finished with you, you're going to be so exhausted, you'll sleep through anything I do to you."

He wasn't exaggerating. He began to make love to her

with gentle caresses and slow, wet kisses. He soon became more demanding, and he brought her to the brink again and again, but each time he pulled back and made her wait. When she finally screamed for release, he gave in. The last thing she remembered was Grayson leaning over her and whispering that he loved her.

He stayed over that night and slept with her wrapped in his arms. When Olivia woke up, he was in the kitchen. She could smell bacon, and she could hear him whistling. She rolled onto her back and stretched her arms toward the ceiling. She saw the ring then, a gorgeous emerald-cut diamond.

Grayson heard the rich, joyful sound of laughter coming from the bedroom. It was music to his ears.

He had his answer.

THIRTY-FOUR

Their wedding was to be a small affair in her aunt Emma's living room. Olivia couldn't make up her mind if she wanted to invite her mother and her sister, but Natalie made the decision for her. She called late one evening, and her voice was absolutely frigid.

"Still blaming me, Natalie?" Olivia asked.

"You are to blame," her sister said resentfully. "I don't think Mother or I will ever be able to forgive you."

"Have I asked for forgiveness?"

"I have a message."

"Oh?"

"The message is from our father. He has such a kind heart."

"Right."

"He said he's ready to forgive you, but you have to face him when you apologize."

There was dead silence on the phone for at least twenty seconds. Then Olivia began to laugh. Some things—and some men—never change. Logan Weston was one example; Robert MacKenzie, another.

It was such a beautiful spring day, Emma decided to have the wedding outside in her garden. By the time she finished with the caterer and the florist, the yard looked like a wonderland.

Dr. Andre Pardieu walked Olivia down the aisle. Her maids of honor were Collins, Jane, and Samantha. Olivia had told Grayson that Samantha had to be at the ceremony, and if she couldn't get leave, then everyone would go to Iceland, and they'd get married there.

Grayson in his tux set her heart on fire. This beautiful man loved her. As she walked toward him, she felt as though she were floating. All her worries had vanished. She was no longer afraid of what might come. With Grayson at her side, she could face anything. He was her lover, her friend, her strength. It would be all right to lean on him every now and then.

There was much to celebrate. Collins had finally received word that she could begin training to become an FBI agent, and she was thrilled. Ronan kept his distance, but Olivia noticed he hadn't taken his eyes off Collins. She couldn't wait to see what might come of the attraction.

Agent Huntsman was late for the ceremony, but he had the most wonderful excuse. He pulled Olivia and Grayson aside to share his news. "I've got a wedding present for you," he began. "We finally caught up with that bitch, Gretta Keene. She was in New Mexico under an assumed name. She's behind bars now. And guess who else?"

Olivia gasped. "Eric Jorguson?"

"That's right. We nabbed him, too." Huntsman couldn't stop smiling. "We've got everything we need to prove Jorguson was laundering money, and now it looks like we'll also be able to go after some of his other clients. It's a mighty fine day, isn't it?"

Olivia thought it was a fine day, indeed. Every one of Grayson's buddies was drooling over Olivia's three best friends. And the girls certainly knew how to flirt, even Jane, now that she was looking so radiant. She'd started dating again and was truly happy.

Ralph and his father were invited—Henry had put them on the list. Mary and Harriet were busy protecting the cake and keeping the boys out of mischief.

Ralph Sr. fell under Samantha's spell. He hung on her every word. She was launching into "the story" when her friends joined her.

"There I was . . ."

Collins, Jane, and Olivia finished the sentence for her. ". . . in seat twenty-eight A on flight twenty-seven forty-three. . . ." Laughter followed, drawing smiles from the guests.

The photographer wanted a picture of the bride with her maids of honor. Olivia gathered them on the terrace. They stood together smiling into the camera. Sam whispered something the others found hilarious, and they had a good laugh.

Contentment washed over Olivia. The Pips were together again. They had come through the storm, and the sun was shining.

EPILOGUE

A year had passed since the wedding, and Olivia had settled comfortably into married life. Patrick continued to keep the household running smoothly, and she helped with carpools and homework.

Grayson hadn't committed yet, but he was giving serious thought to accepting a promotion at the agency. As an incentive, they had agreed to his demands: He could take on individual cases from time to time and not be tied to a desk, and Ronan would continue to be his partner for those investigations. The new position would mean that his work schedule would be predictable and he could spend more time with his family.

Olivia and Henry had become very close. Their busy lives kept them occupied during the week, so Olivia made it a point to reserve the weekends for family activities. One Saturday in late June, Olivia and Henry were at a local farmers' market that was set up on the edge of a city park. She wanted to pick up some fresh vegetables for their dinner, and she'd promised Henry they would see the latest Transformer movie when she was finished. Grayson and Ronan were tying up a case, and Ronan was going to drop Grayson off at the park to meet them and spend the rest of the day with them.

Henry had one of his handheld game players and was

trying to destroy aliens while Olivia and he strolled among the crowded stalls. She kept her hand on Henry's shoulder, guiding him. They stopped in front of a stall containing fresh tomatoes. As she was sorting through them, she glanced across the market to the parking lot beyond. Grayson was walking toward her. Her heartbeat quickened, and her breath caught in her throat. Oh, he was such a handsome man. In all this time together, she still hadn't gotten used to him. Whenever he walked through the door at night, she reacted the same way. Always with excitement and wonder. She thought it a miracle that he loved her.

He reached her and leaned down to kiss her. Henry was so intent on his game, he didn't realize his uncle had joined them.

"Sorry I'm late. After all this time, Eric Jorguson wants to make a deal," he explained. "It's not gonna happen. He can't give us anything we don't already have."

"I can't despise the man," she whispered so Henry wouldn't overhear. "If he hadn't attacked me, I never would have met you."

"Not true," Grayson said. And though he wasn't usually poetic, he added, "We were meant to be together. I would have found you."

On the night of May 11 at precisely eight forty-five in the evening, Finn MacBain stopped being a colossal pain in the ass and grew up. He also became a hero.

Until that Saturday evening, he and his twin brothers, Beck and Tristan, had caused all sorts of mischief. They were daredevils and loved to play pranks. Neighbors cringed when they saw them coming. The brothers weren't bad boys. They were just idiots . . . according to their father, anyway. Smart as whips, but still idiots. Over the years they had built up quite a repertoire of stunts, like the time they strung a zip line from the roof of their house to a huge walnut tree in the wooded area behind the backyard. There was just enough of a downward slope to send them flying. Unfortunately, they didn't anticipate the impact of reaching the tree at the bottom, and they were lucky they didn't break any bones. And then there was the time they tried to build a trampoline. Their parents couldn't even think about that one without shuddering. That was the day they got rid of their chain saw.

The boys especially enjoyed playing jokes on one another. Setting alarm clocks to sound off in the middle of the night, making all sorts of ridiculous things fall when their victim opened his closet door, or wrapping their prey in his bed with Saran Wrap while he slept—their imaginations worked overtime.

The boys didn't limit their tricks just to the family. They had fun with the neighbors as well. When their neighbors the Hillmans returned from their weeklong vacation, they found yellow crime scene tape circling their house and a chalk outline of a body—compliments of Beck—drawn on their sidewalk. The Hillmans weren't amused.

The MacBain brothers were also shockingly ungraceful. It was a fact that the three of them couldn't seem to walk through a room without tripping over their own feet and crashing into a wall or a table. They were growing so fast, it simply wasn't possible to be agile. They were rambunctious and loud and loved to laugh. Even though they were constantly told to "take it outside," they still got into push-and-shove fights inside the house. Heads and shoulders went through drywall too many times to count, and their home was in a perpetual state of repair. Their parents, Devin and Laura MacBain, put the contractor's phone number on speed dial.

The boys were handsome devils, all approaching six feet though barely in their teens. Finn, the oldest of the siblings and the ring leader in most of their schemes, was fourteen and still hadn't shown the least inclination to stop growing. Like his brothers, he attended an all-boys Jesuit high school and was an honor student. He aced every test thrown at him, had a phenomenal memory, and, according to his frustrated teachers, wasn't living up to his potential. He breezed through advanced classes and didn't challenge himself because he didn't have to. He was lazy in that respect. He was also easily bored, and there were times when he actually fell asleep in American history class. Finn didn't have much passion for anything but girls, swimming, football, and having a good time. A school counselor told his parents that their son was too smart for his own good, which didn't make a lick of sense to them. How could anyone be too smart? Several teachers called Finn arrogant, which Finn's father decided was code for smart-ass.

Everything about Finn was a contradiction. His IQ was in the genius range, and on paper he was the perfect four-point student, but he also had been in more fights than Muhammad Ali. He couldn't seem to walk from one end of the block to the other without punching one or more of the Benson boys.

Finn had a rascal's grin and a sparkle in his eyes. He also had a powerful fist and a right hook that was lightning quick. Though he really didn't have much of a temper—it took a lot to get him riled—he couldn't abide a bully, and each of the seven Benson boys was exactly that. They preyed on the younger boys and girls in the neighborhood and got a real kick out of making them cry. All the kids knew they could go to Finn for help if they were being tormented. He wasn't afraid to stand up to the bullies, no matter how many of them there were.

When Devin saw his son's latest black eye, he remarked to his wife that Finn had many fine qualities, but he was lacking in common sense. How else could he explain why his son would take on seven Bensons at the same time?

Fortunately, Finn had never been arrested—none of his boys had—and their father determined that the only way to save them from getting into real trouble was to keep them busy from early morning until late at night, especially now that school would soon be over for the summer.

During the school year, his sons stayed occupied with part-time jobs and sports. They played football, lacrosse, basketball, and soccer. Those were seasonal sports, however. Swimming, on the other hand, could be an all-year sport. This was a revelation that came to him when he heard from a neighbor that there was a brand-new fifty-meter pool just a few miles away at the just-opened Lee Center, where it was believed Olympic hopefuls would start training. He also found out that tryouts for a competitive team were in one week.

That night in bed Devin discussed his plan with his wife. He told her about the Lee Center and the Olympic pool. "I want the boys to try out for the team. I think Finn has a good chance of making it."

"Who does this team compete against?" Laura asked.

"I don't know and I don't care. If Finn makes the team, he'll have to be at the center by four forty-five. He'll swim from five until six thirty. Practice is every day but Sunday," he added, grinning. "It's year-round, too. Even if Beck and Tristan don't make the team, they can do laps with Finn. That ought to wear them out."

Laura didn't see any harm in letting the boys try out. She agreed that they needed to channel their energy into something wholesome and exhausting, and swimming laps at the crack of dawn just might be the answer.

Her husband was just drifting off to sleep when a thought struck her. She poked him in his shoulder and said, "Wait a minute. Who's going to be driving them to practice every morning?"

His snore was her answer.

Without mentioning his plan to his sons, Devin filled out the forms, paid the fee for a family membership, and signed up all three boys for time trials. That evening he broached the subject at dinner. He sat at the head of the table and watched his sons inhale their food. They were good-looking boys, he thought. Their hair was thick and dark, like his used to be before he'd had children. It was streaked with gray now. Beck and Tristan were identical twins. The only way Devin had been able to tell them apart when they were babies was by a small birthmark on the side of Beck's neck. They were exactly eleven months younger than Finn, and for a few weeks each year, all three were the same age. Their personalities were different, though. Beck lived to have fun and had recently become quite the lady's man. He was just now beginning to show signs of having a little sense. Of the three brothers, he was the sweetest and most compassionate, and he definitely didn't hide what he was thinking. Tristan, on the other hand, was the analytical one. He reasoned through everything, no matter how insignificant, and yet he still let Finn talk him into doing the most outrageous stunts. He was generous by nature and would always put his brothers first, but he also took things to heart, and Devin worried he would end up with ulcers if he didn't learn to relax. As idiotic as they sometimes acted, Devin loved the fact that all three boys protected one another. Their loyalty was absolute.

Finn was pushing away from the table and asking to be excused when his mother nodded to her husband and said, "Didn't you want to speak to the boys about . . ."

"Yes, that's right. Now, boys . . ."

"Sir?" his sons responded in unison.

"Did you know there's an Olympic-size pool over at the new Lee Center? Boys and girls will be training there every day."

Before he could continue his explanation, Beck asked, "Girls? How many girls?"

Devin held his patience. "I don't know how many girls."

Tristan frowned as he asked, "What are they training for?" He slouched in his chair, and his hair hung down over his eyes.

"Sit up straight," his father ordered before answering. "The team. They're training to be on the team."

"What does the team do?" Beck asked.

"Compete against other teams," Finn said. "Fastest swimmers end up competing to be on the Olympic team. Right, Dad?"

"Yes, that sounds about right. I'm not sure how it works or how many levels there are."

"You boys love to swim," their mother reminded them.

"I like to swim," Beck said. "I don't know that I love it the way Finn does."

"Finn, you practically lived in the pool next door last summer," Tristan said.

"Yes, I did swim a lot when Justin lived there. We did laps all the time. Then his father got transferred. It's a great pool," he added enthusiastically. "Twenty-five meters, I'll bet. Biggest backyard pool I've ever seen."

"It's not twenty-five meters," Tristan argued. "It's not even close."

"You're fast, Finn. Real fast," Beck said. He decided he wasn't quite finished eating and reached for the bowl of mashed potatoes.

"Did you ever get timed to find out how fast you are?" Tristan asked.

"No. Why would I?" Finn asked.

"We sure can't swim next door anymore," Tristan said.

"Yeah, and it's your fault, Finn," Beck said, waving his fork at him.

"You were told not to play baseball in the street," their mother snapped. Thinking about the incident still made her angry. "Breaking a window isn't a great way to meet the new neighbors. They'd only just moved in," she added. "Mr. Lockhart was quite irritated."

"They were eating dinner," Devin said. "The baseball landed in the middle of the table in the salad bowl."

Beck nudged Tristan. "I'll bet lettuce went flying everywhere."

"This isn't funny," Laura scolded. "One of the parents or one of the girls could have gotten hit in the head."

All three boys leaned forward. "The Lockharts have daughters?" Tristan asked.

"Why didn't you tell us, Finn?" Beck asked.

"I didn't know. Mr. Lockhart stormed out of the house, and I apologized and promised to pay for a new window. He's the only one I saw. Mom and Dad went over later to talk to him."

"Did you see the daughters?" Beck wanted to know. "How many are there?"

"Three," Devin answered.

"What do they look like?"

"That's a shallow question," his father said.

"I'm thirteen, Dad. I'm supposed to be shallow," Beck told him cheerfully.

Devin decided to have a little fun with his sons. "As a matter of fact, I did see the daughters. They're beautiful. Aren't they, Laura?" he asked his wife.

"Oh, my, yes. They certainly are."

Tristan was suspicious. "Beautiful on the inside or the outside?"

"Both," Laura answered.

What their parents failed to mention was the age of the daughters.

"May I be excused?" Finn asked again.

"No, you may not," his father said, his voice a bit sharper than he'd intended. "I want to talk to you about this competitive swimming."

"Okay," Finn agreed, dropping down into the chair again. "What about it?"

"I'd like you to try out for the team."

"Sir, I'd rather not. I won't have time. I've got plans for the summer."

His father rubbed his temples. He could feel a headache coming on. "And what might those plans be?"

"I'm going to work at the Iron Horse Country Club."

"Oh? Doing what?" Devin asked.

"Lifeguarding. I've already done the Red Cross safety thing, and I'm certified in CPR."

"We're all certified in CPR," Beck reminded him. "Dad made us take the course."

"You can't be a lifeguard until you're fifteen or sixteen," Tristan said.

"I'll bet they'll make an exception," Finn said.

Devin closed his eyes and prayed for patience.

"I'll bet they won't," Tristan countered. He reached for another chicken breast with his fork and put it on his plate. Beck took another one, too.

Laura looked at all the empty bowls. There hadn't been any leftovers since Finn had started eating solid food.

"They need lifeguards, and I'm qualified, except for my age, so I'll already be in a pool every day," Finn explained.

"Have they hired you?" Devin asked.

"Not yet. I was going to take my application over, but then I got grounded for fighting."

"Finn, you're not going to work at the country club," Devin said. "Maybe next year," he added to soften the disappointment. "And since you're not going to lifeguard, you might as well try out for the team at the center. Aren't you curious to know if you could make it?"

Finn shrugged. "I guess."

"I'll try out for the swim team if you will," Beck said. "It's a great way to build muscle, and girls like muscles."

"Girls? Is that all you think about?" his mother asked, exasperated.

"Pretty much," Beck admitted.

Finn nodded. "Yeah, we all do, pretty much all the time," he said. He turned to his father, "I'm grounded for another week, remember? How can I go to the Lee Center—"

"I'll lift your grounding Sunday. You're home until then."

"If I try out."

"Yes, that's right."

Finn didn't have to think about it. "Okay, sure. I'll do it."

"Do you think the Lockharts will ever let us swim in their pool?" Tristan asked.

"No." Laura was appalled. "Absolutely not. They think you're all delinquents."

"What did *we* do?" Beck asked. "Tristan and I weren't even home when Finn broke their window."

"You're related to him," she explained. "Delinquents by association."

"That's not fair," Beck complained.

"Life isn't fair. Get used to it," his father said.

"Whose turn is it to do dishes?" their mother asked.

An argument among the brothers ensued—a nightly ritual, it seemed—and they ended it by playing rock, paper, scissors three times until Beck conceded defeat.

As the boys began to clear the table, Devin issued an order. "I want all of you to stay away from the Lockharts. Especially you, Finn. I don't want you to even make eye contact. You hear me? And stay out of their pool, for God's sake. Give me your word right this minute."

Finn wanted to roll his eyes but didn't dare because it would be disrespectful, and he was really sick and tired of being grounded. "Okay," he answered resignedly.

Exactly one hour later, Finn had to break his promise.

His brothers had gone with their parents to Burton's appliance store to buy a new television, and Finn had gone up to his bedroom, which was on the third floor in the back of the house. He was looking out the window at Lockharts' pool, remembering how much fun he and his brothers had had swimming laps last summer. It really was a great pool. The Lockharts' huge deck was about ten, maybe twelve feet off the ground with a thick wood railing surrounding it. It overlooked a concrete patio and the pool beyond. When Justin's parents weren't around, he and Finn would jump up on the railing and, soaring out over the lounge chairs on the patio below, dive into the deep end of the pool and race each other to the steps. Finn always won.

The pool looked especially inviting today. It was so hot, his T-shirt stuck to his back. The central air wasn't equipped to cool the attic bedroom, so he turned on the fan he'd dragged up from the basement and opened the window.

Laughter from below caught his attention, and he looked to see where it was coming from. The Lockharts were having a big party. Finn then remembered his mom calling it a housewarming. Cars lined Concord Street. From what he could hear, there were quite a few guests, and all seemed to be enjoying themselves. A couple of people stepped out on the deck, drinks in hand, then strolled back inside, no doubt because of the heat and humidity.

He really wanted to get in that pool. The clear blue water

sparkled and beckoned. He loved swimming. He forgot his worries, and his mind seemed to clear of all thoughts as he sliced through the water with long, smooth strokes. The faster he swam, the more relaxed he became. His body took over. One of his friends told him he turned into a dolphin in the water. While he was swimming, he felt completely at peace, and at the same time, he felt energized. It didn't make sense, he knew, yet that was how he felt. The more he relaxed, the faster he swam.

He sure couldn't swim tonight, though. He'd given his word to his father, and he wasn't about to break it. Besides, he figured Mr. Lockhart would call the police and have him hauled away for trespassing if he tried to sneak over the fence. No sense tormenting himself by looking at that beautiful pool, he decided.

He shut the window and was just starting to turn away when he noticed her. Man, she was little. She couldn't have been more than five or six, he guessed—way too young to be out by the pool without supervision. Maybe one of the Lockhart daughters was babysitting the little girl, but if that were the case, where was she?

Finn was getting a real bad feeling in the pit of his stomach. The child slowly walked to the side of the pool, but she kept looking over her shoulder. Was she waiting for someone, or was she checking to make sure she wouldn't get in trouble? Maybe she knew how to swim, he reasoned. Still, she shouldn't have been out there alone.

The child sat down, scooted to the edge of the pool, and put her feet in the water. Finn kept waiting for someone to grab her, but no one came forward. She splashed her feet for a minute or two, inching closer and closer until the water covered her knees. She stayed that way for another minute, then tilted forward and began to splash the water with her hands, smiling as she created waves that lapped over the lip of the pool. When she leaned over further to dip her hands deeper, she lost her balance and plunged headfirst into the water. She was gone without making a sound.

Thirty seconds. That was all the time he had, he thought, to get to her. He shouted to his father as he raced down the stairs, "Call nine-one-one."

No one answered him, and he remembered they'd all gone to Burton's.

He ran out the front door, nearly tearing it off its hinges, crossed his and the Lockharts' yards at a dead run, then sprinted up the steps to their front porch. Mr. Lockhart was standing in the doorway greeting a couple, blocking the entrance. No time to explain, Finn decided. He shoved the big man out of his way, and while Mr. Lockhart was bellowing his outrage, Finn shouted, "Call nine-one-one," though he doubted anyone heard him over Mr. Lockhart's roar.

Finn pushed people aside, knocked over a cheese tray and a dining room chair, then slammed through the barely open French doors. He leaped up on the railing and, using it as a spring board, made a clean dive into the pool.

He had the child in his arms less than five seconds later. She was limp and lifeless, and he knew she had water in her lungs. God, he was scared. He had to get her breathing again and fast. Her lips were already turning blue. He held her against his chest as he got out of the pool, then gently placed her on the ground and began CPR.

Finn could hear the CPR instructor in his mind telling him how much pressure to exert. Airway free . . . Don't forget to count. . . .

He could hear screaming in the background, but he ignored it. Suddenly Mr. Lockhart was dropping to his knees next to his daughter. He tried to pick her up. Finn knocked him back.

"Do you know what you're doing?" the desperate father panted.

Finn nodded. His full attention was on the little girl. He kept up his compressions, silently counting as he worked on her.

A woman let out a bloodcurdling scream. "Peyton," she called. "What's happened to her? Peyton . . ."

Mrs. Lockhart knelt beside her husband. Sobbing, she whispered, "Take a breath, baby. . . . Come on. Please, breathe . . ."

"They're coming. The ambulance is on the way," a woman shouted from the deck.

Suddenly, Peyton opened her eyes and began throwing

up a fair amount of water. Finn turned her and held her head until she was able to take a deep breath. She was back with them.

Finn had yet to say a word. Adrenaline was coursing through his veins. Peyton tried to sit up and reached for him. He stood, cradling her in his arms, and only then noticed the crowd surrounding him, all silently watching. Several women had their hands over their mouths. They looked frightened, but as soon as Peyton lifted her head and they saw that she was going to be all right, everyone began to talk at once.

Peyton's mother held out her arms for her little girl, and Finn gently handed her over. Holding the little girl tightly, she whispered, "You're all right now. You're all right," as the tears streamed down her cheeks.

All of a sudden, Peyton's father grabbed Finn. He hugged him and pounded his back. "Thank God for you," he said, his voice quavering with emotion.

Finn thought the man was going to cry, too. When he finally let go of Finn and stepped back, Mr. Lockhart's light blue shirt was soaked.

"How did you know . . ."

"I saw her go under," he explained. "Sir, your daughter needs to learn how to swim. . . . and right away."

"Yes, of course," he said. "Peyton was supposed to be upstairs with the babysitter. . . . I don't know how she got outside. . . . I don't understand how this could have happened." He sounded bewildered as he added, "All these people here, and none of us saw her go outside."

Peyton reached for her father, and he immediately took her into his arms. She put her head down on his shoulder, but she was staring at Finn.

Peyton's mother dabbed at her eyes with a wrinkled tissue as she rushed over to Finn and hugged him.

He was trying to back away so he could go home, but the crowd was squeezing in on him now. They patted and pounded his back, and several women kissed him on his cheek. He was mortified by all the attention. Getting away quietly was out of the question. They were holding on to him, making escape impossible.

The paramedics arrived and quickly checked Peyton.

"This child is lucky someone saw her in the water," one of them remarked.

"Finn . . . our neighbor Finn saw her, thank God. He dove off the deck to get to her, and then he did CPR. He knew CPR."

They asked Finn several questions, wanting to know how long Peyton had been in the water and how long it had taken him to revive her. Everyone was quiet and hung on Finn's every word, but as soon as the paramedics left, they all started talking, and Finn once again was grabbed, patted, petted, and kissed. Mr. Lockhart finally noticed how uncomfortable Finn looked and let him go home. He couldn't get out of there fast enough.

After changing his clothes, he made himself a couple of sandwiches—it had been almost two hours since he'd finished dinner—grabbed a bag of chips and a root beer, and headed into the den. He turned the television on, sat back, and tried to watch a movie. Only one half of the screen had a picture, and it no longer was in color, just a blurry black-and-white. It didn't really matter, though, because he wasn't paying any attention. His mind kept replaying what had happened. He had been so scared that Peyton wouldn't come back, and he thought about that moment when she began coughing. Holding her lifeless body in his arms and helping her breathe again . . . it seemed a miracle to him. The feeling was overwhelming. What if he hadn't seen her? From his window he couldn't see the bottom of the pool. What if he'd been too late to bring her back?

Finn buried his head in his hands while he thought about how close to death she'd been. It had happened so fast. She had gone under without even a splash or a scream, and her short life could have been over in a matter of minutes. What a piece of luck that he had noticed her.

He reached for the sandwiches, saw the empty plate, and only then realized he'd already eaten them.

He heard the garage door open. Shaking himself out of his thoughts, he went into the kitchen and found Beck and Tristan carrying in a huge box with the new television.

"Wait until you see it, Finn," Beck said. "The screen's twice the size of our old one, and the color is awesome."

"I can't watch television until Sunday," Finn reminded him. "I'm grounded, remember?"

His father pulled the door closed. "Help your brothers, Finn. I don't want the television dropped. Put it on the table in the den. Tristan, you figure out the cable hookup for the VCR. Put the old television in the garage."

"Listen, Dad, something happened," Finn began.

"Oh, before I forget, I ordered an air conditioner for your bedroom," Devin said. "It will be in next week."

"Thanks," Finn said. "But listen, while you were gone . . ." he began again.

The door bell rang, interrupting him. "Let me get the door," his father called over his shoulder. "Then you can tell me."

The Lockharts were waiting on the porch. Their daughter Petyon was standing between them, holding her mother's hand. Mrs. Lockhart had tears in her eyes.

Devin's shoulders slumped. "What'd he do?" he asked, his voice deflating as he opened the door wider and beckoned them inside. Before either of the Lockharts could explain, Devin turned and shouted, "Finn, get in here."

Laura saw who was in the foyer and whispered, "Finn, did you leave this house while we were gone? You didn't, did you?" Not waiting for his answer, she hurried to greet the distraught neighbors.

"Did you?" Beck asked.

"Yes," he answered. He couldn't resist adding, "I dove into the Lockharts' pool."

Beck burst into laughter. "You did not. Did you? Oh, man, you're going to be grounded the rest of your life."

"While they were having a party?" Tristan sounded incredulous. "You went swimming while they were having a party?"

"Yes."

Tristan smiled and shook his head. "Why'd you do such a dumb thing? You only had until Sunday."

"You better get in there," Beck said when he heard his father shout Finn's name again.

Laura was trying to soothe the Lockharts. She insisted they come into the living room and sit, hoping they would remain calm while they discussed Finn's latest infraction.

"It's certainly warm tonight, isn't it? Would you like some lemonade?" she asked nervously. She prayed Finn hadn't broken anything valuable.

She noticed Peyton watching her. She was such a pretty little girl, with big blue eyes that didn't seem to miss a thing. Laura couldn't help but notice how quietly she sat between her parents, looking so serene. None of Laura's boys had ever been able to sit for more than a minute without squirming. When they were little, they were always in motion. Now, as teenagers, they still were.

"I assure you that Finn will pay for any damage," Laura began.

Finn laughed. That didn't sit well with his parents. His father glared at him.

"Yes, he most certainly will," Devin assured the Lockharts.

"Your son saved our daughter's life tonight," Mr. Lockhart announced.

"He . . . What did you say?" Devin asked.

Mr. Lockhart explained, and by the time he was finished, Mrs. Lockhart was hugging her daughter and crying again.

While Beck and Tristan were elbowing their brother and smiling, their parents sat motionless, looking dumfounded.

"Over forty people in our house while she was drowning," Mrs. Lockhart told them. "She wasn't breathing. . . . Finn did CPR . . . got the water out of her lungs. . . ."

They talked about how terrifying it had been and how blessed they were that Finn had seen Peyton go under the water. As they were giving their account of how heroic Finn had been, he stood looking at the floor. He wasn't used to such praise.

When there was a pause in their flattering testimonial, Finn spoke up. "Mr. Lockhart, aren't you having a party?" he reminded.

"Yes," he answered and turned to his wife. "We should get Peyton to bed."

Mrs. Lockhart headed to Finn. He braced himself, knowing she was going to grab him again.

As the neighbors were leaving, Laura and Devin followed them out onto the front porch. Beck and Tristan followed.

"Mr. Lockhart, how old are your other daughters?" Beck asked.

"Lucy is six and Ivy is four."

Beck shot a quick accusing glance at his parents, who were trying to hide their grins. While his mother continued to chat with the Lockharts, Beck moved close to his father's side. "You knew they were little, didn't you?"

"Yep," he answered with a chuckle.

"Not funny, Dad."

His father's laughter indicated he disagreed.

Finn stayed behind in the living room while the two families were saying good-bye. He was about to go upstairs when the door opened and Peyton came running back inside. She stopped a foot away from him, cranked her head back, and stared at him for a long minute.

"I was scared," she whispered.

He barely heard her. He squatted down until they were eye to eye. "I was scared, too."

She smiled. Her mother called to her, but she didn't leave. She stared at Finn another minute while she made up her mind. Then she leaned close and whispered, "Thank you." Spinning around, she ran back to her parents.

Finn watched from the window as the parents took Peyton's hands and walked toward their house. He didn't think he would ever forget that moment when he'd lifted her out of the water. What made him turn back and look down at the pool again?

Maybe something bigger was at play here. Maybe Peyton Lockhart was supposed to do something important with her life.